NOORDIN'S GIFT

NOORDIN'S GIFT

Shashi Warrier

AMARYLLIS

AMARYLLIS

This edition first published in 2014

AMARYLLIS

An imprint of Manjul Publishing House Pvt. Ltd.

• 7/32 Ground Floor, Ansari Road, Daryaganj, New Delhi 110 002

Email: amaryllis@amaryllis.co.in Website: www.amaryllis.co.in

Registered Office:

10, Nishat Colony, Bhopal 462 003 - India

Distribution Centres:

Ahmedabad, Bengaluru, Bhopal, Kolkata, Chennai, Hyderabad, Mumbai, New Delhi, Pune, Thiruvananthapuram

ISBN: 978-93-81506-59-2

This edition is for sale only in the Indian Sub-continent, Singapore and the United Arab Emirates.

Printed and Bound in India by
Replika Press Pvt. Ltd.

This is in the memory of my parents, who, after 66 years of living together, died within 36 hours of each other. They read the whole story but missed the book.

Prologue

Thomas

This is my reconstruction of a murder. I put it together from a couple of informal interrogations of one of the murderers; an inspection of the scene of the crime; an inspection of the residence of the victim; conversations with a few of his friends and colleagues; all the reports written by the investigating state police officer and later by the superintendent of the Central Bureau of Investigation who took over the case when the initial investigation turned up the possibility of inter-state operations; the post-mortem report; and several conversations with the professor of forensic medicine – an old professional acquaintance and friend who infers much from bodies but usually keeps his inferences to himself – who wrote the post-mortem report.

I have some considerable experience with reconstructions, so this is credible, even the bits about the dead man's state of mind on the day of his death, though I must admit that some of it is speculative. Forgive the stilted language. For nearly three decades, I have written official reports designed to make conclusions that are either clear without ever being stated, or extremely difficult to arrive at. I'm a policeman, fairly high up in the service, and this is a skill that all of us learn early in our professional lives.

On, then, to Asif.

October 2025

At dawn on what is to be the last morning of his life, Asif comes awake with a foreboding of evil. He knows that he has been on the verge of exposure for some time now and has begun to look forward to the time his charade will end. He has the option, even now, of leaving for the airport and booking himself on to a flight to another city under a false name, but he knows that he will never sleep in peace again, not with these people behind him.

As he reaches for his cell phone to send the usual coded message that tells his handler he is alive and well on this morning, his memory intrudes upon his routine. For some time, he has had a nagging feeling about the latest addition to his limited circle of friends – he has seen the man somewhere, in a different context altogether. Now his memory, which he has been dredging for that face, tells him where. He has seen the man, minus his moustache, in the company of a rabidly right-wing politician.

The choice, he considers brushing his teeth, is between getting caught sooner or later. He smiles wryly as he puts the brush away carefully, and brings out his razor to shave his one-day-old stubble. He doesn't mind exposure and is prepared for the death that will likely follow. What he minds is the pain that lies between the two.

He finishes his ablutions, locks his front door, and crosses the road to the café where he stops for breakfast on most weekdays, picking up a local newspaper as he goes along. It isn't seven yet but the sun is already rising and it is uncomfortably warm, even on this October morning in the year 2025. He finds a vacant table under a fan at the café and settles down for his last newspaper and omelette.

By eight, he is at the bus stop by the clock tower, where he finds his usual fellow-commuter, Imtiaz, waiting. Imtiaz lives with his family friends close by, paying them three thousand rupees a month to put him up in a small room – he shares a bathroom and toilet with the family – and give him breakfast. He prefers it to living alone in the lodge like Asif because his hosts feed him, along with his breakfast, gossip and local news that he'd never get in the lodge.

Passing the lake between the twin cities of Hyderabad and Secunderabad, Asif reflects on the constant weariness he feels. This must be how the hare feels as the hounds bay for its blood, he thinks. Ganesh, his handler, has been telling him for weeks to drop everything and leave, promising him a safe haven elsewhere, in another country if need be. Now, with the danger mounting, he knows that he cannot come out of this alive and admits that he never wanted to.

He doesn't have anything dramatic like a capsule of cyanide. He just hopes he'll have the time and the nerve to provoke them to kill quickly when they do come for him. Meanwhile, he's contented with what he has discovered and passed on to his handler so far, that a certain Afghan named Noordin, now resettled in Kashmir, is up to something dreadful.

His working day passes in quiet flurries of business activity that he can handle with only half his mind. He lunches at the usual restaurant, takes the usual crowded bus back to the lodge at half past six, and has his last supper, a spicy biryani, at the usual café, at eight. He retires with a book at a quarter past ten, a little later than usual, turning out the lights ten minutes later.

They come at half past ten, as he lies awake in the dark,

recounting the events of the day. They do their best not to alarm him. Imtiaz, apparently alone, knocks on his door, chest heaving, saying his brother is ill in another part of the town, asking if Asif could accompany him there. A taxi waits outside. The moment Asif begins to enter it, he knows they are going to take him somewhere quiet to ask him some painful questions. He reaches for the knife in his shoe.

He is faintly surprised to find that he has plenty of time. He's very quick and they are taken aback at his skills and his wiry strength, as he gets away with a scratch on his arm, pounding down the street panting, three of them behind him. As he reaches a corner, he turns around and, when they arrive, runs straight towards them, his knife, sharp-edged but with its blade blackened to avoid glints in the dark, swooping.

In the brief fracas that follows, he goes for the kill, leaving them with no option but to finish him off. He goes down fighting, after injuring two of his assailants, but they flee from his body, avoiding the people collecting there, making it to the taxi, which has followed them.

An hour later, Imtiaz and Sarfraz are being treated for knife wounds by a sympathetic doctor. One of the wounds is serious enough to make the doctor advise a visit to a hospital but Sarfraz refuses to go, and the doctor has to do the best he can. Meanwhile, their leader, Abdul, gets on a cell phone stolen a few minutes ago. 'He's dead,' he tells his own faraway handler. 'We found a name, Ganesh, and a city, Bengaluru.'

'I'll tell Noordin,' his handler replies. 'He won't like it.'

Abdul won't be fazed. He knows that many things can go wrong, especially if you don't have official backing, and if you have to keep your preparations secret. 'We did our best,' he says. 'Allah knows, even if Noordin doesn't. Two of us are with the doctor now.' He disconnects the call, switches off the cell phone, and puts it in his pocket. He decides to get rid of it in a garbage dump on his way back home.

October 2025

If your service in the police forces has been at all sincere, you develop a sense for a case that's coming to a close. Well, the chain of events that started with Asif's death is due to end now, and I fear it will end with a bigger bang than I would like.

One

Noordin

October 2025

Blood defines my life.

Blood is in all my memories. In some, it flows; and in others, it congeals in pools on the street. When I remember my father, I remember blood pouring out of his thigh, his leg suddenly disappearing, sheared off by shards of flying metal – a result of an explosion in a marketplace. When I remember my mother, I remember blood congealing on her headscarf as she lay shot – by an intruder with a machinegun – in her own house.

My friends are my blood brothers in the sense that they have shed their blood for me as I have shed mine for them. No one joins my group in any real sense until he, too, has been blooded.

Blood runs through my dreams, turning them into nightmares. I cannot remember when I last slept well.

I come awake much before first light, fleeing from a nightmare. For a few minutes I lie still, gathering my thoughts, telling myself who I am and what I do.

My name is Shaikh Nooruddin, but they call me Noordin. Friends tell me that some people also call me 'The Ghost', but no one has ever called me that to my face.

I was born in Afghanistan less than fifty years ago, in a village in the Hindu Kush mountains. I am the son of a mother who died when I was two and a father whose claim to literacy was his knowledge of the Quran, the only book he ever read. His literacy was no use against the Soviet bombs that killed him when I was only four, but the stories he told me in those brief years left me with a hankering to read more such, and perhaps to make up a few of my own. So I learnt to read, and began with the Holy Book.

I rise and cleanse myself; it is time for the morning prayer, after which I spend some time with the Book.

If you notice, I say I spend some time with the Book, which does not mean that I read it. I have always thought about the Book, even when I was a child, but in earlier years, I used to think only about how it applies to our modern life, which is, after all, very different from life in the times of the Prophet. But these past few years, I have unfortunately begun to think, not of how it applies, but whether! This is unfortunate because the question has turned the bedrock of my life into sand. I have so far hidden my doubts from my men and will continue to do so. I cannot afford to show doubt while I hold their lives in my hands.

Sunrise on this day in the middle of October is yet to come. After I cleanse myself, I light the lamp before spreading the prayer mat on the packed earth of the floor. I bow east and go through the rituals, following the muezzin's call from the nearby mosque. After I fold the mat away, I get the Book and sit on a rug on the floor with my legs folded at the knee and my bottom on the soles of my feet, a position I can maintain for an hour without trouble. Now, when I am comfortable, I open the Book at a page at random, somewhere in the middle.

I cannot read it, no matter how much I try. I close it gently and hold it on my lap, clutching it tight. I close my eyes and let memories wash over me.

Summer, 1989

At thirteen, I am a veteran of a dozen gun battles. I have helped bring down a Soviet helicopter and killed at least six men. I have shown a group of trapped mujahideen an escape route through difficult terrain and walked thirty miles alone across the mountains with no food and no water to get back to my group. The other Taliban defer to me.

I am an orphan in the process of being adopted. At my uncle's house north of Jalalabad, his plump first wife sheds tears over the scars on my hands and arms, while he rubs his hands in apprehension. The Soviets have left this part of the country, but the AK-47 slung on my shoulder is so much a part of me that even my aunt doesn't find it strange.

None of what I have done seems remarkable. This is just how it is with me. This is how Allah made me. Now I will wait for Allah to let me know how to deal with it.

There has been news, mostly by word of mouth, of the Rabbani government in Kabul. The government hardly works – we get to see little of it in these parts. I often hear Ahmad Shah Massoud, the Lion of Panjshir – which means five lions – and think that he talks sense. However, my fellow-mujahideen think of him as the enemy, the one who consorts with the West, one who is willing to tolerate some of the habits of the kafirs.

Over the months that follow, I watch my fellow mujahideen supervise work in the poppy fields in the mountains. They themselves do nothing; they lounge around and watch; and if anyone breaks their rules, they punish him. Their word is law, and no one can question it. It's a hard life, but after months in the caves just being out in the open is good enough for me. In the evenings, there are meetings around fires, relaxed meetings for the most part, now that the Soviets have left, but occasionally involving punishment.

I hold my tongue, for the punishment is decided by the elders, who, we have been told, know right from wrong – though I know in many cases that they do not. I have seen nothing of life outside the caves and want to learn before I speak.

After the harvest, once the packets of opium leave, there is money to be spent. We go to the nearest town, where we report to the local council before wandering out to the shops.

With us are members of the local mujahideen, who have become an informal police force. They collect money from shopkeepers. 'Taxes,' they say laughingly, 'every government collects taxes.' They collect 'taxes' from opium farmers and from the few traders here. I watch and wonder. In the Book, everything that shakes the mind is forbidden – liquor, music and the sight of women exposing themselves. There's nothing specific against opium, but opium does shake the mind. I know men who used to smoke it before a battle, saying it gave courage, but what it does afterwards is not good to watch. It makes the smoker irresponsible.

I watch Naeem Shaqeer, the leader of the local group, in the formal sense my guardian, whipping a girl, the hem of whose dress went up a few inches in a gust of wind, exposing her ankle. The Book prohibits it, he roars, she must be more careful henceforth. The man with her, her brother, cowers. Some instinct tells me to keep quiet.

Shaqeer is a noisy bully, a braggart. He claims to have killed many Soviet soldiers, and brought down two helicopters, to my one. All the while since we arrived, he has been trying to pass himself off as one better than me. This whipping of the girl is an assertion of petty authority in my presence. In a sense, I am responsible for it.

I remember the Book. It tells us not to waste words. Again, I hold my tongue, difficult though it is.

Thus come the first nibbles of doubt. I listen to the braggart quoting this sura and that, watch him find victory in my silence. I find the whole lot of them quoting from the Book while collecting money from the opium growers. Next morning, as I sit with the Book, I understand that what each one of us finds in the Book is different. It is a revelation as powerful as the Book itself, and the doubt disappears for the time being.

Summer, 1994

The years since the Soviets left have been chaotic. Tribal leaders try to rule but the wiser, older ones have no guns. The ones with guns are not wise; even I can see that. It's even worse, perhaps, than when the Soviets ruled. Gunfire rings in my ears, just as before. I see foreigners – mostly Pakistanis – sneaking around. I wonder what they do, but there is no one to ask, and even if there were, I doubt whether the Pakistanis would answer.

The mujahideen fight among themselves. At times, gangs of armed men roam the streets. I avoid joining any of them, and often thank God that I have the presence of mind and, of course, the weapons – to fend off any attacks by these men.

Into this anarchy comes the vanguard of the Taliban. In a matter of weeks, everything changes. All of a sudden, people are relatively safe; they can go about their legitimate business without hindrance. Shops sprout, their owners safe as long as they pay the Taliban and observe the Sabbath and the rules that the Taliban proclaim to be their Shariat. People begin to go to work, in the fields, at their trades; and the mujahideen, those who are willing, like me, are absorbed into the Taliban.

The Pakistanis recognise the Taliban very quickly. They are very supportive, for they have funded the movement, with American money. Everyone thinks that the new order is wonderful. Afghanistan breathes again; and I am told that I'm with people of honour, as my father told me to be.

I feel some disquiet though. Naeem Shaqeer and people like him are fellow Taliban. Sometimes I feel that family and tribe matter more than religion or principle. Friends and relatives get away with crimes that others would suffer for. There are only a few instances of this, just enough to keep me from accepting the new order whole heartedly.

I will keep my distance.

October 2025

The sun shines through the crack under the door. I have lost track of time remembering these old matters. I rise, first on my knees and then on my feet, with the Book held in both hands. I put it away, in its place on a table in a corner, and make breakfast.

Breakfast is simple. I light a fire – with wood gathered from the nearby forest – and put water in a kettle to boil. I will brew tea, which I drink with salt and milk – goat's milk, if I can get it. This with some naan from last night and some fruit is sufficient for a man of my age. Food no longer interests me as much as it used to. These days, it is more a matter of giving the body enough fuel to keep it going well through the day.

Life is easy here, after what I have known in my own country. In the arid mountains where I come from, water is scarce, as is life, and fuel. Here, in this little green valley, the winters are cold, but no colder than that in Afghanistan, and there is water, enough of it, and the forest provides firewood. Sometimes I feel a flash of shame for feeling rooted here, for it is a betrayal of my country. But I understand that my real country is the country of the heart and mind, and that – for all these years that I have understood such things – has been Islam.

There is no running water or electricity, so everything takes a little more preparation, but that preparation is done here in solitude – something that I have grown to like very much. I eat slowly, savouring the quietness, if not the food itself. Once this simple breakfast is over, my solitude is gone for the day.

The first knock on the door comes a little after seven, before the sun drives the murky fog away. I know it must be Abdul Hameed, who has just returned from a reconnaissance, wanting to report even before he washes himself properly. He must have been waiting outside with his ear to the door and knocked only after he heard me put away the breakfast dishes. 'Salaam alay kum,' he greets me, his breath swirling. 'I have done what you asked me to do.'

'Wale kum salaam,' I respond 'We will talk inside.'

Hameed has spent the last two weeks watching the border, living on nothing, watching the movements of the soldiers across it. He has seen their preparations for the coming winter, watched the patrols, calculated how they are timed, and identified small gaps that few men can exploit. He has always been wiry, and now after this period of privation, his face is gaunt, his eyes deep-set. But then I have never asked him to do anything that I wouldn't, and my face is as gaunt, so he has nothing to complain about. Like the others in the group, he is here only because he is willing to accept this way of life.

I brew more tea for him, pouring the rest of the milk into his glass, keeping mine black. Over the next hour, we go into the details. Shahpur – a grandiose name, or perhaps hopeful – is a small village of some 200 families. In warm weather, most of the men go looking for work. They spend winters closed in their warm, fetid huts, carving or weaving to pass the time. A few, like me, go to India to do what we have done these past many years.

This year, more than a dozen of us will go, separately though, crossing the border at points not more than a two-day walk. We will find our way to Udhampur, where the railhead is. From there, we will take trains to Delhi, or to Jammu, from where we can take other trains to the south. We will all travel anonymously, in general coaches, which are cut-off from the more expensive sleepers and air-conditioned coaches.

There are other groups crossing the border the old way. The big artillery guns have moved from the old Line of Control to the new border, and Pakistani gunners fire a dozen salvos across the border to divert the attention of the Indians, while groups of up to ten armed men sneak across. This is exactly what they used to do across the old LOC, but here, it's slightly easier because the Indians are still relatively new to the nature of the border, and their guns are poorly positioned. Besides, their army seems to have weakened, otherwise they wouldn't have given up the Kashmir Valley the way they did. When we go across, we hear complaints of soldiers being badly paid and overworked, and the new ones, specially the officers, lack the nerve of older generations.

We prefer to scout the border and find weak points, something I learnt during the Soviet occupation when we could move freely across the Afghan-Pakistan border near Waziristan. After we locate the weak points, which change every year because the Indians also work on tightening their border patrols, we sneak across one by one, unarmed, like innocent men visiting relatives. No one has yet been caught because we know the border far better than anyone else.

This is because we keep working on our tactics, another thing that I learnt from the Soviets. Soldiers, like people in any activity, have to learn new ways to use old technology, and use new technology in different ways.

Hameed, though he knows the plans, will not go. He is my age and, with me, the eldest in the group. His injuries have caught up with him. A stiff knee from a firefight in the Pamirs and a painful back from a fall in Waziristan constrain him. He will stay here and keep himself available for emergencies. Someone within a day's walk, with a satellite phone, knowing some code words, will be the link. We have friends all over the world now, so there is no need for direct telephone contact between someone in India and a sympathizer or supporter in Pakistan. We have effective code words, so even if an eavesdropper hears the whole signal, he will still have no idea of what we really speak of. In the old days, the police used to consider a telephone call from India to Pakistan an indicator of terrorist activity. Now, with all calls routed through neutral countries, often a whole chain of them, it's easy to avoid leaving such traces.

There is more news. One of us, Asif, in Indian Hyderabad, has turned out to be an informer. He died before the others could find out whom he worked for, so we must consider the Hyderabad network compromised. We do have an alternative, so this information does not change our plans substantially, unless Asif got wind of the real plan. No one in the Hyderabad network is supposed to know that, but the best-kept secrets always have a way of getting out.

Hameed has to go home, to tend to his fifteen-month-old, orphaned granddaughter, whom he leaves in the care of one of the village women when he has to go away for a few days. But I notice that he is taking time. I get a feeling that he has something to tell me but he is holding it back; I wonder why. He is my closest friend and has been for almost all my life. Perhaps it is something to do with the child. At the door, I ask, 'Do you have something on your mind? How is Fatima?'

He shakes his head. 'There is nothing,' he says, though there clearly is. There must be no such reservations between friends so close. When there is some time I can spend in peace with him, I will ask him about his secret.

Once we have some more information on how many of us are going to get to the target the how and when will be worked out. It is not difficult to choose the timing in India, where the habits of their old rulers, the British, have lingered generations after the rulers themselves left – just after Christmas is perfect. I found that most Indian schools have two vacations – a long one in summer and a shorter one in winter, around Christmas. The Christmas vacation is usually only ten days or so, much shorter than the long summer break. Christmas is more a commercial festival than a religious one, and almost everyone, other than the very poor, shop and holiday. Then there is the New Year just a week after Christmas, which calls for more festivities, and rest after bouts of overindulgence. Also, the police might go on high alert during Christmas but they become lax the following day. At no other time of the year do people compress so much celebration into so short a period.

So we will strike sometime during that one week.

The next question is where. The answer to that has been seventeen years in the making. The planning began in 2008, when India and the Satan America signed their nuclear cooperation agreement.

October 2008

The meeting is as usual in a shabby yellow mansion in the wealthy

Defence Colony area of Karachi, not far from Bilawal House of the Bhutto-Zardari clan – now quiet because Asif Ali is in the presidential mansion in Islamabad. Abdul Ghani Khan, until some years ago a brigadier in ISI, director of counter-intelligence, seems to own this house – seems because with ISI nothing need be what they seem to be – and sends word every now and then that we are to meet in the evening on such-and-such day.

I have been to half a dozen of these meetings. Always present are the brigadier's elder son, Raza, and an anonymous note-taking secretary, who leaves at a signal that I still haven't learnt to recognise. The brigadier welcomes each guest at the door, shaking hands, pretending an equality that has never existed in the world of intelligence.

Only six people attend today's meeting, besides Ghani Khan – Raza and the secretary, of course; Sohail, a serving ISI captain growing old in his rank; Masood Alam, apparently an influential banker; Sultan, a young paratrooper, also a captain, in civilian clothes; and I.

For the meeting, I am an Afghan trader friend of the brigadier's. My name is Murad. I am clean-shaven, reasonably well-groomed, and dressed casually in a pair of jeans and a T-shirt. I have no interest in these meetings, and have said so, but the brigadier insists I attend. 'You're the interesting one, Noordin, the bright one,' he keeps saying. 'You can turn everyone at the table on their heads.'

An early dinner precedes the meeting. It is in the small dining room of the mansion, at the back, near the kitchen. The formal one, by the lawns west of the house, can hold sixty people in comfort, and is far too large for small functions such as this one.

Throughout dinner, the brigadier keeps up a flow of small talk, enquiring about his guests and bringing them out. Afterwards, when everyone is pleasantly full and perhaps slightly off-guard, he throws his visitors a topic to debate. He watches, speaking little, and, as minds warm up and the argument becomes lively, or even heated, he shuts it down with some simple and unexpected conclusion.

Today's topic is TV. We watch Secretary of State Condoleezza Rice shaking hands with India's Pranab Mukherjee after completing the formalities of their civilian nuclear technology and supplies agreement. When the speeches are over, he turns the TV off and turns to me. 'Murad,' he says, 'If we start planning now, Inshallah, you might live to see it through.' He pours himself an inch of liquor from a bottle on the table beside him.

I keep quiet, eyeing the glass. Saying Inshallah while drinking liquor is double blasphemy. The brigadier sees the look on my face and puts the glass down. 'Now, now, Murad,' he says, 'you mustn't take these habits of mine seriously.'

'Yes,' I say. After that first experience with Naeem Shaqeer, I have held my tongue whenever I can. I have found that most people respect a man who holds his tongue.

'Brigadier Saheb, what must we plan now?' Sohail asks.

The brigadier flicks him a glance of contempt. 'Find me a few boys in India, bright young boys who can learn anything. They shouldn't be more than ten years old. Take good care of the boys and their families. Make sure they go to the right schools. Make sure they learn that Islam and technology go together. Light that fire in their hearts.'

'And their minds?'

'Nothing now. Nothing for many years.' He grimaces. 'Maybe the Indians will take care of that themselves. Then we'll see.'

Sohail doesn't see, or at least pretends not to. 'I retire soon,' he says. 'What is it that will take many years for us to complete?'

Sultan, the paratrooper, sits up straight. He is like a puppy looking for adventure. For him, war is glory. He might be a paratrooper, but he hasn't seen anything yet beyond a couple of skirmishes at the border, or the LoC. 'We will have to have someone outside as well,' he says. 'Who?'

'Not you people,' the brigadier replies. He smiles briefly, without humour, 'We cannot afford records.'

'We don't keep records of some of the things we do,' Sultan protests.

'I know.' There's an edge to the brigadier's voice that wasn't there before. 'How did the Indians find Pakistani Army pay books on dead men in Kargil? They knew which battalions those men came from. There must be no records on this one. You will help with the training, when the time comes. Personally. I want a promise now that you will take leave from your unit if need be, but you will be there for the training. Raza will be watching, even if I'm not.'

'Where is the money, Saheb?' Sohail asks.

'This is the trouble with you bastards,' the brigadier says. 'I say, do this or do that, and immediately you ask for money.'

'Saheb,' Sohail says, grovelling, 'you know that you can buy anything in India. With time and money, I can do anything. But without them, I am powerless.'

The brigadier smiles bitterly, 'Masood will take care of that. The money will be there. Start now so that you have time too.'

The secretary leaves and the others soon follow, Raza disappears into a separate wing of the house that he occupies. I wonder where the women are, but do not ask, for it is none of my business where this man and his son keep their women.

When we are alone, the brigadier empties his last glass and turns to me. 'I thank you for your patience, Noordin,' he says. 'Now that we are alone, I have something to say to you,' he smiles. 'You never ask, do you? Sometimes you seem to be made of iron.'

He settles back in his armchair. 'You know, we never look ahead far enough. We never look beyond next year's plan to bleed India, or, if there's a civilian government, beyond the next elections. Zia was the last leader who looked beyond that. I learnt my lessons in that day, and I've never forgotten them.

'This is something that'll work far into the future. I do not see any hope in the next generation for friendship between India and Pakistan. We cannot hope to defeat them in a conventional war for any length of time. We must have with us a means to bring them to their knees – this is ideal. If – when the plans are complete, when everything is ready – there is no need to execute the plan, so be it. Raza will arrange its cancellation. Otherwise, we will go ahead as we deem fit.

'There are people in the establishment here who will want to control this project – to hijack it. They will try to cut our funds off, divert them elsewhere, or even divert people elsewhere. That is why you are here, Noordin. You are beyond this country's government's interference. No one here can stop you.

'Masood will make the money available to you when you want it. He will work out the means to do it safely. Sultan might help, if he is alive when it all comes up. Otherwise, there will be someone else. You can train anyone in the skills required. I know you will, if you have to.

'Your work at the moment is to help the separatists in Kashmir. You are already involved with them. We will be able to make that involvement appear much greater than it is. We will lay down a plan to get rid of some Indian supporters, a few big ones. Can you accept that?'

'I can.'

'After Kashmir is free, we must bring India to its knees. These Hindus must never again threaten our land. No more of their vile bullying.'

'Alright.'

'They are bigger and richer than us. We have no chance of

winning a regular conventional war against them. So we must attack them as a tiger fights the elephant – from behind, aiming for the soft underbelly. So we have something else going on.

'Raza is here. He is committed, and intelligent, but he is not courageous – especially not under fire. That is why he does not wear a uniform. But he is educated, and knows electronics. He will guide you in the means of many things. The National Security Adviser knows of this project… him I distrust the least amongst all these who call themselves patriots, and I have told him about this project because if our plans run into trouble, we must have someone to provide us more.

'We will do this in two steps. First, we will slap them in the face. That will be easy, and I will have that organised separately. They will want a war when we do that. In response, we will take an atomic power station and threaten to blow it up. That will show them their place. They will not have peace, and they will not be able to go to war.

'Your role comes to play in the second step. You must make sure it is taken, even if the first step isn't taken. We must do our best to make sure that our plans stay on course. So make contact with the boys yourself. Go with Sohail and vet whoever he selects. Make sure it all works out.'

As I leave the house that night, I wonder why the brigadier retired a brigadier. If he could plan this well always, he'd have been the general. It's by far the longest term and the most complex plan I've ever seen from a Pakistani spy handler, and I suspect its seed was planted there by someone else. Another Pakistani, perhaps.

The question, as always in this game, is the same old one that investigators ask after a crime – who gains? The Pakistanis certainly do, but is there anyone else?

October 2025

That was how it began, in a shabby yellow house in a humid seaside city. That retired brigadier is gone now, but there is another, a general, in his place, in the same shabby house, with an underground room full of old files and a computer working all the time. The old National Security Adviser, of course, is long gone. He died before the brigadier, and the brigadier decided that the new ones do not need to know. Tying all the strings together is Raza, now middle aged, sitting with the old general. Perhaps, there is someone behind him. I do not know.

So there it rests, in my hands, and in mine alone.

Looking back, I think this was one of the best ideas the brigadier ever had, or probably the worst. At this moment, I cannot make up my mind. Certainly, it is the bloodiest – that much I know.

Two

Ganesh

October 2025

As usual, I'm the first at the office. I let myself in at half past seven, open the windows of my room, and put some coffee in the machine before settling down to administrative matters. There's the usual mess. I run a fairly expensive security outfit that does a lot of work helping corporations keep their secrets. A couple of decades ago, that would have meant a few hundred ex-soldiers working as night watchmen at factories and offices.

No longer. Watchmen are still necessary – in large numbers, for factories, offices, and all those sprouting gated townships as well – but the focus has changed. Now it's information that people look to steal, not materials – client lists, credit card numbers, industrial designs, chemical compositions, marketing plans, dossiers on people, and so on. My key people don't look to catch the occasional interloper climbing over a factory wall; we vet people and design systems to make sure people working with subcontractors don't leave the office with information they shouldn't be taking out, and then implement those systems. Some of these systems are electronic – we have people who work on keeping hackers out, and, of course, hackers trying to break the very systems our people make – and other systems are physical, such as search methods, which cover a broad and changing range of technology, so this is the most hi-tech division. There is occasionally some detective work involved when someone sneaks a list of credit card numbers out of the office, but the idea is to prevent that sort of thing from happening at all.

We also do a certain amount of personal protection. This is mostly for rich people in the private sector, movie stars and so on – people in government get government security – and some foreigners. Bodyguards for hire, in effect. We've lost a couple of people to assassins and suffered the kidnapping of one of our clients. But we've also arranged to rescue kidnapped hostages, though we keep a low profile on that, because it sometimes involves rough stuff that we really want to avoid.

And then there are background checks. Prospective employers, spouses, and landlords – all are increasingly looking for agencies like ours to vet prospective, and sometimes current, employees, spouses, and tenants. There used to be a time when landlords never bothered to verify the identity of the tenants, but with terrorist groups becoming increasingly rich, therefore enhancing their ability to pay large deposits for houses, few landlords want to take risks, especially with bachelors.

So, we're four partners, each looking after a division – perimeter security, systems, protection, and backgrounds. My three partners are all ex-Army, like me. I'm the managing partner because I brought in the money besides my skills. They only brought their skills, which, I must admit, are considerable. The four of us run this outfit out of a gloomy three-storeyed building on the outskirts of Bengaluru, where we started, though now we have spread our business all over the country and have offices in five other cities.

Thanks to luck, timing, and some hard work, we're now considered the best in our field. Business is pouring in; we're doing better than we'd ever thought we would. The ups and downs of the business cycle tend to leave us untouched – bad times, in fact, tend to be good for us. We've been accused of preying on misfortunes, but all our clients happen to be well off, and they've yet to complain, so we ignore the accusations.

Most of our people are ex-Army, with a few ex-policemen thrown in. Ex-soldiers are easy to get if you offer understanding, reasonable money, and an environment where they can use their skills. Ex-policemen are harder to accept because most have already made plenty of money on the side, and we don't want the greedy ones. The best we have, come from the paramilitary forces, the CISF, the CRPF, and the BSF, not the general executive whose people have contact with the public. All in all, a disciplined outfit, and relatively easy to run.

I check my e-mails first. There are the mails that come in on the office machine that the mail server picks up, and which can be read by anyone in the office. My silent, efficient, and highly paid secretary deals with most of them, distributing a majority of the rest to my partners, so I hardly ever get to see them. Then there's the personal e-mail account, password protected, that my secretary doesn't even know about.

The regular message, the one I look for every morning, hasn't come in. My heart sinks as I look at the empty inbox. This is the first time Mahipal has missed the morning ritual, but given the business he is in, your first mistake is your last. Mahipal doesn't really work for the firm. Neither does he work for me, though I pay him what would be a generous salary for someone of his age doing almost anything else. For what he does… is beyond price.

I scan the news on the internet and read, with great weight

on my heart, of a murder in Hyderabad, the knifing of a young man for reasons unknown. His papers identify him as one Asif Jamal, originally from Bengaluru. That's the identity I arranged for him less than a year ago. He knew the risks, and he'd provided information that led to a couple of killings, but that doesn't reduce the burden on the survivor. Not for the first time, I ask myself, what do I survive for?

Mahipal worked for himself. When I had first met him a few years ago, he told me what he wanted to do with the rest of his life, and I helped him along. I got him started along a line of action that he wanted to pursue with all his heart.

November 2020

The firm is less than a year old. We're yet to break even, but we have some reserves and I intend to hire good people whenever I come across any. I've left instructions with the receptionist that anyone coming in looking for work without an appointment should be allowed to see one of the partners, if possible.

Today I'm the only partner in the office, and when the receptionist Jai – short for Jaishree – buzzes to check if I'm busy, I tell her I am. 'There's a person here looking for work, a young man,' she tells me.

'Does he look bright?' I ask.

'Yes,' she says after a brief pause. Then, in a discreet whisper, perhaps so he shouldn't hear, 'He looks mad, actually.'

'Send him in.' If he's nuts and I can do something about it, I don't see why I shouldn't.

The man who knocks before he enters looks in his early twenties, and, as Jai said, 'mad'. There's a glint in his eyes you don't see in a normal person's eye. He places a folder on my desk and waits. 'What can I do for you?' I ask.

'I'm looking for a job, sir,' he says. 'My name is Mahipal Rao, and I have a degree in commerce. That's my CV on your desk, sir.' He's very intense, and I wonder why.

'Sit,' I tell him, and he does, sitting ramrod straight in one of the two hard chairs across the desk from me. In the folder is a CV with the salient points on the first page, details in appendices, the way I like it, so you get an overview at the first look. He's twenty, and has done very well in his final year degree exams. 'With a record like this, you should be trying to study further,' I say.

'I need to work,' he says. 'I've to take care of my younger sister, and there's no money left.'

His father's name, his CV says, is Sreedhar Rao. It's a familiar name. Rao owned an upmarket speciality restaurant in which a bomb went off, killing him and his wife, both of whom were inside the restaurant at that time. Two children survived; this must be the elder, the boy. 'You lost your parents in that explosion three months ago?' I ask.

He nods mutely.

'What would you like to do, then?' I ask, snapping the folder shut. He's too intense, too wound up to get work in any normal organisation, I think.

'I don't know,' he blurts. 'That's why I came here. I thought you could tell me what I can do.'

'I understand your loss,' I tell him, 'and you have my sympathies. But I can't tell you what to do.'

'I'll do anything, sir. Anything at all.' His face twists in pain. 'They just blew up my parents. Our whole life went down the drain. No one knows who did it, or why. I can't leave it at that. If I had the money, I'd hire you to find out who did it, and maybe do something about it.'

'What's the point of thinking like that?' I ask. 'You lost your people some months ago. Isn't it time to move on?'

For the first time, he looks me straight in the eye. 'Do you really think so, sir?' In his eyes are pain and anger and a great hunger for something… revenge, maybe. 'You've been through it yourself.' He's challenging me.

'Indeed I have,' I tell him. 'I'm sorry, but I can't hire you for a job here. But if you'd like to come by Monday evening, at about six, I might put you on to someone who might like to have a chat with you. Leave your CV with me.'

'Thank you, sir,' he says, rising. 'I'll be here on Monday, at six.'

Six days to Monday, that gives me time to run a few background checks on him. For that someone who might want to speak to him is myself, but I need to be sure of him beforehand. I pick up the intercom and leave word with Mahesh – that's the partner running background checks – that Mahipal Rao needs to be vetted.

The vetting process includes getting someone to talk to the subject's friends. It's possible to find out his political orientation, history of drug abuse, peccadilloes, everything, in a few days. The report on Mahipal is on my desk on Saturday, first thing in the morning. From what Mahesh's people have understood, he's determined and intelligent. Champion material; actually, a soccer player who gave up the sport to work at his studies, and did very well at them.

The explosion, that cost his parents their lives and their entire life's work, came from a lunch box in a carry bag from a high-end supermarket that somebody had left at the takeaway counter of the restaurant after placing an order. Surviving witnesses said that a clean-shaven young man placed an order with the counter person, said he'd be back in ten minutes, and disappeared. A few minutes later, the bomb in the box went off.

The bomb hadn't been the usual easy-to-buy but hard-to-mix ANFO – ammonium nitrate and fuel oil – but instead a kilo of plastic explosive that had probably been smuggled across the new border a year earlier, and had been set off by a simple electronic timer. Everything in the package except the plastic was freely available in any city anywhere in the country and could have been fixed up by anyone who knew how bombs work best. It had been packed with nails and steel balls, like an anti-personnel mine, and the lunch box, which had a reinforced side, had been placed with the strong side against a wall so the blast was directed into the restaurant hall, where over fifty well-heeled people were eating. Also in the hall was a salad counter, manned by Mahipal's mother, Susheela.

When the smoke and dust settled, eighteen people were dead, including Mahipal's father. Susheela suffered blast and shrapnel injuries and spent a month in the hospital before dying. Fruitless efforts to save her life in a posh hospital cost more than the restaurant was worth. Mahipal and his sister, Neena, who were at a friend's birthday party when the bomb went off, escaped.

Investigations afterwards had revealed little. The police had put out an Identikit picture of the youth who placed the bomb, but he seemed to have disappeared. Forensic tests established little beyond the contents of the bomb itself, and that it had been exploded by a simple timer.

On Monday evening, Mahipal looks a little more hopeful. 'This might take some time,' I tell him. 'A late night.'

'I can't be late, not beyond nine,' he says. 'My sister's alone at home. I can't leave her alone there.'

'We'll go there, then, if we can speak without being disturbed or overheard,' I tell him.

He hesitates, 'Then, will you eat with us if it's very late?'

'I'll take you both out to dinner afterwards instead,' I offer.

He grins for the first time, and his face lightens up dramatically. 'Fine,' he says. 'Let me call and tell her.'

Home is a four-bedroom villa in an expensive gated township

not far from the office. Neena, short and slight and waif-like, opens the door, and he shows me into what seems to be a study upstairs. I question him about how much money they are left with after the blast, and all his answers match with the background check: His parents had been deep in debt, having expanded their restaurant recently, and there was little left for the children. The restaurant, of course, is gone, and this house is mortgaged. He and his sister have enough to see them through the next few months, and that's it. 'Now you know why I can't study further!'

There are loans available for good students, but I don't tell him that. It's clear he doesn't want to study. 'What would you like to do?' I ask.

'I want to get back at whoever did this to us,' he replies. 'The police are doing nothing at all.' Bitterness creeps into his tone. 'They're too busy looking after VIPs to bother about us.' After a brief pause he says, 'My sister's getting married in a few months, and after that I'll be free.' That, too, was in the background. His sister was engaged to a young businessman in England.

It's written all over his face, the anguish and the anger. 'You won't do any good getting worked up about it,' I tell him.

'You know what it's like,' he says, looking up. He looks me straight in the eye again. 'You do know.'

'I do. The someone I mentioned the other day is me. I have something you can do, but it's got nothing to do with the office. It's risky, and you'll have to spend some time preparing yourself.'

'What is it?'

'Essentially, you need to be a hacker. You need to hack into not only a computer network, but also into a community. Learn Urdu and Arabic. You're already familiar with communications technology. Get yourself thorough with it. You should figure out the safest way to send e-mails. Then, go where I tell you, and see what happens.'

October 2025

He understood immediately, of course. I had six months or more to watch him, during which I got him false papers – starting with a government-issued identity card – describing him as Asif Jamal, son of a used-furniture trader in Shivaji Nagar. He went to school, learning a little Arabic and fluent Urdu – of the flavour spoken in Bengaluru, a far cry from that of Lucknow or Bhopal – and brushing up his computer skills. He saw his sister married and settled in England, and gained, with a few props, the ability to change from a bearded, skull-capped young man with fiery eyes to a clean-shaven nerd in minutes. But when he got into his role, the glint of madness that I thought I'd seen in his eyes on our first meeting, disappeared.

I learnt what to get him to do from the history books, from Israel and the Palestine. In the early years after Israel came into being, a large proportion of its people were immigrants. When their intelligence services got going, there was a large supply of immigrants willing to go back to their lands of origin, so getting undercover agents was easy. If Mossad or Shin Bet wanted to insert an agent into Syria, for instance, they had no trouble finding a Jew who had come in from Syria and could go back and be an authentic Syrian. But by the 1970s and 80s, with the supply of immigrants decreasing, the agencies found themselves running out of authentic infiltrators and had to go back to training people who went under cover.

India's intelligence agencies have similar problems – besides the corruption and the lack of motivation, of course. Though about a tenth of the regular police forces are Muslims, there are only a handful of them in the covert agencies, RAW and IB. The agencies have little trouble infiltrating Hindu fundamentalist outfits, but Muslim groups become a problem. Not that the agencies particularly care. Few agents care about the results they generate, and the senior officers in the IPS who work for RAW use postings for rounding out their CVs and spending some time overseas, rather than doing any serious intelligence work.

As for me, I needed information, some of which would be best gathered by an infiltrator. Here was one, at last, committed and probably, trustworthy.

In the beginning, he was spectacularly successful. He divided his time between Bengaluru and Hyderabad, hanging around mosques, and with his show of quiet devotion, attracting the more fanatic element in the crowd. He was a sort of lightning rod that led me, within months, to groups making bombs or smuggling equipment that could be used for assassinations and explosions in crowds. On two occasions, I did what I could – illegally, of course – and told my conscience that the killings I committed would save more lives later.

My original intention was to supplement what he ferreted out of fundamentalist Muslim groups with information I gained from other sources. The other sources made me uncomfortable for a variety of reasons. First, they worked for one government agency or another, and usually had their personal axes to grind as well; so anything you got from them had its own spin.

Second, working with these sources brought, on lonely sleepless nights, disgust at myself. I have contacts – not friends, mind you, though you might catch me having a drink with one of them on a quiet evening – in the police forces of all the states in which we operate. The firm can't survive without good references from senior policemen. In one way or another, I've bribed them, fixing little things for their friends and relatives, paying them off, doing all kinds of greasy things that would have my grandfather – or, for that matter, my father – turning in their graves if they'd been buried instead of being cremated! What I did with these people went completely against my instincts; much more so, to my surprise, than eliminating someone I knew would be happy to let off a bomb in a marketplace.

My grandfather was a soldier, and so was my father. As an only child, I never considered a career other than the Army. Granddad wouldn't have wanted me to leave the Army. Dad advised me against it. 'You need work,' he said when I told him I was thinking of quitting, some months before he died. 'You're not in the Army for the money, and this place won't keep you busy enough.'

'This place' was the family land near Virajpet, some 200 acres of land, under coffee. A tiny plantation, but we grew specialty coffee that sold well. We had a bunch of workers whom we looked after much better than the average plantation did, and they stuck by us to the extent that we had grandchildren of Granddad's employees with us.

Granddad, a former infantry lieutenant colonel who had served in World War II, looked after the estate until my father retired from the command of a division – also infantry – somewhere near Ferozepur in Punjab. By then, I was already a major and Granddad often said that I'd do better than Dad, and become lieutenant general, even though I was a bloody sapper and not an honest infantryman.

On one of his last lucid days before he died, at the age of ninety-three, he told me, 'Boy, play it straight. It doesn't matter what rank you make, what arm you serve. Don't give in to the crooks. There are too many of them around these days.'

The gravelly parade-ground bellow I remembered from childhood had given way to a hoarse whisper, but even that whisper had bite. I knew exactly what he was talking about. In his day, the Army had been honourable. In Dad's day, the elite units had escaped the worst. By the time I got my commission, we were scraping the bottom of the barrel and were still thirty percent short on officer strength. Poor pay, rigorous service conditions, obsolete equipment, not enough rest, and widespread corruption had reached right down to battalion commanders and junior officers who helped themselves to mess funds; quartermasters who demanded supplies that disappeared; doctors who sold certificates; and people willing to pay for plum postings at Army HQ in Delhi. Engineers I knew paid to avoid postings with sapper squadrons, preferring appointments as garrison engineers in rear garrisons, where they could make plenty of money on the side. 'Right,' I said. 'I intend to do just that.'

'Good lad. Your father was lucky. You might not be. Don't blame yourself.'

Dad wasn't just lucky. He took a route that kept him clear of the paperwork and retired one of the best field-grade commanders in the Army, an earnest proponent of the Cold Start strategy, leading a crack division in the northwest, poised against what we thought was the best of the Pakistani Army. He spoke little, closed his eyes to the skulduggery going on around him, and stuck to the front teeth of the Army, where the corruption was least. If he'd had a little less backbone and a little more skin, he might have risen higher. For himself, he was doggedly honest, and his men invariably said he took care of them. Mom didn't like it, being stuck in out-of-the-way towns and, worse still, being separated from him while he was off in the forward areas where they didn't permit families. But she, too, understood him, and while she complained most of the time, she backed him up when it mattered. That made all the difference. The only advice he ever gave me was to try to get a secondment to a paratrooper commando battalion. He pointed out that it would encourage the paper-pushers at the HQ to keep me in the teeth. Good advice, it turned out to be. I completed the course and spent three years doing things I don't want to talk about except in that they equipped me for much of what I was to do afterwards.

But it all came to naught seven years ago, just before Dad retired – the second partition. The politicians gave in to the pressure and let go of Kashmir. Kashmir, they said, was too expensive to keep, in blood and in money. Neither the blood nor the money came from the people who made the decision; the money came from taxes and the blood mostly from soldiers and defenceless civilians.

They took their time working out the details – three years of waves of violence, of polarisation. At first, they thought that Kashmir would form an independent republic, but a quick referendum revealed that Kashmiris wanted to be united with their brethren in Azaad Kashmir, or PoK as we knew it, and they acceded to Pakistan months after gaining their independence.

The secession of Kashmir, and its accession to Pakistan a year later, took the backbone out of the Army. Nearly a hundred thousand uniformed men, including at least one lieutenant general and four major generals, put in their papers within a year of the secession. Almost all were hard-bitten veterans of conflict, from the units that made up the sharpest of the Army's teeth. What remained was the dispirited tail, and perhaps a bit of rump occupying the Army HQ, mostly paper-pushers.

The decision to let Kashmir go had been made before Granddad died. He had seen it coming, and had also observed the fall in standards. So had I. I, too, was one of the hundred thousand who quit. But I had other reasons to quit.

March 2019

I've no great love for Delhi, and whenever I have to be there I don't get out of the Army Enclave at Dhaula Kuan unless I have to. I'm here for a brief course at the Indian Institute of Technology – a technical thing on testing construction products for integrity – and have my cell phone switched off for the duration of the presentation.

A uniformed clerk raps on the door of the classroom, and the instructor, a lady colonel with no idea of combat conditions, excuses herself before calling him in. The clerk hands the instructor a slip of paper, salutes, and leaves. The instructor looks, her eyes searching for someone. They come to rest on me. 'There's an urgent message for you,' she says. 'Call this number.' She holds out a piece of paper to me – with my name and a cell phone number written on it.

I switch on my phone and call the familiar number. It's a senior colleague Dinesh, also posted at the sapper base in Bengaluru, where I am. I make a video call; and when Dinesh picks up his phone, I can see how troubled he is. 'What is it?' I ask.

'You'd better come back now,' he tells me. 'Look up the news. There's been a blast in a mall.'

'Hold on a minute.' I put him on hold and get on to a news website on the Internet. The red banner across the bottom says 'Breaking News'. The scrolling message beside it says, 'Blast in Bengaluru's Pegasus Mall: 21 feared dead, 55 injured'. My chest fills, my breath stops. Manju, my wife, was supposed to take my parents shopping there today, for buying things in anticipation of my return home in a few days. 'Dinesh, where are you?' I ask.

'At St. John's Hospital,' he replies. 'That's where they took everyone.'

'How are they?'

He hesitates. 'That's for the doctors to tell you.'

'Who's hurt?' I ask.

'Gayatri's unhurt,' he replied. 'Your father covered her. Everyone else is in the hospital. Someone has informed Manju's parents; they're on their way, with her brother.'

At least there wouldn't be any immediate cash crunch. 'Let me find out about the flights.'

'You do that, and let me know.'

Flying is expensive, but tickets are easy to get. I book myself on the next flight to Bengaluru, leaving in an hour and a half. That leaves me just enough time to pack and get to the airport. Someone will get me through security faster than a civilian can hope to get through. The instructor is indifferent, the rest sympathetic, but not overly so. 'Don't worry,' they say. 'Hope for the best.' By the time I'm ready, there's a jeep waiting, with a police escort out front. Someone must have pulled strings.

I keep the news channel on all the way to the aircraft. There've been two explosions side by side, the first smaller, perhaps to get people to look up, the second the killer, a powerful bomb loaded with shrapnel – nails and balls – that did the actual damage. Dad must have reacted instinctively to the first blast – the result of a lifetime's training. The wounded have all been taken to St. John's Hospital, the one nearest to the mall – important during peak hour traffic – and one of the largest now in the city. It's well-equipped, but Dinesh's words and tone don't leave much room for hope.

Getting to St. John's from Bengaluru's airport could be a long nightmare, but there's a jeep waiting for me and the driver has a flashing red light on top. Dinesh, who's in the jeep with me, says little on the way. There is nothing to say. About six hours from the time I first spoke to Dinesh, I'm at the hospital, with the uniformed driver working his way ahead through the crowd of relatives and newsmen milling in the lobby, all sort of held back by a line of policemen. As I pass, a dishevelled plump woman grabs my arm. 'Help me,' she says. 'My daughter's in there. They won't tell me anything about her or let me see her.' She looks at me, senses something, and says, 'You have someone in there?'

I nod, and she continues. 'They're not letting people in. Am I different from you just because you have a uniform and I don't? Don't you people think I'm human?'

I see the tears tracks down her cheeks. Sympathy overwhelms me. 'Why aren't they letting these people in?' I ask a police inspector standing by.

He takes a lazy look at my epaulettes and paratrooper badge and decides finally to answer. 'VIP protection, sir. Minister inside.'

'So why can't this lady see her daughter?'

'Minister come out, lady go in.'

I clamp down on my urge to hurry and look behind. A lady subaltern hovers a few feet away. She catches my eye and approaches. I look at her name tag, and ask, 'Lieutenant Sinha, would you mind frisking this lady?' I point at the plump woman. It's not part of Lt. Sinha's job, doing this sort of a thing, so I can only ask.

Lt. Sinha is game. She nods, and inspects the woman's ID, a driving licence, before patting her down. Sinha asks a couple of soft questions, then reports, 'She's clear, sir.'

Dinesh and I take her along into the corridor leading to the lifts. The inspector glares, and a couple of men from my unit fall in behind us. The inspector backs off. We walk along bright corridors smelling of antiseptic, go up ramps designed for gurneys, and reach our destination, three floors above. One of my men takes charge of the lady and I go into the room where the doctors have got Manju on a drip, tubes going into her nose. Gayatri flies into my arms, wailing, and we hang on to each other. 'What about Mom?' I ask. 'Dad?'

One of the doctors looks at me. 'Your mother and father?' He shakes his head. 'We couldn't save them. Sorry.'

I squeeze Manju's warm hand, but there's no response. I'm numb.

October 2025

Part of me is still numb. Manju never moved again. She hung on for three days, her life reduced to blips and jagged green lines on a monitor. I sat by her, wondering if she dreamt, and hoping that her dreams were pleasant. On a sunny spring morning, an eternity after the blasts, she passed quietly on. I lit her pyre three days after I'd done the same for my parents, dried Gayatri's tears as best I could, and held back my own.

A week later the lady who had appealed for help to see her daughter got in touch. She had remembered my name from my name tag, and, having remembered the insignia on my epaulettes, had been told my rank. Her daughter was better, she said, when she called me. She offered condolences. She'd seen my parents' names in the newspaper, and figured out I'd gone to see them. 'How's your wife?' she asked.

'Gone,' I said. 'Six days ago.' I didn't tell her how empty those days had been and how difficult to live through.

She offered more condolences before coming to the point. 'You saw what I went through; so, can't you, being an officer after all, get these people in uniform to be more humane?' she asked after a bit.

I explained that I was a junior officer; and in any case, security matters for ministers and such were handled by the police. I thought she was being crude, doing this to me now, but I could see her point of view – who else could she go to? In that instant, I decided that the time had come to leave the Army. I couldn't work for such a government. Gayatri was all I had left, and I'd make sure she got the best. Nothing else mattered.

There was no means then to tell what the future held, but even if I'd known, it wouldn't have changed my decision, even though I had some unfinished business left.

April 2012

A group of twenty Taliban associates from Kandahar have crossed the LOC into Kashmir somewhere near Drass, a few kilometres west of Kargil, at one of their favourite crossings. A Rashtriya Rifles (RR) battalion from Kargil moves in to isolate the group, with two companies cordoning off the Taliban and another offering a mobile reserve, though mobility in these hilly areas is questionable.

Warm weather and unseasonal rains have turned rocky hillsides slippery, and green areas into mini swamps, so the cordon is increasingly difficult to maintain. The area is thinly populated, and the RR battalion has got all the residents out into a camp set up for them.

I am scouting the area for signs of a build-up of men and materials; no one wants a repeat of the Kargil conflict, which nearly grew into a war. The RR battalion commander knows that if he waits long enough, the fugitives would run out of food and ammunition, will have to give up. He is preparing for a mini siege.

However, a new problem has come up – a sniper. The man seems to be crossing the cordon almost at will, usually by night, like a wraith. He's already taken out one of the company commanders, a senior non-commissioned officer, and two jawans. The men are afraid because the sniper strikes without warning. Standard counter-sniper measures mean locating the sniper, pinning him down, and then hitting him with overwhelming superior firepower. They haven't worked because of the terrain and the weather. The man gets away before the RR men can get into position. In these conditions, a one-man or two-men team can move much faster than, say, a section of riflemen. 'Oh, boy,' I think, the sniper in mind, 'you're good.' Only one way to get you – you don't expect a sniper to come after you.

The idea crystallises. I tell the RR CO, 'I could go in there with a buddy and bring a few of them down.' He doesn't like it much, partly because it's not in the book, and partly because the best snipers are NCOs, not officers. Officers normally don't go out hunting on their own. But he knows that Special Forces men don't respect the hierarchy the way regulars do, so he agrees.

The men hunker down. The cordon becomes a defensive operation, aimed at keeping the fugitives inside rather than closing in on them. And I go after the fugitives with a spotter, a veteran from my own unit. I've got map coordinates of where the fugitives were last seen, and some idea of their numbers and equipment, and a radio for the RR to let me know if they're spotted.

On the second day, I spot three men in a bunker against the steep hillside. It's camouflaged, but I spot the gun slit from 400 metres. From then on, it's a matter of waiting. I get one and in the panic that follows, I get another two. A barrage of return fire misses me because I've skipped twenty metres by the time it starts.

Now that we've spotted them, I call in artillery, and a brief bombardment encourages the rest of them to surrender. The sniper gets away, but from the captives we get a name – Noordin, the Ghost, an Afghan mujahid.

I have an account to settle with him.

October 2025

I never did settle that account. I never encountered him after that, but I always thought of him with a sneaking respect because he could have attacked the civilians in the camp and driven the RR unit back but he never did.

But news of the man kept filtering through, and I followed him when I could.

Three

Thomas

October 2025

I tend to be regular, almost mechanical getting to work. Every day, I take the same route at the same time, in the same car with the same driver, and my colleagues keep telling me I'm being stupid because regularity makes me vulnerable. I smile when anyone tells me this to my face, and say, 'I must be the most harmless policeman in the country. Why would anyone want to kill me?'

On my way back home, I tend to wander a little. Sometimes I go to a bar for a drink or two – usually small – and sometimes I visit a friend. This is a cover. I occasionally have to meet my controller, and the purpose of my evening wanderings is to conceal these meetings. The trickiest bit of all this is getting past my own security detail, which is headed by an inspector of the Delhi Police whom I have selected for his incompetence. I smile without humour thinking of the man – dull but well-connected; he has been foisted upon me by a superior. And every senior policeman needs some deadwood serving under him, to take the blame if nothing else.

On this warm October evening, I have to meet my controller again – after a gap of months – and have made plans to be available to him by half past seven in the evening. I will go to a bar, slip out of the rear staff entrance, which my security detail don't know about, and a waiting car will take me to the meeting, in a safe house sanitised by the controller's staff, none of whom is American.

I try to rise early, in the hope of having my breakfast alone, in peace, but am unlucky today. My wife, Nancy, whom I encourage to stay in bed late so that I can get away before she rises, is up at half past seven, an hour before her regular wake-up time. She arrives at the breakfast table when I am midway through, to ask when I'll return in the evening. 'Late,' I tell her, and, leaving my breakfast unfinished, pick up my briefcase and call for the driver over her rising protests. I know I'll have to pay for it when I return, but I cannot afford to be late for this meeting, and I need some time at the office to prepare.

At the office, the headquarters of the National Investigation Agency, I plough through my early-morning paperwork, finishing it by eleven, complete my rounds, and find myself more or less free. One of the advantages, I've discovered, of being with the prestigious NIA is that while there's a great deal of work, there's also the freedom to schedule it to suit one's convenience.

The most important of the investigations I head presently is a terrorist attack at a temple in Madurai. The NIA was called in two days after the attack, for protocol demands that the state police call in the NIA only when they come across something big or complex or sensitive enough to be sure that it's beyond their own capabilities to handle smoothly. In this case, the Madurai police should have reasoned it out immediately, but they didn't; so we lost at least a day.

Three devotees were killed, and one acolyte. None was wealthy, or connected. The laboratories determined that the plastic explosive used in the blast was manufactured at an ordinance factory near Murree – not far from the Inter-service Intelligence's school in Pakistan – and they called us in. I know that I will not get far with it. I'll have a few suspects rounded up and interrogated, and have chargesheets filed against them. After that, the case will wander along the labyrinths of the courts and be forgotten. I also have a rough idea how the explosive arrived in the country, across the border with Nepal at Raxaul, where the men at the customs checkpoints are among the most venal in the country.

There is no evidence that will stand up in court. I have this knowledge from long years of observation. I'll file this bit of information somewhere, and use it to make inferences that might come in handy later. I have accumulated many of these bits of information and have turned a surprising number of them into assets. A gentle telephone call to a member of parliament telling him that his secretary is involved in a drug ring, for instance, has earned me both money and a string to pull.

I didn't always think in these ways. As I sign off on a memo that mentions the damage done at the Madurai crime scene by ham-fisted local policemen, at my team's inability to get uncontaminated forensic evidence – the memo will come in handy years from now, when the prosecution fails to establish its case – and the delays in referring the case to the NIA, a stray thought catches me off guard.

'How did it come to this?' I wonder, remembering what I was thirty years ago.

∽

Summer, 1995

One of the eighty odd men and women to complete the basic training course at the Police Academy in Hyderabad, I find myself the assistant superintendent in charge of a rural *taluk* of Bhatkal district in Karnataka. This is my first independent posting and I find life outside the academy to be a great deal more interesting once I come to terms with my independence. My immediate boss, the district superintendent, is only a few years older; and, while he doesn't interfere, he is always available for guidance.

He hands me my first real case, which I find interesting as well as challenging. An insurance salesman, a youngster of some twenty-eight years, has been knifed to death in a crowded street. I decide to follow up on the investigation myself, visiting the scene of the crime twice, and personally interrogating three of the witnesses. I understand a few essential facts – the murderer knew what he was about for he found his victim in a crowd, knew exactly where to stab him, and left the knife behind but no fingerprints. Typical of a professional killer. Investigations so far have revealed that the victim was a harmless professional, moderately successful, married two years ago.

Investigations need to be done carefully. The purpose of a typical police investigation is not just to find out who did it, but also to enable the prosecutor, through careful collection of evidence, to prove in court that the accused is indeed the culprit. Investigating strategies must consider the Evidence Act – most of which is dreadfully out of date – and the nature of the judge conducting the trial. The sequence in which evidence is put forth, and the maintenance of its integrity, is as important as the sequence in which the parts of a skyscraper are put together. In both, investigations and construction, the end result won't hold up if everything isn't done right. Of course, a crooked judge –

and there's no shortage of those – can turn all this inside out, but the quality of the investigation always shows in the reports.

Reports of investigations, too, conform to a format. They can seem complete while leaving out large parts of the evidence available, or actually collected. That's at the discretion of the investigating officer. An investigation conducted by the book can ask all questions that seem right while missing the point altogether.

I hark back to the lecture sessions at the academy, which were led by a senior officer with the Intelligence Bureau, one Rahul Sadasivan, who has concluded many tricky murder cases during his tenure with the Central Bureau of Investigation. He is something of an icon in the service, a man with a reputation for being fearless and incorruptible. They say he's missed promotions a couple of times because he didn't hesitate to antagonise his own seniors, besides politicians. He's known to lead a simple life and is accessible to the public who might want to complain about police behaviour in his jurisdiction.

When the inspector in charge of this case fails to come up with a viable motive, I get suspicious. Officers of my rank rarely participate in investigations We generally point the way and let juniors do the legwork. In this case, that won't do.

So, despite being short of time, I take over the case, and following Sadasivan's guidelines, look for something that doesn't fit. A month after the murder, I meet the victim's widow, a voluptuous young woman in her early twenties whose grief seems to have been short-lived. A little questioning reveals that she is ambitious and wants far more than her late husband would have been able to provide. But where would a young woman from a good family, and not much exposure to the world, find access to a professional killer? And how would she pay for it?

A little observation reveals more – the widow has a lover, a middle-aged, married and very wealthy mine-owner with political ambitions, who has often contributed generously to the coffers of the ruling party in Bengaluru, and, as a consequence, has managed to get the investigation slowed down.

Local knowledge is always useful. I have learnt Kannada, the language of this state. Now, on the principle that petty criminals, if used judiciously, can offer leads to larger criminals, and armed with my knowledge of the language, I develop my own network of informers in Bhatkal. It's not easy, getting away on my own, but I do; and the rewards are great. Within weeks, I discover more about the several hundred policemen in my jurisdiction than I would have in the entire two years I expect to spend in this posting. My immediate subordinates, it turns out, are very different from what I'd imagined them to be.

The inspector in charge of this case, for instance, I'd always considered him to be a plodding, unimaginative man with no personal initiative, honest, miserly, and most concerned with living within his means. From one of my older informants, an alcoholic pickpocket and small-time burglar, I discover that this inspector, now nearing retirement with no further promotion possible, has still managed to build a rather lavish house in his hometown, besides getting his daughter married off very well – all on the income of a relatively minor government official. I check his background – he could have inherited money, or married it – and find that his ancestral home is less than two kilometres from the mine owner's. From there, it becomes easier. The inspector's house, I find, is valued officially at less than a quarter of its market value, and his daughter's dowry paid largely in gold and cash.

I find the killer, too, a professional from another district. He's been seen in the area, following the victim around. But I cannot establish the link between the mine-owner and the professional – they have always dealt through at least two levels of intermediaries.

I manage to get the inspector suspended and later dismissed

from service, the mine-owner involved in several criminal cases, and myself a name as someone incorruptible, competent, and persistent. At this time, I am sure that I am all those things. I certainly look it – lean and tall and straight-backed, severe in my crisp khaki uniform. For a short while, I am proud of myself. I write to Rahul Sadasivan, telling him how useful his lectures have been. He sends me a gracious handwritten note in reply that I file among my most precious possessions.

Summer, 1997

A few years later came my first promotion, to a superintendent with independent charge of a district, and marriage to Nancy. The parents arranged it – essentially, my father and hers – and promised each other that Nancy and I would marry, very soon after my training. Informing Nancy and me of the deal was secondary, we get to know only months before the event, when the parents need to fix up the details.

Nancy, an only child, is probably impressed by my position in the police services. She only knows of the sub-inspector in charge of the local police station, an unsavoury man himself, feared by everyone on the street, wealthier than most, and piling it on hand over fist. Her cousin, recently married to another policeman, an inspector, seems to be doing well. She thinks that being married to someone an order of magnitude senior to these men will bring her unimaginable wealth and position.

I demur. I have asked around a little, and know of her father, who owns a coffee plantation in the hills near Kottayam. He has been involved in many questionable deals, some of them in collusion with local government officials. Then Ammachi tells me the story. They are broke. An uncle has challenged her right to a valuable patch of land, her inheritance, and the case is likely to drag on for at least a decade, or probably two. I meet the uncle, to try to persuade him to settle out of court, and discover that he thinks he is right. He will not back off an inch from his position, which is that the land is entirely his. 'I know you're in the police, boy,' he tells me as I leave, 'but don't think I fear you.'

'You have no need,' I tell him.

He laughs, 'Do you expect me to believe that? I know who you're marrying and why. But just remember – whatever you do to me, I'll do twice to your parents and your sister. They have to live here, even if you don't.'

He has a loud voice in the church hereabouts, and with local politicians as well. I privately think his case against Ammachi has some legal substance, but cannot say so. In any case, I have no intention of using whatever little influence I have with the local police to interfere with him. 'Let's not look at all that,' I tell him. 'Let the courts decide on the property and leave it at that.' I turn my back on him.

Nancy, despite my protests, brings a large dowry that is set aside for the man who is to become my brother-in-law, my sister's husband. I am in debt, to Nancy and her father, with no way of paying them back. I am trapped.

Spring, 1998

What little charm Nancy has fades away quickly. As we set up our house, I discover that she is more than a little spoilt. She likes to have her way and throws tantrums, often in front of visitors, even my subordinates, when she doesn't get it. She has no qualms about misusing whatever power she thinks I might have. Matters come to a head when she comes to me with a registration number. 'Find out who was driving this car,' she tells me. 'He should be taught a lesson.'

'What has he done?'

'Find out yourself!' she shouts. 'What kind of a policeman are you?' she retreats to the bedroom, slamming the door.

At the next opportunity I ask my driver what happened. He tells me that she was in a hurry to get somewhere and asked him to rush. A cab ahead of him refused to give way. My driver forced his way past, forced the cab off the road, and slapped the cabbie because he, too, thought the cabbie should be 'taught a lesson'.

A telephone call is all it takes to have the cabbie traced and taken to the nearest police station. I have left instructions that I should be informed when he arrives, and that he should be treated with caution. I cannot bear the thought that my relatives should misuse their position. I speak to him on the phone, asking him to meet me directly. He turns out to be middle-aged and sober, with no record of bad driving, a steady worker, paying off his loans more or less on time. It turns out he was taking someone to the airport and was in a bit of a hurry. He still doesn't really understand why he'd been forced off the road by a police car ferrying the wife of a police officer to a private function. He seems apathetic to the treatment he's got, though. I see his point of view, and, in fact, share it. The attitude of many of my colleagues has begun to disgust me. They think of the public as subjects, or people to be milked. 'Your driver took fifty rupees to give my keys back,' he tells me.

I take a fifty-rupee note out of my pocket and he smiles. 'What are you giving me that for?' he asks, his anger and resentment breaking through his apathy. 'I've lost a day's business coming to the police station and then here, waiting to talk to you. I've been dragged out of my car and slapped and insulted by one of your people. I'll fall behind on this month's loan instalment because of all this nonsense. What are you trying to prove by giving me this money?' He takes a deep breath and apologises.

'I shouldn't speak to you like that,' he says. 'Please forgive me… I have a family to feed.'

I put the note back in my pocket with a deepening sense of shame and helplessness, and send the cabbie away. Later, when the driver asks me what happened, I tell him that in my opinion, the cabbie was entirely right. Nancy gets this from him by evening, and that night, we have the loudest and most serious quarrel of our life together. I tell her at the end that she is free to do as she likes, but will not misuse any of the petty authority she thinks she has because of my position, and that she will keep her rancour to herself in the presence of others. For the first and only time I threaten her – anytime she breaks these rules, I will make sure her father, whom she drags into every argument, suffers at least as much as I do. That is the end of the fight.

I am glad Nancy and I have no children. In the first few years, I force myself to bed her sometimes. With the passing of the years, with Nancy growing fat and ever more shrill, I give up even that – much to her relief, I think.

Perhaps sexual frustration makes her even more unpleasant. I hear every evening of how a cousin of hers, married to a sub-inspector in the Karnataka police force, posted somewhere near the border with Kerala, lives better, has more servants, goes abroad for holidays, and is generally more content.

Two years into the marriage, her father asks me to 'fix' a relative in what he considers a lowly job, as a constable. Lacking the spine to refuse point-blank, I evade, and do nothing. Their contempt for me grows, as does my isolation, from her and from my own parents, who wonder what I am trying to prove.

Spring, 2000

Three years into the marriage, with my second promotion to a senior superintendent, I find an oasis in the desert of my life – another woman – in a moment of disturbing serendipity. Her name is Mridula, and she is the widow of a fellow-officer, who was killed as he left his mistress's abode… apparently. She grieves little; the marriage had been rocked by her late husband's serial infidelities, and she was separated from him. She lives in Delhi with her two children, determined now to manage with the small pension the government gives her, supplemented by a salary from the NGO where she works.

I have worked under her husband, and have met her once before, which was an awkward meeting. On an official visit to Delhi, I take a break to pay her a visit and offer condolences. I find her home small but comforting, the children gap-toothed but engaging, and I stay longer than I'd planned. Over the next eight months, I find myself looking for reasons to visit Delhi, and when the opportunity comes to join the CBI and move there, I grab it… though I detest the city.

After moving to Delhi, I pursue her actively. The feeling that my life is spinning out of control grows, until I conclude that I have not really chosen any part of my life – even this one pleasant part. I gravitate wherever my nature and my circumstances take me. A voice somewhere in my head tells me that this is just an evasion of my responsibilities, but I ignore that voice. In Mridula I find comfort, at last, and a reawakening of lust. I plan. I arrange for her to move to a place where I can meet her discreetly and create for her a wholly false new life, with a husband away most of the time.

She tells me that she will never be able to acknowledge me; that her children must grow up without the baggage of a scandal. I agree. Friendship and occasional meetings are sufficient, and I soon find myself liking the children.

Quietly, in my office in the CBI, I learn the ropes of negotiating bribes, taking them discreetly, and making the money seem innocent. Unlike some of my more acquisitive colleagues, I am willing to sacrifice a large percentage of the takings in return for safety, and, over the years, Mridula finds herself a consultant with a number of organisations that she doesn't know about, collecting cheques on which she pays income tax, paying off loans that materialise out of nowhere. At first, she is bemused, but takes things in her stride. I explain to her that for our relationship to continue, she must. She must also save, I keep telling her, because there is a limit to what I can make on the side without serious unease. Since the money is all apparently legitimate, she must invest what she can, ensuring comfort in her old age.

And Nancy continues to sneer at the salary that I take home to her.

∽

October 2025

I find a message on the new communications system just implemented at NIA HQs. Rising costs have forced staff cutbacks. Intelligence agencies have tended to be as bureaucratic as any other government office, senior intelligence officials think like other bureaucrats – one sign of the clout a high-up carries is the number of staff assigned to him. The regular police, the IB, and the CBI all continue to think of power in terms of manpower. One of the trappings of power is personal staff. Even retired officers tend to grab what they can. As a result, the law enforcement system needs large numbers of clerical and other staff to function properly.

The ultra-secretive Research and Analysis Wing has never been a regular bureaucracy and has always been run as its chief, an innocuously designated secretary who reports directly to the prime minister, thinks fit. But the government has tried to experiment with the NIA, still in its teens, to create an organisation that runs without too many junior staff. For one thing, the more people in an intelligence agency, the greater the expense of vetting and recruiting them and then training them. And the more the number of people, the higher the chances of people being bribed or turned by another agency.

The NIA has done away with some of the trappings. Every official is supposed to be highly computer-literate and should be able to operate with as little paper as possible. Every official is aware of the risks of sloppy computer security, myself even more so than others. I know that the others laugh at me for being so particular, but I don't mind. I've developed some unusual skills. I've worked out the passwords of several fellow officials from the way their fingers move on keyboards, practised reading text upside down and at odd angles, and learnt the Hindi slang that some officials use under the impression that my Hindi is no good. So I get to read messages that I shouldn't, but no one knows about that.

This present message is a circular from my opposite number in the IB. It's some follow-up about false identification papers on a dead man in Hyderabad. The police found, some weeks ago, on trying to contact his next-of-kin that he isn't the Asif Jamal his papers said he was. The middle-aged lady at the Bengaluru address on his card said that while she did have a son called Asif in Hyderabad, the man in the photograph was Karim, Asif's friend. She didn't know where the false Asif hailed from, and, when questioned, neither did her son, the real Asif. The news went up the police ranks and on to the IB, which passed it on to me, for my name is on a list of officers to whom reports of such incidents must be circulated. I followed up and suggested a watch on the fundamentalist Hindu groups who might be trying to penetrate Pakistani terrorist networks. This present message names three such Hindu organisations that are worth watching because they get money from abroad.

I've already been through the records of two of these outfits, and both seem clear. The money coming in has been accounted for – it's gone into a college, a hospital, several schools, and an orphanage. I suspect the schools teach their students a little Hinduism besides the regular government-approved curriculum but that, as far as I've been able to make out, is negligible. The man who's made this report has done it just to give the impression he's working.

But the message breaks through my preoccupation. I've spent considerable time on trying to find Asif's real identity without success. Competition among intelligence agencies is fierce. This man could well be part of an operation being run by another agency, or even someone on his own. I've been through what NIA records I could find, but have found nothing that could involve a man with a fake ID in Hyderabad, definitely not a youngster in his twenties. A few secure telephone calls and some more searching has yielded nothing from the IB or RAW.

So who could it be?

Something strikes me as odd as I break for lunch, which I take, as usual, in the officers' dining hall on the ground floor. Lunch at the office is never particularly good, but then I look for sustenance in food, not pleasure. Besides, it keeps me from eating too much. Ten minutes later, I am back at my desk, looking through my diary of notes – all unbreakably password protected – that lives on a flash drive in my office.

I have indexed these notes myself and can look among them along the lines that the official database doesn't offer. I look for unusual killings and find eight. I discard six of them – one is a teenage suicide, another a drug overdose, and the rest murders of known dangerous criminals. But two recent ones catch my attention.

Both victims are men, killed by shots from a powerful rifle fired from far away – at least 600 metres in one case and 800 metres in the other. The rifle is a high-end sniper rifle, one of the few models used typically by Special Forces soldiers of any of a dozen or more poorer countries, including India, meaning it's not the best or the latest, but adequate in its way.

Even more interesting than the mode of the killings was the evidence found on the victims and in their temporary residences. They were involved in what might be called terrorist conspiracies – one of the dead men turned out to be an explosives expert retained by the Lashkar to improvise bombs meant to go off in crowded marketplaces or on commuter trains. The other was in the process of moving a cache of weapons from one safe-house to another.

Investigators seemed to have assumed that they were eliminated by a Lashkar sniper for suspected treachery. But the leads generated by the killings led the police to two detailed plans for mayhem in Delhi and Mumbai, and on to a ring that smuggled weapons and other material into India for groups like the Lashkar. Even though the killer – the investigators believed strongly that the same sniper shot the two – was never found, the various agencies involved came away feeling that they had gained. I have the self-congratulatory memos to substantiate all this.

Going through these lumps of turgid writing, I know that these two deaths are linked to the death in Hyderabad. I put the notes away to prod at another hunch – vigilante. It's unlikely to be a single man, because the kind of information required to pin down these two men takes a fairly efficient organisation with resources and time.

Dwelling on this produces conflicting emotions. Disgust, aimed partly at myself for being a part of such a lethargic and self-serving establishment; relief that someone has finally woken up to ignore the establishment; and more disgust that I, as a part of the establishment, will have to go after this bunch who are doing my job for me.

But then, doing my job properly is a sure way of losing it, as I discovered long ago.

December 2014

The NIA is relatively new but it is staffed by old hands, some of them very wily. The chief, the director general, is a former deputy DG of the IB, and not a friend. Directly under him is the additional director general, under whom are two inspectors generals, one for Investigations, that's me, and another for Operations and Coordination.

On paper, our mandate is clear. We take up everything involving weapons of mass destruction, delivery systems, terrorism, and so on. We could be called in by state governments or have something pushed into our laps by another central agency that encounters a case involving our specialties.

Nothing works that well, because of the people involved, and, more significantly, the jealousies. There's the usual inter-agency conflict, where you learn the value of information, and its different forms. The CBI, my old agency, has been investigating a sitting MP in Mumbai who is accused of bribe-taking on a breathtaking scale.

Investigating a powerful politician is always an uneasy process. I always think of Shakespeare and turbulent priests when I think of these cases, because the man himself usually doesn't interfere with any of us. Instead, his friends in the police – all established politicians have friends in the police – misdirect the CBI's investigators.

They have many ways of doing this. One of the most powerful tools in an investigation is the informer. Each policeman has his own jealously guarded set of informers. Local police simply refrain from telling CBI investigators, who aren't familiar with local conditions, about local informers. Alternatively, they might offer informers who have been primed to misdirect investigators. The onus is always on the investigator because he has to prove that the accused is guilty because any gaps or inconsistencies in the evidence are sufficient for a good lawyer to get charges dropped.

In the course of their investigation, the CBI investigators find that this MP has been taking money from a young businessman who's been smuggling explosives. The businessman is the scion of an industrialist, who happens to be well known for his honesty and philanthropy. The case is too hot for them and ends up with the NIA field office in Mumbai on the grounds that the explosives might be used by suicide bombers.

The field office runs into a wall very soon. Since this is a high-profile case, with the MP making threatening noises about harassment, I push the investigators and discover that there are so many intervening layers between the MP and the money that it's next to impossible to prove that he's taking any.

On a visit to the Mumbai field office I run into an inspector, who, like me, took a transfer from the Maharashtra State Police to the NIA, and find him deeply unhappy, so I invite him to a private chat after working hours. He says he's been sidelined by his boss, the superintendent in charge of the field office, and regrets the shift. The superintendent is a by-the-book man, while the inspector prefers to refer to the seat of his pants. A series of inexplicable but accurate hunches running counter to the superintendent's deductions has put him in the chief's bad books.

The inspector has a network of informers that is now almost moribund. I tell him to revive it and report directly to me for the time being, which he is glad to do. In the office next morning, I ask the superintendent if he can assign that inspector to me for the next few weeks. The superintendent demurs. 'He's not of much use,' he tells me. 'You must have seen his ACRs (Annual Confidential Reports).'

'That I have,' I reply. 'If he turns out as poor as that, I'll replace him.'

The inspector, to my delight, does his rounds and revives his network in the next couple of days. We discover, after doing the rounds of several bars where the ungodly find their entertainment, that the smuggling ring has been around for some years, and operates under the benevolent eyes of a group of police and coast guard officials of all ranks, who have got themselves involved in it to the extent that they simply call it 'The Fund'.

The principle is simple – crime is too big and too profitable to leave to the criminals. It must be regulated. A single large shipment of drugs or arms brings the dealer more profit than a middle-level police or customs officer would earn in his lifetime. A little blindness of the watcher eases everyone's life. But how does the watcher – now no longer a watcher – deal with his money?

This is where 'The Fund' comes in. It runs a set of accounts with highly secretive Swiss banks, into which large pay-offs go. Monies transferred to these go to Middle-Eastern countries where income tax does not exist, in the form of consulting or other fees, and thence to other accounts in Europe and the US where they are used by children or other relatives of the officials who have chosen to turn a blind eye to the pipeline. Also paid are politicians, taxmen, and sundry others who might do the damage. The incredible advantage, I discover, is that policemen deliver both the threat and the bribe. People who stand in the way tend to be steamrolled by a variety of means, ranging from simple harassment by the local police to having relatives treated in imaginative fashion by men who make a profession of pain.

Large companies, Indian and foreign, use the money to facilitate the release of bank loans, to get rid of awkward employees, to pay off safety inspectors at factories, to get power at low rates, to get questionable goods past customs inspectors, to intimidate debtors and owners or properties they covet, and so on. Companies participating in 'The Fund' are responsible for four-fifths of the advertising revenue that the media gets – enough to ensure that no investigative journalist ever accuses a member of 'The Fund' of wrong-doing.

One in every five senior police officers is a member. There is, in fact, a waiting list, and, for some, a membership fee, paid usually in favours or, occasionally, in blood. The ones willing to pay the most to keep the pipeline under wraps are my colleagues from various law enforcement agencies, the major beneficiaries of 'The Fund'. Over the weeks that follow, the inspector and I receive, in equal measure, sticks, in the form of threats of painful death, and carrots, in the form of offers for membership of 'The Fund'. Free, of course, for now.

I follow up, among the juniors, and the messengers, to discover who thought it up. I run into a dead end, and a surprise – the present manager of 'The Fund' is a relatively junior police officer, up from the ranks, who retired as a deputy superintendent with Mumbai's crime branch. One free evening I pay him a visit at his anonymous single-bedroom flat in Borivili.

Children play in the concrete parking space below, and fit young men in strange haircuts lounge in the corridors, quiet and watchful. A dark man with scarred hands and a pot belly mans the old lift. It's very clear that no mischief will be allowed in this neighbourhood!

As for the man himself, his ears sprout hair, and he wears an undershirt, baggy trousers, and worn blue rubber slippers.

He reads the local newspaper while his wife chops vegetables in the kitchen. The only things that stick out are the air-conditioner and a modern – and very expensive – computer with all kinds of gadgetry.

He knows who I am and why I am there. He greets me with words of respect and a smile that taunts. I honour his home, he says, and wishes it could be more suitable for a man like me, but this is all he can afford, and he has peace here. There is an *akhara*, a gymnasium, nearby, where young men learn sports, body-building wrestling, etc. He is too old and weak to use such a facility, of course, but he contributes what he can, from time to time. The young men of the neighbourhood are grateful and always around to help if he needs them. They are like his children, devoted to him.

His sons, he tells me, have become big men in Europe, with growing business interests. He never dreamt that he, a humble government servant, would ever see his sons grow so big. The smile widens. He is grateful to farsighted seniors like me, he says, and his sons will be happy to have me visit them.

'Where?' I ask.

The smile widens further. 'Wherever you want. In whatever company you want, and for as long as you like. If you had a daughter, my sons would have been happy to arrange her wedding in Geneva, by the lake, on a midsummer's night. If you so desired. With the chief minister's blessings.' He offers more, probing for a weak spot.

With some difficulty, I smile back and turn down the offers. 'The time isn't right.'

His pate gleams under the tube light, and the smile dwindles. 'If you had a daughter, you'd probably find the time right. Perhaps you like your wife, despite the inconvenience she causes in your life. I've helped some of my friends deal with awkward relatives too, just at the right time.' The smile disappears, and he rises. The meeting is over.

As I leave, I wonder how a simple smile can taunt and threaten at the same time. Persuading the inspector to become a part of 'The Fund' is simple. His boss assures me that those ACRs will be revised and future ones will glow. As for me, I walk away. I will keep my silence for nothing. There are limits to what Mridula will accept. But that one action establishes me as an enigma at the office. My colleagues have no idea how to deal with me, which is exactly how I want it to be.

October 2025

Life in the office became easier after I discovered 'The Fund', for now I knew what made the most of us in the service tick… in a word – greed. 'The Fund' united politicians and bureaucrats, and policemen and businessmen into one entity that managed crime. Organised crime was no longer the phrase; managed crime was more like it. It left no one untouched, even the ones like me, who watched, cowering, from the sidelines.

My colleagues still have no idea how to deal with me, but over the years, they seem to have lost the diffidence they had earlier. To them, I'm still an enigma, but harmless, and perhaps a bit of a bumbler. Sun Tzu would have approved.

Four

Noordin

October 2025

Sohail and Raza, and, I presume, the brigadier's secretary, knew who I really was. Others who attended the meetings never did. Masood Alam, for instance, who made the money available to us for the project, never knew. Masood arranged for the donations to the trusts, expenses for the boys, and so on, from London. I never knew much about that. The equipment we needed came when I asked for it, even after I learnt that Masood had died. Sultan, the paratrooper, probably didn't. He, too, died, but we never found out how, where or when. He was with a secret commando force at that time and might have been killed in action.

Sohail died in a traffic accident some months after he retired. He used to like cars and had acquired what by Pakistani standards was an expensive one – and sporty too – a Toyota Camry. I wondered where he got the money for it, and whether his accident was really an accident. His widow complained that the insurance was insufficient for her to live on after his death, which was strange, since she got his pension anyway, and that was all they would have had, unless, of course, Sohail had something else squirreled away that she couldn't take on her own.

Regardless of all that, Sohail did much of the essential work for the project. He bumbled and toadied and stole, but somehow accomplished whatever was required of him. Allah provides all, but sometimes in strange guises.

August 2009

In the ten months since the meeting at which the brigadier told him to find boys, Sohail has been busy looking for them. All must be literate in English, the brigadier has ordered, and good with numbers for their age. All must have suffered. All must be in situations where they have no great future to look forward to.

Finding such boys has been difficult, even in a country with over 208 million Muslims, of whom at least a third are dirt poor. Sohail has a network of informers all over western India, Some of them don't know he is Pakistani; he is simply a trader friend from Punjab, who drops in every now and then and gives them a good time. He has spread the word that he has been asked by a charitable trust to find good bright boys who will go to good schools and do good to the community later. There must be no advertisement; he says, 'Everything must be strictly word of mouth.' At Friday prayers, the word spreads.

Sohail has found three boys, Rustom, Adnan, and Karim. Rustom's father is a tailor, and he is one of the four children. He goes to school, but his father plans to get him to join the business in a couple of years. Adnan's father makes and repairs shoes, and is indifferent to his son's needs. He leaves the care of his children to the mother. Karim's father is dead, a victim of the Godhra riots of 2002, and his mother works in households to earn them a living. She wants Karim to study, but can't afford to send him to school.

We meet again at Ghani Khan's house, Masood the banker, Sohail the sweaty spy, Raza, and I. There are others, but for these few weeks, others come in only for specifics. 'We must take the ten per-cent route,' Ghani Khan decrees at the beginning of the first meeting.

Asif Ali, Mr Ten Percent, as he used to be called before they made him president, is cunning in ways ordinary people do not comprehend. Ghani Khan learnt from him, but Ghani Khan's ten percent is based on something else.

The principle is simple. Infiltrate a running charity. Pump cash collections – from, say selling drugs – into a charity, one that will ask no questions about the source of the money. There are many such organisations, most of them NGOs supposedly working towards AIDS awareness or on feeding the hungry. Find a genuine charity, put in the money with a condition that some of the money be used for activities that the donor specifies. This, we have found, should not be more than about ten percent of the NGO's total expenditure. Anything up to ten percent stays unquestioned.

The Jamaat-ud-Dawa have been using it for some time now. The bulk of their income, from sources legal or otherwise, is spent on charity; so if one of the leaders gets into trouble, hundreds, if not thousands, of people will happily go out on the street in protest.

With most practical governments this is insignificant, but western governments, especially the US, are easily swayed by public demonstrations. It is a cover that has worked again and again, and will continue to do so.

Masood comes up with his list of charities, some ten of them, and Ghani Khan asks our opinions. I offer none, for I know less of these matters than anyone else at the table. We decide, eventually, on three of them, all with Saudi Arabian contributors and a few Japanese as well.

We have more NGOs to vet. For many weeks, Sohail visits the brigadier every Sunday carrying a sheaf of papers. The three of us go through these papers, which describe various Indian NGOs. We are looking for one that's new, run by someone hungry for publicity, and well connected. It must also have trustees with some political clout, preferably relatives of parliamentarians. An MP on the board would be ideal, but might not be possible.

Masood calls from London. He has the modalities ready. He can shift money around wherever we want him to. Once we decide on a couple of NGOs, we're ready. As we look through the papers, we discover that our problem, at least in the matter of NGOs, is a problem of plenty. We need only one and there are thousands.

The brigadier has spent more time planning the operation. This time, he tells Sohail, everything will be different. The brigadier wants an extra layer this time between himself and the boys. He has his people influence a trust in London, the Al-Noor Foundation, which is paid through a bank in the Bahamas. Sohail, now in his last year with the ISI, will follow this up. Since he will retire in a few months, and the project will come to a climax only after at least ten years, he is safe.

Sohail is fat and bald and sweats all the time. He is nervous about his future; he has told me of his three demanding daughters and sole spendthrift son. They like music and dance and parties, he tells me, and to provide for them, he has had to bend the rules a little. I don't know if Sohail stole any of the money meant for the three boys' families; he probably did. He tells me often that his colleagues are greedy, unlike him, but every other colleague of his that I have met says much the same. For them, one's own thieving is just a little commission to help things along, while everyone else's is greed.

He has persuaded the brigadier to settle for an Indian NGO to use for the project – Jeevan Prakash Education Trust, run by a board of trustees amongst whom are strong liberal voices and the younger brother of a minister of the Delhi cabinet. The managing trustee is a former movie actress who spends far more on her appearance than on her charitable activities and has as much TV time now as she had during the best years of her acting career. Sohail himself – using a false identity, of course – takes me along to meet her.

Her name is Maithili. She meets us in an air-conditioned office in a skyscraper in an emerging new suburb of Gandhinagar, Gujarat. 'We don't have a permit to accept contributions from abroad,' she tells us when Sohail explains what he intends.

'That should be no problem for someone as well-known as you are,' he says. He has already found out that there is a thriving industry in New Delhi, selling these permits.

She preens. 'I suppose I know enough people. We'll take care of it in a couple of weeks.'

'I can promise from my side that there will be no interference. Until the boys complete their schooling, we will take care of them. Within reasonable limits, we will give you whatever you think the boys require – books, tuition, whatever. We will also take care of your expenses in these matters because we want you to give us your best. You have a lawyer amongst the trustees; you can let him draft an agreement to this effect, and I will make sure that we do our best to cooperate.'

'We might have to send your boys to schools run by Christians, or Hindu missions.'

'We have no objection to that. We want the best for the boys. Development comes before religion.'

'Very good.' We can see the calculation in her eyes. Here is something to add to her liberal and secular credentials, and perhaps her bank balance. Finally, almost as an afterthought, she arrives at what both Sohail and she claim are the most important people in the project, the boys. 'When shall we meet the boys, then?'

'We can start next week if you don't think it essential that we wait for your permit.'

She won't go ahead without the permit, but with help from her fellow-trustee in Delhi, she arranges for the permit in ten days. Three days later, we are visiting the boys.

We first go to Karim's house, in Godhra, smallest in a line of squalid huts with tarpaulin roofs. Strangers to the mohalla are treated with suspicion, and we are watched all the way to the house. We don't go in; a lady comes out and speaks from her doorstep. We don't bother to try to hide anything because we know that she will tell everyone in the mohalla anyway. 'I manage the JPET (Jeevan Prakash Education Trust),' Maithili tells Karim's mother, Zahira. 'We'll try to get you a good future. A better future than you can otherwise afford.' She has said nothing about Al-Noor and us, and Sohail doesn't push.

'What does that mean?' Zahira is sceptical. I understand from the background information that many organisations approached her after the killing of her husband, but all had let her down because she had her son to look after and couldn't spend time running after them.

'Education for your Karim and a little less of a struggle for you to survive.'

Her face turned fearful. 'Will you take him away?'

'No.' Maithili is at her most earnest. 'Not until he finishes school. After that, it's up to him.'

She is still suspicious, not being used to being given things without strings. 'What will we have to do?'

Despite the suspicion, there's a tiny shift in her stance, and Maithili catches it immediately. 'Karim will have to concentrate on his studies. You will have to shift to Baroda.'

'Why?'

'The best school there is better than anything here, and it's not too far away.'

'How will we survive there? I don't know anyone.'

'We'll get you a house for rent. We'll take care of Karim's expenses. We'll find you work. If necessary, we'll help with expenses until you can take care of yourself.'

'How do I know...?' Her voice, laden with worry and uncertainty, yet lit by hope, trails off.

'Come with us to Baroda,' Maithili offers. 'We'll all drive down there, you and the boy and us. You see the place and the house we've got you. It's a good house. Then you decide.'

'How will I pay the rent?'

'We'll pay the rent. No problem.'

'Why are you doing this?'

'We've heard that Karim is bright. He's good at his studies. We want him to become great and lead others.'

Karim, who has just joined in, perks up at the mention of a drive to Baroda, and tugs at his mother's black dress. Zahira comes to Baroda with Karim. A fortnight after that meeting Zahira is settling down in Baroda, looking for work, with her son going through the admission procedure for the school. Others have told me that admission to the school was so much in demand that the management asks parents of prospective students to pay large sums of money to get their children in.

I cannot imagine a school demanding money from its students. None of these is a real school. They are factories where students are taught subjects that will enable them to make money. None of them teaches the beauty of Allah and the mysteries of the Book.

That one visit is sufficient for Maithili. She sends her assistant, much less glamourous and much more effective, with us to the other boys. Maithili is apologetic on the last occasion we meet. 'I have meetings here,' she tells Sohail. 'Another project has come up.' We know, of course, that she dislikes going out in bright sunlight. It makes her look her age.

Rustom and Adnan are less trouble. Their families are poor, and their parents eager to get the boys off their hands, and into good schools. Both go to residential schools, one in Delhi the other in Agra. Both are placed in schools that demand that residential students write to their parents regularly, which was difficult because both sets of parents are illiterate: They will have to get the postman to read the letters to them, and write out their replies.

Everyone is happy – the boys, their parents, Maithili, Sohail, and, of course, the brigadier.

October 2025

Keeping in touch with Karim and Adnan – Rustom is in reserve elsewhere – in the last two years has been difficult. Both have risen in the hierarchy of work, Karim faster than Adnan, and both have to be careful in their movements. We have had to create fictitious friends in neutral countries, keeping in touch with each other electronically without letting an incriminating word or phrase into the communication. So we talk of the target city as 'Aunt Sadia's home' and the event we plan as 'Uncle Rehman's gift'. Messages can be traced easily by the police – the new systems are much more sophisticated than the old method of tracing IP addresses – and ciphering algorithms are easier to crack, thanks to more powerful computers. So we use codes based on books. Sometimes we use one-time pads – still the only unbreakable system available – but only when we have to, because it's very slow and cumbersome.

Over the last few years, Indian intelligence officers have extracted e-mail IDs, codes, and personal information out of them, often with torture, or more dangerously, drugs. We have done what we could to make sure that if anyone who is taken under arrest has the means available to take his own life, but sometimes that fails, as in when an injured mujahid is captured unconscious or when the mujahid's nerve fails him, which does happen occasionally. These intelligence officers impersonate the captured mujahid in an effort to extract more information from the network, so we now preface and intersperse any electronic conversation with a series of personal questions that should trip up any impersonator.

Sohail set up all this in the last months of his life. But these difficult matters are only matters of finding practical solutions. We did the most difficult parts of what we had to do with no effort at all – lighting the fire in the minds of the boys. That the Indians did for us.

June 2020

The rains are delayed and the summer's heat is building up. The sun sets in Delhi these days around half past seven, and it stays bright until around eight: Buses and trains are crowded well into the night.

At four in the afternoon on 4 June, people begin to pour out of offices, schools, and colleges. The heat beats down upon the people on the streets, the noise, and the press of the crowd. Fights break out. At five, a bomb goes off in a crowded mohalla in Janakpuri – populated largely by pandits who have fled Kashmir after the second partition – sixteen people die and over fifty are wounded. Eyewitnesses claim to have seen a bearded young man leaving the bomb in a heap of garbage and disappearing down a nearby street that leads to an area populated by Muslims.

One of the victims is an active member of the rightist BJP. His fellow-party men protest at the appeasement of minorities; visible beneath their rhetoric is fear, as always, that Hindus and Hinduism will be swamped. Hindu fundamentalists take retributive measures in Delhi and elsewhere, and Muslim groups retaliate. Over the next two days, fires rage. More people die, both Hindus and Muslims, more Muslims than Hindus. It's like partition all over again.

The narrow streets around the spot where the bomb went off make vehicular access next to impossible, and police find it hard to enter the area, hence, have far less control over the carnage going on there. But by the third day, they arrive in force, on foot, heavily armed, staging a march through the locality, bringing back a fragile peace. The state government appoints a commission of enquiry into the massacres, offers compensation to the bereaved and the wounded, and goes back to its usual business of making money. Other state governments follow suit. No one is satisfied. Both Hindus and Muslims, ignorant of who started it all, seethe under a forced calm.

I am with the boys. Two of them have completed engineering degrees from good colleges. They have finished their examinations and await their results, and both are confident they have done well. The third, Rustom, has just been accepted as a doctoral student into India's best-known institute for physics in Bengaluru. They know me as a trader with money to spare and a sympathiser with Muslim groups. We are in Mumbai, a city where it is easy to disappear or to live in anonymity for a few weeks. From here we will go to Deolali, where we can disappear into the forests for some time to complete some elements of the training that are still incomplete.

Once these boys get to work, we will not be able to train them. They will, of course, be able to practice their skills on their own, but training and further indoctrination will be next to impossible. Both the engineers are active men, their childhood of hard labour endowing them with a degree of hardiness unusual among their peers. I asked them many years ago to start learning karate, and they have both earned black belts in the discipline, thereby acquiring some essential skills without my involvement.

October 2025

The history of these boys brings to mind my own. They are young, but I was younger when it all began. Father brought me up all by himself during those early years. When the Taliban asked him why he didn't get married again, leave me to a new wife – there was a shortage of men in those days of war, and he would have had no trouble finding a willing bride – and spend more of his time fighting the Soviet, he replied that I was special. He saw something in me that they didn't, at least not then.

He would feed and clean me in the morning and leave me in the hut – all huts were left unlocked, for theft was unimaginable in those days – for the day when he went out. He would come back for brief lunch and be off again. He would return by evening, before dark, to spend time with me, and show me the Book, and feed me again, and put me to bed. He was around all the time, his presence comforted me even when he was busy with something else. At first, I used to cry when he left, but soon I got used to his absences, and learnt to expect him after some hours.

Spring, 1981 – Winter, 1982

I am four or five years old. I have got used to being alone most of the time; the hut in the village is safe, and there are women nearby with their own children to look after who keep an eye on me. There is little to play with, but one of the women has made a sort of a doll of rags and given it to me. I am fascinated by its colours and hang on to it.

Uncle Lala comes visiting at an odd time. His face and voice are strange; he looks angry, but speaks softly. He picks me up and holds me tight for a little while. I find the smell of his clothes – normally almost as comforting as my father's – disturbing, and start crying for Father. He pets me for a while, and, when I don't stop crying, shouts at me. More from surprise than anything else, I go quiet. I look in his eyes and see something that scares me even more. I keep quiet. I remember always that Uncle Lala, perhaps without intending to, taught me to be silent.

He tells me that Father will never be back. When I ask where he has gone, Uncle Lala says he has gone to Allah. Others amongst the neighbours have gone to Allah, last among them the old man next door. I know now that Father will not be back. Ever. There is a stone in my throat that catches my breath. I want to cry out, but keep quiet.

They lead me out to where Father lies. He does not move when they touch him. At first I think he is asleep, but he does not move, and his face and hands are cold, like stone, and his wooden leg lies beside him. Again I want to cry, but keep quiet. Uncle Lala begins to shake, and I see tears on his face. Then I, too, begin to wail. After a while, both of us stop. Uncle Lala holds me tight. 'The Russians did this,' he said. 'The Russians took his life.' He pauses, and sniffs. 'We have to pay them back. Nothing else matters.'

Afterwards, I go with Uncle Lala to his hut, where his older wife takes charge of me, the younger being busy with her own children. She is kind, but she keeps stopping me from doing anything. I was free with Father; with her I feel imprisoned. So when the Taliban come to take me along, I go happily.

I sit in a bag on someone's back in the sunshine, and then there comes the first sound of what I later learn is small-arms fire. I am terrified. I sink into the bag with my eyes shut tight, trembling, too terrified even to cry out. After a while, the sounds die away. Soon the men in the group are up and laughing and shaking hands with each other. The leader pats my head, and so does everyone else. I am still afraid, but keep quiet.

I have just survived my first firefight.

By night, we are higher up and it is getting cold. We go to a cave. It smells very different from the hut, and I am afraid again. But there is some light from lamps, and the sound of men talking. I know they are talking of me. Soon I go off to sleep.

When I wake up, it is still dark in the cave. Then the men lead me out into the sunlight. They do not clean me as my father did. I have to wash myself under the supervision of one of them. The water is very cold, but I do not make a sound.

Later, we reach my uncle's house in a town. There are more people here than I've ever seen before. Uncle – my father's younger brother – is lean and tall, just like my father, but his house is noisy with quarrelling children and his new wife has a sharp voice that I fear. The men talk, and soon the group takes me back to the caves, though I want to stay in the city with all these people.

We go out from time to time. I learn to sit quietly in a bag hung from someone's back. But now Ghulam Rasool, the man in the group who will take care of me, makes me walk longer distances. My legs get tired, and they hurt, but Ghulam makes me keep going.

It is always cold, and I am always hungry. I am tired of walking; I am tired of the darkness in the cave. I want my father back.

Those were miserable months. Things stayed much the same for years afterwards; but in one way, they did improve. Another orphan boy arrived.

Spring, 1984 – Spring, 1985

Abdul Hameed, my age, and quiet like me, is smaller and restless. His mother took care of him, so he is better clothed than I am, and he is as afraid as I am. We sleep together, holding each other because it is warmer. We play, and sometimes we quarrel. But at night, in the dark, we reassure each other. I read the Book the way Father taught me to. I have learnt the letters, and soon I read suras that he didn't teach me. Sometimes there are new words that I don't understand. I ask Ghulam, but he doesn't know either. He asks me where I found these words and I tell him I found them in the Book.

Other groups visit sometimes. Then we are brought out and exhibited and petted and fed better. One day, another group visits; and this time, too, we are brought out. But this time, we are not fed or petted; instead, we are told we are going to another cave far away from here. Ghulam carries me. Shamshad carries Abdul Hameed. We go to another crowded town, and from there we take a bus to another, and from there it's some more time on Ghulam's back before we reach our new caves.

These are the same as the earlier ones, but the group is different. Ghulam is gone, and in his place comes Shahabuddin to take care of us. I ask him the meaning of those new words, and he asks where I found them. He, too, knows the Book, and he tells me what the words mean.

Then he asks me how I learnt, and I tell him I learnt by myself, after Father taught me how to recognise letters. He smiles, and asks me to show him how I read. I spread the mat, sit on it, leaning forward slightly, as Father had showed me, and recite, rocking slightly with the rhythm of the words. He gets me books with the letters of a new, strange language, written from left to right, with two of every letter. I learn to read the letters, and to speak them as Shahabuddin teaches me, but the words confuse me, because the same letter can be spoken in different ways. I keep trying.

Soon the nature of life changes. There are more food items and blankets. There is more water, too, when I need to wash, and a new prayer mat, and new clothes to replace the old rags that I wear. When I see that there are none of these for Hameed, I protest; and Hameed, too, gets these things. We are happy.

But soon there is more learning to be done. We must learn to walk the mountains, Hameed and I. Shahabuddin takes us out, and we learn to keep up with him. In the beginning, it is difficult, and my legs and chest hurt. Hameed is often reduced to tears – and so am I… sometimes. But Shahabuddin keeps us at it until we can go no further. We learn to ride mules, to stay on their backs as they wind their way through the rocky paths in the mountains, to bear the cold and inactivity, and to keep watching for signs of danger.

One day we go a long way across the mountains. Hameed and I are empty-handed, but all the grown-ups carry large packs, and there are mules to carry more. When Hameed and I are tired, we ride the mules. At the end of the ride, we are on the floor of a valley, surrounded by high rocks, and cut off from the sight from above, except from directly above.

There we meet just two people; both are dressed as we are. One has black hair and brown eyes, just like us, and speaks like we all do. But he is different – though he tries to be one of us. The other has yellow hair and light eyes, and is clearly from somewhere far away. Shahabuddin tells them how I read the Book, and of my gift with languages. The yellow-haired one laughs and pats me on the head. He speaks to me in a strange language. When Shahabuddin tells me that he is speaking to me in the new language, I realise that I do not understand a word of what he says. He says some words slowly, and I understand a few; now I know how different the same language can sound! This is very confusing.

Over the months that follow, the yellow-haired one sends books, and I learn his name – Mike. I learn even to speak like Mike, for I can hear the rhythms in his voice quite clearly. Sometimes I ask a question the way Shahabuddin would ask it, and answer as Mike would, and everyone laughs, and pats my head.

Then Mike gives me two more books with pictures in them. But these are not storybooks – they are about weapons. Thus begins my own journey of learning outside the Book.

October 2025

At the time Father died, the Soviets, by virtue of their extra firepower, had begun to dominate our mujahideen bands. But by the time I began to learn the manuals about field-assembling rifles and the use of Stingers, the tide had turned. The Soviets had learnt their lesson and knew that they would be driven out of Afghanistan sooner or later. Their officials and ministers, safe in Moscow, watched their country bleed to no purpose. By the time I fired my first shot, the Russians were retreating. The mujahideen bands had, by then, formed larger and more purposeful groups than the roving bands of a few dozens that ambushed Soviet convoys in the early days of the resistance.

I was part of a company of some 200 men, without uniforms or drill practice or any of the things that make armies presentable, but we thought out tactics to use our country's terrain to our best advantage, knowing that no outsider would really learn to use it that well. While the best of the Soviet soldiers could come into the mountains after us, there were few of them. The vast majority stayed in their BTR-70 armoured personnel carriers and tanks, and helicopter pilots learnt to fly high to avoid being brought down by Stingers.

Mike kept up limited supplies of Stingers and other weaponry, including a few sniper rifles that I learnt to use, to bring down Soviets from far distances. Thinking back, I feel that was the greatest test of my resolve until then – bringing down a calculated target from a faraway hideout.

September 1988

It is clear to everyone now that the Soviet Army is withdrawing. The convoys are heavily guarded, and helicopter raids into the mountain caves have almost ceased. Even when they do raid, they do it ineffectively, from altitudes sufficient for the pilot to take evasive action when he sees a Stinger being fired. They have got used to our tactics, and we to theirs.

Now we are harassing them out of the country. One tactic, used rarely but effectively, is to block a road where we expect a small convoy to come through, and when it stops, to finish off the seniors, usually officers, with sniper fire. The rifle is a Remington 700 that Mike provided, with plenty of ammunition.

My first kill as a sniper is from about 400 yards. As a small child, I developed the ability to be still… now I use the ability to hide behind a notch in the rocks where I can rest the rifle, because I am still not strong enough to aim it accurately, or even carry it, for a long time without tiring my arms. So Shahabuddin, who is still with me, has carried the rifle for me, and later hands it over for me to use. This is not how the manual says it should be done. The sights should be zeroed on before I use the rifle, because we don't know what bumps the rifle has suffered in transit, but we can't do that.

So Shahabuddin hands me the rifle, with its 10-power telescopic sight. The sight magnifies objects in a strange fashion – everything looks flatter than it really is. A human head at 400 yards through a telescopic sight is like a football at 40 yards. Without a sight, it would be too small, really, if you want to aim at the centre of it.

I concentrate on getting the details right. We know where the ambush is. Ideally I should have the sun behind me when I am ready, so no one can catch the shimmer of the telescope's lens in the sunlight. I am about 40 yards above the road. This will make the shot more difficult. Wind blowing down the valleys here is unpredictable, so I might have to take an extra shot if I miss, and manage to see where the first bullet hits. It seems quite complicated and I am nervous. Shahabuddin senses my nervousness and pats me on the back. 'Remember your father,' he whispered. 'Remember Allah.'

Lying on the cool rock in the shade I think of my father and his stories, and of how he died at the hands of the Soviets and I'm not nervous anymore. This one is for you, Father, I tell him, and imagine him nodding in approval.

We have slid a boulder partway across the road, blocking only part of it. A BTR should be able to find its way past with a little backing and filling, so the driver won't be suspicious. A regular ambush would force the convoy to stop and people to come out to inspect the road and the block. Someone is likely to get out, and not with the usual caution, so I should get at least one without delay. We have the escape route fixed in our minds. From here, we move another 200 yards to the shelter of another rock, from where we can shoot pursuers.

A few months ago, I had helped hunt a helicopter. The man with the Stinger was Altaf, an Afghan born in Pakistan. We saw the helicopter far away, and Altaf aimed the Stinger. It began to hum, telling us that it had sensed the aircraft, but Altaf didn't fire. He waited a lifetime before he fired, a lifetime during which my stomach turned to water. After he fired, we saw the missile hit, and one of the engines blow up. After that, there was nothing the pilot could do. Afterwards, Altaf told me, 'You must be patient. You must let him come so close that when you fire, he can't get out of the way. You must time it right. Always!'

A strange peace descends upon me – the reticle of the sight defines my universe, and in it the crosshairs are stark and clear. The shot itself is anticlimactic. My breath steadies out on its own, as I wait for people to emerge from the BTR. In this peace, there is no urge to shoot, to finish it off or to flee before the pursuit begins. The first man emerges from the BTR, and then another, and I inhale before steadying out again. My eye fits on to the reticle and the man's head floats into the crosshairs.

The shot is fired almost before I realise it, and the head disappears from the sight. There is just enough time to turn to the second man, and bring him down too, before the others rush for cover. Then Shahabuddin takes the rifle and slings it on his shoulder, and the spell is broken. The two of us – Shahabuddin carrying my rifle slung across his back and his own AK, ready for pursuers – climb silently towards our hiding place, from where we can see if anyone is pursuing us.

There is none. The Soviets simply collect their dead and move on after an hour's wait. We, too, move on.

October 2025

I was mistaken, for there was pursuit. The dead pursue me even now. Even Mike, with the yellow hair. I was to shoot him with a rifle he had got for me.

December 2002

There is news of a suspected informer, a villager who disappears into the mountains for a day or two at a time. His hut has been searched in his absence, but nothing has been found.

The Americans have driven us back. They have bombs – called daisy cutters – to get us out of our caves. They always attack from air, from beyond the range of our weapons, and drop bombs they have developed that will explode in the caves.

They can penetrate far deeper than the Soviets could ever do, and many from amongst us have died. But most of us have chosen to retreat into Pakistan; into a territory that, though formally Pakistan's, is ruled by local despots with small private armies beyond the reach of the government. We are safe in the Pakistani territory, where the American aircraft don't drop bombs, though they do fly.

Over the last dozen years, our lives have changed dramatically, but in some ways very little. Once the Soviets left, there was a brief interlude of peace and celebration that very soon gave way to fighting amongst the groups that had forced the Russians out. There were plenty of weapons, all stockpiled during the years of the occupation, when the Americans gifted us small arms and anti-tank and anti-aircraft missiles in large quantities. There were also gifts – similar weapons – from Osama bin Laden and his Al-Qaeda.

Most of these arms have found their way into the hands of private armies, and the farming of poppy has spread wherever there is enough water in the mountain valleys. Opium is easy enough to get from the flower, though refining it into morphine requires some equipment and time, and refining that morphine into heroin takes even more equipment and time. That the Afghans don't have, so the opium crosses the border to Pakistan – the highway from Jalalabad to Peshawar is the pipeline – in trucks, and from there it goes all over the world.

Since the Soviets left, some of the mujahideen have found their way into Kashmir via Kashmir. There they find themselves at home... in Azaad Kashmir, under Pakistani supervision. With tacit American approval, they have fought for the freedom of the rest of Kashmir. In the dozen years since they shifted to Kashmir, they have done considerable damage to India, particularly to Kashmir.

More doubts have arisen. Kashmiris practice a lax form of Islam – they tolerate too much. To my mind that still does not justify the slaughter of people who are not a part of the oppressive Hindu regime. What is the point in using a bomb to kill people at a marketplace? I have withdrawn from this movement, though I do occasionally go to India to disrupt the activities of the government there.

So now our old friends, the Americans, are attacking us because they and our other friends, the Al-Qaeda, are enemies. Americans have turned from godless but tolerable aliens into devils, and are doing to us what the Soviets tried to do all those years ago.

And now there is news of an informer in Waziristan. This is an Afghan who came into Pakistan with the waves of refugees that came with the American attacks. His movements are suspicious, and my brethren among the Taliban tell me that he is meeting an American intelligence man. They want to catch him, but I counsel patience – if we follow him instead, we might catch the American.

They are not happy, but relent when I insist. And so we follow him, and at the end of the journey, we find him visiting another village a day's march away through the mountains. He walks almost all the way, and so do we.

This village sits on a plain ringed by hills with a small stream flowing nearby. It is a collection of mud huts baked yellow in the sun, with flat roofs and very little by way of ventilation, grouped around a rough square in the middle. The outsider's hut is towards the periphery, three streets from the square, and has a little enclosed compound in the front. The walls around this compound, no more than twelve feet by fifteen, are high enough to prevent anyone from looking over them.

The occupant of this hut comes out into the compound; there is something familiar about his walk. It takes me a few seconds to place him… Mike. The hair is red now, dyed perhaps, and he has grown fat with the years, but his walk is unmistakable. 'What are you waiting for?' the Talib with me hisses in my ear. 'Finish them off.'

So it has come to this – with a rifle that he got me, I am going to take his life. The same peace comes upon me. Almost automatically the rifle aligns itself, and I feel the cool wood of the Remington's stock on my cheek. The sights are properly zeroed; and at 600 yards, I should be able to get these two with ease. I have learnt to read the wind from signs – the flight of birds, a plume of smoke, leaves waving on a tree, a drying garment flapping on a washing line, a long stem of grass bending before the target. *Mike, you taught me well.*

This time I steady my breath and squeeze the trigger consciously, the way Mike taught me to, and he falls, less than a second before the shot that takes the informer.

Goodbye, Mike.

October 2025

Mike never relents in pursuit. 'You screwed up, kid,' he says, in the accent I have learnt so well, addressing me as the teenager I was the last time he saw me, towards the end of the Soviet pull-out from Afghanistan.

I did, in his words, screw up. The Talib who told me to shoot took the blame that should have been mine. Seeing Mike there caught me off balance. I should have thought it through – instead of killing him, I should have been patient, and taken him alive. He and the informer would have been more useful to us alive than dead.

Especially Mike. When the Americans discovered that a CIA agent had been killed, they took revenge. It was easy, making a bomb fly slightly off target into a village, killing dozens of people whose deaths were covered by the innocuous phrase, 'collateral damage'.

I respected Mike more than the American soldiers. The American soldiers in Afghanistan never faced the enemy without a substantial advantage in firepower, technology, and armour. For every American soldier dead, ten Taliban died, and ten civilians, half of them women and children. No mujahid ever faced an American on anything like level ground. The women and children in our villages had no more chance of surviving than the people trapped in the twin towers on 11 September 2001.

Mike took risks. He might have been a spy, but he was courageous.

So, when he looks me in the eye and points at the crowd of villagers who died to pay the Americans for his life, I cringe. Americans permit collateral damage, but not Allah the Merciful.

Is this the price I pay for that peace that comes in battle?

12 September 2001

I have been shot in the left arm in a raid on an Indian police camp in Baramulla. I was already out of the cordon when I was injured, otherwise I would not have escaped with my life. In the three days since the raid, I have covered more than 200 kilometres by bus and shared taxi on a forged identity card, using my clean-shaven face and English to get past police checkpoints. The effort has weakened me considerably. Now, at last, I am safe, at least for the time being. I am very fortunate and relieved, for once you are injured in a firefight with the police, your chances of getting away dwindle to next to nothing.

Sitting in a hotel room in Muzaffarnagar, I review the news that greets me. Ahmed Shah Massoud has been killed at the orders of Osama bin Laden and his partners, the Taliban, controlled by the Haqqanis. They have the support of Pakistan's ISI, for Massoud was – by Osama's and Haqqani's standards – a moderate who was willing to talk with the West and coexist with them.

Massoud is something of an icon for me now. Between 1981 and 1985, when I was just beginning to read and write, he survived at least ten major Soviet campaigns, aimed specifically at him. The only time I saw him, he seemed to have a charisma that no one else had, least of all the soft-spoken Osama, in whose mind rages the fiercest hatred I have ever come across.

The bad news does not end with the piece about Massoud. In the morning, I hear the news of the aircraft crashing into the twin towers. The US has a history of violence against opposition. Enemies of the country might claim to have defeated it in Vietnam, but only at the cost of unknown millions of lives against about 60,000 American.

The lesson is clear – if you are poor, you can fight America only on the terrain you know, and only if you are willing to spend thirty to fifty lives of your own per American. Afghanistan cannot afford it. The Vietnamese could, which is why America lost that war, despite losing less than 60,000 lives versus over three million Vietnamese.

Knowing what the Americans did to Iraq over a decade ago, I fear the backlash against Afghanistan. American intelligence will certainly be able, over the days and weeks, to see where Al-Qaeda is hiding. Al-Qaeda might manage to escape over the border into safe havens in Pakistan, but Afghans in the mountains will pay. The Americans will indulge in an orgy of blood-lust, and salve their consciences by paying out money to establish a puppet 'democratic' government, as they did in Germany, Japan, and South Korea.

They think they can buy people with money, but they are careless about how they spend. They hand money over to the ISI, and the ISI spend it where they wish. If the Americans had had a little more sense, they would have seen to it that Ahmed Shah Massoud got some of that money they gave to ISI.

American rhetoric about democracy is just that; they have supported violent anti-democratic regimes in South America, the Philippines, Iran, and elsewhere when it served their interests to do so. But they have a history of hypocrisy. They imported slaves who made them rich, then freed the slaves and now make war against anyone else who uses slavery. They drove the Native American from his land, established themselves in it, and now the old natives eat crumbs from their table. They used an atomic bomb on the Japanese, and now try to stop anyone else from using one.

Their bluster is only a cover for their calculations. I hope they get their calculations wrong, as they have often got done in the past.

As the weeks pass, the Americans zero in on Al-Qaeda, and Osama bin Laden. They mount a search for him, and decide that he is in Afghanistan.

Allah help Afghanistan; no one else will.

October 2025

The boys are as willing as I was. They have yet to kill, or to face their own ghosts. In all probability, they will not face any, because they are unlikely to survive. It seems a pity, having taken all this trouble over all these years just to have them die in a flash.

The flower of our youth died in war; the few who survived were soon forgotten, and the dead were considered the most fortunate, for they were with Allah.

No longer.

December 2008

Only a little more than a month after that meeting at Ghani Khan's mansion, I am back in Karachi after a few weeks in Peshawar, now staying in a small, cheap hotel near the city's main railway station, a hotel where the rooms have neither telephones nor TV sets. Both are available though, in the cramped lobby downstairs, where the watchful clerk permits the use of the telephone, usage to be billed separately, and a TV set is perpetually tuned to a free 24-hour news channel.

Around eight that morning, I'm on my way back to my room after breakfast with a fellow Afghan refugee at a small restaurant near the railway station and stop to watch the news. One news piece takes pride of place – the attack on Mumbai. Even as I watch, live shots show black-uniformed soldiers rushing into the Taj Mahal hotel and loaded stretchers being carried out. Over and over, they show a young man with an assault rifle firing at people at random.

Dear God, what are they doing! If this is in the name of Allah, these men will be forever damned.

I go up to my room, but can't sit still. Every hour I come

down to look at the TV, and the news they show is still the Mumbai attack, though now they talk of the hundreds dead and more hundreds wounded, of the damage to the hotel, and then the lone man taken alive. Already they speak as if the Lashkar is behind it.

In one sense, this is worse than the 9/11 attack on the US. This is a long drawn out massacre by trained killers, not a series of suicidal pilots flying into buildings and personal oblivion. From what the news channels carry, the Indians are furious – strangely, their fury seems to come from the number of rich people killed.

The Indians are sheep led by pigs. They are neither made for anger nor can they keep it up. It will all die down in a few months – instead of the usual few weeks – and we can get back to business as usual. That is the best – from our point of view – part of the Indian system. For some weeks or months, there will be more checkpoints, more checks, and more people, mostly innocents, picked up for questioning, but the lasting effects will only be on the security of the pigs.

But this attack is wrong. I would support any attack on an Army base or a police station or a government office, but these are relatively innocent bystanders. They don't make the law nor do they ask their police to commit atrocities in Kashmir.

After it's all over, I call on the brigadier. He has never refused to see me, although when he is busy, he keeps me waiting until he finds some free time. On this occasion, he is free, and Ali takes me to him in minutes.

We are alone in his book-lined study overlooking a lawn. He is soft-spoken and knowledgeable, as always. Had I not known who he is, I would have thought that he is a professor in a good university. 'Well, Noordin,' he says, shaking my hand. 'What a surprise!'

'I came across a bigger surprise,' I tell him. 'The one in Mumbai.'

He grimaces. 'What a completely useless thing to do,' he says.

'Is the Lashkar behind it?'

'I think so... and some of my old colleagues too. This will isolate us.' He turns on the TV set in a corner. 'Let's see what they're saying.'

The Pakistani channels are equally furious, saying that the attack is a Hindu conspiracy just as the bombing of the twin towers was a Zionist conspiracy. 'Would you like to watch an Indian channel?' Ghani Khan asks, and changes over without waiting for me to reply. Apparently, he has special equipment that enables him to watch almost any TV station in the world.

'There are elections coming up in a few days,' Ghani Khan tells me. 'Ignore the noise on the TV; that's just the better-off in India making noise. We'll find out what the commons think of the attack after the elections. I don't think they care all that much. The noise is mostly from the better-off liberal bunch, which is no different from the better-off liberal bunch here.' The contempt in his voice comes through loud and clear. 'We need them. We need them to make noise on the streets, so we can point at them and say, "See, this is a free society; here is dissent for you. They say what they like and we do nothing to them."

'The world doesn't know that the trouble comes from the underside of the society, from the people who are not heard. These people will continue to make noise. You must not listen to them, Noordin. They can be persuasive, but you must keep your mind clear.'

'I will do that,' I tell Ghani, 'but I will have nothing to do with these butchers.'

He smiles. 'When you pick up petty criminals and give them training and weapons, this is what you get, Noordin. The next group will be hitting back at us, like the others in the FATA are doing now. No thinking man would support it. I don't expect you to. They've all forgotten Zulfikar Ali's promise – we will fight for a thousand years if need be.

'So now they don't look beyond the next summer, or as is the case with some of my colleagues, the next annual report on their performance. They try to keep their superiors happy. Some of them think they fight for Islam and they keep the rebels happy. Neither works; we have to be professional about it. We must avoid collateral damage; it will only turn others against us. We kill a thousand Indian soldiers, and no one will protest. We kill a dozen unarmed civilians and the world will go against us… at least for a few weeks.'

October 2025

Ghani Khan was right about the voters. Those elections after the Mumbai massacres showed that most Indian voters didn't care about terror, and soon the reasons for that were clear. The Indian government spent more on protecting a few thousand influential people than it did to protect over a billion citizens.

To most voters, a few rich people dead didn't matter very much, because they'd been seeing it amongst the poor for a couple of decades, and some of them were even happy that the Lashkar had begun to aim at the rich instead of them. And then there were the numbers. India averaged well over 900 deaths a day from traffic accidents and only about two from terror. It was no surprise, then, that the voting public didn't care.

It's much the same now. But then, it's much the same in Pakistan, and not very different in my native Afghanistan, and in my adopted Kashmir. Since they're not so very different in these matters, as in many others, why fight?

Of late, Mike has begun to ask me this, too, and I have no answer for him. *Why do you trouble me so much, Mike?*

Five

Ganesh

October 2025

Evenings are the worst part of the day. I postpone going back to a cold and empty flat as long as I can. But tonight I leave earlier than usual; I am going out. Dinesh keeps in touch. He stayed on in the Army after I left, and is a colonel, commanding a battalion in Ferozepur, Punjab, not far from the border. He is in Bengaluru now, on leave, and has called me home for a meal.

He lives in his own flat in Whitefield; a flat that no honest Army officer would be able to afford. After that blast in Bengaluru, I quit. Dinesh stayed, but turned. Would I, too, have done the same if I hadn't had the family acres to fall back on? I don't know, so I don't judge him, but I always wonder when I see him what Granddad would have thought.

His elder son, Kartik, opens the door; he is ten now, a little older than Gayatri, and growing fast. Dinesh stands behind him, smiling. In the year since we last met, he has lost weight and gone grey. He's forty now, still young for a colonel, but the stress is showing. It's as if he has shrunk in some way. He's been like that for some years now.

November 2019

It's over seven months now since the bombing of the Pegasus mall. The police arrested three men for it in the middle of April, and say that their interrogations have revealed that these same men were responsible for another bombing last year, in Hyderabad. Others are saying that these are innocent men, trapped by circumstantial evidence, that the police have been coming down hard on Muslims, and that the real bombers are elsewhere – an old refrain.

Last month, a former chief minister of Bihar joined the chorus of these others. He is a minister in the Central government; there is a by-election coming up in his parliamentary constituency and he needs the votes of the Muslims who constitute a third of the population there. The mathematics is easy enough.

I put in my papers in April, and will be relieved in a few weeks. Meanwhile, there is the question of what to do. I am on leave now, busy with the family acres, which in a few weeks will go to a neighbour, who, knowing the value of coffee, is willing to pay any reasonable price I ask. I have time to spend finding out what the police is doing.

They tell me nothing. Dinesh tries to help by finding out what he can. His cousin is a senior policeman with the Anti-Terrorist Squad, the ATS, which has now expanded into a national entity with jurisdiction over all crimes deemed to be committed by terrorists.

When I call Dinesh at eight in the evening, he sounds tired. 'What's the matter?' I ask.

'Nothing,' he says. 'Look, my cousin Anil says he doesn't mind you calling him directly. Why don't you take his number?'

I wonder why he sounds dispirited. He has, after all, some good news for me, in that I can get my information on my own. But I don't probe, fearing to pry into his life. After I hang up, I call Anil; he's at work, he tells me, and I could meet him, perhaps for a drink and dinner. When I suggest one of the better hotels, he agrees. 'Make it around nine,' he says. 'I'll find you in the lobby.'

A woman from Virajpet, near Mysore, a widow whose late husband spent most of his life working on our family acres, is installed in my flat to look after Gayatri, so I can afford to spend the odd evening out. I try to keep this down to once a week or less, and have managed well so far, thanks to telephones and the increasing ability to communicate electronically.

I'm in the lobby of the boutique hotel – whatever that means, besides that it is expensive – at five to nine. No one sitting on the plush sofas seems to be Anil, so I wander around, looking at some of the displays in the shops. At five past nine, a plump, greying man approaches me. 'Ganesh?' he asks. When I nod, he holds out his hand. 'Anil.' His grip is firm, his voice steady. 'Shall we go get a drink?'

The bar is almost full; the steward leads us to one vacant corner table. He seems to know Anil; he takes my order, then turns to Anil and asks, 'The usual, sir?'

After he brings the drinks and a small plate of fried junk food and nuts, Anil asks, 'What do you want to know?'

'How the investigation is progressing,' I tell him. 'When will the case against those three men go to trial? What are the chances of getting a conviction? What do we know about who sent them?'

'You know this is off the record. You never came here. We've never spoken of this.'

'What about the waiter?' I ask.

'He won't remember you, only me. I pay cash, so there won't be any trail.'

'As you wish,' I agree.

'The investigation is more or less complete. We have enough evidence to go to court now. The chances of getting a conviction against the bombers are fair.'

'Good.'

'There's more. The investigation will go on for some more months, certainly until after the by-elections next year. The chargesheet will be filed only after that, which means that the case will come to trial only late next year. There could be changes by then.'

'What do you mean?'

'Investigating officers could be transferred, documents misplaced, confessions found invalid, procedural lapses discovered, contradictions found in forensic reports… it's no simple matter.'

It begins to fall into place. 'Is there anything I can do to change that?'

He shakes his head. 'You Army men are so simple. You see something and react. Will convicting those three men bring back your family? Or are you concerned with some version of justice?'

It's just a hope that there's somebody trying to pick up the pieces, a hope that Gayatri will be safer in the years to come. I keep quiet. The man across the table is a practiced interrogator, so he doesn't mind the silence much. After a few minutes of nothing, he gives up. 'What are you thinking about?' he asks.

'Who's behind the blasts?'

His lips widen in a smile. 'How many steps behind these three men? Just behind them is a Lashkar agent, and behind him an ISI handler. Behind him and his bosses? Well, it goes beyond people. History, you could say. Zia-ul-Haq, the CIA, all the way back to Adam. Where do you want to stop?'

'With the ISI agent it becomes the work of the Pakistani government.'

'They'll deny it. We have no proof really, just pointers.'

'The Lashkar guy?'

'Safe in Pakistan, somewhere in a tribal agency, past the reach of the Pakistani government. They practice deniability over there, you know, just like we do. Or perhaps, it's the other way round. We learnt some of it from them.'

Again there's silence. This time I break it. 'Who's responsible for what happens to the investigation over the next few months?'

He smiles again. His teeth gleam in the semi-darkness. 'Why? Will you finish him off?' He laughs softly. 'There's no single person responsible. The system fixes it so that if you want to take revenge, you have to take on half-a-dozen people. You fix one of them and you can be sure the rest will come after you.' He sips from his glass. 'Look, most of the time we know what's going on, but won't do anything unless there's something in it for us.'

I blank out for a moment. This is the system I joined the Army to defend. This is what runs this country I call mine. How could I defend it? 'I'll think on it.'

'You must. Also consider this – more people die every month in traffic accidents involving buses than in terrorist episodes every year. That makes your bus driver more of a terrorist than all these fellows. Does that stop you from going out on the streets?'

'No.'

'I hope you get the point.'

'I do.'

'What are your plans?'

I clench my teeth for a moment to stop myself from saying or doing something that will give me away. 'For the moment, trying to get my daughter's life back on track and then, trying to get a business going.'

'What business?'

'Security. That's the only business I know.'

'There's competition. A hundred thousand recent ex-soldiers.'

'True. I'll be hiring some of them.'

'Where will you be based?'

'Here. I know this place. I have friends here. I also have some reserves to last out some years if the business doesn't take off.'

'Let me know if I can help.' He finishes his drink, looks at my empty glass. 'A refill?'

I shake my head. 'I'll take your leave, if I may. The earlier I get back to my daughter the better.'

He nods. 'All the best. Keep out of trouble, and, remember, we never met.'

October 2025

Kartik is comfortable with me. He runs into his room to bring out the new chessboard his father got him just yesterday. It's second-hand actually, fifty years old, and all wood, black and white showing up as heavy dark walnut and some yellow wood I can't identify, all handmade and very expensive. It must have cost Dinesh a packet. 'How come?' I ask them both.

'I'm going to attend classes,' Kartik announces. 'Starting next week, as soon as we get back to Delhi.' Dinesh is posted in NOIDA, which is adjoining Delhi, now practically a part of the city.

'Good you don't go for video games,' I tell him.

'But I do!' Kartik protests. He brings out a new Sony game machine, a virtual reality game that comes complete with a light helmet that makes you think that you're actually in the game. It's a great deal better than the old games in which you only pushed buttons to make characters move on a screen. With these modern games, you put on the helmet and pick up your sword and shield, and the real world is cut off. It's frighteningly real inside. I'm afraid of getting into one of them, but Kartik manages with nonchalance. It's a great deal more strenuous than the old games, because you actually swing your arms about and have the option of weighting your sword and shield so you get some exercise during the game. Most people don't use the weights, of course; certainly not Kartik, but it's something to think about, the way games have developed.

Bhaskar, the younger boy, about four, has just discovered colours in the form of crayons. He tries to colour the back of my hand bilious yellow to lighten it, failing which he wanders off to inflict colour elsewhere.

Dinesh brings out the whisky, a good Laphroaig, and his Goan wife Jenny smiles, serves appetizers to go with the whisky, and disappears with the children. When we're finally alone, Dinesh gets down to business. 'There's a company here that needs someone to check their security,' he tells me. 'Anil knows some of the directors. It should be a good deal for you.'

'I'll follow it up,' I tell him. 'Thanks.'

He's a little shamefaced. 'Anil's decided he's given you enough. From now on, it's the usual.'

Anil usually takes two percent up front as a finder's fee. As he can't take the money, he has registered a company in his wife's name, a vague marketing services provider, to which his commissions are paid. Thus far, he's charged me only one-and-a-half percent because I'm Dinesh's friend, and both of us have done well out of it, but now he thinks it's time. He thinks I'm established well enough to pay him full fee, which is a fact. 'No problem,' I tell Dinesh. 'We can afford it now. We're profitable enough, thanks to people like him.'

He's still uncomfortable. He's never forgotten that the case against the three accused youngsters failed on technical grounds – discrepancies in forensic reports, faults in police procedure, and so on, as Anil had forewarned me. The judge had upbraided the ATS and let off the accused. Anil lost a promotion and made so much money on the side that he could have retired then and spent the rest of his life in utter luxury anywhere in the world, but chose instead to shrug off the disgrace and stick to his profession to make even more. He's still raking it in, and when he will eventually retire in a couple of years, he'll have a few lucrative consulting contracts to keep him busy.

'I don't know what to tell you,' he says.

I wonder for a while whether to put him out of his misery. There are sides to Anil that Dinesh doesn't know about. Anil likes his girls young; and while he doesn't hurt them, he likes to scare them. Someone in the backgrounds division ran into one of the pimps who procures young girls for Anil – he needs a regular supply because he can use a girl only two or three times, no more – and set up a trap. Anil gambols naked with a thirteen-year-old Manipuri girl on a SafeWrite – an expensive sealed one-time recording device that can't be overwritten or tampered with in any way, and is, therefore, acceptable in court – locked up in a safe somewhere.

Anil got an anonymous message and a copy of the contents of the SafeWrite with a threat attached – all organised by Mahipal. No money, of course, but information. All information transferred electronically across a series of servers that leave almost no trail. Ever since, he's been feeding us information that we've used in ways that I hope have made life safer for the average citizen.

He's also named others who might be vulnerable to a little pressure, so now we have half-a-dozen more SafeWrites sitting in that safe. One of the people on a SafeWrite in the safe actually got in touch asking us to trace the blackmailer. We had to turn him down, telling him we were too busy to take him up just then, but he did turn some more business our way.

So now I have four people like Mahipal pulling strings on

these people – one of them is a woman politician with a taste for young boys and gold jewellery, both expensive habits paid for in cash with the slush she gets through a protection racket – and having most of them think they're getting away lightly. I put all the information together, and then, sometimes, I put some skills to use.

December 1998

Granddad is an avid photographer and birdwatcher. Mom and I are with him for the Christmas break because Dad is somewhere he can't take us, and I am bugging Granddad, following him around. He keeps telling me to be careful not to make noise, but I can't learn to be quiet. After a couple of days of this, he sort of loses his patience. He doesn't raise his voice, but makes it very clear that I either learn to be quiet or keep off.

'I don't know how to be quiet!' I protest. 'You have to show me.'

'Will you listen carefully and do exactly as I tell you?' he asks.

'Yes.'

'If you do, I'll show you how to use my camera on Sunday evening,' he promises me.

He has this nifty Hasselblad with a dozen lenses that he keeps in a cool black carrying case that he won't even let me touch. Granddad has never broken a promise to me, and I'm stunned into silence. I only nod.

Next morning, when he comes to wake me up at half past five – we have to catch the birds at first light, and therefore be out in the dark – I'm already up and putting on my shoes. We go out and I get my first lesson in keeping quiet. By Sunday afternoon, I'm managing much better than before, though still not well enough to make Granddad happy.

At four, he calls me to his room. It's large and sunny and has some furniture he treasures. He opens his cupboard and brings out the Hasselblad. 'You haven't done as well as I'd hoped,' he tells me, 'but you've tried, and you put your heart into it, so here's the camera.' He gives me a guided tour, and I'm lost pretty soon. I also manage to get Mom at an awkward moment when she's eating cake and spilling crumbs.

There are four more days left of the break and I spend most of my time out with Granddad trying to get up to his standards. This time the terrain is tougher. The first morning, I have to bite back a cry when a few ants climb up my leg and begin to bite. I hold back tears, but let out a sniff. In the sunlight an hour later, Granddad notices the marks on my calves and looks closely at my face. He doesn't say anything then, just pats my head. Later, when I show him a swelling leech on my thigh, he smiles benignly and lights a rare cigarette. 'These things are useless,' he tells me, holding up the lit cigarette, 'except for getting rid of leeches.' He holds the lit end against the purple body of the leech and it drops away.

I begin to learn to cope with insects and worms, and to watch out for snakes. Granddad tells me that in another few years, I'll be able to give him lessons. On the last morning, we get back to the house, tired and a little dirty, and get cleaned up before a late breakfast. Mom, who's already had hers, sits with us until Salma, the cook, calls her into the kitchen to decide what we're going to have for lunch.

Granddad takes the opportunity handed to him by her absence to offer me some of the coffee brewed specially for him, strong and black, that he likes to sip slowly after a morning ramble around the estate. He pours a little into a cup that he pushes across the table to me. I glance at the thick dark fluid inside – it looks like some terribly powerful cough syrup – and finish it off at one gulp, the way Granddad does when there's only a little left in the cup.

It's so bitter it almost makes me cry. I hold back my tears and wonder how Granddad could actually like this filth. A breathless minute or so later, I manage to say, 'That's good, Granddad, but right now I have to go to the bathroom.' I had to wash my mouth!

Later, at Mangalore's Bajpe Airport, from where we catch the flight back to Delhi, Granddad doesn't hug me as he usually does when seeing us off. Instead, he extends his hand and shakes mine. 'Next time, we'll make a real woodsman out of you,' he says. 'And when you grow up, you can have that camera.'

I board the plane feeling very grown-up, but wishing somewhere that he'd hugged me as usual. The taste of that coffee lingers. That, and the memory of something Granddad told me after we had spent fifteen minutes hiding in a thicket of bushes waiting for a shy tailor-bird to emerge from its nest, 'You must forget yourself. For all of us, it's normal to try to stand up and shout, "Look at me!" You must learn not to do that.'

October 2025

It took me eight years to get to like that coffee, and much less to learn the craft. On the next vacation with Granddad, I began to learn to stay silent, to disappear into the background, and to steady the camera. By and by, Granddad taught me to shoot weapons, and I discovered that a good eye and a steady hand are useful there too. Later, in the Army, I had plenty of opportunities to sharpen my shooting skills. But the most important lesson came from Granddad that October morning long-ago, the lesson about forgetting myself.

I still have the Hasselblad, now stored away, and a love for still photography. I have several other more modern digital cameras, which I get to use less than I'd like to. But there were some other little things I had to get to take care of what I had in mind. These, again, came from people in the Army.

March 2013

This time of the year, the snows begin to recede and the trees appear, leafless and stripped. This time of the year, the Pakistanis follow their annual pattern of emerging from their camps across the LOC to try to come into Kashmir to wreak their usual mayhem. The attacks have increased in the recent past, and people at the front, like me, are beginning to wonder about the effectiveness of our observation mechanisms at these points. It seems to us that they have far more local support, not only here, but in the rest of the country, than they did some years ago.

They have also begun to get more sophisticated weapons into the country. I've noticed several sniper rifles, including a rare Dragunov from the old USSR, probably captured from some Spetsnaz group before 1989.

There's a definite difference in the pattern of their strikes. The people most vulnerable to their strikes used to be the poorest, the least able to protect themselves, with bombs placed on bicycles in crowded markets, rarely in upmarket shopping areas, where security is tighter and guards and police more watchful. There's also a difference in the strikers. They're increasingly better educated, speak fluent English, and are capable of getting into an upper-middle-class environment without trouble.

Back when they used to strike more or less at random, the victims tended to be relatively poor. The government could make sympathetic noises, pay out a little money, promise that the bombers would be caught, and forget all about the strikes. After all, people in the government who made these decisions – all civilians – were well protected. The uniformed forces and the poor provided the blood.

Now, the upper class is beginning to feel the threat. There have been bombs placed outside government offices earlier, but in the last couple of years, there've been bombs inside offices. They've only killed junior employees, clerks, and a few supervisors, but all members of powerful unions. So, government offices now are more tightly guarded. The terrorists have caught the shift and are now aiming at the haunts of the rich, which means they have to have people capable of entering a shopping mall or an expensive movie theatre without arousing suspicion. These places are also guarded, but by private security outfits that have no legal standing, and often wouldn't know what to do with a weapon if they ever caught one being smuggled in, because police response to calls from such places is very slow.

Groups of jihadi organisations have got together into a sort of loose confederation. Wherever there are guns, there are usually drugs to pay for them. The large profits from Afghan morphine pay for the smuggling of weapons that are stockpiled with sympathisers, who give them to any organisation when need be. There's more money now, and hence better weapons.

The presence of sniper rifles points to the evolution of jihadi groups to the point where they will get at specific targets with minimal risk to themselves, at substantially better training. It also points at the availability of special ammunition, or, perhaps, even of the possibility of the jihadis reloading their own. I'm beginning to suspect that such jihadi activities in India are going to expand in entirely new ways.

As they get more sophisticated, the jihadis' need for money will increase beyond the limits of what they can get from their drug-running activities out of Afghanistan and what they can beg from the ISI. They are going to diversify into crime – kidnaps for ransom, protection rackets, and, through the contacts available via Dawood Ibrahim, gangland in general. Jihadis have hitherto kept out of straight organised crime, but now it's too lucrative for them to ignore; and it also cuts off the possibility of their returning to Pakistan, which is important, because the Pakistanis would like to export their violence. More money also means more opportunity for sleepers, which is worrying. Our bureaucracy in Delhi is riddled with Pakistani moles. God knows what direction they will take in the years to come.

Meanwhile, I hear of a brother officer being involved in the 'diversion' of captured weapons and ammunition. I track him down one evening and confront him, and find that it's not just him but a network of officers and men involved in stealing captured weapons. They simply refrain from reporting certain captures, especially of caches away from jihadi hideouts.

This officer, an infantryman, doesn't smell of corruption the way some others do, and I ask for an explanation. He offers one which is straightforward. The groups are doing it with intentions that seem good. There's too much corruption in the government. No one seems capable of stopping the jihadis and matters are getting worse. They intend to create a small stockpile of weapons they can use later or give it to someone who can. They have no specific plans, but are in touch with former soldiers who might be willing to participate in some vigilante action.

On impulse, I walk away from the man. 'Keep it discreet,' I tell him. 'I'll keep it to myself, but you might run into someone who won't.' Later, he seems to have acted upon that advice, for I hear no more about the ring.

October 2025

After I quit the Army, I traced this infantryman, Ashok. He had retired early and was 'underemployed' in his hometown, putting in twelve hours a day, six days a week, administering a large private hospital, with no prospects of better money or advancement, and children to put through college.

January 2020

Finding Ashok has been easy. I run an Internet search for his name. The search engine finds three retired soldiers with that name, but only one commissioned officer. I check their ages and he looks the possible one, the officer. The address and telephone number of the hospital where he works are right there. Just to be doubly sure, I check with his regimental centre whether this is the Ashok who served at such-and-such station a few years ago. They confirm the posting, and I know I've got him.

When I call him and identify myself, he recognises me immediately. 'Are you going to make trouble?' he asks. 'I have a family and I will keep them safe, you know.' The tone is casual, the threat unmistakable.

'Quite the contrary,' I tell him. 'Let me buy you lunch.'

'I'll lose a whole day coming to Bengaluru,' he says. 'I can't afford it.'

'I'll come there this Saturday,' I offer.

'I work Saturdays,' he says. 'My weekly holiday is Sunday, when I can manage it.'

'Well, Sunday it is then.'

'What is this about?'

'If I could tell you on the phone, would I offer to drive 200 kilometres each way to see you?'

'Fine,' he says. 'Do you know your way around here?'

'Just tell me where you want to meet me.'

He names a restaurant. On Sunday, I arrive there half-an-hour early. I park a hundred metres away and watch for him. He shows up twenty minutes later, looking wary, and looks around at the number plates of cars in the parking lot through his aviator glasses. Old habits don't change.

Five minutes later, I enter the restaurant and find him examining the menu. He's taken off his glasses but his eyes are hooded. He starts aggressively, in the manner of one whom fate hasn't treated well recently. 'There's no such thing as a free lunch,' he says. 'What do you want? Are you going to rake up the past?'

'No, I came to find out how you're doing.'

'Isn't it obvious?' he barks. 'Dead-end job, terrible hours, lousy money, the works. Why do you want to rub it in?'

'Not really. I thought I'd offer you something better instead.'

'What?'

'I've got into the security business. Help me run it. We can work out a good package for you. Much better than the deal you've got.'

'Why?'

'You'd fit easily. I can trust you. We can work together.'

'What if I say no?'

'We finish our lunch and I return to Bengaluru. Simple.'

'No skeletons out of old cupboards?'

'Not a rattle. But I'll keep the offer open for a while.'

'Seven years, nearly, since we last met. You've kept your word,' he says. His tone is different.

'Don't worry about that business,' I tell him. 'It stops with me. Have a drink.'

Suddenly his face changes. The desperation shows. 'I think I will,' he says.

'Why are you stuck in this lousy job?' I ask him.

'I'm religious,' he says, 'so I visit temples every now and then. In one of them, I met this guy called Swami Suryaprakash, who they said was involved in those killings of Muslims in Mangalore. You remember?'

Suryaprakash was charged with planning the murders of two members of the South Indian Mujahideen who were suspected of murdering a whole family, and released because of insufficient evidence. Suryaprakash, too, was cleared. I nod.

'Well, the police took me in. For questioning, they said. They didn't arrest me or anything, or even take me to a magistrate. They'd come every morning for a week, take me off to the station, keep me there for a few hours, sometimes all night. They kept asking me about Suryaprakash, but nothing about the old days. Soon I figured they didn't know about all that. They had to stop all that because I stuck to my guns, but they made my life very unpleasant, I can tell you.'

'How?'

'Sleep deprivation, the odd beating, threats to pull my kids in… the whole nasty business.'

'Drugs?'

'They cleared Suryaprakash before they got to that. Later I found out that they just round up old Army guys on suspicion – their own form of profiling. Then I got sacked because my employers didn't want a guy whom they might drag off to jail any time. This is the only job I could get afterwards.'

'We can fix that.'

'How do I know you'll stay in the business?' he asks. 'Start-ups are having a tough time.'

'I have the reserves to hold out for at least a couple of years. You know that.' He knew of the family acres.

'What do I do?'

'Run the nuts and bolts.'

'Are you alone in this?'

'No. I've got two others, both ex-infantry, easy to deal with. You know Mahesh Naik. He last served with 5 Kumaon.'

'Yes. Where do you operate from?'

'Bengaluru for now; all over if we get lucky.'

'My wife will have to find work there. She'll have to give up the job she has here.'

'No problem.'

We order lunch and discuss specifics. I discover that he's horribly underpaid. We work out a package that'll keep him satisfied. As lunch arrives and we finalise his package, he grins. 'The hospital wanted to keep me on my toes; they can sack me at a day's notice. They insisted. I insisted that the arrangement be reciprocal, so I can quit the same way. They agreed. Now I look forward to walking out on them.' He's not vindictive, but after all these years walking towards a dead-end, he looks forward to telling his employers where to get off.

I wish him joy of it. 'Don't worry about references,' I tell him.

October 2025

He reported for work the Tuesday after we met. The weekend after, he'd found a house and moved his family over. Through him, I found a relatively easy way to find untraceable weapons of all kinds. A few months after I got him out of the woodwork, he quietly offered me his personal stockpile of weapons any time I wanted it. When he made the offer, I got the impression he didn't quite know what to do with his rifles.

Though he never told me why he acquired the rifles and then passed them on to me, I could guess. That bit about his being religious said it all.

December 2020

After Gayatri's accident, I find myself trying anything for solace. I'm Hindu only because I was born into a Hindu family, but essentially I'm an atheist. I don't think I'd be different if I were Christian or Muslim, or something else by birth.

For many weeks, during long walks in the morning, I watch a number of people trying to find some comfort in temples. I follow them. I pray as best I can, but find no comfort, and after a few visits to a temple, perhaps seven or eight, I give up. There are, however, people at the temple who notice me. After my third visit, a man in saffron – a monk – accosts me on the way home. 'You don't know me,' he says, 'but I know you. My condolences, your losses have been grievous.'

'Thanks,' I reply. 'Please do introduce yourself.'

'My name is not important,' he says. 'It's what I stand for that matters. I'm a great supporter of the defence services. Our country needs people like you.'

'I'm not in the services anymore.'

'I know why you left. The services are no longer what they used to be—'

I'm getting a little irritated. I don't like strangers talking to me about matters I consider private. 'If you could tell me where this conversation is headed…'

'A man like you must be terribly frustrated at the system. There are many like you, fed up with the system. We should all fight it together. After all, we have a common identity – the Hindu identity.'

'Perhaps, but my religion is my business… and mine alone.'

'Come, come,' he insists. 'You must let us help you. We must protect our heritage.'

'I'm not sure you can help.'

'Oh, yes, we can,' he suggests. By now I'm intrigued enough to listen to him. He speaks of a common glorious heritage, of eternal truths, and a common enemy. He speaks of raising the means to fight the common enemy, and of my skills being essential for that battle. He never gets down to specifics but he does paint a picture of a Hindu India that isn't to my atheist taste. I hear him out that day, and a couple of times later, then disengage myself quite firmly. He never comes back.

Ashok, too, must have been through something similar and had probably taken a few steps more than I did, but he disengaged at the right time.

I, for one, am glad he did.

October 2025

Ashok turned out to be a find, an excellent administrator, who, within a year, was running the outfit with no trouble at all. All of us partners found ourselves leaving much of our work to him. Besides, after we decided to let him do it his way, he was running the industrial watchman division practically on his own, and very well. So when, two years after he joined us, I proposed that he be made a partner, the others agreed without demur.

As a partner, he did what he had been doing all along, and, with the addition of a secretary and an assistant to his staff, took on more. He was also the first of the partners I let into my secrets – I found his help invaluable.

He keeps my secrets because he still burns. He was, by his lights, an honest soldier – he did his best on the front line with the rest of us.

To have come back home and end up in trouble with the police was the last straw. Most of us ex-soldiers – and, of course, serving soldiers – still seethe at the thought of being thrown behind bars by people like Anil. We haven't done anything wrong, and the few who might have harboured thoughts of hitting back at terrorists are actually doing the job the police should be doing, but are too corrupt or lazy to do so. Crooked politicians are involved, and so are crooked cops and crooked bureaucrats. They all get away, but not soldiers.

For instance, anyone can get an identity card in a false name, with a non-existent address, for a few thousand rupees. With an identity card, for a few more thousands, you can get a driving licence and even a passport. With all that, you can get a phone card. The people who take the money are touts and clerks but it goes up all the way to senior bureaucrats, who prefer to hide their heads in the sand, and politicians, for whom the extra income through bribes has become essential. None of these people has been caught. None has been dragged out of his home with his head in a sack, to be beaten by the police and injected with truth serum. None has been sentenced to years in prison, his reputation in shreds, permanently unemployable, branded a traitor.

But soldiers who try to hit back at terrorists in the absence of any serious attempt by the system have been through all this. Part of it is because of the training – they're trained to stay away from politicians who might help them. Part of it is because they're safe to profile – there is very little political backlash when you put a former soldier behind bars.

So, it's not worthwhile being a soldier. Best to stay back and raise a family as best you can, and keep them safe, and make what money you can out of a job or a reasonably honest business. I don't know what Granddad would have said if he were around… I'm glad he isn't around to see all this. He would have been incredibly sad.

Anil was right about most things, but one thing he got seriously wrong was the bit about the rest of the half dozen coming after me if I got one of them. I could have got all the seven-or-so officers involved, without Anil and his bunch even getting a sniff of who was getting after them. But then he had learnt to go by the percentages, and there are cases where the percentages mislead.

In any case, the information he gives me under duress is worth far more than the percentage he takes on the business. I don't grudge the money he makes out of me by way of commissions.

I wish I could tell Dinesh and put him at ease, at least with me. But I can't, at least not now. There's too much at stake, and I don't know if anyone has got his hooks into Dinesh the way I have mine into Anil. But one of these days, when I know it's safe, maybe I'll tell him. Until then, he'll have to suffer.

Six

Thomas

October 2025

I take a break from this vigilante to prepare for the meeting with my controller, who calls himself Tony, which is obviously a fake name. I'm reasonably sure it's fake because when we first met, he said, 'The name's McAuliffe. Tony McAuliffe. Call me Tony.' I know Anthony McAuliffe was a fairly well-known World War II general, so I think he picked the name almost tongue-in-cheek.

I have no idea what he will want from me – he might just want to give instructions that will keep me subtly busy for the next few months, or information – but I dislike surprises, though some of the most delightful events in my life have come as complete surprises. One of the routine jobs I do for him is to tell him of the progress of our investigations of possible terrorist jobs, especially those that might be backed by Pakistan, and I have no qualms about giving him this, even if he is somehow passing it on to the Pakistanis, because nothing ever comes of these investigations. We get some evidence, some pointers, and some leads; and the Pakistanis either ignore all of it, or deny whatever they can.

He also asks me, occasionally, about foreign-policy matters. I know little about these, but I do have inputs on how the elements of foreign policies are formed; and, as an investigator of crimes, I have to be watchful and careful of those that might have their genesis abroad. I also have to be more than a passing acquaintance with the foreign policy of his country, amongst others.

I have felt like asking him which industry group he works for. The US foreign policy might be a disaster, but it's just an extension of a very simple corporate policy which clearly states 'don't lose clients'. That's been the reason for their otherwise morally inexplicable support of some of the most unsavoury dictatorships in every continent but their own; and perhaps Antarctica. I haven't bothered because it won't ruffle him one bit.

He is unfailingly courteous, in the manner of the old British aristocracy, though I have always known him as an American. The one time I misled him, he made it clear, without being in the least ruffled or offensive, that he was ahead of me, that my information was only corroborative. After that, I've been careful with him – sharing any information that comes through 'regular channels'. He might have a minister or two on his payroll, and it wouldn't do him any harm if he lets one of those know that I have other sources of information.

Is he equally collected when he deals with less savoury others, I wonder, or does he consider me as the most unsavoury, a crooked policeman making the best of his position?

This evening, as usual, he greets me in the quiet hall of one of his safe houses and offers me a drink; he invites me to sit across him on a comfortable wing chair that has been out of fashion for half a century and pushes a bowl of salted cashews within my reach. We could be sitting in a plush club of a century ago, with subdued lighting and wood panelling on the walls, and copies of paintings of dead animals for people to contemplate whilst eating dinner. But then, everything I do and say is being recorded from half-a-dozen different directions in very high-definition, and I can't afford to miss a step.

This time I'm done with my report in fifteen minutes. Tony has obviously tapped one of his other sources. Without effort, and in seconds, Tony changes the tenor of the meeting, and I find that we're chatting about why the chief minister of Delhi attended yesterday's cricket match and matters of equal importance. I've been through this before, and know that Tony is always trawling, and telling you in many ways that he knows more about you than you yourself do. 'You really should listen when people tell you to keep changing your schedule from time to time,' he suggests. 'You stick out.'

'I don't mind,' I reply.

He smiles. 'Please don't be difficult. You're quite an asset, an irreplaceable one, in fact. We wouldn't want you to go missing one morning.'

There's a hint of command in his voice that I don't like. He has me by the short hairs, and his country is rich, but essentially he's a middle-level bureaucrat with field experience, a large budget, and many toys. His country's foreign policy has arguably had the largest number of disasters ever. They don't seem to have got anything right since World War II. For a brief moment, I consider reminding him, but it doesn't seem worthwhile. Don't let the pinpricks get you, I tell myself, outthink the man instead.

So I smile back. 'Thanks for the warning. I'll keep it in mind.'

'Do. I'm grateful.'

This marks a subtle shift in the relationship. Until now, he's been taking information from me. This is the first time he's given me a piece of information explicitly, and it tells me much. It tells me of my value for him, and that he has sources of information that I should review.

I survive the rest of the meeting on autopilot and break off as soon as possible, quoting personal reasons – that he never questions – for wanting to go back home. I take the car he provides to the back entrance of the bar at which I've left my official car waiting. All through the drive home, I keep thinking of Tony and why he's telling me to watch out.

In the first place, Tony is far lower down in the hierarchy of his agency than I am in mine. He wouldn't presume to order me without a pressing reason. Therefore, he must have something specific about a threat to me. Second, Tony has no idea of the kind of information that I have access to. I have so far given him only such information that anyone in my position could have got legitimately. Since there is no threat to me visible on the Indian official radar, he must have got wind of a threat from somewhere else. He is what the CIA – or whatever agency he works for – calls a South-Asian specialist. There are possible threats to me from the Chinese, Pakistanis, Bangladeshis, or maybe even Nepalis, all within his area of operation... which means he has sources in one or more of these countries. But then, I know that, just like I know that Tony isn't based in India – he just visits from time to time, and perhaps visits the others as well, buying and selling information back and forth.

We reach the back of the hotel where I gave my security detail the slip, and I sidle inside, going to the bar via the toilets. I must have gained a reputation as an alcoholic from visiting all these bars in the evenings, but that is all for the good... or so I think. After a while, I get into my car for the half-hour drive home to Nancy.

Nancy in a rage, especially after the quiet meeting with Tony, is unpleasant in many ways. She has aged and her voice has roughened very fast. She greets me with a stony silence that lasts all of two minutes; when she finds that I don't respond to it she explodes. 'How dare you treat me like this?' she screams. 'Especially after all that my father did for you!'

October 1997

I arrive at my parents' house near Kottayam a few minutes before midnight, looking forward to a good night's sleep after putting in a hard day at work, and then taking the flight from Bengaluru to Kochi and a cab thence. Achan and Ammachi are waiting, looking downcast. When I ask them what the trouble is, they explain – the father of the groom wants more. He wants another ten lakh rupees, far more than they can pay. They can just about borrow that much if they mortgage everything they have, but failure to repay the loan will result in their losing their only home.

I tell my parents that they should just call the marriage off. They can't afford a relationship with such a mercenary family: The groom's family will just keep up the extortion, even after marriage. 'Who will marry her?' they ask.

'She's educated,' I tell them. 'I'll help her find a job. When she's independent, she can choose her own man.'

'What about the money we've already paid?' they ask.

'Get it back.'

'Will you help us get it back?'

They already know the answer to that – I won't. What with my principles and their need to keep face within the only community they've known, we're all trapped.

October 2025

That's only the beginning of the tirade. I ignore her and go straight to my study, where I settle down in front of my computer, which is connected to the computer at the office. I'm not quite aware of how it's done, but I do know in the normal course of events, a computer at home linked to the office computer is totally unnecessary.

Nancy's voice penetrates the door. I cannot bring myself to divorce her – the money she brought, an amount I wouldn't have been able to earn legitimately, enabled my sister to marry into a good family. I cannot bring myself to feel angry at her. Any anger I feel is directed at myself for not having the backbone to send her back home to her father.

The computer takes a minute or two to come on and I turn my mind to other matters. You see, it's the same old thing about trappings – the more you have, the bigger you are. In the NIA, you don't get too many people, but you do get lots of expensive technology instead. So the big chief – officially, the director-general – has got to be wired up; and since he might ask any of his lackeys, such as me, for information at any hour of the night or day, the lackeys, too, have some of his privileges.

So we have large amounts of money invested in a wireless network connecting our home computers with the one at the office. It's supposed to be secure – the techies say so, but I really have no idea whether it is.

The egos of a whole parade of senior officials shows up in the specifications of the system. The typical policeman wants to know what everyone is doing without letting anyone know what he himself is up to. So, all these senior men rejected the idea of leaving a trail. The ones who enforce the laws don't themselves like to be bound by a computer system.

So here I am, using a set of typed passwords rather than a system that recognises thumbprints, voices, or retinal images, all of which we could have implemented with ease. It eases my burden, making it possible for me to steal passwords without being caught.

Out in the hall, Nancy gives up on me. One of these days, she'll cry on her father's shoulder, and he'll call me, telling me coldly and sadly that his daughter is a good girl. I'll evade, and after a few days of strained peace, she'll erupt again. At least I have the comfort of a liaison, of small children who are looked after. I don't think Nancy has that. I won't add to her burden by reacting.

On balance, any threat to me must come from the Pakistanis, for I haven't been after people from any other intelligence services. And, I must ask, does Tony have a few senior Pakistanis in his grasp just like he has me? He must; officials there are even more venal than the ones here. Is he feeding them bits of information? He's just fed me one.

Is he working for them?

I've never really thought this through before, I realise. All I thought until now was that I was handing over secondary information to a neutral party; and, in return, getting Mridula a comfortable future. That kept conscience at bay. But I don't think so now. He's been using me much more sharply than I'd thought. He's been sifting what I tell him, extracting the few grains he needs from the material I gather for him so rigorously.

The one possibility I've been shying away from has caught up with me; for a moment, I just sit, trying to grasp the enormity of my misjudgement of the man, of the situation, and of the significance of the information I've fed him. It's like the customs men who let a whole container full of weapons into the country after having been bribed into thinking it was some big politician's private stash of imported furniture or agricultural machinery. They were disgraced, but, like all government servants, saved from punishment of any real consequence. Their ill-gotten gains were left untouched and their families left alone.

He's not really working for them, of course, that's clear. If he were, he'd simply tell them to keep off me. He's playing both sides against the middle. For the time being, they're doing something that suits him, and he doesn't want to upset anything by telling them to keep off me.

Now what could that be?

I can't get to the bottom of it. I've just got on to the question, and I take time to recognise patterns. I can only think of one man who would be much better than me at this.

July 2010

I have been with the CBI and lately the NIA for some time now, and find myself settling down to life in the capital. I am not happy, but there is certainly much to be happy about. There is Mridula, and the children, who are now well into their teens. They are both at exclusive boarding schools not far away, and I am glad because I can spend time with Mridula without their getting to know.

All this subterfuge tires me out. I wish I could leave Nancy and stay with Mridula and her children. I can't. Perhaps I lack the killer instinct.

The children are both away, sleeping over with friends, and that presents an opportunity for a night with her – rare during the childrens' vacations. I am heading for her flat when I get a message from a visitor, a senior in the service, one I cannot refuse. He is a deputy director of the IB, and I have met him several times in the past. Now he is close to retirement; he has only months to go or maybe weeks.

His name is Rahul Sadasivan, the doyen of investigators. Every time I've met him, he's contributed something to my knowledge, something important. He maintains his reputation for utter, fearless integrity. They say that even ministers walk softly around him because he knows so much about them.

I return to my office and find him sitting quietly in a visitor's chair. He is a lanky man, simply dressed and soft-spoken, but charismatic enough in his own way. He rises when I enter and holds out his hand for me to shake. 'Good evening, sir,' I greet him.

'You were on your way home. I apologise for holding you up.'

'That's all right, sir, I was on my way to meet a friend. He can wait.'

'I'll keep this short. I wonder if we could go out somewhere.'

'The Club?'

'Right.'

'We'll take my car.'

'Sure.'

At the club, a white-uniformed bearer settles us in comfortable armchairs across a low table in a discreet corner of the barroom, brings us our drinks, and disappears quietly. 'It's awkward, what I've come to tell you,' he says. 'That's why I didn't want to speak in your office.'

'Go ahead, sir. No problem here.'

'As you know, I will retire next month.'

That's only a few days away. I must have miscalculated. 'I thought there were a couple of months left,' I tell him.

'Quite right. But I have some accumulated leave that I can't encash, so I'm leaving two months early.'

'We'll miss you.'

He grins, his face lighting up. 'You will, I know. I still remember the letter from Bhatkal.' The grin fades. 'Others might not miss me so much! You might have heard that I don't take money for favours. Or even favours for favours.'

'Yes.'

'It's true. I never have, never will. No matter what.'

'Yes.'

'That's not all… I believe that do what you have to do. Don't let the politicians tell you what to do. They decide policy, they might even give you a basis on which you should prioritise your work. But they don't interfere with cases. You don't let them. Understand?'

Indeed I do. Every tenth major case involves someone influential, at least indirectly. Every now and then, I get calls from people in the legislature, or even in Parliament, saying that I must do what I can for someone in trouble. I politely promise to do what I can, and let the investigation take its course. I've got a name for being, well, uncooperative. I'm aware of it, and I've kept it that way on purpose, though I could have increased my earnings fivefold or more with some help from the odd MP or MLA or minister. 'Yes, sir,' I say.

'Keep it that way. It's very important.'

'Yes, I will.'

'Sometimes, just sometimes, it might even do you some good. You might get work somewhere.' There are plenty of semi-government jobs for retirees from the bureaucracy and the police services. 'I've got many offers myself; to be on some committee or other.'

'Congratulations, sir.'

'Premature, I think. I'm not taking up any.'

'Why not, sir?'

'Whoever made the offer thinks I'll miss my income and the privileges that come with a police job. Certainly I will, but not enough to be manipulated afterwards.'

'I get it, sir.'

'Politicians come and go. You stay in the service for your whole life. That gives you a tremendous edge.'

'I do see that.'

'I hope you do. I like what I've heard of you. Don't give in. Keep yourself straight. Be prepared to accept the consequences. I can assure you that a suspension or punitive action of the kind soon becomes bearable if you know you've done the right thing. And there's always your enemy's enemy to help you out.'

'Yes, sir.'

He finishes his drink and stands. 'It's been good talking to you. I've been watching you all these years; and now that I'm retiring, I want to share with you the most important things I've learnt from my thirty-odd years in service. Forgive an old man for talking too much.'

'You're not old, sir,' I assure him.

He smiles and shakes his head. 'Being old is in the mind, and I find myself doing the things most old people – with nothing much to do – keep doing. Talking too much, repeating myself, taking too much time over simple matters... well, it doesn't matter. I'll have all the time in the world for that.'

Seven

Noordin

October 2025

It is a week since Hameed completed his reconnaissance, and we are ready to move, the six of us who will take part in this mission. We leave separately, over a week or so. The leave-taking is formal, and stretched out, for we do not know whether we will return or not. The women stay inside their houses; I can hear some of them weeping. The men gather solemnly, to hug, to wish each other well, and, most importantly, to wish us all success.

I will cross the border and find my way to Ramban across the hills. We have cut it very fine. Another week and the border will be impassable, and getting to Ramban through the country is next to impossible for a lone man. But some of the habits I learnt from fighting the Soviets all those decades ago come in handy now, for I can move across the hills better than others fifteen years younger.

I will take a bus to Jammu, rather than to Udhampur. Jammu is much larger and more crowded; losing myself there is relatively easy. Udhampur is smaller, and the Indian Army's 15 Corps headquarters is here, with the commanding general's house on a hilltop. All the way to Jammu from Ramban, it's difficult for an outsider to hide. The population is fairly stable, neighbourhood's small, and strangers stick out, except in Jammu itself, which now resembles an armed camp. I will have to get on to the train from Jammu, and get past Pathankot into Punjab before I can relax just a little.

We have learnt to use conditions to our benefit. In most of Afghanistan, there are few people except in the bigger cities. With natural disasters, wars, and the terrible terrain, the population hasn't grown much. But here, in this gentler land, every town is crowded, as is every village; and, when we travel, every bus and every train is crowded. It is easy to disappear into the crowds, especially in the poorer areas.

Now, having walked across the border in the hills, through gaps in the Indian patrols along the fence, I reach Ramban towards the middle of the morning. As soon as I reach the bus stand, a bus from Jammu pulls in. I am relaxed that my travel-stained appearance will cause no comment. I find a room in a small lodging house by the bus stand, where I do my prayers and clean up. From here, it's only a few hours to Jammu, and when I board the bus after lunch, I am in garments that would excite no comment in any north Indian town, pyjama and kurta with a shawl to keep the cold out.

I am in Jammu before dark and get off the bus at Raghunath Market, near the temple, and find another small, cheap lodge where the clerk puts my name in the register without even looking at my face. In the small, warm, airless room on the second floor, I finish my evening prayers before going out for a walk in the crowded market. As I leave the power fails – this is common all over India – and when I ask the clerk, he says it's an hour's load shedding.

Scattered lights come on as people turn on generators here and there. Only the bigger shops have them because only they can afford diesel. Others who have inverters, turn them on, but even those are only slightly cheaper than generators – most shopkeepers use candles and kerosene lamps. Electric three-wheelers ply silently, their lights dimmed.

In the dark I look around and find a place for the evening meal. It is a small, crowded, cheap restaurant where I find a cramped place on a bench along a narrow table. I order, and while waiting, listen to bits of the loud conversations doing the rounds. The government has just raised the price of petroleum products and electricity, so bus fares have gone up considerably, as has the price of cooking gas, which is becoming more difficult to find.

The people here are easy victims. Leaving a bomb under this bench and disappearing into the night would be easy – a kilo of plastic explosive with a sufficiency of shrapnel packed into it would devastate the place. I can't bring myself to contemplate that kind of violence now, though that is how most groups like to operate – hit vulnerable people and get away quickly, in the dark. Victims are easy to find anywhere.

In a burst of déjà vu, I find myself remembering a similar occasion a few years ago, but nearly a thousand miles away, and in a very different context.

December 2015

It's been a momentous year. The Indians have announced that they will be leaving Kashmir in three years. The northern part of the Indian province of Jammu and Kashmir will become the Republic of East Kashmir in three years, during which the Indians will decide exactly where the new border will be, withdraw their forces and administration, and leave Kashmiris to prepare to take over their own land. Meanwhile, the Kashmiris must write their own constitution and prepare to deal with their erstwhile oppressors on an equal basis.

I, too, am light of heart. Kashmir is my adopted country. I have never spoken of it, but I feel at home in it. To any Afghan from the mountains, it is a gentle land, with plenty of water in its rivers and a winter milder than the Afghan one, at any rate. I have been taking some time off in the valley, living in the sunlight, hoping for more for Afghanistan.

Of late, there have been events that cause disquiet. Some of the more militant separatist groups have already begun to label Kashmiri elements in the administration 'collaborators', and plan vengeance upon them. Others have begun to plan their own version of ethnic cleansing – the elimination of non-Muslims to establish a land of 'pure' Islam. Other groups have decided to continue their struggle to get Kashmir to accede to Pakistan, on the grounds that the Indians who have just cut Kashmir free might change their minds any time.

Lahore's rich continue to live as ever. I have a meeting with the director of ISI's Joint Directorate of Counter Intelligence, a brigadier named Haroon Sami. Sami had hopes of being promoted to a much higher rank, but his love of rich food and his physical laziness have given him hypertension, and he has been told he cannot rise any further. He has heard of me from his predecessor, who has now gone back to the artillery division, and is not sure whether to bully me or to be servile.

It's a year since Abdul Ghani Khan died. Ghani Khan's plans have been taken over by his chosen successor, another retired ISI officer, one Major General Irshad Junejo. But even Junejo doesn't know about the three boys, who are now young men in the best technical colleges in India, and what they are intended for.

Sami has heard rumours that Ghani Khan was up to something,

and is trying to get it out of me by pretending to know more than he does. He has taken me to Lahore's best restaurant, where you pay through the nose for the privilege of being served any liquor that can be disguised as a soft drink. So now he is drinking rum with Coke and is trying to persuade me to join him in the hope that the drink will loosen my tongue. At the tables around us are some of the wealthiest of Lahore's citizens - successful businessmen, a police official in uniform, and a few Army officers I know by sight, some of whom make more money than these businessmen.

Sami prides himself as an interrogator but has never questioned someone in a hurry - with the enemy knocking at the door and the floor slippery with blood, with the lives of men depending on the answers. He has no nerve. I turn down the drink, and let fall driblets of half-truth that will keep him busy investigating his colleagues - the ISI officials I've met have an abiding fear of their brother officers. The sole exception so far has been Ghani Khan, and I hope that Junejo, whom I have never met, will also be one.

Sami is too full of himself - of his resentment, of what he thinks of his own capabilities, of what he can do for me that no one else can - to be a good interrogator but he's too old now to learn that. I doubt he can really listen to anyone, a must for any successful interrogator. After the first couple of drinks, he isn't even aware that his voice is rising and is perhaps audible to people at the next table.

I question him about his own plans and he makes the mistake amateur interrogators always make - he boasts. He tries to persuade me that his people are as powerful in the rest of the world as they are in Pakistan, and that he himself is at the top of his organisation, forgetting that he was complaining minutes earlier that his department is running short of money, and that he wasn't getting his due from his superiors. I listen quietly, nodding from time to time, trying to extract some wheat from the volumes of chaff.

There is more cause for disquiet. The movement for accession to Pakistan will soon be gaining force and will become violent. There are weapons to be channelled into Kashmir to ensure a period of such violence so that the Kashmiris beg Pakistan first for intercession, and then accession. 'Money for these and other plans is pouring in,' Sami boasts, 'from the poppy fields of Afghanistan.'

After the meal, he offers to take me wherever I want to go in his black Volvo, with its efficient heater, but I tell him I'd prefer to walk. He looks bleakly at the wet night – it's been drizzling for some time now – and then at me, as if to say I must be mad, but I smile and wave him on.

Afterwards, I take a walk around the city, habit driving me near the railway station, where the odd stranger won't be noticed. It's well past ten, the kebab stalls are still open, and so are many shops, and the dormitories and hotels. A train must have arrived, for a crowd pours out of the station as I pass by. Taxis and three wheelers throng outside, competing for passengers.

The power fails, leaving the area in darkness. Out come candles and lamps, and here and there a generator comes to life. The city becomes surreal. In the uneven darkness, I immerse myself in a part of the crowd, moving along with it to the bus stop nearby. Just then I find a restaurant for a late-night cup of tea and sit to listen to what people are talking about. The conversation is mostly about how difficult it's been since the military government took over, how difficult it is to get good meat, and how fuel prices have really shot up, especially of cooking gas, which all these people use. A man, leader of a group of three men in frontier garb at a nearby table, shows with his hands the size of a leg of goat that you could get for a thousand rupees a couple of years ago, and what you get now.

Less than an hour ago, Sami paid more for each drink in that restaurant than this man and his group are paying for their entire meal. Is Sami the kind of person I want for an ally? Are these men not victims of people like Sami?

Certainly they are, but Sami is no ally. Thinking about it, I find that the old brigadier, Ghani Khan, had some integrity, as does his son, Raza, whose only weakness is his physical cowardice. They spent their lives trying to make something of their country. To be sure, they broke some rules, but just like Sohail, they did what they had to.

Sami has no such quality. Who is Sami looking out for – himself? His countrymen? Islam?

I stop in my tracks. For the first time, I ask the question – who am I looking out for?

October 2025

The answer is yet to come. I have tried to put it to myself in another way – where do my loyalties lie? The answer here is a little easier. My loyalties are for my God and Islam, for the country of my birth, Afghanistan, and for my adopted country, Kashmir. Then there is the next question – in what order? There is no answer yet.

December 2017

My adopted land is being torn apart, and I dare not intervene.

The Indians are withdrawing from Kashmir, to Jammu. The new border, negotiated by the Indians and a consortium of separatist groups, passes through what the Indians called the Jawahar tunnel, which permits almost year-round access to Srinagar from Jammu. Their troop strength is down to a quarter of what it used to be, and the guns have been taken off the LOC.

Fortifications along the new border are coming up, and now it's clear that the three years of time that the Indians wanted for preparing their new border is insufficient – the way they are going now, they will need more than ten years.

I drift back and forth across the LOC; no one really cares. Many of my fellow-countrymen have come across the LOC into Kashmir, along with Baluchis and runaways from the FATA, bringing with them their favourite small arms and their tendency to be violent. Honour killings, once unknown in Kashmir, have become common.

There has been a vacuum, with no one really governing the country. The Indians are too busy getting themselves out without too much damage, setting up the new border, and figuring out ways to weaken the movement in Kashmir to accede to Pakistan. Most of the Kashmiri police have been labelled traitors, and Indian Quislings, and are too busy protecting themselves to police anything. The administration has come to a halt because no one is clear about what to do.

Tourism has shrunk to almost nothing, although foreign journalists abound, most of them hovering around the bar of a new hotel that offers liquor. Many businesses that flourished supplying goods to large Indian troop formations have collapsed since the withdrawals began.

The police themselves have been decimated. Those who served the Indian administration have been labelled collaborators, and, with the first of the major troop withdrawals, been targeted by the separatists, who have set up their own kangaroo courts. Some of them have been killed – shot dead by passing youngsters on motorcycles – or blown up. At an average, one bystander has been killed for every such 'collaborator' shot or blown up; many of these bystanders have been women or children who have died just for being where they were.

Non-Muslims, especially Hindus, have been 'encouraged' to leave – their properties bought or taken over at unbelievably low rates. They have been harassed out of their homes if they refused to move out and a few killed or injured in knife attacks or beaten by groups of angry youngsters. Behind all this is the Lashkar-e-Tayyeba, now out in the open.

They operate even in the villages, collecting taxes, telling farmers what to grow, for they need the cash. They have planted opium wherever they can. Opium is a hardy plant and grows reasonably well in the southern parts, on higher ground where the water doesn't stay long. The crop pays well, but the Lashkar or the Taliban take most of the profits. The Lashkar is rich.

It is a time of great tension, though not for me personally.

I travel. Raza occasionally calls me for meetings, and again I pretend to be Murad, the easy-living Afghan. He asks me to stay back after one of these meetings. 'I'm afraid, Noordin,' he tells me as he sips from his tumbler of whisky and water – he has inherited some of his father's habits – in the shabby yellow mansion. 'I am afraid of many things.'

'Name them,' I tell him. 'Sometimes just doing that drives the fear away.'

He sits quietly for a moment, his eyes turned inwards. 'I have two fears,' he points out, 'one immediate, the other a long way off.'

'Tell me the immediate one first.'

'The ISI men are after me. They know Father started something long-term.'

'How?'

'From the money. The Americans tried to buy off a few mujahideen through ISI. They routed some of the money through Father. Father knew it was useless trying to bribe the mujahideen, because they'd just take the money and keep doing whatever they wanted to do, so he diverted some of it to your project.'

'He must have covered his tracks.'

'He did. But you know how obsessive the mujahideen are. They got a ballpark figure on what he'd diverted – it's much more than Father really got, you know – and started working backwards from that. They keep asking themselves – if he took that money, as we know he did, it must show up somewhere. It's not shown up in his private life, because he's got no house, no cars, nothing that he didn't have before, and his son lives exactly the same as before. They've got no assets abroad, no bank accounts in countries with strict confidentiality and no extradition treaties. Besides, he just wasn't that type. So he must have set the money aside for some project we don't know of. What can it be?'

'Have they got at Masood?'

'Father was good at what he did. They did get at Masood but they can't understand anything from what he tells them.'

'What do they want?'

'They want to know what happened to the money. They'll want to take over the project if they get to know of it. What saves us is the infighting amongst them… you know how it is.'

'Yes.' Amongst officers in the ISI, as in practically every intelligence organisation, the man who starts a project or an operation is responsible for it. Every major project is run by a committee, the idea being to have it reviewed by many heads, and to provide it a wider range of resources than would be possible otherwise. It never works that way, though. Each member of the committee, knowing that he is safe, interferes to his greatest advantage. ISI officers tend to be a little more venal than others, that's all. Ghani Khan knew exactly what he was doing when he left this to me, and covered up the money trail. 'Will anything specific lead them to you? Or to me? We don't need to worry about them sniffing around without evidence.'

'I don't know. I hope not.'

'Do you have an escape route?'

'Yes. But if I leave here, I won't be able to help you anymore.'

'You'll do a lot more damage if you get caught. Go ahead and run if you have to.'

'Thanks. Now for the other one. It's the money. It's always the money. The Americans might get on the money trail. You know how they are; compared to them, our ISI men are pussycats. If they come behind us, their follow-up will be relentless and hi-tech. For all we know, they're already on to us, and we don't even know it.'

'Yes. Your father was aware of that. He warned me about the Americans. We'll have to be more careful. Their satellites can be fooled, and our codes are still strong. The key elements of the plan are nearly ten years old, and the money trail almost as old. We've spent very little after the money for the boys was paid to the NGO and the rest transferred to my various accounts. One thing we know about the Americans is that they can be even more short-sighted and vicious than the ISI.'

'I hope you're right, Noordin.'

I begin to feel that the brigadier should have found someone else to carry on the project. Raza just doesn't have the nerve. He must have thought that Raza's knowledge would keep him alive.

October 2025

These last ten years have been relatively quiet. I have found myself withdrawing from operations that make me queasy. After that meeting with Sami, I began to isolate myself from the gangs that indulged in shameless revenge, in the gross public humiliation of 'collaborators', and the massacre of non-Muslims. I do not think there is anything 'holy' in killing defenceless people at random. I have persuaded the men around me to think similarly; those who do not have left for other groups whose values and ideas match their own.

Summer, 2010

I have been watching the Palestine. The Israelis have attacked ships supplying essentials to Gaza, and the world is outraged. What kind of inhumanity is this?

Our network is now worldwide. We are all interlinked – the Taliban, the Al-Qaeda and the Hezbollah. I am known across these networks for what I did as a young boy. Although I have done nothing in recent years to compare to that, they treat me with some respect.

After much consideration, I think of something useful that I can do. I can find my way into a military installation in the US and blow myself up, along with any soldiers who might be in the vicinity. I have the skills for it, and I can do real damage.

The Taliban have dispersed. The Americans have made it clear that they have no heart for a long-drawn out war. Now they plan to build up their forces in Afpak for one hammer blow before leaving the Afghans and the Pakistanis to pick up the pieces. Their foreign policy has never been as short-sighted as now; we will just wait out and, when they leave, return to action.

The leadership – leaders of all groups meet in a conclave to which I have never been invited – decide upon courses of action that involve any action bigger than a small raid. What I have proposed, a strike in the heart of America, is significant enough to require a meeting of the senior-most leadership.

The leaders decide that I am too valuable to be wasted on a suicide mission. However, they think I am an inspiration for younger men, inexperienced lads – I don't understand how they think suicide bombers can gain experience. Will they pick dead bodies to do similar things? I am to train these boys instead, to inspire them.

Just months later, one batch of six boys is ready. My heart sinks when I see them – they are all in their late teens or early twenties, all from poor families in the mountains, all deprived in one way or the other. They think they will be heroes, and their families will be feted for the rest of their lives.

They are also believers. The depth of their belief takes me by surprise. They imagine the depth of my belief, and expect some kind of religious discourse. I, too, take them by surprise.

I talk of the Israelis.

There have been many successful suicide bomb attacks in Israel and there could have been many more if they had not been as watchful as they are. My fellow Taliban might speak of them with contempt, but I respect their fighting abilities and their intelligence. A long time ago, they went through everything they knew about suicide bombers and made a list of signs by which to identify one.

Now, I tell these boys that the checklist of about a dozen points should tell them what not to do, how not to behave. I go through the list with them. I tell them that they must dress appropriately, mustn't mumble a prayer or stare blindly ahead or keep both hands hidden. After we have been through the list, I tell them they must behave as if they are going to meet relatives they don't particularly like, carrying a surprise gift.

This raises a laugh of sorts even amongst that gloomy bunch. That is the last I see of them alive or free. I don't even know their names or where they come from; all I know is that they will blow themselves up in Afpak or in Iraq, if they can find their way there.

Months later, I begin to see the results of the session. One of the boys has killed himself in Kandahar, taking two American soldiers with him. Also killed were four Afghan civilians who just happened to be passing by at the time.

Were those civilians devout men, unable to be with the Taliban because they had families to look after? I begin to question these tactics that involve indiscriminate killing even further. Killing our own is no way to fight the enemy.

At one time, I thought civilians in the US or Israel were fair targets, but now I question that, too. Killing a harmless Jewish clerk doesn't seem the way to heaven, even the clerk in question might pay taxes that pay for the Israeli Army, or vote for politicians who blockade Gaza.

I will support no more suicide bombings in civilian areas. Killing the defenceless is not my way.

Winter, 2020

A group of Taliban meet at Islamabad, formerly Anantnag, south of Srinagar. The Taliban have refrained from renaming some places because they continue to maintain the fiction that Kashmir is an independent country – Anantnag was called Islamabad even before the partition. But that fiction is increasingly difficult to maintain, now that the Taliban's version of the Shariat is in place in all of Kashmir.

On our way to Islamabad, in Qazigund, we stop to talk to the local council of elders, and they persuade us to watch an example of the Shariat in action. A woman is to be stoned to death for speaking to a man not related to her. My companions join in the stone-throwing. I stay away, pleading ill-health, knowing that if I am at the ground and do not throw a few stones, I will be considered a suspect.

The others return, glowing with satisfaction, but their

satisfaction is no different from the pride of Naeem Shaqeer. Again, I hold my tongue. Again, I wonder what this means.

October 2025

I use the 'facilities' that these gangs have in common, the systems that deliver explosives and weaponry – that is all. Even that is becoming difficult, for I fear the network has been compromised over the last few years, though the organisers deny it. They are businessmen; they are willing to write off a percentage of what they bring into India. As long as their losses stay below that percentage, they don't really care: The money they earn from smuggling arms and Afghan morphine keeps them in comfort.

The power comes back and I can see the people around me. They don't look at all different from the ones in that Lahore restaurant – all victims. Is there anything I can do to improve their lives? I do not know, but slowly I am beginning to think that I can't.

Eight

Ganesh

October 2025

I leave Dinesh's flat at half past ten; at this time of the night, traffic thins out and I get home in fifteen minutes. It takes me another five to reach my flat from the gates of the apartment complex. First, there's the check at the gate – a watchman checks the underside of the car for bombs with a mirror on a stick. He then checks the registration number off a list on a clipboard and the parking sticker on the inside of the passenger-side windscreen for validity. Then he looks inside the car and the boot, just in case I've been forced to smuggle someone else in. Only then does he open the inner gates. There's another check in the lobby – this time it's my fingerprint, besides the visual identification. And then, finally, when I get to the door of the flat, I run my own checks before entering, just in case someone is masquerading as a maintenance worker or a utility representative has booby-trapped something inside.

As has always been the case so far, there are no traps, booby or otherwise. Sometimes I wish someone would try to get through all this security.

Anil was right about lots of things; for instance, more people die in traffic accidents caused by badly driven buses than in bomb explosions and other terrorism-related incidents. I keep wishing they'd show the country's score for the year – for this one, it'll be something like:

Terrorists: 1,600

Buses: 4,500

Or

Terrorists: 1,600

Road Traffic Accidents: 10,500

Include the wounded, and the accidents column would have an even bigger lead.

Sometimes I think we don't really want to reduce these numbers. Of course, with population about a billion and three quarters and birth rates showing only a small decline, lives perhaps don't count much, unless the dead are close to your heart.

Gayatri used to get off her school bus across the road, where Usha, the widow from Virajpet, would be waiting to collect her. One warm summer afternoon, the year after the bomb blasts in Pegasus, Usha and Gayatri were crossing the road when a bus, ignoring a lollipop man, mowed them down. Gayatri never moved again and Usha's broken legs meant six months in a hospital, after which I sent her back to Virajpet on a pension.

That was easily the worst day of my life.

March 2020

School traffic begins at one. Bengaluru's schools, unable to cope with the crowd of new students, have switched to a shift system to accommodate the rush. The first shift runs from six in the morning to about half past noon, the second from one to half past seven. No one's complaining too much – more jobs, more profits, and, for harried parents, a set of timings that don't interfere too much with work timings.

Among those who can afford it, there are maids to take care of children while their parents are at work. Then there's a whole generation of latchkey kids, typically ten or more years old, who return home to fortress-like apartment blocks, who help themselves to warmed-up snacks out of the oven and wait alone until their parents return or leave when their parents are both out at work.

Gayatri has the second shift, which means an hour of fighting peak-hour traffic on her way back, so she reaches home at half past eight, just in time for a quick bath and a meal before turning in. But there's no pressure on her to get up early, and I manage to spend some relaxed mornings with her. Also, I am almost always home to read her something as she goes to bed. A couple of times a week, I'm home early enough to pick her up at the bus stop.

Lollipop men abound, to help groups of schoolchildren cross streets safely at bus stops. There's always one where Gayatri gets off her bus, and I'm always reassured by the sight of the old man in his bright fluorescent orange – and hence very noticeable – uniform with his lollipop-shaped board stopping traffic to lead a waiting stream of children across.

And then, one windless March evening, the unthinkable happens. A driver loses control of his bus and ploughs into the children. The lollipop man, from devotion to duty, or perhaps just plain courage, does his best to cover his charges, putting himself in the way of the bus, now slowing, but still dangerously fast. Some of the children leap to safety, but Gayatri, Usha, the lollipop man, and two other children don't make it in time.

Three hours later, in the hospital, a nurse wheels Gayatri's still and unbearably small form out of the operation theatre. Her face is unmarked and, for a moment, hope leaps up in my heart, but fades when I touch her.

I don't remember much of what follows. Mahesh, the only partner in town, has been around for a couple of hours now. I vaguely remember him holding me, that's all. I didn't weep for Manju or Mom or Dad, but now something explodes deep in my chest and all I remember is coming home in the small hours, thinking at first that I've been having a nightmare, then finding the reality to be worse than any nightmare.

Two months later, for the second time, I meet Anil. This time about Gayatri. Again, he invites me for a drink in an expensive bar at night. This time, though, with Gayatri gone, I am in no hurry to go back home.

Now that I can recognise him, I arrive a few minutes early, as is my habit, and find him already seated at a table in a dimly lit corner from where he can watch the front door and the service entrance with hooded eyes. More or less as I'd expected, for I'd earlier assigned one of my discreet colleagues to survey the place. Anil, too, it seems, has a commendable habit of arriving early.

By now, I've discovered a few of his less commendable habits, too. I won't mention them to him, of course, for I'm happier with him thinking of me as the simple soldier he said I was the first time we met. His underestimation of me comes in useful all the time.

When he sees me crossing the hall to his table, he stands up. 'Condolences,' he begins. 'Late, but sincere.'

I nod. 'Thank you.'

He takes off his glasses – photo chromatic and reflective – and polishes them before putting them in their case on the table. His left eyebrow goes up. 'The same questions?' he asks.

The waiter arrives with a menu card for me – Anil apparently is a regular here, too – to take my order of vodka and lime, and I wait for him to go a few tables away before replying, 'I'm afraid so.'

The eyebrow goes down and he contemplates the glasses in their transparent case for a moment before he replies. 'The answers are much the same.' He clears his throat, 'Another dead end for you.'

It really is a dead end for me. Without Gayatri, I have to struggle to get through each day. But I must have some details, and I know more than to ask who's responsible. 'Could you be more specific?' I ask.

'The driver has disappeared. He got his job with a licence issued in what seems a false name. The address on it doesn't exist. We've been trying to trace him. The owner of the bus obviously isn't responsible, but he's willing to pay you off, not you specifically, but anyone in your position. Some form of compensation. He knows you've just got into business.'

Something breaks in me. It had weakened when I spoke to Anil about the investigation into the blasts; now it's gone. By now, I'm quite sharp at keeping my emotions buttoned up. 'I don't really need the money,' I tell Anil, 'but I do want to know what he's offering for Gayatri and Usha, the lady who was with Gayatri, and for Prasad, the lollipop man.' Prasad, of course, bled out on the road and Usha is still in the hospital with two broken legs.

Anil names a figure, and my stomach clenches tight. It seems so pathetically little. Is that how much a life costs? Anil seems to sense my thoughts and continues, 'He told me to tell you that when a bus runs someone down he does his best to ease matters. He certainly offers more than the government. The victim or his people get a fairer deal than they would if someone pursued the driver and got him in prison.'

I tamp down the urge to finish this man off right here, then smile and ask, 'What about making sure he doesn't do it again?'

'Will jail do that?' Anil asks, sounding dangerously reasonable.

'One experience like this is enough for most people. Be practical. That driver's going to be extra careful the rest of his life.'

'What about the owner?'

'Accidents cost him. Payments like this. The bus being off its route. Time lost. Finding a new driver.'

The trouble with what Anil says is that it makes a perverted kind of sense. I sit still for a minute or two with my eyes closed, unaware of anything but the growing urge to retaliate. Then I say, 'Tell this man, whoever he is, to arrange for an anonymous donation to this Chennai-based orphanage called Udhavum Karangal. He can take care of Prasad's people, too. Double the figure.'

'Very good,' Anil smiles. 'You've grown.'

His approbation grates. *Granddad, forgive me. You knew what you were about. I wish I did.* 'I'd like to meet this guy,' I tell Anil. 'Just to get a sense of the man.' I don't really know why.

'What exactly do you mean by that?' Anil asks. His posture doesn't change but I can feel his antennae standing up.

'It's always good to make personal contact. You never know when someone might come in useful.'

'At last, we're on the same wavelength. This calls for another round,' he says finishing off the contents of the glass in one gulp.

As he smiles, I knock back my drink, and he orders another for me. As I sip the second vodka, I find a smile somewhere and notice Anil relax just that little bit more. *Granddad, Granddad, I wish I could talk to you now.*

'You need to unwind a little more,' he says. 'You know what they say about all work and no play, don't you?'

'Yes. I intend to do just that.'

'You'll be much happier that way.'

I give him company through another couple of rounds. I don't drink much and I can feel my speech slur, but I'm aware of whatever's going on. I slur a bit more than necessary, and when, an hour or so later, it's time to leave, Anil tells me I shouldn't drive home on my own. 'Good advice,' I tell. 'I'll take a cab.'

'Do that,' he says. 'I'd have offered to drop you off, but I have another person to meet here.' Does he spend his nights hanging around these bars or what, I wonder to myself, and walk unsteadily across the lobby towards the road.

April 2020

Anil has been as good as his word. A few weeks after our chat, he calls to give me an address and a time – three on a Sunday afternoon. 'The man you want to meet is Ramakrishna Gowda. His brother is the minister of finance in the Karnataka government, and far more powerful than that position might lead you to believe. He himself is in the security business, but in a different way, so I don't think you need to think of him as competition.'

I've done my own asking around. Gowda's in the security business all right – he runs a protection racket. He moves around the town in a custom-bodied SUV that his driver leaves unlocked on the premise that anyone – members of the traffic police force included – who touches the vehicle is liable to lose an arm.

The power, such as it is, seems to have gone to his head, for he's lax. His movements are predictable, the quality of the people around him variable. He lives in a white house set in an acre of lawn near Chikballapur, some fifty kilometres north of Bengaluru, almost twenty kilometres from the airport. Four armed men at the gate stop my car and their chief tells me to get out. While he pats me down, another opens the door and goes over the seats with a loop at the end of a stick, and a third looks at the boot. A fourth looks cursorily at the underside with a mirror at the end of another stick. For a long moment, all four are occupied. Any passerby could take the lot with an automatic weapon. Ramakrishna Gowda's attitude seems to have percolated through to the bottom of his pyramid; it's not much better inside. The switchboards for alarm systems are in plain view, and his men out of shape.

The man himself is dark and squat, with a thick layer of pudge covering what seems to have been a lot of muscle, like a heavyweight wrestler gone to seed. His voice is a pleasant rumble, and his smile infectious. He has charisma, and when he shakes my hand, I find that his grip is hard and immensely powerful. When he speaks, it's clear that his English is limited. 'Accident very sad,' he says. 'Driver careless.' He raises his hands. 'I beat him. I beat him myself. Never again.' He sees an underling approach with a tray. 'Have coffee. Special coffee.'

I can feel the power of his personality. His special coffee isn't a patch on Granddad's, but it isn't bad either. He continues after a sip and a brief pause. 'Anil. Anil tell me about your family.' He shakes his head. 'Very sad.'

'Yes,' I nod.

'Your family gone. But you not alone. I there.'

I drag the words out of a throat that doesn't want to collaborate. 'Thank you.'

'What I can do for you?' he inquires. 'You new in security business?' He smiles again. 'I fifteen years in security business. You want contacts? No problem.'

It's true. The businesses under his protection haven't suffered anything more than petty thefts. The only problem is that he charges thrice what I would for the same service, and demands a large portion of it in cash, to pay for his acquisitions of land and for the other even more unsavoury bits of his business. *Granddad, I have to do this. For Gayatri. For Manju. For Mom and Dad.* 'You have a lot of experience in investigations.'

He laughs. 'Fifteen years. Lot of investigation. You want

recommendation? See, you cooperate in accident, I cooperate here, everybody happy. I give recommendation.'

'That's alright. You know about my family. The bomb in Pegasus.' He nods and I keep going. 'Well, nothing's come of the case. Maybe you could help.'

'Those three men. Still in jail. You want to do something? My men in same jail.'

'No,' I explain. 'Not those men. The men who sent them.'

His good humour disappears as if he's switched it off. 'You speak to Anil?'

I nod. 'Anil has his limits.'

'What he say?'

'He said it's difficult to get proof.'

'Yes.' He flips the switch again. 'You go Delhi? I got friends there.'

'I go there once a month. More often if necessary.'

He nods. 'No problem.' He waves and a goon appears beside him. He says something to the man in Kannada, and moments later, the goon brings his writing pad of the finest paper. He scribbles on it with a gold Mont Blanc, rips off the sheet, and hands it to me. 'You see this man. I call him now.' The goon hands him his cell phone, and he speed-dials a number. His voice is low, but clear. I hear him telling someone that I will get in touch, and that I am to be helped. The phone's built-in camera clicks a picture of me, and he fiddles with the buttons, sending my photograph along. 'He busy now. See him in June. July. Give time to find details.'

'Thanks.'

He rises. He's given me sympathy, coffee, and a contact. Unless I have more business, I should take myself off. I find a card in my hands with Gowda's name and a cell phone number. Nothing else. 'Personal line,' he says. 'I only pick up. Any time.'

October 2025

The moment I decided to do something about Gayatri's death, the pall of fatigue that had descended on me lifted just a little. It must have been because I suddenly found something to do that seemed meaningful, though I knew that no revenge would ever bring her back or make mornings easier to face. What I did afterwards came in a way I've never been able to explain, as if someone else with a taste for revenge had got hold of me.

July 2020

Ashok has been with us for three months, and is already making his presence felt. He has more or less taken over the Industrial Perimeter Security Division (IPSD)– providing watchmen for factories besides sharing some of the administrative load otherwise shouldered by Mahesh and Vivek –the remaining partners – and me. He concentrates quietly but fiercely at work. Not the smallest detail slips his eye. He already knows almost all the many hundred men in IPSD by name and has most of them sized up. Most of them being former soldiers, know exactly how to deal with him.

Ashok likes to get to work early, sometimes even ahead of me, preferring, if necessary, to leave early too so as to get home at a reasonable time. When I ask him why, he grins. 'First, the Army taught me to get out of bed early. Then, with two kids getting ready to go to college early in the morning, home is not the place to be. It's much more relaxed in the evening when they get back.'

By and by, I might need a good rifle to bring down someone from a distance. I ask Ashok if he still has access to those weapons he and his group stashed away a couple of years ago. 'I don't know about the others,' he replies, 'but I know where my personal stash is.' He flicks a glance at me. 'You can help yourself from it whenever you like. It's only a couple of hundred or so kilometres away. We'll have to go there together the first time, but after that you can dig it up whenever you like.'

'Thanks, I'll let you know.'

'Look, you don't have to explain anything. The less I know the better. Okay?'

'Okay.' The more I see of this man the better he seems, as a colleague and even as a man.

The next Sunday we're on the road to Bengaluru. Well past Hassan, we exit the highway on to a rutted secondary road, and park the car in a thicket at the verge almost five kilometres away. He leads me behind a rocky knoll, where by a gigantic grey boulder, he points out a spot. 'They're packed well enough to last years,' he tells me, 'greased and so on. You know the drill. You'll have to go a metre down – too deep for a casual treasure-hunter – before you hit the outer layer of plastic tarpaulin.'

'Thanks again.'

'The stash wouldn't have been here if you'd split on us,' he reminds me. 'I don't plan to use it at all.'

'Do you mind if I shift it?'

'Go ahead. I don't want to know if you don't want to tell me... actually, I don't want to know at all.'

Another few weeks later, I revisit the spot, and recover the bag of weapons. It's very heavy, some sixty kilos – one .50 calibre anti-materiel rifle, two sniper rifles, two designated marksman rifles, a laser range-finder, image-intensifiers, ammunition, packing material, gun oil and grease, cleaners, the works. In the dark I open it, and check individual rifles before rewrapping them and taking them out to the car. Later that night, I bury them again, distributing them over the hectare of land around the old house in Virajpet, which I know like the back of my hand, taking care to place them near spots that snakes guard.

One of the sniper rifles is a long-barrelled Barrett that I've used before, an excellent rifle equipped with a custom-fitted 12x sight and infrared sensors, just in case I want to bring someone down at night, which I do. Active infrared won't work at any great range but there's also passive infrared, which instead of putting out an infrared beam, just intensifies available light to the maximum possible. That should be enough.

I have to zero the sights properly, and to do that I head out to Virajpet, where I can get into the hills and find space to calibrate the sights at 300 metres. This is well short of the range at which a trained sharpshooter can bring off a head shot, but I'm out of practice. Besides, I don't need the range for what I need to do. There's not enough ammunition, so I have to collect the cartridge casings to take home and reload. Bullets are hard to come by, so I'll have to make them myself, which will compromise accuracy. There should be enough for me to take care of this job; I'll look after the reloading when the need arises.

In any case, now I have four rifles which can't be traced back to a person or place – two from our own Army, written off as combat losses, and two captured but never recorded.

October 2025

I spent several weekends figuring out what to do. I couldn't leave any of it to colleagues, and since I had to do it all during my spare time, it stretched out over several weeks. The man in question was well-known, a bit of a gangster, and, more importantly, related to a prominent local politician. He was both indiscreet and regular in his habits, and therefore easy to trace.

December 2020

Ramakrishna Gowda divides his time between Bengaluru – where he has several dozen buses, a construction contracting business, and an automobile dealership – and Mangalore, his hometown, where he has an expensive hotel where he entertains himself in complete privacy.

He can fly the distance between the cities but prefers to drive in his SUV, stopping off at Hassan, where he has a farm. He tends to leave Mangalore early in the morning, beating traffic congestion and getting to Hassan by mid-morning, and proceeding onwards after a leisurely lunch, getting to Bengaluru by about dark. Bengaluru to Mangalore, however, he likes to do at night, leaving at ten, after traffic has eased off, and speeding along the highway to get to Mangalore before first light, an hour or so ahead of the long-distance buses from Bengaluru. He employs a fast driver, a hoodlum who also serves as his bodyguard, and tends to honk his way past vehicles that get in his way, and occasionally slows to hurl abuses at slower drivers who hold him up. Another bodyguard, who doubles as a spare driver, travels in the front passenger seat.

The route takes him through Coorg district, hilly and fertile, not far from the family acres, where the roads wind up and down mountainsides, and there are plenty of blind curves and hairpin bends. At this time of the year, there is a mist just after dawn and visibility can be very poor indeed. I doubt if anyone will do a detailed forensic examination on a car that's crashed in an early-morning mist in these parts – knowing the backlog in the labs and the costs of getting tests done – both reasons seem reasonable enough.

So what we need is a crashed car and the bus-owner dead inside. The driver is collateral damage. I have no qualms about him.

I've waited at this curve several times, at a hairpin just west of a high orange sodium lamp that lights up any vehicle coming along well enough for me to read its registration number. I don't want to stop the wrong car. The barrier on the outside of the curve is just a fence – it's only for show, and past it is a thirty-foot drop. The curve itself is sharp enough to make vehicles slow down to fifteen or twenty kilometres an hour, and most drivers take it in first or second gear.

If there's one thing I've learnt in the Army, it's to keep things as simple as possible. To make the driver slow down a bit more, I leave a football-sized lump of stone on the road just a little before the hairpin, positioning it such that the driver won't be able to take the best line through the bend, from the outside to the inside at the apex and then out again. I use my own jeep to push an opening in the barrier at the side of the road. Then it's a matter of waiting.

The SUV, squat and ugly, appears on time, just before four; and from fifty yards, getting the off-front tyre with a good rifle is easy enough. As the driver and the man in the front passenger seat step out and inspect the flat and curse, I make my way to my jeep, with false number plates, and draw up behind Gowda's car. 'Can I help?' I ask, getting out.

The driver-bodyguard, a squat dark man who habitually wears tight short-sleeved T-shirts that display his biceps and tattoos on his arms, is bent over the wheel, tightening the nuts. It's easy enough to knock him out and turn the rifle on the other hoodlum, and then on Gowda. In less than a couple of minutes, they both are out cold, the wheel nuts are checked, and the car, with a stone tied to the accelerator with a nylon line, and an extra litre of petrol soaking the highly inflammable interior, goes through the gap. The car has automatic transmission, so no one's going to ask why it was going so fast in first gear. It falls the thirty feet, but the low-speed impacts don't cause enough sparks to make the tank go off despite the petrol. A flaming oil-soaked rag tossed in through an open window makes a satisfactory blaze, with the tank going off seconds later. I'm on my way as fast as I can.

If they trace anything back to me, I'm fine with it. There's no one waiting for me; and in the worst case, a few years in prison isn't intolerable. These days, they drug you for almost anything. If they do that, I'll probably reveal that I got the weapons from Ashok, and take him, too, with me. If that does happen, I will at least make sure that his wife and children live in reasonable comfort for the rest of their lives.

October 2025

The car burnt well. They had to do DNA tests to establish that the corpses were indeed that of Gowda and the driver and bodyguard. But the police never came anywhere near me, and Ashok is still doing well at his job with the firm. They assumed it was an accident, and the autopsy was sloppy enough not to catch any discrepancies – like why there were contusions on the back of the bodyguard's head, which hadn't burnt completely, and so on – and point at foul play.

People might have put two and two together – people like Anil, maybe – but I never got to know of it. Anil and I met a couple of times after that incident as he had to point a couple of clients in my direction and take a percentage. On both the occasions, I had a few drinks with him, but he never asked me if I had anything to do with Gowda's death, or about the taste of revenge, which he would have, if he'd had any idea.

For a few months I wondered if I'd done the right thing by finishing off those guys. Each time I thought of Anil and his smile and the money the bus owner had been willing to offer in exchange for Gayatri's life, I got convinced that I had done the right thing.

Soon after the killings, I found my second, and perhaps most powerful, ally, one with even fewer inhibitions than Mahipal.

November 2021

The firm's name has spread, and finding talent has become slightly easier, but I still keep the door open for people walking in looking for work. But Sushil Tikkoo is not a normal walk-in – Mahipal has told him to get in touch with us if he wants something interesting to do.

Sushil is tall, fair-skinned, and light-eyed, with angular features and a sparse beard. He and Mahipal have been learning taekwondo from the same Korean immigrant – whom I, too, know – for many weeks now. He's presently a marketing executive for a firm making soap and feels completely out of place in his job. Somewhere underneath that layer of indifference, I sense a different character. In his resumé, which he offered on entering my room, he says he's worked with different employers in Delhi, Srinagar, and Bengaluru. I put the folder containing his resumé down on the desk and ask, 'Why are you looking for a change, Mr Tikkoo? And what kind of work would you be looking for?'

He grins. 'I'm tired of selling soap,' he says. 'Can you blame me for that? I don't know what kind of job I'm looking for, but Mahipal said you have openings for all kinds of people.'

'Did Mahipal tell you he doesn't work for us?'

'Yes,' he replies. 'But he said he visited you, and you put him on to his present employer.'

Mahipal's present employer is a consulting firm registered in the name of someone who doesn't exist, with a registered office in Mangalore. The address serves its purpose in many ways; and the vague definition of his duties enables him to travel and be away for long periods, without arousing suspicion.

Mahipal has sent this man here because Sushil, too, is a victim of separatist violence. Sushil is Kashmiri, and his parents were forced to move to Delhi when his paternal grandparents and sister were killed in a grenade attack on their shop in Srinagar. As refugees in Delhi, they lived for a while in a one-room set in a slum, with no running water and only occasional electricity, before desperation drove them back to Kashmir. Back in Srinagar, separatists made an example of his family. His parents were murdered one night – he was the only one who escaped. Ever since then, he's been drifting. He hasn't been able to study beyond a basic degree in commerce. He's bright enough to get to wherever he wants to, but doesn't seem that committed.

'Don't you think you could study further?'

He shakes his head. 'I tried. I enrolled for courses in business. It didn't seem relevant.'

'Relevant to what?'

He shrugs. 'Anything. It seemed unreal.'

I know the feeling in his eyes. Nothing seems to matter any longer. He has to find his own moorings, find out what he needs to do to bring that meaning back into life. I can only offer a little advice, which might not be relevant either. I tell him so.

'But can you get me in touch with someone who might offer me more meaningful work?' he asks.

'Not unless I'm sure you'd fit, that you have something to offer.' I look him straight in the eye. 'What I've got from you so far is this – you don't like what you do, but you don't know what you'd like to do and can't even think of anything you'd like to try. Put yourself in my shoes – what would you do?'

He nods. 'I see what you mean.'

'Have you been to a doctor?' I ask. 'A good counsellor might help.'

He nods. 'I met a psychiatrist,' he says, 'but he didn't seem to have anything to offer.' He grins again, a tired grin. 'He told me much the same things you told me; I've to find my own way back to life, all he can do is nudge me along from time to time.'

'What do you do in your spare time?' I ask.

'I have a bike,' he says. 'I spend a lot of time on it, especially on weekends.'

It turns out that he's spent a large part of what little he's inherited on a small sports bike that he takes out every weekend. His face lights up when he speaks of biking, and at last I have an opening. 'Take me out for a ride this Sunday,' I tell him.

'Why?' he asks. 'Are you also into bikes?'

I shake my head. 'Past tense,' I say. 'Too old now, and too slow.'

'Sure,' he smiles. 'I'll pick you up at half past six.'

Sunday is far enough for me to check him out, and Mahesh does his part well. Again, the facts in his resumé are borne out, but his character remains hidden. The most important question remains unanswered – what makes this man tick? A long, probing conversation with Mahipal elicits little that might help.

On Sunday, I get a little closer. On the little passenger seat of his Suzuki GSR 450 – the seat is removable, a thin pad bolted on to a metal plate at the back – and clad in a helmet, leather jacket, and stout shoes for protection, I feel the wind in my face after many years. A little outside Bengaluru, on the near-empty road to Mysore, Sushil opens the throttle wide, and soon we're flying along the countryside at speeds that terrify me, but leave him completely unmoved.

Afterwards, I invite him for lunch where I offer him a beer. He refuses. 'Don't you drink at all?' I ask, though I know he does have the occasional beer.

He grins, his teeth flashing, his face lighting up for the first time since I met him. 'No booze can give you a high that even gets close to doing a 200-an-hour down these roads. I only wish it could be 300!'

Now I know. This man needs risk to get him going. Today he doesn't have the patience to invest a few months in learning, the way Mahipal did, so we need to get to what he can do right now. But then, there are some things he can do right away, in Kashmir. 'Would you like to try something that could make your 300 seem safe?'

He sits up straight. 'What do you mean?'

It's fundamentally this – various separatist Kashmiri groups acquired arms and people capable of using them. They have been joined by various men of violence from Pakistan's FATA and from Afghanistan. I think they're going to try to rebuild Kashmir as a tourist destination and use the tourism to conceal some high-volume drug traffic. If they can get half the tourists that used to visit Kashmir in the safer periods, they'll be able to have as many mules as they like carrying their product all over the world.

What they already have is a pipeline into India for arms. They've bribed people at key points on the border, and have other routes including at least one from Karachi to points along India's western coastline, and another from Bangladeshi ports to spots on India's eastern coast. They've kept drugs off this pipeline because these arms are meant for people whose ideas of revenge are drastic, to say the least. Their arms clients also provide their poppy fields protection back in Afghanistan.

I need someone to follow up on the pipelines, to know who's getting what, where, and when. Mahipal has already got into one of the groups there that arrange delivery in South India, but that group has no idea where it all comes from. A Kashmiri infiltrating a Pakistani supply group would be invaluable. I don't know if Sushil will do it; but I know that if anyone can, it's him.

I can't tell him all this in so many words. I'll have to break it to him gently. Over ice cream, I start. 'There's a friend of mine who might want you to do something for him in Kashmir. Would you be willing to go back?'

'I don't mind,' he says. 'What have I got to lose?' He continues after a brief pause, 'It depends on what your friend gives me.'

'What if you went back as someone else? As, say, Majid Khan of Hubba Kadal and not Sushil Tikkoo?'

He's wary. 'Now, why would your friend want me to do that?'

'That's up to him, really. Thing is, are you game for it? And if you are, what do you want for it?'

'What about the ID card, passport, etc.? You can't just walk into Kashmir, you know. You have to have all these papers and shit.'

'Yes. He'll get you all that.'

His eyes widen. 'You can get me a passport?'

If you know how, it's easy. The Kashmiri authorities are perhaps even more venal than the ones here, especially with Kashmir in the mess it is now. 'Not me. My friend can.'

'What is he? A secret agent or something?'

He's a blackmailer of sorts, but I don't say that. 'He's got friends, let's say.'

'What would he want me to do?'

'He'll have to tell you that himself. I can only fix up a meeting with him.'

'How long will I have to be away?'

'A fairly long time – months, a year, maybe more. Not immediately, of course, but by and by.'

'What do I do about my bike, man? I can't just dump it.'

'I'll look after it for you. If you want, I'll buy it from you and sign an agreement to sell it back to you when you get back. In any case, I'll take good care of it.'

He lowers his eyes for a while. 'Give me a few days to think about it.'

Next Sunday, he agrees, on the condition that I return his bike to him in the condition it is now.

October 2025

Sushil did what was expected of him and more. Given the papers, he learnt to submerge himself into his surroundings and spent months in Srinagar without trouble, before travelling to Lahore and surviving there as well, pretending to be a Kashmiri handicrafts trader or a worker for a fictitious Karachi-based NGO. The first time he came back, I returned his bike to him. He took it for a spin next morning, and later told me that the high was gone. 'What about 300?' I asked. 'Would you like a bigger one?'

He shook his head. 'No, man, all that stuff, it's for kids.' He smiled at me and winked, knowing very well what was on my mind. Two days later, he sold the bike and got himself an ordinary commuter bike. He grew a neat beard; and to some considerable extent, gained depth and dignity. He never speaks of bikes now, though he does occasionally look at pictures of fancy ones in magazines, and sometimes watches a Sunday race on TV.

When I spoke to him first, I thought his primary weakness would be his impatience, but he surprised me. Gathering any meaningful intelligence requires patience and steadiness of mind. He had both in good measure, and they kept him alive and well.

Now I have a little something for him to do, something that he will understand. I want him to get Mahipal's body back from Hyderabad. It's the least I can do, after getting the boy killed.

Nine

Thomas

October 2025

The vigilante. I put him on the back burner for a while, but he pushes his way forward again.

I'm at Mridula's flat; tonight is one of those rare nights of quiet, of peace at her house. It's well after midnight and I lie sleepless, listening to faint traffic noises and crickets in the trees outside. I've had to retreat here to decide what course I should take – here, surrounded by the people who matter, I might think more clearly than in the office or at home.

What do we have on him? We know he shoots well – 800 metres isn't beyond his capabilities. If we assume it's not some disgruntled Lashkar sniper picking off former colleagues, it has to be someone from the elite units of the Army, or the Navy or the Air Force, or a policeman from the National Security Guards or some such outfit. The few civilians who can shoot as accurately are very well off, and end up participating in shooting competitions: None of them are likely to indulge in this kind of mayhem.

It's someone with money and resources. Therefore, it's more likely to be an officer. He's no longer in service: He wouldn't have the freedom to move around if he were. It's unlikely to be a woman as they still don't allow women into the Army's Para Commando units, or the Air Force or Navy equivalents, or, for that matter, the police. So, it could be a former officer from the Special Forces, well off, with the flexibility to move, and sources of information that we don't have.

Someone like that should be easy to find, with the kind of databases available with the government these days. They're all secure databases, with nothing that might encourage a teenage hacker to break through the walls, and I can't access them without a series of approvals, which in turn require much paperwork.

Besides, if I make this official, the vigilante is done for. They'll go after him with everything they have, because a loose cannon is the last thing the system wants. I want to keep them off him for two reasons – one, a sneaking respect for what the man is doing, and, two, a feeling I'll be able to use him to neutralise some of the damage Tony and his government can do to us.

Now I understand what was niggling at me – this uncertainty about what to do with the vigilante. Now that I know that I have to try to get him to work with me, I'm relieved. Sleep comes, finally.

I'm awake at five, as usual, and get ready without disturbing anyone. I'm all ready to move in twenty minutes, but Mridula wakes up as I'm putting on my shoes. 'Why are you going so early?' she asks.

One of the difficulties with leading a double life is that there isn't enough time. 'Something to do with work,' I tell her.

'You were preoccupied yesterday,' she says, standing. 'You look better now. As if you've fixed something.'

She's perceptive; that's one of the things I like about her, but the problem is that she takes it for granted. I nod. 'Yes.'

Instinctively, I hold her hand and pull her down to sit beside me. 'There's something big coming up.'

'At work?' she asks, unwilling to ask for specifics.

'Yes. I've made some mistakes, and perhaps found a way of fixing them.'

Even without lights, I can sense her mood darken. 'Will you be in trouble?'

'It's possible. You'll be safe though.'

'I'm not afraid,' she says. 'It's just that… I worry about you.'

On impulse, I speak from the heart. 'Don't. I just wanted to tell you that being with you has made life worthwhile. I forgot about honour for a while and now I have a chance to get it back, so perhaps I will. That's all.'

She looks down. I know her eyes are wet. It's difficult for me to leave, but the longer I stay, the more difficult it'll get; so I squeeze her hand and move on to the hotel outside where I've left my car.

Back at the office, I get back to the vigilante. I plough through my meetings like an automaton and find that it's afternoon before I can even start chasing this man.

Any further search would be impossible without computer systems. I log in as a colleague, and get lists of officers with Special Forces training who have left their respective services during the last ten years, and are now under the age of fifty. While there are a few such ex-policemen, the number of Army officers who have left is staggering – it runs into a hundred or more. Of course, there was that wave of early retirements following the second partition. Many career soldiers, veterans of the worst skirmishes of the last three decades, quit. They are irreplaceable, though the government won't admit it.

I can't cut down the list of a few hundred officers on this database without setting off some warning bells. Some of the information I want is in the computers under the control of the Army HQ, and I do not have the permission to check their records directly. But I have figured out how to use the account of another colleague who investigated the role of former Army officers in the training of a group of Hindu militants, who wanted to cross over into Pakistan and raise hell there.The investigation continues, and, while it lasts, as it will for the next few years, I will have access to some of the data in the Army HQ computers.

I have to get four different streams of data together. First, the regular service records of these officers. Second, something more about their personal lives or as much of it as the Army keeps on record – their marriage, children, and so on. Third, their financial records or as much of them as I can get from the records. This would typically include records of payments made to these officers, and lists of their assets, bank statements, and income tax documents acquired from the declarations of income and assets at the beginning of their careers. Fourth, and the trickiest, details of what they've done during their stints with their respective units.

This is going to take weeks. But I don't think I have so many weeks in hand. But I do have that list of several hundred officers, and I must think of some ways to eliminate men from it, at least provisionally. What they call a quick and dirty job.

An officer, with Special Forces training, under fifty, well-off or rich, with a cover so he can travel all over. Is that all?

Isn't he likely to be a bachelor, or, at least, someone with no dependants?

This last query throws up only one name. And he is a bachelor. I look up his service record, and find, buried under a lot of officialese that the man would have been cashiered if he hadn't quit. How could that be?

I search again, looking for people who've lost family, and

discover that there's a little ambiguity in the way the records are kept. A widower with no children wouldn't show up in response to my query because the system looks only at whether he's married or not. Ambiguity.

So I look for widowers or divorcees, with no children or deceased children. The list is now down to a few dozen. I download the records of these men to read at home.

At home, barricaded behind my study door, with Nancy watching one of her favourite game shows, I sit down to read about the professional lives of some of the best of the country's former soldiers.

Another little worm at the back of my mind suddenly comes forth. I remember a conversation with a retired brigadier, an infantryman and former commando. 'They encourage us to bring the bodies back,' he had said. 'Buddies! You don't leave your buddy behind. It's not something that is said, it's implicit in all the training.'

If my vigilante is a former Special Forces soldier, will he try to get back the body of the young man we know as Asif? This is something I follow up on my own. Hospital records show that the body has been lying unclaimed. The autopsy has been completed, and the body will lie for another week in the morgue before it is buried – as far as we know, the deceased is a Muslim – at public expense, in a pauper's grave.

Since the dead man has false papers, I must assume that whoever he was working for can manufacture more false papers. I must also assume that his hometown was Bengaluru.... I'm making too many assumptions, I know, but I'm not really assuming anything, just following a series of hunches, which a policeman has to do, and trying to explain them afterwards.

I have a lecture coming up at the Police Academy in Hyderabad. I'll visit the morgue the day after tomorrow. The vigilante knows that any effort to get the body out through regular channels will only draw attention to him, so he'll either break in or…

Or what? I can't help smiling. Few systems work the way they should. I'll check what other bodies have been taken out of the morgue in the last few days. The people at the morgue can be persuaded – with cash, of course – to mix bodies up. There is a small chance of another unclaimed body similar to Asif's being in the morgue, in which case a substitution would be simple. The morgue is a part of the government hospital; people go in and out all the time, and security is lax, as it is almost everywhere VIPs don't go.

It's not so easy to transport a corpse from Hyderabad to Bengaluru. The chances are that it would have been flown over, since our vigilante seems to have money. So I'm going to check with all the airlines about corpses flown on that route over the few days after Asif's body was deposited in the morgue. These days, crematoria and graveyards require the production of death certificates before accepting bodies for disposal. That might give me a lead.

My friend the professor will come along – it'll cost me a bottle of scotch or an equivalent – to make sure that the body in Asif's box is indeed Asif's.

Assuming that he's based in Bengaluru will also cut down the list. Am I sacrificing too much for speed? Perhaps not. The man is probably based in one of the larger cities, which should make him easier to find, and I'm just picking one out of perhaps a dozen possibilities.

I sleep.

Ten

Noordin

November 2025

I shall soon be past Jammu without trouble. Over the years, I have learnt to make myself inconspicuous, which is more difficult than it seems, for any effort at making oneself inconspicuous usually has the opposite effect.

I chose a train that starts in Jammu, and got to the platform early, getting into the first coach behind the engine. There are two such coaches at each end of the train, with benches and backrests of planks and a luggage rack above each, large enough for a man to sleep on. I have only a small bag that can serve as a pillow. I climb on to a luggage rack, tuck the bag under my head, and prepare to sleep well for the first time in a week.

This train is bound through Delhi for Patna, where I am headed for the time being. Patna is the capital of what must be India's most lawless state, where anything can be purchased cheaply. In earlier years, whenever I was on the run, this was where I headed. Getting out of here is easy; this state has a border with Nepal, the former Hindu kingdom, and crossing it at Raxaul is easy. Getting back into India from Nepal is also easy, at the border crossing near New Jalpaiguri, not far from the Air Force station at Bagdogra.

As I say, it is easier to disappear in Bihar than perhaps anywhere else in India. This is where officials are most corrupt and policemen easiest to blackmail. This is where you have small factories producing illicit, unlicensed firearms – crude shotguns and pistols that are unreliable at any range beyond a few feet, and rifles that might blow up in your hands any time you shoot – for gangsters. This is where contractors will sell you any amount of gelignite. This is where the government loots the poorest of the poor – every few years, when rivers swell and their banks burst from rains heavier than normal, people starve because the money for such emergencies has been stolen.

Fifteen minutes before the train is due to leave, every seat is taken, and there are more people climbing in all the time. Most carry bottles of water, as I do, because drinking water is just not available. Of course, there are taps at every station, but there are crowds at every tap, and the water is such that it will definitely make you ill. Bottled water, too, is available, but one bottle in three is counterfeit, filled with tap water and chilled to just above freezing point so that no one drinking it will be able to taste it properly. I cannot afford to fall ill now, so I take precautions, carrying water that I have seen boiled or filtered properly.

The train starts on time, without warning, beginning to move gently forwards. From now on, there will only be routine checks for tickets, and the odd pair of armed policemen hurrying by, looking for obvious explosives or known criminals whose faces are on the 'Wanted' posters at every railway station. Within minutes, knowing that perhaps the most dangerous part of the journey is done, I fall asleep.

I wake to the noise of people clapping and singing. Below are a group of Hindus returning to their homes in Odisha after six months, building a temple in Jammu. One of them belts out a devotional song in Hindi, which is close enough to Urdu for me to understand – it is a hymn to Lord Ganesha, after whom my adversary is named. Others sway to the beat of the song, some with eyes closed in devotion. At least fifteen people are crammed into two benches meant for ten. More people stand between the two benches, and a vendor selling tea and snacks forces his way through. The two ceiling mounted fans are on, and the windows are open, but it's stifling.

Even in the hubbub, I manage to doze off. Prayer in the manner prescribed is impossible on a journey such as this, and I keep my prayer mat inside the bag, reciting the prayers in my mind at approximately the right times. I pray and drift in and out of sleep, and, in the warmth and security of the crowd, relax.

Some sort of order has forced itself on the crowd below. Families have begun to share water and stories, and, eventually, food. A ticket examiner forces his way through, looking at everyone's tickets and writing something indecipherable on them. He doesn't even look at the faces of the people offering him these tickets to check. A man travelling with his wife and two children asks if there's room ahead, in the sleeper coaches. The examiner responds rudely, asking why he didn't reserve his seats earlier. Unforeseen circumstances, the man explains, a birth two weeks ahead of time. 'Well,' says the examiner, 'then you have to take what's available or fly your private plane wherever you want to go.'

The petty official goes to the next compartment, and the people in this one relax, and return to whatever they were doing before the interruption. All this, I think, is entirely familiar. It's the same in Pakistan, where I've travelled much more extensively than in India.

A man sitting below looks up, catches my eye, and smiles. When I smile back, he asks if I'm alright. 'You've been lying there quietly all this time,' he explains. 'I was wondering whether you were unwell.'

'I'm alright,' I tell him. 'I'm tired, that's all; many nights without sleep.'

'Would you like some water? Something to eat, maybe?' he asks, holding up a bottle and a little packet of food.

'Nothing, thank you. Just rest.' I try to sit up. There's just enough head room for me to sit cross-legged if I stoop a little.

'Do you mind if I join you up there?' the man asks. 'It's very crowded down here.'

'Come on up,' I tell him, and he scrambles up, much to the relief of the man who was at the receiving end of the ticket examiner's sarcasm.

At close range, he's younger than I thought, in his mid-twenties maybe, with the big strong hands of a workman. It turns out he's a carpenter by profession, and works making temple doors and such. Again he offers me food and water, and this time I take a sip from his bottle. Soon the ticket examiner forces his way back through the crowd, back to wherever such men go.

'What an arsehole,' the carpenter says, shaking his head. 'Did you hear what he told our brother below, with the wife and two children?'

'Yes,' I say. 'He could have been more polite.'

'These bastards don't care,' he shakes his head in disgust. 'These guys can't be fired. They take bribes when they can, behave like little lords, and there's nothing we can do about it...' He stops talking to think for a moment. 'Actually, these railwaymen aren't so bad. At least this man has to take the trouble to walk all over the train for eight hours before he can go home. There are these other little fellows in government. Clerks. Babus.'

The frustration in his voice is clear. 'What have they done to you?' I ask.

'I travel a lot,' he explains. 'I leave home for six months at a time, and each time I've to find a place to stay. Each time I have to struggle to get a gas connection or a cell phone connection. In Jammu, I can't use the cell phone card I use at home because it becomes too expensive, so I have to get a local connection. To do that, I have to give these guys some proof of my address. They insist on a driver's licence or a ration card or a voter's card or at least a lease agreement. My licence, ration card, and voter's card are all based on my home address back in Cuttack, and we poor people don't have lease agreements – it's all based on word of mouth. So where do we get the papers from? I don't, so the clerks take a thousand rupees to give me a paper that'll get us a phone connection or a gas connection or anything else. They take your money, they spit in your face, they make you run around, and you have to take it because the alternative is that you go without what you want, which you can't afford. So these little bastards rule us. If I had a gun, I'd shoot them.'

He seems to be an angry child. A rare imp of mischief takes over me. 'Don't be so angry,' I tell him. 'Cool off, otherwise you might do something you might regret later on. We sometimes overreact when we're upset.' I pat him on the shoulder and smile. 'I know just how you feel.'

He gives me a sidelong glance. 'I thought you didn't fit here. You look the type who travels with a reservation. What are you doing here? Didn't you get a reservation?'

'I'm a mechanic,' I explain, 'and I'm also poor, maybe a little better off than you, but I've worked twenty years longer than you for that. I always travel like this, though I can afford more now. Habit! I feel at home.'

'You must have seen all this,' he tells me. 'Don't you feel the same?'

'Yes,' I tell him. 'I've felt it for a long time.' I smile at him. 'When I was your age, I might have been as angry as you are now.'

He suddenly laughs. 'I'm getting married next year,' he says. 'I've been engaged to this girl for a long time, nearly two years. I've wanted to have a small house of my own before we got married, and it's taken a long time. I started working when I was sixteen. Now I have a house of my own. See, I need a phone connection to talk to my fiancée. This time the bastards kept me waiting three weeks before giving me one.'

'So you spent three weeks without speaking to your fiancée?'

He blushes and laughs. 'Yes,' he says. 'I lost my cool thinking of that.'

The train, which has been slowing down through this conversation, stops at a station and vendors board the train before it stops, blocking the way for passengers trying to get off. The chaos inside the coach increases and we watch from above as passengers with baggage and vendors with their trays and cans of goods swirl below. In the couple of minutes that the train stops, the swirl builds up and ends miraculously, with passengers who want to get off doing so, and vendors managing to sell tea and snacks and collecting money and returning change. A few minutes after the train moves off, we are a little more comfortable, since more people have got off than on.

The wind is stronger now, and colder. The carpenter shivers, and reaches out to fetch a shawl from a bag hanging from a hook between the windows. He covers himself and settles down again. 'I was thinking of what you told me about anger,' he says. 'You're right, and I know it. My work is mostly in temples. It's something I like to do. It's my form of worship, and it's a privilege because it brings me close to God. Working like that, I shouldn't worry about these little things.'

'Yes,' I tell him. 'You should keep doing what you should be doing.' Suddenly I'm tired, bone-weary.

He gives me a strange look. 'Yes. Are you religious?' When I nod, he continues. 'Are you Hindu?'

I shake my head. 'I'm Muslim.'

'Ah, well,' he says, 'it makes no difference. If your heart is in your work and you remember your God once in a while, that's enough to make a man rich.' He smiles at me. 'I'm rich.'

When I smile back, he looks at me strangely again. 'You're tired,' he says. 'There's space below. I'll go back down. You rest.' Without waiting for a reply, he slithers down. He looks up at me. 'Sleep, Uncle.' He uses the Hindi word 'chacha', meaning father's younger brother. 'You speak wisely. Tell me if you need anything.'

I lie down again. These attacks of weariness have been coming off and on for the past few months. I have medicines to help, but don't use them because they cause other troubles. The doctors tell me there's nothing more they can do unless I leave myself completely to them, and that is not possible yet without endangering the project.

August 2025

The stomach aches come often and eating is difficult. I throw up more often than I used to, and occasionally there are spots of blood in what comes up. I have tried many of the herbal treatments available around Shahpur, but none of them has made a difference. A few days ago, I gave up and went to the doctors at Sher-e-Kashmir Institute of Medical Sciences, SKIMS, in Shoura, Srinagar.

This is a government-run institution; out-patient treatment

should be free, and in-patients charged very little, but you have to pay little bribes to all kinds of people if you want to get meaningful treatment. I have been through a series of tests and scans that cost so much that I had to augment my resources from the emergency funds I had kept aside as backup in case Masood's arrangements fail. Now I wait to see the physician who prescribed all these tests.

The doctors themselves are supposed to be fairly competent. They are among the best in all of Kashmir, which, unfortunately, isn't much since the Hindus among them fled years ago, and no one comes from outside to replace them. There are no women among the staff – women, by government edict, stay at home.

But the doctors do not ask for bribes; the ones who do are the staff – the clerks, the nurses, and the technicians who run the labs. I have decided now that I will not pay any more bribes.

The doctor calls me in after a two-hour wait. He tells me to sit down, and with a professionally inscrutable face tells me that I have tumours in the stomach and the liver. From the test results so far, he says they are likely to be malignant. This can be confirmed only after a biopsy, which he can schedule for any day this week. 'Alright,' I tell him. 'When?'

'Tomorrow,' he says. 'We'll make a tiny incision in your abdomen and get some tissues out.'

'How long will it take?'

'A few minutes. We can do it with local anaesthesia. You'll be able to go back home in the evening.'

'And the results?'

'Two days after the test.'

'Can we do it today?'

'No,' he says. 'The specialist has to be booked earlier. Tomorrow is the earliest we can do it.'

Next morning, I report to him at eight, and am back home

by six. This is not home. It is the house of relatives of someone in Shahpur, sympathisers with the cause, whom I have known for many years. They do not know why I am here, and I prefer to keep my purpose to myself. I have to keep myself alive for the project – what happens afterwards is immaterial. I am tense… I wonder why? I do not particularly want to stay alive, but some instinct within me does not give up.

Two days later, I see the doctor again. He tells me what the scan says, what I already know deep in my mind. I have a cancer. One that started in the liver and spread to the stomach, and to the gullet, which accounts for the difficulty in eating, and in keeping food down. He has referred me to an oncologist a few doors away, for treatment.

The oncologist does not keep me waiting. He recommends that I start a course of drugs immediately – a course of six injections spread out over about four months, with scans after every second injection. 'I have heard that these injections are not very successful in cases like mine,' I tell the doctor. 'What do you think?'

'We don't lose hope,' he says. 'We have to keep fighting.'

'What happens if I do nothing at all?' I ask.

'The disease will spread. It will weaken you, cause much pain, and eventually kill you.'

'Over how long?'

'It's a matter of months, or a year.'

'How long will I be able to function normally?' I ask.

'That varies from person to person,' he says. 'It depends on your tolerance to pain, to fatigue, to illness. Since most of your body's resources are used up in fighting this illness, you are likely to be more prone to picking up infections that you would not otherwise, and you will feel tired very easily. This will get worse.'

'I have some important projects on now,' I tell him. 'I can start the treatment only after that, in January, perhaps.'

'It's already late,' he says. 'Any further delay and it will spread to other organs, and become more difficult to treat. Even a week's delay in the treatment will decrease the chances of the success of the treatment.'

'Can I take some treatment for the pain and the fatigue?' I ask.

'Certainly. But the effects will be purely temporary, and will decrease as the disease progresses.'

'Can you tell me how many patients you know have recovered from this stage of cancer with the treatment you prescribe?'

He looks me in the eye. 'Look, if you want to argue against treatment, I have nothing to say. I speak in your interest.'

'I understand what you say,' I tell him, 'but I cannot detain myself for treatment this year. I can come back here only early next year and put myself in your hands, but not before.'

He shrugs. 'It's up to you; you have to decide what you need to do and what you don't. All I can say is that if you don't come in immediately, your chances of beating the disease decrease every week.'

'Fine,' I tell him. 'What I have committed to is very important. I cannot give it up. But I will come back to you on New Year's day, if I can.'

He smiles wryly. 'Alright. I'll wait for you.'

November 2025

During these spells, I find it difficult to concentrate. Lying on the bench in the warm coach amidst the noise of the other passengers passing their time socially, my mind drifts off once again to Naeem Shaqeer and his immaturity. We met again in the aftermath of the 11 September 2001 bombings, on the border with Pakistan. It was a time of turmoil in the area, for President Musharraf was under pressure to prove himself to the Americans, while he had to keep the loyalties of Pakistanis in the FATA to stay in power. I had found my way into Kashmir and decided that I would live there. I had even found Shahpur, and built myself a wooden house there, not far from the stream that carried snowmelt down to the Chenab through the year. That done, I went back to Islamabad to tell my handlers from ISI that I would be based henceforth in a part of Kashmir then occupied by India. Then I met Raza to find out how I could get in touch if I needed to.

March 2004

I meet Raza soon after seeing the ISI men, and he approves of what I was doing. 'They'll find it easier to get at you there,' he says. 'Stay there, and make sure you have a clear line of communication, and we'll be fine.'

'I don't know much about communications,' I tell him.

He smiles. 'I do, but what I'm going to do isn't technical. I'm going to have telephone code messengers.'

'I don't understand.'

'It's like this – there are too many messages flying around for anyone to monitor manually, so practically every country, the developed countries especially, use computers to monitor messages, and program them to set out an alarm whenever they come across a key phrase, such as 'nuclear device'. Any such message is then further analysed by a computer, and if it has more phrases that sound dangerous, it gets to a human analyst, who then decides what needs to be done about it.

'This could include trying to figure out where the message came from and where it's going. As far as I know, only the IP address of the sending computer is traceable; if that's available, they should be able to trace the computer in a matter of hours.

'When I want to pass on a message to you, I call someone

in Geneva using a code. He converts that one more step and passes it on to someone in Helsinki. That person converts it into something else and passes it on to Paris, from where someone calls you with the message that you decode.

'The trouble with passing messages through chains like this is that it's cumbersome and expensive, besides it also takes a lot of time. But we've got ways around some of those things now. We can send messages over the Internet, so expense is no longer a problem. We've got to pay local people, usually shady characters involved in illegal betting or pornography or something like that, to pass messages on for money. We've also got volunteers, thanks be to Allah, because that helps keep expenses down. We can also automate some of these steps – have a computer program do the conversion and forwarding of an Internet message – so that helps us further.

'Whenever it's a telephone message, we make sure a public telephone is used. When it's an Internet message, we use an anonymiser to remove the IP address, just as an extra security measure.

'When we're done with all this, we'll be able to send you messages through five or six intervening layers, all isolated from one another. There's very little chance of such a message being intercepted.

'The trouble is that the system takes a lot of time. We'll automate some of it so you can get your messages quickly, but that won't have any human layers in between, and you'll be dependent on the Internet. We'll use direct radio or telephone messages only in an absolute emergency, and even those will be coded.

'We can't use such complex systems for routine messages, but, for projects like yours, we will. We must make sure no one, not even someone from our side, gets a whiff of what's going on.'

November 2025

Raza's efforts seem to have paid off; so far there has been no interference. Raza was right about keeping our project a secret from our side. I understood how twisted intelligence matters could get when, after meeting the brigadier and Raza, I took a trip to Peshawar to meet some old friends from Afghanistan who had settled nearby. One of them dealt in stolen arms.

April 2004

Naeem Shaqeer leads a small group of men loosely allied with the Taliban. They drift across the border from time to time, depending on which side is being raided by whom. They have to suffer assaults from heavily armed American soldiers led by aircraft, and, sometimes, artillery, on the Afghan side. They wait out these assaults in their caves. The Americans travel in convoys, much as the Soviets did, but are far better equipped and supplied, and have, therefore, lasted longer. American soldiers spend much less time in Afghanistan than the Soviets did; they average less than a year here before being sent back home while the Soviets averaged three years. They eat better. In the last few years of the Soviet occupation, their soldiers were so ill-equipped that they ate meat once a week, if that often: So the Afghans rarely faced the combined air and artillery barrages that the Americans pour down on them from time to time.

Across the border, raids by the Pakistan Army are far weaker, and relatively easy to evade because the Taliban have many informers, some in the headquarters in Islamabad. A few of the informers are in it from fear – in the Soviet years, many ISI officers helped themselves to the American money intended for the mujahideen. The mujahideen know of a few such people, and have threatened to inform the headquarters about the embezzlement, so now a few colonels and the likes in the ISI have per force become informers.

Shaqeer, the toady, caught several ISI men helping themselves, and encouraged them; he did it out of fear then, but is now reaping the rewards for it, in the form of informers at ISI headquarters. He survives by selling the information to other mujahideen bands.

We meet in Peshawar, where he has come to sell some weapons he acquired recently. He does not reveal where he got them from, and no one asks. He asks for payment in American dollars, and gets it, because the weapons are well maintained, even if they are old. We have both gained experience in the years since we last met, but I do not think either's character has changed one bit. His strut turns into a crawl when I cross the street to meet him, but he manages a smile. 'Noordin!' he exclaims. 'What brings you here?'

'Old friends,' I tell him. 'And you?'

'Weapons.' He cannot help crowing. 'I captured a lot of American weapons and have come to sell them.'

'What weapons? How did you happen to capture them?' I ask.

He evades, which means he must have stolen them from where someone else cached them after taking them from the Americans, or they are from an old American stash. Details of the weapons themselves will reveal something of their origin, as he must have realised by now. 'An odd mixture,' he says. 'How does it matter, now that someone else has them? Come, let us celebrate!'

He drags me to a restaurant where he insists on buying me too large a lunch, none of which is wasted because we eat in a group. There is nothing to celebrate, for neither of us is particularly pleased to see the other, but he insists and I agree. As we sit, we are joined by others from his group. They have all heard of me, and from the way he speaks, his purpose is clear – he wants to establish his familiarity with me to his men.

Towards the end of the meal, we are joined by a quiet, dark man in traditional Baluchi dress, with the embroidered skull cap characteristic of the region. He wears aviator sunglasses, which many of these men do now, but something about him does not fit. He is wary of me, too, when Shaqeer introduces me to him, and soon I understand why – he does not smell right for a man who has spent the morning tramping around the market in the hot sun. He has used an expensive American deodorant, which people don't usually do in these parts, which means he must be faking, which in turn means that he can only be an ISI agent operating undercover.

Shaqeer does not seem to know that this man is an ISI agent. I finish my meal before the others do, and excuse myself despite Shaqeer's pleas to stay on. I wander off and wait for the ISI man, who now calls himself Majid, to appear. Unless I'm mistaken, he will be in a hurry to get away, to report that I have turned up in Shaqeer's company. I have nothing to hide and don't need to interfere with his report, except that ISI officials are so suspicious that any such association automatically means that they will watch me for some time. That is likely to be awkward at this time.

I catch up with Majid three streets away from the restaurant. 'Change your deodorant,' I tell him.

He gives me a sickly grin. 'Don't you like it?' he asks.

'It gives you away,' I tell him. 'Also, if anyone from the Pakistani government hinders me with stupid questions in the near future, I will know you reported on this meeting.'

He mumbles something. I ignore it. 'It will not be difficult to find you afterwards.'

I turn and walk away, exposing my back to him in a gesture of utter contempt that I do not feel. This is only some half-trained peasant lad doing what he has been told to. If he is not sufficiently equipped to do it well, that is the responsibility of the men who sent him here. Either they picked the wrong man for the job, or they didn't train him enough.

I do not understand why they waste their time on people as useless as Shaqeer; the only explanation is that it's someone in ISI whom Shaqeer is blackmailing, who has sent Majid here in the hope that he will turn up something incriminating against Shaqeer.

All the ISI men I have met complain that they have insufficient resources to do what they are told to do. If they did their work with any commitment, they wouldn't have to waste their resources on jobs like Shaqeer. ISI men, indeed all Pakistani soldiers, are much better paid than their Indian counterparts. You rarely see an Indian soldier, no matter how highly-placed, in an expensive restaurant or bar in Delhi. Islamabad's expensive hotels and restaurants are full of middle-level and senior Army men. The Indian soldier has no real authority with a civilian outside his jurisdiction, but in Pakistan, the soldier can get away with anything.

Despite these advantages that the Pakistani soldier has, I cannot help feeling that he is fundamentally more corrupt. Perhaps it is because he is exposed to corruption – as the Indian bureaucrat is – but I don't really know.

Why are there such corrupt people in the land of the pure?

November 2025

I emerge from my reverie wondering again why have I taken sides with the Pakistanis in Kashmir, my adopted land? The fatigue has taken hold of me as has a fever. My mind wanders, and I cannot help it. Is it the illness, I wonder, or the medicine or is this what is really in my mind? Or is the medicine bringing out what's in the depths of my mind?

What did the Kashmiris get from their secession? In old days, they had Indian soldiers all over and feared for their lives. The laws were secular, which is another word for ungodly, and women had their place. Now they live under the Shariat, and their life has become orderly once again. The pagan temples are gone, and so have the tombs of the Sufi heretics where even the idol worshippers came.

But this good Islamic government is only in the cities, most of which have new names, rather than the old. Back in Shahpur, things have not changed much. Perhaps not much change is required.

The questions persist. If life has not changed, have the Kashmiris gained anything? On the one side there is the Shariat, which is good. On the other side though, there is poverty, and many public punishments – whipping and stoning and the cutting of hands. There are people who grow opium and harvest it and keep some for themselves or sell to locals instead of handing it over to the Taliban. As a result, there are more drug addicts than before. More Kashmiris go unwashed and unfed these days. I don't know.

Has Afghanistan changed? Perhaps yes, I think. But then again, perhaps not. Afghans go unfed, ill, dirty, and cold. That hasn't changed.

I must think it out for myself. There must be a way.

November 2011

We are winning against the Indians. They will soon declare a second partition, and all of Kashmir will be azaad. But for those like us, who live by the gun, death by violence is always in the back of the mind. It is, for us, the normal state to be in.

I am in Peshawar, in a private house, in a room that has been converted into a hospital room. The patient is Shahryar, named after one of Afghanistan's old warlords. This Shahryar, too, once promised to be something of a warlord.

I still remember our first meeting, a few days after the incident with the helicopter. He had Abdul Hameed and me picked up from the village and taken to his own camp, near Khorram shehr. He was an inspiration then, a laughing bandit whom everyone feared. Since then, he became powerful and well-known but didn't seem to reach the heights I thought he would.

Now I find his room difficult to enter. He has gangrene from a gunshot wound he took while evading the Americans. Someone is changing the dressings and the smell is enough to keep most people at bay. I walk into the room and find him lying stoically silent while fresh dressings go on. When the dressing is done, he takes a handful of tablets with a sip of water, wipes his mouth with the back of his hand, and tells his two young attendants to leave us alone.

Despite the pain and the fatigue, he finds a smile for me. 'Noordin,' he says, 'I thought you'd forgotten old friends.'

I hold his hand in mine. 'You were always a leader. Too far ahead to be my friend.'

He shakes his head. 'People change. You've grown. I wouldn't presume to guide you now.'

I smile at his modesty, knowing that it is genuine. 'Whenever I found myself at a loss, I used to ask myself how you would handle whatever was going on. Most of the time, I got some answers.'

The same shake of the head. 'That's you, not me… Noordin, my time is over. Don't argue. You and I both know it.'

'Yes,' I tell him.

'Then listen to me carefully.'

'Okay.'

'Don't take anything for granted. Don't take Islam for granted.

You know what Islam means, don't you? You listen to God. Does God speak to you? No. So do you listen to the man who says he knows what God says? Does God speak to him? No, and no. So, make up your mind. You've read the Book, and you've lived thirty years. Think for yourself.'

'Okay.'

'Remember Ahmed Shah Massoud? He wanted to follow the Book for himself, but didn't think it necessary to force it on other lands, other countries. Do you think that was wise?'

'Why do you ask that?'

'You have a hundred different voices saying different things, all claiming that they speak for God. Which is true?'

'I don't know.'

'Good. Then think about this. The God who made us all – do you think He needs our help for anything? Our support?'

'No.'

'Look to yourself, then, and let God take care of the unbelievers.'

'Yes.'

'If someone speaks ill of God, how do you react?'

'I don't know.'

'If God wants, God will take care of them. Okay? Think it out for yourself.'

'Why are you telling me this? Isn't it blasphemy?'

'All I'm telling you to do is think. Think about the nature of God. Think about what these men tell you. Decide for yourself what fits and what doesn't.'

I think again of Shaqeer, quoting from the Book, of his falsehoods and his weaknesses. Shahryar's words strike a chord in me somewhere. I nod. 'I'll try to think it out for myself.'

Shahryar nods. 'Good. Follow your heart.'

'You sound as if you didn't.'

'Yes. There have been times I didn't think clearly enough and ended up doing wrong. It's no use talking about those matters now, but you must think for yourself.'

'There's more to it.'

'Of course there is. Look, you and I, we are Taliban. Students, seekers. Our way is inwards, to understand ourselves, to understand God. Now tell me, what's been happening?'

I see it; it's been in the back of my mind for some time now. 'The innocents. They're getting killed in our war.' These are the stone-throwers. Our allies, the Lashkar, have been telling youngsters to gather stones, and when a protest is called, to throw them at policemen in large numbers. The policemen at first defend, but when the stones don't stop, they go on the offensive, with increasing force – tear gas, rubber bullets, and eventually, real bullets.

It's the youngsters with stones who have won this for us, not our weapons.

We should not have done this. I see it more clearly now. The wounds will not heal. We have created a monster. Now we must create new enemies for the youth to focus their anger on. Even if Kashmir is free, the war will go on.

Is this freedom?

November 2025

Now, a dozen years after Shahryar's passing, I still remember what he told me that day. He faced his death with courage; I hope I will face mine with as much. I haven't flagged so far, and I think I can take some more pain without much difficulty.

On matters of right and wrong, I struggle with my thoughts. Sometimes I know fear, when I question some of the things I learnt in my childhood; when I question the Book. At such times, I am glad to have Abdul Hameed with me. He might not be a great fighter but he has an instinct for good and bad that I have found reassuring. I will speak to him soon about all this… he might have advice for me.

Once this project is over, I can face death with a clear mind. Just this one last thing to do. Afterwards, I will tell Allah that I did the best I could. I always tried to do my best, though I must admit I have made mistakes.

On that note of consolation, I drift off once again into slumber.

Eleven

Ganesh

October 2025

I learnt a bit about intelligence work in the Army, where every large unit has its own intelligence officers, who work mostly with signals intelligence (sigint) and, if they're lucky enough in counter-insurgency operations, with human intelligence (humint). The big stuff, electronic intelligence (elint), and some sigint such as extracts from data got off the satellites and e-mails and so on, is processed by a different agency in Delhi, but I never got anywhere near it. Even so, I did figure out that very little of it is about James-Bond-style operations saving the world, or about stoking the fires of resentment wherever necessary and converting it into violence.

Mahipal and I spent some time on the information he's been bringing back in lumps. Most of it is about getting into the enemy's head, which requires enormous patience and analysis, of putting apparently disparate, small items of intelligence picked out of a sea of information. The trick lies in picking the right bits of information out of that sea, and that, I learnt is a separate talent all by itself, and one that I don't have.

Trouble is, it takes a long time finding out whether you have it or not. You have to work with the data all the time, looking for patterns. There's more than enough data, and plenty of patterns too – the trick lies in picking the right pattern.

There's only one way to learn that trick, and it's a long and difficult one – you work with your data, making predictions, checking them out. Over the years, if you have the right kind of mind, and the right kind of memory, you'll find yourself getting an increasing percentage of those predictions right, and, once in a while, making guesses that seem almost uncanny.

If you have the talent, you can develop it, but, as I said, it takes years. The problem is, the intelligence agencies, like all the other arms of the government, take bright young people out of college based on how they do in a series of examinations and how well they impress a group of bureaucrats. Anyone with an unconventional mind is out of contention for any senior job with intelligence. And no young high-flyer is interested in spending three to five years poring over data only to find that he doesn't have the talent to be great at it. Even if you have the talent, it's almost automatic that you go no higher, something no career intelligence officer would like. So, few people volunteer for an analyst's job. Those that do are people who think a few years as an analyst will round out a resumé sufficiently.

And so, no matter how bright the intelligence men might be, few of them, if any, have a feel for what they work with. Of those few who do have a feel for their data, only a small number can get their predictions right – very few get, or even understand, the internal shift that comes with being right.

And then there is the matter of wanting to please the boss. Given the ambiguity of conclusions in intelligence work, it is one of the most dangerous of inclinations; but in a culture that degrades risk-taking and values conformity, it is inevitable. The Pakistanis suffer from this even more than we do. One night, soon after I got my commission, Granddad told me something he got out of a Pakistani officer captured in the 1965 war.

On 2 September 1965, a young captain deputed in the Pakistani IB got a message from an Indian source that India would attack Lahore and bomb Rawalpindi on 6 September. He passed the message on to his immediate superior, Ehtisham Hussain, who, in turn, passed it on to the director, one A.B. Awan. Next morning, Awan summoned Hussain and the captain. 'Do you know,' he asked the captain, 'the damage you can cause if this report is accepted and it turns out to be fake? Which it certainly is.'

'Sir,' responded the captain, 'suppose we have this information and do not tell anyone, and Lahore is attacked on 6 September, what will you do to me?'

'I will hang you,' retorted Awan. So the message was passed on, with the marginal noting, in bureaucratic style, that it could be treated for what it was worth in the light of other intelligence, and the rest is history.

Finally, the strong chain of command in the intelligence community deters analysts or even operatives from going over their boss's head to, say, the chief of an area desk. Every desk man rewrites every report as he or she sees fit. So, in a system as hierarchy bound as ours, honest opinions are at a premium in most intelligence agencies.

The formation of an umbrella agency to coordinate these different agencies has made a small difference in that it can cut out some of the inter-service competition, but there's nothing it can do about faulty or insufficient basic data, and therein lies the rub.

Knowing all this, I encouraged Mahipal – my first-ever private intelligence operative – to be as independent as possible and to learn from mistakes rather than cover them up. It worked. For the first few months, he came up with choice morsels that turned out to be false alarms, but he soon got into the spirit of the thing, and his later reports were solid, even brilliant in parts.

April 2023

I'm in Hyderabad on business and take the opportunity to spend some time with Mahipal, who has been here ever since he went underground. He has friends all over now. He meets me in a small restaurant near the clock tower by the lake that divides Secunderabad from Hyderabad. I fail to recognise him when he accosts me. He has grown a full beard, changed his spectacles, lost some weight, put on a black skullcap, and acquired a little stoop. When he asks me the time in Urdu, I look at my watch, for he even sounds different. He reverts to his normal voice to ask, 'Why do you think I asked you the time when I have a watch on my wrist?'

I look up in surprise, managing to keep my mouth shut as I do so. He's taken me aback, and I'm pleased to break a big smile. We shake hands, and he sits down to tell me what he's been doing.

He first made contact with a group of fundamentalist Muslims who till now pursue the Bangladeshi writer Hafiz Mohammed, whose famed expose of the Jamaat and its extreme and violent forms of Islam led to his exile to Europe. A demonstration by this group, led by a sitting MLA, during Mohammed's truncated visit to the city, brought Mahipal to the notice of some local arms smugglers. His face – not recognisable as such – was on TV the next day, and he had no trouble establishing his credentials with them in the days that followed.

Hyderabad has been, for many years, a hotbed of ISI-sponsored activities. It's been relatively easy for the Pakistanis to establish themselves here. The groups fed by the ISI don't even know that their masters are in Pakistan. They think they're working for the betterment of the Indian Muslims, and that the violence is aimed at bringing forth to the government the extent of ill-feeling among Andhra's large and heterogeneous Muslim community.

Mahipal believes that some long-term planning has gone into creating this support base. He makes his reasons clear. 'I've worked out the basics that groups such as the Lashkar – for that matter, any rebel groups – need. The first is money, meaning cash, and the means to handle it without getting caught. They make a lot of money by smuggling drugs out of Afghanistan, from ISI slush funds, mostly diverted American money, and from collections from the general public. Most of it is cash. They use their charitable front men to bring cash in and transfer it into safe accounts all over the world from where they can use the money at will. The charity actually uses eighty percent of the money it gets; only a fifth is diverted, not enough to prejudice the effectiveness of the charity.'

'Very good,' I tell him. 'What else?'

'They need a refuge somewhere, a place where they can hole up when people get after them. That they have in Pakistan. And it's a good refuge because the Pakistanis are nuclear, so no one wants the country to disintegrate, and they can't attack it head-on because they don't want to start a nuclear war. Now the refuge stretches into Kashmir as well.'

'It isn't safe.'

'They lose a few people now and then, but rarely the key men – yes, they're all men, no women, unlike the Palestinians – or large numbers of low-ranking men. They have their own cannon fodder for all that; and in any case, they have a huge pool of talent to pick from. One out of every ten petty criminals in the major cities is available because they keep in touch with gangsters for their drug business. Then they have their own indoctrination schools. You know all that.'

'Indeed, but not as pat as you do.'

He grins. 'You haven't spent as much time with these guys as I have. They're scary.'

'I imagine so. And?'

'They need material – small-arms, explosive, the occasional larger weapon, a small rocket launcher or an old Stinger or something. They have a pipeline into the country for that, running parallel to their drug smuggling systems. Actually, this is what got me thinking… there's some long-term planning going on. I discovered that they actually engaged a few senior MPs in it, mostly in Bihar.'

'Why Bihar?'

'They have pals in Nepal. The get the stuff across the border at Raxaul and hand it over to the MPs, who then have it shipped to Patna or wherever in their cars! A hundred kilos at a time, maybe, but over the years it builds up to a lot. The point is that they cultivated the MPs well. They pick the right guys, the guys who win elections over and over, find their weaknesses, and home in on them. Sometimes they select women, sometimes wayward children who need to be rescued, sometimes large amounts of counterfeit Indian currency. It varies. So they've been building up the pipeline for ten years now, and it's solid.'

'Why?'

'Look, you have this crooked MP who thinks he's into a minor smuggling racket in return for favours, right? He tells his pals, spreads the word around, and more of them get trapped, and can't get out. I believe he's got a dozen Bihari MLAs working for him.'

'Is that it?'

He holds up a hand, ticking off his half-a-dozen points. 'Money and financial systems, a refuge, a pool of talent, a source of arms with a delivery system, a means to indoctrinate, and local support. This has been coming up for years, chief. Years. They're up to something big.'

ഗ

Sushil has been finding out about the differences in the operation of the various separatist groups. He's the one who confirmed that they have a common pipeline that delivers weapons wherever they are required. Being caught with weaponry is one of the biggest risks that a terrorist takes; once that risk no longer exists, these groups find themselves safer. The risk is passed on to the men who move these things around – the drug smugglers, who have a cosy relationship with people in the law enforcement agencies – and get away with the application of grease most of the time.

Now Sushil has a Pakistani passport issued by the passport office in Karachi. It's strange how similar the processes of the Pakistani and Indian governments are. Sushil went to Karachi and got himself a ration card. It cost him about one lakh rupees. I managed an appointment letter in his name from a friend in a British concern – a friend willing to back up his letter with a telephone call, if necessary – and he went off to meet an influential police officer who, understanding the urgency with which he required his passport, expedited the issue: for a consideration, of course. Besides, the Pakistani government is still, in its own lazy and confused fashion, bending over backwards to keep Kashmiris happy. Confused because its Foreign Office tends to take a lenient view of Kashmiris, while the police and their IB take the opposite view, and lazy because neither of these does much for anything other than their own benefit anyway.

So now Sushil has a legitimate Pakistani passport identifying him as Irfan Khan from Srinagar in Kashmir. He also has, separately, an Indian passport identifying him as Sushil Tikkoo from

Bengaluru. Both are equally valid, and as long as he remembers where he is and comes up with the right passport on demand, he's going to be alright.

He now needs to be able to move freely. The patrols on the Pakistani side of the border don't stop people from getting across. Rather they encourage people crossing over, assuming they're all militants crossing into safe havens. Sushil gets across with ease, but getting from Kashmir to, say Karachi, to identify the weapon pipeline from, say Peshawar or from the new munitions factory at Bahawalpur, is another story. How he's done so much is a mystery to me, and every now and then, I find myself wondering if he's been caught and turned. But his information has always been complete and spot-on, and, more importantly, he hasn't seemed ever to ask for information that he doesn't need.

He has, astonishingly, made contact with juniors in ISI, low-level field agents looking for reliable information on Kashmiris. They've been trying to persuade him to go to India to get information on RAW's plans for Kashmiri separatists, now, ironically, fighting to get Kashmir to secede from Pakistan. The Pakistani government was initially taken aback by the strength of this movement, which it thought would fizzle out once India moved out.

It hasn't, and the old JKLF – Jammu and Kashmir Liberation Front – has reformed under the name UKLF – United Kashmir Liberation Front – and just isn't giving up. Their old enemies, India's IB, have been helping them along, as have the Border Security Force. It's strange how groups change allegiances, but the one big advantage when old enemies like this become friends is that they know each other very well, warts and all, and expect no more than the least.

November 2024

Sushil has arrived to brief me, to check his bank balance, and to reconfirm his roots after a few months of being under cover. The firm is raking it in and I have no trouble paying his expenses out of a slush fund that we keep for 'entertaining' clients or their representatives.

'How did it go?' I ask.

He's been in Muridke, near Lahore, before spending some time in Skardu, in what used to be PoK, near the Army base there. From there, following rumours, he moved off to FATA, where, he says, there's a new camp which has come up recently, one run jointly by Al-Qaeda, Taliban and Lashkar. It's in the hills, near Orakzai, miles away from anywhere. It's an isolated kind of area, but he's established himself in a village some thirty kilometres away that seems to be the base from which supplies go to the camp.

Working these things out has taken time. Wherever you go, you have to find out the normal pattern of activity, and then look for deviations. Working out the 'normal' pattern in a place like Orakzai is difficult because the pattern keeps changing – the normal business of the place is war. It's taken Sushil some patient months for acclimatising himself, learning the language, and watching patterns. Here he's with an NGO working on child welfare. One of the things he's discovered is that people here are touchy about their children. He nearly got into trouble before he got anywhere when he said something that his audience thought suggested that they weren't capable of taking care of their own children. He also found that working men with children were suspicious of him because the children were in the care of their mothers most of the time and the fathers thought he was after the ladies.

But he's grown past all that and has been accepted by the locals as the visiting eccentric. He's got friendly with the shopkeepers, who, being traders, are often the easiest to get to know; over a period of weeks, any regular customer who doesn't put on airs becomes at least a neutral, if not a friend.

He's got plenty of news and an air of excitement. All that work is paying off. 'There's some new activity in the camp,' he tells me.

'What kind?'

'I don't know,' he replies, 'but what I do know is that they shifted everyone out of the Lashkar camp a few weeks ago. Then they brought in a new set of instructors, and a separate bunch of students. You know how it is – at a time, they can put seventy or more guys through one of these camps. Well, they just got about thirty or so guys in there now. Half strength. Stricter rules. No one in, no one out, except the odd instructor. I don't know what they're doing, but I know they've bought things such as climbing equipment, short rations, and stay-awakes from the shops around. I've heard a chopper up there from time to time, and it looks like they're planning something big. Looks like they're going through some special drill. I heard they've been making models of something in there, plywood models they can dismantle and reassemble.'

'Any ideas what kind of special drill?'

'The climbing stuff; they probably plan to rappel down some place. They might want to hit the dam at Baglihar, but that's not going to do them any good.'

'You are right. They're not likely to get into something that'll bring floods downstream, and bugger up the water agreement.'

'The railway line?'

'Not good enough, unless they blow up a train as well. But that would just be random violence unless the train is carrying something special. However, if it is, there'll be enough guards to deter thirty men.' I wish we had access to satellite photographs – the ones you get these days are sharp enough to show the pimples on the faces of some of the young lads they get! I'll have to talk to someone in military intelligence to find out what's happening.

'They've got an old paratrooper NCO training them,' he says.

'How do you know?'

'The bastard flaunts his para badge when he's drunk. Do you know, they have the same thing we do, blue wings?'

'I know. But drunk? In the Army of the Islamic Republic of Pakistan?'

Sushil grins. 'All those bastards drink, especially in cold weather. This guy has an excuse. He's got lots of broken bones, he says, which begin to act up in cold weather, particularly when it's wet. Like now. The only way he can handle it is with booze, which he gets without problem.' The grin widens. 'Murree rum is what he likes best, but he'll take anything else if he's desperate enough. I know.'

'Any idea how high they're jumping from?'

'Low, 500 feet,' he says. 'He gets pretty contemptuous of these guys after the fifth peg. Says when he was their age, he could land on a target six feet across from 5,000 feet. These guys get blown a hundred feet off target, jumping from a chopper hovering 500 feet up.'

'Takes some practice getting it right.'

'Hey, Chief, you've done this shit, haven't you?'

'Long ago,' I tell him. 'Long enough to have forgotten.'

'You're younger than that NCO,' he says. 'Umm, any broken bones?'

'A couple. One from a fall off a tree when I was six, the other from bumping into someone on a cricket field. I dropped the catch, by the way, and got no sympathy for my efforts.'

'Maybe I should get you drunk,' he says. 'Good stories I will get then.'

'I don't think so. I served during a quiet period.' Time to change the subject. 'Do you know what kind of chopper do they use?'

'Not very big,' he tells me. 'It was an American make, a Bell Civet. A five-seater. It's an evolution of the old JetRanger.'

'That's a civilian machine,' I tell him, 'and too small to handle bad weather or long distances. Most Civets go to businessmen or politicians wanting private helicopters to fly short distances in good weather in urban areas. It's too small for defence services work, which means that someone must have bought it for civilian work. What are they doing with it in Ozakrai?'

'I have no idea, but the NCO being there tells you something, doesn't it? That the Army backs it up.'

'Are you sure the trainees are learning to handle it?'

'Very sure. The NCO tells me a couple of students are learning to fly it.'

Stranger and stranger. Maybe the money trail will throw up some more. 'The money for all this?' Their funding is based on collections from the public who support them, and grants from ISI which are dependent on the government in power. For now, grants are being sanctioned rather fast because they have to have an enemy to focus on.

'They're collecting money outside the mosques,' he says carefully. 'They're getting blankets full of money.' These days they have four masked men, each holding the corner of a blanket, outside a mosque. People emerging after prayer drop whatever money they want into the blanket, which is whisked away when full. The four men, who are all armed, watch who pays and who doesn't, and are known to have long, sharp memories for faces. People tend to contribute even if they don't really want to, but most volunteer. But contributions like this don't pay for helicopters. Even ISI grants won't run that far. Getting a pilot good enough to teach a bunch of kids is easy, but learning to fly involves a certain amount of theoretical knowledge, which I don't think any NCO has.'

'Do you know of any officers coming in?' I ask.

'No. The only officer-grade man is the pilot, and he's a civilian. The NCO thinks he's a poof. Probably because he doesn't drink his rum neat.'

If the students are learning to fly, that can only mean one thing – they mean to fly a five-seater helicopter to the target, or somewhere near it. The rappelling equipment means they'll come in from above.

Now, what could that mean?

If the special session at the camp has begun only weeks ago, there's probably something planned for the second half of the coming year, because these training sessions last a few months. The middle of the year, in the middle of the rains and the bad weather generally, is not a good time to launch an operation, so whatever it is they're doing will happen after August or, perhaps, September.

If the coast guards aren't asleep, and the radar defences are fine, these Lashkar men won't be able to get into India along the coast in one lot. They won't be able to do that across a land frontier either, and they would definitely not want to raise eyebrows by having two dozen fit young men fly in together. Therefore, if they have to get into the country at different points and then assemble, we're looking at something happening by October or later.

They can't smuggle in a helicopter; they'll have to get hold of one locally. How are they going to do that? No one in India rents out helicopters without pilots; it's not like renting out a car. If they're going to hire one and take it over, that will reduce the capacity of the craft by one, and they will also need to get rid of a body. Three men in a chopper are going nowhere without ground support. The rest of the people being trained on the ground must be that support.

These guys are quite professional. They use backup teams and so on, which means that the job is meant for a dozen people or less, assuming that not all the people going through the training will be involved in whatever they want to do. Now what could that be?

'What do you want me to do next?' Sushil asks.

'Can you go back? Keep an eye on that camp?'

'Sure,' he replies easily. 'I'll keep you informed.'

'Watch out for odd movements.'

'Not to worry, boss,' he says. 'You've taught me enough.'

'Get out before it's too late. Don't hang around when you know you shouldn't.'

'I know.'

'I'm repeating myself because we are always – always – working on incomplete information. Keep looking at it long enough, and you will begin to see patterns. Right now, you might not be able to see them, but I do. What you get means more to me than to you. So don't hang around waiting for that last bit of the puzzle to fall into your hands. Sorry for the lecture.'

'I get you. One whiff of danger and I'm out of there.'

Meanwhile, Mahipal has more to tell. Mahipal has been in Hyderabad for the last eighteen months, getting familiar with a group that call themselves the Deccan Fidayeen. They are so taken with his knowledge of the Internet that they have put him in charge of all the communications. They use coded messages, keys to which are not known to Mahipal, but there are some in the clear, which he has been passing on to me electronically.

Some of the messages are about suits. What suits, I ask him, but he doesn't know. Why should they be talking about suits?

'Don't forget this,' I tell him. 'If you come across another reference to suits, let me know.'

I wish I had someone I could trust in the intelligence services. The guys who can be bought can't be trusted to give me all they've got, and the ones who can't be bought – yes, there are a few of those too – won't give anything away. They must be getting inputs like this from all over the place. Perhaps they're piecing something together. It seems ironic that to understand what's going on, I have to have someone spying for me in Pakistan, and someone else eavesdropping on intelligence services in India.

October 2025

There's a mail; Sushil has got in touch. He's been reading the news, and knows that Mahipal is gone. He's shocked and angry and afraid, which is all perfectly normal. I reply telling him to get to Hyderabad as soon as possible to retrieve Mahipal's body. I won't get in touch with Neena, now married and living in London, until I have the body. I don't know what to tell her, but I've done this before. I was hoping when I left the Army that I wouldn't have to do it again, but here I am – doing the same thing all over again.

The police will be looking out for claimants to the body, of course. They don't have independent storage for bodies, so this one will be in the largest and oldest of the government hospitals in the city – the Nizam's. Sushil will pick up Mahipal's body, but the paperwork will show that he's taken the body of some other youngish man. There are enough venal people all over to enable this.

I'll have the body cremated here. I call the crematorium myself, and as I force myself through the arrangements, I find myself thinking that this is the first time I've had to do this for a brave young man whose courage won't be recognised or understood.

Twelve

Thomas

October 2025

This vigilante sniper has really gotten under my skin.

At the Police Academy, I deliver my lecture on autopilot, and am surprised at the applause and the praise afterwards. 'You spoke well,' the commandant, a very senior policeman, tells me at the dinner afterwards. 'They will remember it.' I certainly won't.

Afterwards, I spend time with their computer system administrator, also a uniformed police officer, one Ajmal Khan, about a decade younger than I am. He asks to meet me, and I invite him out for a drink the day after. We find ourselves in a bar in Banjara Hills, and he tells me why he wanted to speak to me. 'I want a transfer. To the NIA.'

'What makes you think I can help you with that?' I ask.

The subservience he showed at the Police Academy, in the presence of others, has disappeared. He is two rungs down the ladder from me, but his tone is that of an equal. 'I helped set up the computer systems you use at the NIA, you know. We had all kinds of problems getting people to agree on the kinds of systems we should use.'

'I know that,' I tell him. 'I attended some of those meetings.'

He grins. 'I've seen some of the minutes of the meetings and your observations.'

'So what?'

'The others were into protecting their own little spheres of influence, or their expertise. You were one of the few who really wanted the system to work. We got some good points from you. The way the system was designed originally would have let us work out who used the system from which computer at what time and so on… A basic log of anyone on secure databases. You wanted that.'

'Yes, I remember.'

'Some of the seniors didn't want that bit of the system implemented. The excuse was that such a system might compromise the safety of the undercover operatives they run.'

'I remember that, too. I also remember that the excuse was overworked, and that I was outvoted.'

'You were. Well, the computer people left that bit of the system in. They only disabled it.'

'So?'

'So I managed to enable it again, I can do it whenever I want to, and I've been watching the logs. It seems you have a lot of colleagues visiting you, using your computer to look at various things.' He smiles. 'Even when the office logs show that they're far away from your office at that time….'

This is a stand-off. He might have caught me with a stolen password or two, but he can't really threaten me with it. If any of this does come out, it'll finish him off in the service. I smile back. 'Few people are going to like it, you know, that their movements are logged,' I tell him. 'Perhaps least of all the minister.' The minister being talked about here is the home minister, a relatively – very relatively – straightforward man who wouldn't have been the home minister except that he had the prime minister by the short and curlies after the elections.

'I know what you're trying to do,' he says.

'What?'

'Take the credit for what the others are doing.' He sits back and takes a long sip from his glass. 'It's obvious you're not making anything on the side.'

The moment of fear passes. That's how a climber would think. I see an opening. 'I'll help you,' I tell him, 'but you'll have to help me as well.'

'How?' he asks.

'I need access to certain secure databases.'

'I'll give you whatever I can, but you have to tell me what for.'

Now he's bargaining, looking for more seniors to pressure. To outsiders, members of the service present a united front – like wagons in a circle – but rivalries within the service are incredibly vicious. The plum posts – the ones offering money or power – are available only to officers close to retirement age. In your last three years in service, you have to make sure you have enough to retire on, to send your children to foreign schools, to live in pleasant houses with gardens to relax in and servants to take care of everything, as it is when you are in harness. This man is past forty now, and has some more years to go, but he seems to be in a hurry. There's no real strength to his position. 'That won't be possible now,' I tell him, 'but we can think about it in a year or two.'

'A year or two? Do you expect a change soon?'

'Yes.'

'Ah! I can wait. What kind of database?'

'Army ones.' I lower my voice, forcing him to lean forwards.

'Looking for retired Army officers who might be linked to some recent violence. They have a network. And sometimes the people; some states are slowly passing details on to us.'

'So you're going to pre-empt them?'

'Yes. And I want something out of RAW sources.'

'What?'

'Their files on the Americans.'

'Not the Pakistanis? I'd have thought you'd want that.'

'No. It's easy to get information on them. It's the Americans who are the shadiest.'

'I'll do what I can.' He smiles happily. This is politically correct, career enhancing, and secretive. This is his idea of a professional heaven. I smile back, for I might have got a handle on McAuliffe. *Tony McAuliffe, I'm coming for you.*

The professor is about to retire and is happy to spend some hours reminiscing over a delicately flavoured meal in one of the city's older restaurants. His children are all grown up and far away, and he intends to spend his retirement in the garden he couldn't tend to while he worked. I can see him pottering about, as happy with the flowers and the lawn grass as he was with decomposing livers and body fluids.

By half past nine, when the plates have been cleared, he shows no sign of fatigue, and when I bring up the Asif Jamal case, he looks up, bright-eyed. 'Have you discovered where the boy came from?' he asks.

'No,' I reply, 'but I do have one matter to check. At the morgue, without a fuss and without anything getting on the records.'

He's happy to help. 'Of course,' he says. 'Now?' His enthusiasm reminds me of a puppy I got as an eight-year-old.

'Why not?' I summon the driver, and we move on.

He gives the driver directions to the Nizam's Hospital – old, prestigious, and, like many of its kind, run-down and busy. The morgue is in the basement and is supposed to be guarded round the clock. We find a sleepy clerk in charge, who doesn't recognise the professor and tells us to come back in the morning. The professor rages into his cell phone. And a minute later, the clerk's intercom rings. He picks it up and mutters, 'Yes?' Moments later, he looks up in fear, and within the next few seconds, we're inside the morgue, looking at rows of lockers.

The locker room smells of decomposition and disinfectants, and is cold enough to give me the shivers, which the clerk and the professor don't seem to notice. The clerk has looked up his computer to find out the locker in which the false Asif Jamal is kept. We get him to unlock it and tug the long drawer out.

Inside, wrapped in a white sheet, lies a body. The sheet is stiff with moisture at freezing point, and crackles when the professor pulls it away, exposing the face and shoulders of the corpse inside. One look is enough for the professor, 'This is the wrong body,' he thunders at the clerk. 'I want every drawer in here examined, and Asif Jamal's body found! Now!'

A flurry of activity follows; and while it's on, I commandeer one of the staffers to look at the records of bodies removed from the morgue in the weeks since Asif Jamal arrived here. There are six – I list the names of the dead and the names and addresses of whoever claimed them. The vigilante has been here to bribe someone to release Asif's body while the paperwork shows another. He came back for the body.

Now that I have a lead, the lack of immediate resources to follow it up frustrates me. In the normal course of events, a few telephone calls followed by official e-mails would have fetched me information on who booked a coffin on which flight out of Hyderabad, or who booked an ambulance to carry a body out of the city on the dates on which these six bodies were released, but now I will have to wait.

While waiting, I think some more about what I'm going to tell this vigilante when I track him down.

∽

There seems to be no way to find out who took the body out of the morgue. The paperwork is all there, a driving licence number and so on, but all that leads to a dead end – the address on the licence is false. I leave the professor embarrassed and apologising for the corruptibility of his staff. To console him, I tell him some truths about some of my colleagues. 'I can't even sack the man,' he tells me. 'Any action like that and the staff go on strike and the hospital just stops functioning. These days, your income is not based on how much you contribute but on how much trouble you can make for everyone else.'

'Don't go down that road,' I tell him. 'You'll end up very lonely.'

He nods. 'I'm glad I'm out of this. I'm going back to my village, where I'll live on my pension. And play chess.'

'When I get fed up of the city, I'll come visiting,' I reply.

Back in Delhi, I find that Ajmal is as good as his word. I find that I have access to all kinds of database except the ones with the banks, which Ajmal can't get into. A former, well-off Special Forces officer, based in Bengaluru, should be easy to find now. A list of half-a-dozen early retirees comes up, ranging from a thirty-year-old major to a fifty-year-old full colonel. Ajmal's access isn't good enough to get me into the Army's classified archives, where you can find the operations that some of these Special Forces men have been involved in, but the decorations tell a story of their own. Other retirees are disabled – one a double amputee in a wheelchair, another blinded – all very unlikely.

There is another possibility though – someone, probably a

retired Army officer, has found a retired Special Forces NCO and is paying him to do all this. I've come across officers who generate that kind of loyalty amongst their men. I extend the search which brings up all the retired officers, and the number swells immediately to several hundred – too many for me to follow up. I restrict that to people of some wealth – who pay significant amounts of income tax – and the number shrinks to less than a dozen.

So now, I have eighteen names to work on. I get their backgrounds out of the database, and one officer's history leaps out – one Lieutenant-Colonel Ganesh Cariappa, applied for voluntary retirement in 2019, which was granted in 2020, now CEO of a firm specialising in industrial security, most of it hi-tech. He's had a three-year secondment to 9 Para, and details of most of this period are under wraps, but the list of medals says something of the man.

Son and grandson of soldiers, a widower who lost his wife and parents to a bomb in a mall in Bengaluru, and his daughter to a wayward bus a few years later. He's well off, with the proceeds from the sale of several acres of land growing specialty coffee, and the income from the security firm of which he is a managing partner... the other partners are all former soldiers, too. The firm has branches in all the big cities, and he's out of town half the time...

I remember the bombing. No one was ever prosecuted for that. Three men involved got away for lack of evidence, and a senior police officer was censured for sloppy work. If ever there was someone with the means and the motive for being a vigilante, this is the man.

I do something I often tell people never to do without digging much further – follow a hunch. His daughter was killed when a bus driver lost control of his bus. The driver fled and was never caught. Colonel Cariappa seems most unlucky. People destroy his family and get away.

A little more follow up reveals that the owner of the bus died in a traffic accident some months later. He was the brother of a minister, that one…

Did he die or was he killed? He was in an SUV with a driver-cum-bodyguard. Both died when the vehicle crashed through a barrier on a hilly road and went down a near-vertical slope.

There are plenty of photographs taken from the ground and from satellites. The investigating officer doesn't seem to have done a thorough job because there's nothing in the report about skid marks… and there are no skid marks in the photographs. If the driver had slept off and hit the barrier at high speed, the vehicle should have gone much farther than it did.

Cars contain so much plastic and other inflammable material that if they catch fire, they burn up completely. Petrol found on the scene, a litre or two used as an accelerant, wouldn't raise suspicion. Convenient, perhaps, for someone looking for revenge.

Was it an accident or did the colonel make it appear to be an accident? Was he an officer but not quite a gentleman? The investigating official, an inspector from the records, was overloaded, and wanted to get rid of this file as fast as he could. Otherwise he'd have noticed all this.

I'm glad he didn't.

Another thought rises as I shut down the computer. Will the good colonel come after me if I confront him? If this man is indeed who I think he might be, I don't want him doing that. For the first time in many years, I find myself looking forward to the chase – it doesn't matter if I end up being the prey.

Thirteen

Noordin

November 2025

When I wake up, most of the lights in the coach are out and people are dozing – some sitting on the benches and others on sheets or even newspapers spread out on the floor. The shutters are all down, but there are gaps between the windows and the frames which brings in a cold draught that keeps the air inside fresh.

It's half past midnight in my watch. I have no idea where we are right now, but I do know that we should be in Patna in another seven hours or so. These few hours of sleep have not refreshed me, I need some more, and there is plenty of time. I find my way to the toilet to ease myself, and when I return to my temporary bed, I close my eyes and prepare to sleep.

Sleep doesn't come. Memories come instead.

May 2004

These are the hottest weeks of the year in Pakistan, with a month to go before the rains arrive. I am in sweltering Karachi, to meet the brigadier one more time before returning to Kashmir. I am nearly half-an-hour early at the yellow house and Raza greets me. He is bare-chested. 'I was preparing for a shower before the meeting,' he tells me. 'Father is getting ready. Make yourself comfortable. Ali will look after you.'

Ali is the steward. We have known each other for a couple of years, and I keep my distance because Ali is more servile than he needs to be. 'Get the newspapers for the past week,' I tell him.

Afghanistan is not far away, and the newspapers are full of news about the country. About the failure of the government to keep the country together, about the warlords who have taken over large parts of the country, about the security system falling apart when the Americans – there are soldiers from other countries as well but those are all American stooges – leave, and so on. Tucked away on an inside page, I find a reference to a few Taliban killed by an American patrol on the Afghan side of the border.

From what I understand, it seems that the Pakistani Army has attacked a Taliban stronghold by the Afghan border in Waziristan, driving its occupants west across the border, into the trap laid for them by the Americans – one of the rare successes these people have had against the Taliban here. The news item is a clear photograph of the dead Taliban lying in a row, and among them is a familiar face – Naeem Shaqeer. One eye has been shot out and his headdress is askew, but his face is unmistakable.

So that was why the man with the deodorant was following us around! I thought he might be after me, but he was after Shaqeer. I take a closer look at the photograph, and with a lurch in my chest recognise another dead man's face – this one is peaceful, almost as if he were asleep. It is Uncle Lala, Father's friend, whose wife cared for me for a while after Father died. I don't know what he was doing in Shaqeer's company, but he did have relatives amongst the mujahideen and would have joined them if he hadn't had a large family to support. He certainly wasn't part of Shaqeer's gang.

The Americans speak in glowing terms of the cooperation of the Pakistani Army and crow over the deaths of sixteen Taliban. I don't know what they mean by the word Taliban, but if they include people such as Uncle Lala in that group, they don't know what they're talking about. Even Shaqeer, for all his bravado, is a small fry; no mujahid group would have let him anywhere near action. With this massacre – for massacre it is, this killing of innocents and minnows – the Americans think they've achieved something.

Raza soon joins me, freshly showered, and dressed for the occasion, casual but elegant. I point out the newspaper item to him, saying, 'I knew this man. He was one of the Afghan mujahideen.'

Raza nods. 'I know,' he says. 'I didn't know him personally but I know quite a bit about him. Was he a good friend of yours?'

'No,' I reply. 'I just met him a couple of times, and I wasn't really impressed. It's just that he reminds me of...' I can't find the right word. 'Probably, some remarkable days from the past.'

'He was a traitor,' Raza says. 'Back when the Soviets were around, he was talking to them. When the Americans came, he wanted to talk to them. We thought it best that he and a few others like him be sacrificed to keep the goodwill of the Americans. You know how it is – when the Americans take a few lives, they go away happy. They don't understand yet that there are others to replace the ones they kill.'

'So you bought yourself some credibility with Shaqeer's life.'

'Not me. The Army. Now the Americans are more inclined to believe that we're serious about helping them with their war on terror.'

'What about the others?'

'All were part of Shaqeer's group. All equally available to the Americans.'

'All of them?'

'Every single one of them.'

I do not react, though I know this is a lie. Raza perhaps does not know, sitting so far away from all the violence and the dirt, what really happened. Perhaps Uncle Lala, too, was 'collateral damage'.

'This one isn't my fault, Mike,' I tell the ghost who sits permanently on my shoulder.

'No,' Mike agrees. 'But do you really believe that? Don't you think Lala would have been saved if you'd finished Shaqeer off earlier?'

I do. I could have saved Lala. I put the thought aside and turn to Raza for the briefing he is supposed to give me. Later, when I board the train back to Rawalpindi, from where I will head for Azaad Kashmir and then to Shahpur, the thought resurfaces and keeps me awake. But then I have trouble sleeping anyway. All those ghosts don't need to sleep, and they keep me awake too.

November 2025

Remembering people such as Shaqeer and Sohail confuses me. They are both gone now, gone so many years, but I remember them because of their flaws. Both were on our side, and both deeply flawed. Would the good that they did outweigh the bad?

These questions have come up increasingly often since I fell ill. I don't know if it has to do with my illness, or with my age. Now, in the darkness, it strikes me that I should not be asking these questions – they are for Allah to answer. Judgements such as these are not for the likes of me. It is disrespectful to ask. But the questions come up, and I can only keep them at bay; I cannot force my mind not to ask them.

So I try to turn my mind to the eventualities of the next few days. I have a valid Indian passport to show if I have to prove my identity. I have used it to make a couple of trips abroad – one to Malaysia and another to Indonesia – besides a few to Kashmir. It's now only a few months short of expiring, and if I were the person I said I was while applying for the passport, I should be applying for a new one now. But this one will keep me going till the end of this project, and I don't want to think beyond that now.

Again my mind goes to a flawed person, this one on the other side.

January 2016

I am in Patna now, about the small matter of an Indian passport for myself. With my fair skin and brown hair and sharp features, I can pass myself off as a Kashmiri Pandit settled in Delhi. I have also shaved my face clean for the purpose.

First on the list of people to meet is a bureaucrat, a relative junior, what they call a joint secretary – in Delhi, a non-entity. This junior, Altaf Kamal, has a weakness for young boys, something that one of our smugglers knows. The smuggler, Moin, has been providing Altaf with boys, and now Altaf has come to Moin's help in the matter of the passport.

Altaf himself has nothing to do with the issuance of the passports, but knows someone in the Indian Ministry of External Affairs – I always wonder why they don't stick to the conventional 'foreign affairs', but Indians have this urge to be different even when it doesn't make sense – who just might know someone there. Altaf has demanded that he wants to meet the applicant first. 'I can't recommend just anyone to Mr Sharma, you know,' he has told Moin over the phone. 'I have to make sure.'

'Of course,' Moin replied. 'Please tell me when it's convenient for you to see this friend, and what papers he must bring along.'

'He must have some identification,' Altaf said. 'Something with his address.'

'Sure,' Moin replied. 'The boy is perfectly legitimate.'

'Otherwise you wouldn't be bringing him to me, would you?' Altaf asked, laughing. 'How about 11 a.m. on 15 January?'

'Perfect,' Moin replies.

So here we are on this Thursday morning, waiting to see Altaf at his office. We wait in an anteroom until his personal assistant summons us, a matter of a few minutes, and then we're drinking tea out of good china in the warm quiet of his office. 'I hope we're not disturbing you,' Moin says.

'Not at all,' Altaf replies, looking up from the file he's working on. 'All this can wait.'

'I know you're very busy,' Moin says. 'We'll keep this as short as we can.' His tone is servile, as is his manner, but something in his body language signals a threat.

'So, what can I do for you?' Altaf asks, closing the file and tying it up.

Moin produces the papers he's got – a driving licence in my name, with my photograph and address on it. 'This friend of mine needs a passport in the next two or three days,' he says. 'He needs to go to the Middle East to meet a sheikh there.'

'For a job?' Altaf enquires.

'No, no,' Moin says, 'for a manpower supply contract. See, he has friends in villages all around Delhi and in UP. Skilled workers and professionals. So you see, when people in the Middle East look for skilled men, Arjun here can supply them quickly if the terms are good enough.'

'Then what's the hurry?'

'Sahib, you know how competitive it is in those parts. Every time anyone here gets a hint of such a contract being available, people line up. This sheikh is going to decide in the next few days who he's going to appoint, and Arjun must see him before that.'

'I don't know how quickly we can get your papers processed,' Altaf says, 'but we'll do it as soon as we can. Do you have the application with you?'

'No,' Moin tells him. 'We've handed it in at the passport office three days ago. Here's the reference number.' He hands across a slip with my reference number on it.

From what I have seen, the governments of both the countries thrive on inefficiency. The poorer the quality of the service they deliver, the more people they have begging for them. Elections make very little difference because the part of the system delivering these services is still in the hands of petty officials, no matter what their rank. In the early days of every military government in Pakistan, people would say that matters would improve now that the government could look beyond the next election, but the relief never lasted more than a few months, or a year, at the most. Then people began to say that any elected government is better because they at least have the choice of throwing it out if it doesn't perform.

In Afghanistan, in my youth, we fought for something very visible – we had to get rid of the Soviets and their puppet Najibullah. Now, when I travel through India and Pakistan, and see how similar these countries and their peoples are, how similar their troubles are, I wonder whether what we are doing is worthwhile.

I cannot wonder for a long time. Altaf is quick and efficient. He speaks for a few minutes on his cell phone, points the camera at me for a short while, and gets an acknowledgment. He disconnects and turns to us again. 'That was my friend Asim at the passport office,' he says. 'He's the passport officer there. You have to meet him tomorrow morning at 11. Go to his PA, tell him your name, and say you have an appointment. If there's any trouble, call me.'

'Did he say how long it will take?'

'Oh, a day or two. You should have it by the end of the week or maybe Monday.'

Moin speaks. 'What can we do for him?'

Altaf laughs. 'Speak to his PA. You'll have to pay, of course, but he won't take it directly. The PA will tell you the procedure.'

Suddenly he looks uncomfortable. 'What's the matter?' Moin asks.

'I told him you're looking for a contract in the Middle East,' Altaf replies. 'He might increase the price a little. You know how it is.'

Moin does indeed. 'That's alright,' he says. 'We are prepared to pay any reasonable amount.'

Altaf smiles in relief. 'Then I hope Asim won't be unreasonable.'

November 2025

I consider getting up, but a wave of fatigue keeps me lying down. There's nothing to do, in any case, until the train reaches Patna. There I can rest for a couple of days.

These flawed people are not entirely useless. Lying here, thinking of Naeem Shaqeer and the manner of his death, and the closeness of my own, one aspect of life becomes very clear. I spend most of my time trying to exploit the weaknesses of people. I have never really concentrated on trying to see their strengths… only their weaknesses. People like Altaf have helped me not voluntarily but at gunpoint. You push a button here, issue a threat here, offer a sop somewhere else, and matters work your way.

Even my own men, the men I know will follow me at the cost of their lives, I have only used in similar fashion. I have turned their strengths – their loyalty – into their weakness. I can lead them wherever I like, especially now, since this is clearly the last time I will lead them, but the truth is that I have been using them.

Who has been using me?

The force of the question wakes me up completely. I am tired but clear-headed, thanks to the hours of sleep I have had since boarding this train. I have slept better than I do in my own home in Shahpur. I again feel an unnecessary twinge of guilt at the thought. The middle of an operation is not the time to ask such a question, not when there are so many operational issues yet to be resolved.

No matter how hard I try, I cannot concentrate on operational matters. Perhaps I only think I am clear headed, like youngsters who have smoked hashish. Now it seems that I am a complete stranger to myself.

I used to be sure of myself; now I am not. Is it the illness, I wonder, or age?

My mind wanders to the first step that Ghani Khan had planned. I told Raza about it.

December 2017

'We should do it in Goa,' I tell Raza. 'The timing is critical.'

'That I can understand if you're going to do the big thing between Christmas and New Year. I can also understand placing the first move in Goa. But you never told me what it is.'

'The preparation starts a year beforehand. Six of us check into the Leela – that's one of Goa's most exclusive beachside hotels. Three men and three women. You know they don't allow private beaches anywhere in India; that works to our advantage.'

'How?'

'Our people scout the place, work out a proper cache for the arms, and generally make themselves pleasant. They will tip well, say the right things to the right people, and flash a little money at the casino, perhaps. They stay a week, and make friends.

When they leave, they promise to return the next year. If the hotel permits, they book their stay for the next year's Christmas week right then.'

'It's going to be expensive.'

'Your father diverted enough from the ISI funds and the Americans to take care of all this. He was totally committed to it.'

'I know. He was in Dhaka in 1971. He spent a year as a PoW in India before they repatriated him. He wanted revenge. He burnt with it.'

'He got it with Kashmir, didn't he?'

'He didn't live to see it. Pity. And it wasn't enough. He wanted them to have bloody noses for a long, long time.'

'This should be bloody enough for anyone.'

'Not for him.'

I remember Ghani Khan telling me about his son's lack of physical courage. The old man didn't seem to mind; he just made sure that Raza didn't get into a position where he needed such courage. Now I can't help asking, 'And for you?'

Raza smiles. 'I never wanted any bloodshed except on his account. I grew up to stories of what he wanted to do… That's still there. Otherwise, nothing. You still haven't told me what you've planned.'

'Understand, the details are flexible. We have to be able to change matters until the previous year.'

'Of course.'

'So we are back to the first year. Our people stay at the Leela in Goa. They check in early, maybe weeks ahead of the tightening of security for Christmas, the rest of the team members will check into a cheap, small place on the beach, one without security checks – there are plenty of those within a couple of kilometres of the Leela.

'They meet at the right time, which should be at the height of the Christmas Eve party with firecrackers for camouflage, and enter the Leela, and maybe the Holiday Inn, which is next door along the beach.

'Getting the weapons in won't be a problem even if the first team doesn't get a place by the beach. They can hire a car, put all the stuff in the boot, and drive to the beachside somewhere in Cavelossim. No problem getting into the hotel, because the beachside won't be as easy to protect as the main entrance. The lighting is poor after dark, and there would be too many people around for the police or security guys to be really effective.'

'What do they do?'

'There should be plenty of notable people around – movie stars, businessmen, foreigners… even Israelis… to take hostage. That'll keep their security apparatus occupied. While that's on, we sneak in with the big one. They won't know what hit them.'

'It's all very big and very expensive because of the preparations.'

'Your father planned it that way. Spend thrice what you would otherwise, but make sure it works.' It's strange. The brigadier had a nose for the money, and Masood followed up. They put the funds in real estate around Karachi and Islamabad, where there's plenty of unaccounted money, and in Jewish-run mutual funds, which have been really fruitful. That Jewish money is paying for most of this.

Except for a couple of operations going awry in the last few years, it has generally been safer for us as compared to the old days. We have a pipeline running drugs and guns into India – opium from my old homeland and weapons from around there. I hear that Goan politicians are for sale; one, who has been in the legislature for years, helped with a ring to bring drugs in for tourists. Once the smugglers got him into the racket, he had to help with the guns. Now he is their pet dog. Then his son got into trouble with some girl, and the smugglers got him out of the country before the police could get him. The legislator we have picked up will make sure our shipments get to the right place at the right time.

With all this, the expenses have come to matter less. We have been more successful, with fewer men lost; and now I find that all this is not a lot more expensive than before, and the results of this project are infinitely more dramatic. It goes much further than holding a few movie stars hostage.

'Worthwhile, I would say,' I tell Raza. 'Worth every bit of the expense.'

November 2025

Last year, the men went to Goa, and established themselves there as free-spending businessmen from the Middle East – Iranians, who are welcome in India. They were planning to take on Malaysian identities, but decided against it because the accents are very different.

It will soon be time for me to send the signal telling them that their bit of the project is on. They must be incredibly brave men, living all this time with the knowledge that few, if any, will survive into the new year. They are committed. Their leader knows that he is a part of the diversion and will almost surely die. He looks forward to it. In one sense, I am abandoning those with him – they know of their impending death, but not its purpose.

Their strength of will shames me. For their sake, I experimented and found the leak. I had it plugged, too, but I am still not sure that that's the only leak.

August 2025

Several operations that I know of have failed in the last few years. All seem to have been sabotaged.

All were carefully planned. One was a strike at the Army base in Hyderabad; another was an attempt to finish off a leading politician in Gujarat. Neither was foiled by the police or by the intelligence agencies. In each case, one of our men was killed a few days before the operation and left with clues pointing at the operation and at the other men involved. In each case, the police came to investigate the murder, found the clues, and proceeded to break the cell. The leak seemed to be at the point where the materials were delivered to our people.

Everything pointed to a group in Hyderabad. I had no way to tell who the man was, but I did have a list of people and the security procedures they'd been through before being accepted. Back to the basics, I thought, and had the antecedents of every man in the group verified. I asked my people to recheck, over the objections of some of the seniors. I just could not trust anyone.

The recheck raised doubts on three people. Doubts on two were put to rest, but the third man turned out to be an impostor, one Asif, a youngster with computer skills, who had apparently contributed much to our communications system.

He must have known that he would be caught, for when my men caught up with him, he was prepared. They had to finish him off before they could interrogate him. I felt more than a glimmer of respect for him when they told me what happened.

We tried to find out whom he worked for, which Indian agency, but all our sources said he was working on his own.

We stopped discussing it after that, but I couldn't keep the thought out of my mind – what if this one worked for a group outside the government? A group like my own? I wouldn't be surprised to see such groups because the government clearly does not care about the average Indian.

November 2025

How much do governments really care about the average citizen? From what I've seen of the Pakistanis, they care even less, except the elected governments, only during the election time.

How my mind drifts.

Do the Pakistanis care about me? Why do I owe them any loyalty? I have Pakistani friends, but then I have Indian friends as well, and American, and Afghan, and Bangla and Chinese.

From my childhood, I've been taught not to question some parts our lives, some of the teachings in the Book. Now, with death approaching, these teachings have begun to seem empty. The question comes – what have I done with my life? If I have to meet the Creator soon, what will I tell Him?

One thing I will tell Him is that I have lied.

I have lied, not casually, but in defence of what has become, in these last few weeks, the most important part of my life. Not an event or an object, but a person. It is difficult for me to think in these terms, and I recoil at the words, but here they are – the love of my life.

He is forty, ten years younger than myself, and I have known him for half of those. For fifteen of those, we have been clandestine lovers, enjoying each other's company whenever we have been together. He is Kashmiri by birth, and this is one of the reasons why I consider Kashmir my new homeland.

He is worth more to me than life itself.

He does not live in Kashmir. Our political views are similar, and we have some common friends among the brethren, whom he has supported with gifts of money and arms, occasionally offering to transport weapons or drugs, but he is not involved in any of my operations. He might have some vague idea that I am involved in some of these things, because I am rather well-known among the brethren, but he has no specific information.

He respects me a lot; in the beginning, he almost feared me. Now that fear has gone.

I have asked him very little about himself. He has been vetted by some friends among the brethren, and that is good enough.

I am going to Patna to collect some papers; papers of a new identity. At the end of this operation, I intend to disappear and spend what time I have left with him. These are papers I have arranged myself, for myself, through a new person, without involving anyone from any of my mujahideen allies.

I will collect the papers and proceed to Chennai, where he lives. I will give him a surprise. He will be overjoyed to see me.

His given name is Ahmed Kabir, though the world knows him by another, and the brethren by yet another. I am one of two or three people who know this name.

Fourteen

Ganesh

Neena at first blames me for her brother's death. 'You got him into all this,' she said fiercely when I picked her up at the airport. 'Otherwise he'd have been alive now.'

Granddad taught me long ago that most of the time it's best to keep your mouth shut; and so, I didn't respond to her anger. She had just lost her only sibling, and needed someone to blame. I happened to be handy. I put her bag in the back of the car and drove carefully out of the airport complex towards the hotel, where I'd booked her a room for a little rest before the cremation.

Forty silent minutes later, she sniffed. 'I shouldn't have said that,' she said. 'He came to you. He was much happier after that.'

'Feel free to say whatever you think,' I said neutrally. 'People have said worse, and I've survived.'

A passing flicker of a smile broke through the misery on her face. 'He liked working with you,' she said eventually. 'He thought a lot of you. I think he was obsessed. He just wouldn't get over what happened to Mom and Dad. But he never spoke of what he was doing.'

The difficulty in dealing with families was never so great.

In the Army, I'd never had to explain to a grieving woman that her husband or son or father or brother had died trying to do something worthwhile. I'd have liked to tell Neena just that, but couldn't. 'Neither can I,' I said. 'Industrial secrets.'

'I didn't know it could get so bad.'

I would have liked to tell her that he died easily because he faced the enemy at the right time. Otherwise she wouldn't have got a body to burn, an urn of ashes to keep on her mantelpiece in England. 'They must have mistaken him for someone else. Or it was just bad luck.'

'The police must be at it. Tell me if they find anything.'

'I will,' I promised, 'but I don't think they will.'

She sniffed again. 'I shouldn't be saying this, but I thought he was looking for something like this.'

'Don't dwell on that,' I told her. 'Be proud of him. He didn't give in. He didn't make it easy for them. He did what he could to stop them. Surely that counts for something.'

She wept openly then, and again at the crematorium some hours later. I took her back to her hotel room, and back to the airport the next day. At the departure terminal, she looked washed out, as much a waif as she had been when we first met. I'm not good at farewells; and when she looked back to wave, I wished I'd been able to offer something more substantial than a rather distant word of comfort.

Later that night, I couldn't sleep. I'm not doing this again, I told myself. I can't face this… I can't face people like Neena, not on my own.

∽

Sushil has gotten into the spirit of the thing. A little money, applied judiciously amongst the staff of the hospital, has gotten him some information. A senior policeman named Thomas, from

Delhi, visited the morgue with a professor of forensic medicine, discovered that Mahipal's body had been replaced by another, and began a search.

More digging reveals that the policeman is with the NIA, which means he has all kinds of information at his disposal. The NIA investigates terrorism, and nothing else, and has access to all kinds of government database. In theory, they're supposed to take permission, but in practice, it works otherwise. A telephone call is all it takes for the permission to come through.

In any case, now they know that Mahipal, using his fake ID, was involved with a terror group. Since there is a real Asif Jamal, they will work out that the ID is counterfeit. How much more time will they need to find that the body was actually Mahipal's? If they get as far as Mahipal, will they eventually get to me?

Government officials tend to close ranks in the face of an investigation, even the ones that don't take money on the side, because their jobs are also under threat. This, simply, is the reason why it's easy to get a fake ID. The NIA will force their way through though, so it all depends on the official who authorised the issuance of the fake ID. If he's no longer at his job – been promoted or transferred out, or if he's retired – they'll take a little longer to find him. From there, to the agent who got me the documents is another long step… since agents pay off everyone involved – ministers and union officials all get a cut – this agent will have some protection, but the NIA will work its way through that as well.

So how much time do I have? A week, perhaps. If this Thomas character has looked at a crime database and tied those two dead Lashkar men together, he is going to put a lot more together, which means my operation is at risk. If I go down the tubes, what happens to my partners?

This stunt, getting Mahipal's body back, has put us at high

risk. I did it because I can't imagine leaving a buddy behind, and Neena's visit has made it worthwhile, but I'm worried that Sushil might get caught. Time to get him out of trouble under a false ID. If I tell him about the risk, he's likely to laugh and tell me that the best way to stay out of trouble is to disappear into Kashmir, or even Pakistan, but I think it's beyond all that now. The NIA will not give up easily, and they have tremendous resources to not let the matter rest.

I decide to tell Sushil. What about my partners? I think we swing sufficient influence now that if I tell them, they'll get away.

One possible way out is to finish off the agent or the official in question, but I can't take that route right now. Finishing off a Lashkar operative or a bully-boy and his bodyguard is one thing, but finishing off a clerk in a government office is another. It's something I can't understand. This clerk in his office making money on the side to sign a bit of paper is as dangerous as the Lashkar man because without these corrupt clerks, the Lashkar men wouldn't be able to operate. But I can still not bring myself to kill him, probably because if I start killing men like that on a matter of principle, I'll have to finish off perhaps a fifth of all civil servants and many more politicians.

Maybe I can end it all now. I should find out what this Noordin cat is up to, and stop that. If I get killed in the process, no one else will be hurt.

You see, I feel exactly the way Mahipal felt. I have more resources and I know more, so I've kept going longer and done more damage, that's all. Otherwise all of us want the same thing at the end.

I sleep then, better than I do on most nights.

∽

I wake up late; this is one of those rare mornings when I'm going to be late to work. It's almost ten when I finally reach office. There's a message from Sushil – he wants to go back to Kashmir or other parts southwest. I reply telling him we should meet first, as soon as possible.

We meet at a restaurant outside the town, a dhaba frequented by truck drivers, where the food is simple and good, and lights dim. We sit at the back, hidden from the road, on plastic chairs, eating tandoori chicken in battered metal plates. 'I don't know how long we can go on,' I tell him when we're comfortable. 'It's time you took off.'

'We can't stop this stuff in the middle,' he says. 'That would be a waste of everything I've done so far. Besides, we're just this far away from finding out.' He holds up his left hand, forefinger and thumb a millimetre apart.

'He who runs away lives to fight another day. Clichéd, I know!'

'Who's going to catch up?' he asks.

'The police.'

'With whom?'

'Either of us. I can't tell now. All I know is that there's some senior official from the NIA on our trail.'

'How do you know?'

'The guys you set up at the hospital in Hyderabad. They called to say that this guy from the NIA turned up with a professor of forensic medicine, checked out the body, discovered the switch, and left rather frantic.'

'It's only the cops, Chief, you can stall them.'

'Sure I can,' I tell him, 'but if the cops know the Lashkar will know very soon after. They have their own sources, better than mine. They have more money. And if they get to know… well, you know what happened to Mahipal. We can't have that happen to you, can we?'

He chews on this for a moment. 'I can't believe you're just

going to pull out. Look, they're going to catch up with you anyway.' He thinks for a moment. 'You're going to do this on your own, aren't you, Chief? You're going to take them on anyway because you're not going to disappear the way you're telling me to.' He grins. 'You can't fool me, Chief. Mahipal, you, me, we're the same. You're looking for a way out, just like me.' The grin widens. 'If we'd been in your army, you'd have had me up for insubordination for what I'm going to say.'

'Nonsense. You saw what happened to Mahipal. I just don't want the same thing to happen to you.'

'Look, I know what Neena said to you, okay? She told me she regretted blaming you for it. I know the risk… I've been taking it all this while. Don't even think of getting me out of this. We keep doing whatever we're at, and we'll deal with whatever comes along. But it doesn't mean we don't prepare as well as we can.'

I argue with him for half an hour, but he refuses to budge. Considering the way we've been working all along, I can't really order him to back off; so I give up and get back to the office for the rest of the working day, during which I use routine work to pacify my mind.

At home, I go through my fitness routine – a forty-minute exercise regimen that keeps me reasonably fit, requires little space and no equipment – before assembling and warming a basic dinner.

I can't eat. Seated alone at the table, looking out the window at Granddad, I find myself thinking almost automatically, 'What can I do with this boy?'

By and by, reason returns. There's nothing to connect me to Sushil except for the stunt in the hospital. I can still make arrangements for him to disappear – there are plenty of countries where biometric measurements aren't mandatory, where the appearance of his characteristics won't ring alarm bells, and I can make sure that he has enough money to make a start anywhere.

I'll tell him to continue, but on the condition that he will pull out and disappear the moment the police get to me. It might be cutting it a bit fine, but that's the best I can do.

ᔕ

What Sushil said about suits sticks in my head. Several possibilities come up, none of which seem right. Uniforms of sentries, so they can infiltrate something? These days, guards at any major establishment are identified electronically. Good suits in which to enter some kind of gathering? Guests at gatherings that likely victims attend are also screened. My people do a lot of that sort of thing, so the suits can't be a disguise.

Protection, then? With a thump, my mind jumps to another kind of suit altogether. CBW suits. Radiation suits. Plywood models. Put the two together and you have very few options. With thirty men, they're not going to get into a proper military establishment.

Why didn't I think of this before? Could they be planning some sort of assault on, say parliament, with a chemical weapon that they can set off a mile away and then infiltrate the building? They wouldn't need the helicopter then. They need suits only if they're planning to attack a CBW facility in India, which doesn't really exist. That leaves only nuclear stations.

They plan to attack – to create a distraction at some point and infiltrate the compound and attack. But then they'd need some scientific knowledge, some training of specific controls in a power station. It's not easy to learn, even for someone used to reading manuals. Dear god, they have someone inside, someone who knows how to do a great deal of damage.

What kind of training would the man have? The few scientists I know tend to trust people within their circle; they are not very aware of hierarchy and are always anxious to explain. A bright technician could do it.

Just one? I have no idea. It's just past one in the morning, and I know someone who might possibly help, one Sridhar Ramanathan, a retired physicist, widowed and insomniac, who spends his nights playing chess online with unseen adversaries all over the world, adversaries whose ELO ratings he knows better than their faces.

∽

'If it's not a matter of life and death, call me in fifteen minutes,' he tells me. 'Let me finish the games I'm on now.' He hangs up. He has ultra-fast broadband and plays with half-a-dozen people simultaneously, switching from game to game with blinding speed.

When I call him fifteen minutes later, he's alert. 'What kind of an emergency is this?' he asks.

'I'm not sure,' I reply. 'Perhaps you could tell me.'

'You've left the Army,' he says, 'and if you're in a situation where you need me to clarify something, you must be badly out of your depth. I suggest you go to the government. I can give you names.'

The man is disturbingly straight. 'Umm.... I can't do that just yet.'

'You have information that would incriminate yourself?' He laughs. 'I thought as much. You'd better come over.'

'Now?'

'If you want to wait for a more civilised hour, you'll spend a couple of hours in the traffic. If you come now, you'll be here in twenty minutes.'

Twenty-two minutes later, I'm ringing his doorbell. He opens the door himself with liver-spotted, unsteady hands. I can smell the whisky in his breath. His eyes widen as they go to the package in my hand. 'Laphroaig and quarter-cask at that! Must be something big you want!'

'The biggest favour I've ever asked for,' I tell him. 'Just between us.' He's alcoholic, and I have reservations about letting him know what's on my mind because if anyone finds out that he knows, he won't be able to take any serious questioning. But then, he's asocial, and I know he won't talk voluntarily. Good enough, I have no choice.

'Come in, boy,' he says, standing aside, showing me into his sad dark house. He's always called me boy, claiming to be unable to remember my name. A single low-wattage pedestal lamp glows in a corner. He brushes papers and a chessboard off a sofa to make room for me to sit. 'You know where the coffee is, if you want some. I can't offer you anything else.'

He hasn't been sober since his wife died ten years ago. She held him back, and after she died, he climbed into a bottle and hasn't been out since. Drunk or sober, he's one of the most intelligent men I know; and for someone that intelligent, he's been doing some very stupid things. He's an old schoolmate of Dad's. He had a few good acres not far from mine; his equally intelligent son, now a professor in Cambridge, has fixed his financial affairs so that he has a reasonable amount of money to live on. He has nothing to fear, nothing to lose. When I step into his dark house, it strikes me that we're similar in that, if nothing else.

'What is it, boy?' he asks when I've made myself comfortable on the sofa and refused coffee.

'I have a feeling someone's going to try to hit one of our nuclear power stations.'

'A feeling? Nothing more?'

I tell him about the suits, and he laughs. 'Look, nothing can protect you from a nuclear incident at close range. It might protect you from a small level of radiation from, say, the irradiated water coming out of one... how much do you know about these things?'

'Nothing,' I confess. 'I know a little about how they're guarded, but that's it.'

'Okay. Let's make some simple distinctions to start with. One, the newer reactors have better control systems; they are automatic-fail safe, so if there's a problem, parts shut down without manual intervention. So if at all they're looking to hit a power station, they'll go for the older ones, the ones built with Soviet help. Two, they can try to take over a power station and threaten to blow it up, but after that, every stable government in the world will join in the hunt. Three, they can actually get into a power station and set off a Chernobyl-type event, which makes it a suicide bombing on a large scale. In any case, they'll need specialised knowledge, which means that at least one of the men in the attack team is properly educated, or they have people inside. More likely than not, they'll have a man inside because the specifics of every nuclear power station are different.'

'I got as far as figuring out the man inside,' I reply. 'Didn't know that the older plants are more vulnerable.'

He grins. 'The Americans took us for a ride in every way on that deal. They didn't give us technology, they didn't allow us to reprocess; in addition, they limited their liability in case of a disaster.'

'You were against the deal when it came up, if I remember.'

'I was. Not just with the technical bits, but also the commercial part. You know, that's where they should look first, where the money is. That always tells you what they're trying to cover up.'

'They didn't listen to you?'

'No. I didn't expect they would, because someone influential must have been paid off. And I was past caring… I still am.'

'Then why are you helping me out?'

'In the the memory of your father. When we were in school, we had decided to be the best at whatever we did, you know. He was going to be the Chief of the Army, and I was going to get the Nobel Prize. That never worked out. We both discovered that more than anything else, you need political skills to reach the top. He learnt to live with it, but I drank and played chess instead.'

After a moment's silence, he continues. 'Back to your earlier question. All our reactors – all of them, without exception – have enough built-in safeguards so nothing like Chernobyl will happen here unless someone makes it happen. And even that is difficult, unless you have people who are willing to die doing it.'

'Our older reactors are of Soviet design. I thought they'd be similar to the Chernobyl one.'

'Chernobyl's was what they call an RBMK type reactor, which is no longer in use. Its advantage, essentially, was that you could change fuel rods without shutting it down. That's no longer a priority; we're quite willing to lose a couple of days of power generation for refuelling. Now, back to your question.

'So you're looking at a suicide bomber with at least a master's degree in physics, experience with a power plant, and expertise in how control systems in a nuclear power plant work. If the idea is to hold the plant hostage, he must be assisted by others who are trained enough to break through security in a nuclear plant. But then, you know more about that than I do.

'In any case, it's not a small thing to organise, and it requires knowledge, planning and money – many years of it. The question then is, how did they get away with it for so long?'

'I have no idea. They must have slipped through the cracks in our intelligence apparatus somehow.'

'We must start with the assumption that the Pakistanis are behind this plan. There might be others behind the Pakistanis, but we cannot allow that to change our focus until it has either happened or we have stopped it from happening.'

'Right.'

'You're here as a private citizen. Ergo, no going to the police or intelligence agencies.'

'Right again.'

He looks at a tatty calendar on the wall. 'When do you think it'll happen?'

'Christmas – New Year week.'

He's silent. Then, holding out the bottle he says, 'That gives you time to get thoroughly drunk before we all go up in a puff of irradiated dust.' He grins. 'You wouldn't do that. You'll keep at it, won't you?'

'I'm afraid, I will.'

'Let me explain some basics about nuclear reactors. First, they work on fission, on big atoms breaking up into smaller ones, and letting off some strange particles in the process. That generates heat, which produces steam that turns on a turbine, which brings you electricity. Okay so far?'

'Yes.'

'Each atom that breaks generates particles that bump into other atoms, and give them energy, and make them break up. This process generates more particles that cause more atoms to break up, and so on. A chain reaction. Beyond a point, critical mass, if the reaction is left to itself, you'll have more and more particles breaking up until all the fuel is consumed. This could happen in a fraction of a second – that's how a bomb works, releasing enormous amounts of radiation and energy. In a civilian reactor, the chain reaction is controlled or moderated. A variety of means exists for this: You could use water under pressure or what they call heavy water or even uranium compounds dissolved in water. We tend to use pressurised water or heavy water.

'Water cools things down; it flows through a set of coolant pipes under pressure. Any loss of pressure, anything unusual, and the reactor will shut down. So you have to damage the reactor and destroy its control systems, most of which have backups and backups of backups, to do any serious damage.

'You can do this only if you know exactly what you're doing, and since procedures vary from plant to plant, often from reactor to reactor, you can't do any damage based on theoretical knowledge, no matter how much theory you know and how bright you are. Ergo, an inside man.'

'What about the suits? You said they're useless at close range to a reactor incident.'

'They are. The suits might give the attackers the impression that they're safe from radiation sickness. Either that or they're going to hold the power station hostage…

'If you know where they're going to hit, and you have access to someone who can help you go to the government, you could increase security there and put every technician through the scanner. So, what are you going to do?'

'Try to figure out where first, and then figure out how they'll come in.'

'I haven't been much use.'

'You have. At the worst, I can go to the government, even if it gets me into trouble. I can try to inform someone anonymously, maybe.'

'Yes, try that. This is too big for you on your own.'

'Thanks.'

Back at home, I begin to wonder about Sushil's information on helicopters and rappelling. If they intend to arrive in a helicopter, there must be a helicopter service available near the power station. It can't be a service at the power station itself, but it's got to be nearby. A helicopter can't go very far without being detected – at the most, fifty kilometres or so, because if it flies low enough to avoid detection by ground-based radar, it'll still be heard on the ground, and someone or the other will report it.

Helicopter bases tend to be well guarded. The invaders wouldn't want to break into one. Sushil mentioned that the training is being done on a Civet, which means that they're not going to use one very different. Helicopter taxi services don't use such small machines; they prefer bigger ones, which will carry more passengers and can handle bad weather better.

Could they be planning to steal one? A private helicopter, maybe, parked at some rich man's house? How can I get a list of all private helicopters in the country? There must be someone at the DGCA keeping a list of these things. It shouldn't be too difficult to get a list of small private helicopters in the country, and from there, it would probably be possible to eliminate some possible points of attack.

Whom do I know at the DGCA?

Fifteen

Thomas

Access to the RAW database and the IB one as well has been very useful. Tony McAuliffe isn't Tony McAuliffe; he is probably one Stephen Hawker, and he is definitely not of the CIA. He is, in fact, a member of Consular Operations, part of the US Department of State, a much smaller and altogether less noticeable intelligence agency than the CIA.

I prefer to work at the office, where Nancy can't get at me. I have practically stopped going home now, except to sleep and change clothes. I continue to do that only to avoid complications caused by talking about my personal life. I wouldn't normally care, but I don't want Nancy and her complaints using up my time until this operation is over.

In one very negative sense, I am glad to go through these packets of information, for they show how silly intelligence agencies can be. Our own are no exception – IB, NIA, CBI, all apparently with different briefs but with colliding jurisdictions, compete for information, both to collect it and to deliver it to the right person. So do the CIA and Cons Ops.

Two dossiers, only slightly different, exist on Stephen Hawker;

one dossier is with RAW and the other, a much slimmer one, with the NIA, compiled mostly from IB sources. First, he's a case officer, which means he runs local agents. The dossiers themselves reflect the strengths of the agencies that have compiled them: RAW's dossier is far more detailed on the subject of Hawker's activities outside India, while the NIA dossier contains more on what he has done inside India. I'm relieved to see that my own relationship with Hawker figures in neither dossier.

Neither dossier mentions his presence in India at the times he's met me, which means he has false documentation to get him across borders with ease... nothing new for Cons Ops agents. Both mention that he is currently posted in Tajikistan, north of Afghanistan... convenient for someone who wants to operate in AfPak and India.

The American immigration system demands biometric details to avoid this kind of misuse of false documentation – if you've been to the US, and your fingerprints and retinal ID are in the database, you won't be able to enter the US with a false passport even if it's supported by background information from the government that has issued it.

Hawker hasn't been to Pakistan lately, according to the dossiers. He, too, must be visiting there with a false ID. It's a smart thing to do, to position yourself in country A and raise havoc in neighbouring countries B and C, without being noticed by the intelligence agencies of any of these countries.

The first thing to do is to find out how he arrived in India, and how he got through immigration without alerting our intelligence. He must have a generous allotment of false identities, all backed up by the US government. A look at our immigration database turns up an answer – he's come in as James Carver, an in-between who vets service providers all over Asia, and has interests in India, Pakistan, Bangladesh and Nepal. He's also been going into

Tajikistan, where RAW has some facilities. The photograph on the computer's display is Carver's passport photograph blown up – it's Tony McAuliffe, alright. I can tell.

He must have had nerves of steel, my friend Tony. It's a gift to be able to switch seamlessly between identities. Even remembering one false persona is hard enough… to change among four or five of them is both difficult and dangerous. One slip and you're gone. And Tony has been safe, in and out of half-a-dozen countries in the region, with intelligence men behind him, for the past eight years or so, from his record. He's come here from the Middle East, of course, Palestine and Lebanon and Iran, so he's had the frontline experience to teach him the basics. Not your usual spy, this one. He's smart, he's capable, and he's dangerous.

With a little help from the vigilante, I can trap him. If the colonel is as big an expert as he seems to be, it'll be a breeze. Hawker has been well trained – Cons Ops trains its people better than the CIA does, and the CIA's case officer training used to be comparable to that of any Special Forces training – and must have years of experience detecting a tail or a watcher. The colonel should be able to handle that – he's probably one of the best, has comparable training and experience, and, most importantly, is on home ground and relatively undetectable, unlike a tall, pale-faced blonde American.

If the colonel is willing and able, we will put up a show that will get Tony to talk. I look forward to the interrogation that will follow his capture.

It's high time I got in touch with the colonel.

∽

These are places I haven't been to before. The possibility of violence, of violent death, usually in the background for every policeman, no matter how senior, has forced itself to the forefront. There is the risk that Hawker will not give in, that the colonel, however good he might be in the field, might fail this one time. I must admit the possibility, then, of not having a future after this.

I must settle matters with Nancy, no matter how unpleasant it may be. There's not much to settle, since Mridula is a completely independent part of my life. Nancy will get my pension, which might not be much by her standards, but is quite enough for a single person with no dependents to live on with dignity.

Mridula... well, she has enough to see her through, her late husband's pension and what I've got her so far. I feel a twinge – no, more than a twinge – when I think of her. She has made life bearable these past few years and, perhaps, added a touch of humanity to my soul. Her children are grown up now. I hope they will think well of me.

I must also hold Ajmal off until this is over. I suspect that all kinds of mayhem will occur towards Christmas, that this case will reach its climax then. Ajmal will be a part of the collateral damage, but he is self-seeking and would pretty well think of a way to save his own skin.

Then there is the possibility of disgrace, of being caught as a loose cannon. The NIA will try to distance itself from me, but I have enough dirt on my colleagues and even a minister or two to reduce the consequences to nothing more than being forced to resign, which means I will have my pension, if nothing else. Come to think of it, if I'm going to leave the service, I might as well leave Nancy. I think Mridula and I have the means to get by even if Nancy gets half my pension.

Now that's a good thought. There is, perhaps, a future.

But I am stuck in the past. I am reminded of my own dreams of long ago. Like any youngster fresh out of the Police Academy, I dreamt of heading one of the premier enforcement agencies –

IB, NIA, CBI – and serving as National Security Adviser before retiring to a quiet, book-filled life back in Kottayam. None of that has worked out. I used to blame Mother and her tears for it. Now I don't. I'd have been in much the same position professionally even otherwise.

November 1999

There are the fast-track men, and there are the others. You can make out the fast-track ones easily. They're the ones who get the jobs that require intimate contact with the political leadership. Beyond a point, you have to deal with politicians, with ministers, their subordinates, and sometimes their families, who are the worst of the lot, arrogant and demanding. If you can take all that, and your luck holds, you'll end up as a top cop somewhere, with the possibility of a freebie – a governorship somewhere, at best, after you retire. Much of it, of course, is simply a matter of being in the presence of the right VIP at the right time.

I have acquired a name in the service for sobriety and integrity. I am in line for a fairly high-profile job with the anti-terrorist unit of Karnataka, but I am passed over. It's not the end of the world, of course, but I know now that my future in the service is limited. I will never hit the top, not in this state.

I have a friend with contacts, a fellow-policeman who has relatives who do some relatively innocuous strong-arm work for a politician. I invite him for a drink at the club one evening, and when he joins me, I ask him why I missed the bus. He takes a sip before replying. 'You remember that murder case? The old one, in Bhatkal?'

'Yes,' I reply. 'That got me a sort of name.'

'Exactly,' he says. 'That got you a name.'

'So?'

'So everyone thinks you're too straight. You won't cooperate if the need ever arises.'

'Look, I was just doing my job. As I have been trained to do.'

'True. But others don't like it… Look, this anti-terrorist thing is very sensitive. It sometimes happens that a minister's PA, or someone he trusts, recommends someone who's had some sort of contact with a terrorist. A friend of a terrorist happens to belong to the same village as the PA, visits the city looking for work, and happens to meet the man. It's just coincidence. But if you follow your anti-terrorist guidelines strictly, you'd have to interrogate the PA. You have to handle these things tactfully. The people in the ministry aren't sure you can be tactful enough.'

'You mean, everything I get should go to the politicians first?'

'Not just that. You might have to act upon someone who's… inconvenient. The other day, there was this man who used the Right to Information Act to dig up some dirt on the Bengaluru South MLA. The MLA gave the SP a call, and that was it.'

'What do you mean?'

'Someone from the local station went to his house every night for a week. They'd pick him up, take him to the police station, ask him questions about some crime in the neighbourhood, and take him back home after a couple of hours. That cost him his job and his friends. They let him go after that. Nothing illegal in that – you can take any person into custody for a couple of hours. As long as the entries are in the general diary, and the person isn't ill-treated – and this man was treated with courtesy, offered refreshment, and taken back home in a police vehicle – there's nothing much you can complain about. Would you care to get something like that done?'

I doubt it. I remember Nancy wanting me to interfere with that cabbie just last year. I'm not willing to get into that kind of thing. 'No.'

He leans back. 'You see?'

'Yes.'

'When you have the seniority, they'll push you into some place where you can't do any damage. Some kind of post that has the usual trappings and nothing else. You'll retire from there with your pension and go home quietly. Unless you're a little flexible. Or you have some dirt on someone really high up.'

'Right.'

'So take my advice. Get out of here. Get into one of those central agencies. They look for people like you. There's less interference there, most of the time.'

October 2025

So it's not Mother's fault.

But I haven't lost that name after all these years, after all those favours I've taken. But I've also done others professional favours, and now I think I'll ask for some back.

∽

The first is to get in touch with someone who is still in Bengaluru. I need to get to Anil Krishnan, the man who messed up the case of the blasts in the Pegasus Mall. I'm surprised that he's still alive – could it be that Cariappa hasn't figured out that Krishnan's contribution to the investigation was way too large? Does Cariappa have a weakness that Krishnan has figured out? Or is Cariappa using Krishnan in ways that I don't know. Cariappa is, after all, in the security business.

One way to work it out is to look at Cariappa's business dealings. Cariappa runs a security service, a very well-known firm, with three partners, all former Army officers like himself, though none of the others has any Special Forces experience. Cariappa used to be an engineer officer, but the others are all infantrymen.

I find the firm's website. Ah! Six branches. He has reason to travel far and wide. Clients all over Karnataka – that's where they're most spread out. Makes sense, because they started off in Bengaluru, and Karnataka is Cariappa's home state. Let's see what the airlines say about Cariappa's travels!

This man is a character. He is resourceful and well off. He has no family – no one to lose. Rather, no one else to lose any longer. That makes him dangerous. There's no trace of any association with Hindu fundamentalist outfits. Going by the records, he's a good businessman, hardworking, no bad habits, takes care of himself, and has a good, even if rather austere, life for someone in his position. He's good at keeping a low profile, and that, to my mind, makes him more dangerous.

The good colonel is worth watching.

Sixteen

Noordin

November 2025

My work in Patna has taken one morning. My old contact Altaf Kamal, the one who likes young boys, has been transferred, but he remembers me, and a phone call is all it takes to fix the papers. In the evening, I head to the railway station to board a train to Chennai. This trip will be different. The discomfort of the earlier trip took a few days to wear off, and I do not have many days to waste. I will, therefore, travel in relative comfort and arrive in Chennai in better shape.

There is no question of flying. I avoid situations that put me in contact with large numbers of policemen, as security checks at airports always do. Taking a train involves nothing of the kind; there is so much traffic that any checks must be random, and no one these days checks a clean-shaven, middle-aged businessman with a small, expensive-looking suitcase.

For the next five days, I will be out of touch with my allies. Two of those will be spent on this train, and I hope to spend the last three with Ahmed Kabir. This might be our only chance. This is one thing I must do when I have the chance. This is the first time I have deserted my allies, and I hope it will be the last.

On the train, the air-conditioning is on, and it's cool inside my coach. I am on my seat fifteen minutes before the train is due to start, but there is no place under the seats to place my small box – all the room has been taken by a group of three men with plenty of luggage. They seem to be well off, plump and loud as such people all over this part of the world are, and lacking in courtesy. They have spread themselves out, and I have only a corner to squeeze myself and my luggage in.

A porter comes up to be paid for carrying their bags; they offer him a note without looking at him. He protests that it is not enough. They laugh in his face and one of them says, 'Take it or leave it, but don't hang around. Else we'll show you what we can do.'

I turn away, wishing I had travelled the cheap way. I take my bags and climb up on to my berth to settle down to think and rest, but I can't sleep. The train starts on time; I feel the jerk as it moves off, and my mind settles. Fifteen minutes later, the ticket examiner comes and, when I offer him my ticket, signs it without even looking at my face.

Sometime later, the men below open a bottle of soda – even from above I can smell the alcohol in it – and bags of savouries. They eat and drink, laugh and chat, and, as time passes, get mildly drunk. When I can't bear it any longer, I climb down from my berth and go looking for the ticket examiner to see if he can give me a place elsewhere in the coach. I find him filling some forms in the next coach, and he seems to sympathise with my need for some quiet.

'Please go back to your place,' he says. 'I'll be there in fifteen minutes to see what can be done.'

Half-an-hour later he's back. 'Sorry,' he tells me in a discreet whisper, 'there's no one willing to exchange. No one wants to travel anywhere near those men. They're friends of a minister.'

I climb on to my berth and try to sleep. After a while, the men quieten down a little and speak of women they have known, discussing them like sacks of flesh, and my mind drifts off into my own memories of women.

∽

Winter 1987

The Soviets are retreating. They know the signs. The common troopers eat a regular hot meal only once a week or so, and the junior officers rarely come out of their compounds. Senior officers travel in convoys with plenty of machine gun support and armour.

Their helicopters no longer harass us in the valleys. When I was small, we hid when their gunships, the terrible Hind Mi-24s, came along. Now we have Stingers with which we can bring down these gunships, and we know how to use them well. The helicopters still come, but stay above the Stinger range, but they can't do much from that height.

Occasionally, one of them strays into our Stinger's range, and we shoot almost immediately. They are still quick enough to evade, but with one rocket out of ten, we hit a gunship. One hit gunship in four limps back to base: the others crash. Two out of three of the crashers go up in flames on impact. But every once in a while, the craft doesn't burn, for whatever reason.

We salvage what we can from these crashes – arms, ammunition, and medical supplies, which are not as good as the Americans give us. In fact, we have so little medical equipment that we take whatever we can and store them.

We also take any men left alive. We leave behind the dead and the comatose. Everyone else is taken. Some are killed nearby, some at one of the encampments, and the rest are handed over to the villages nearby – the villages these men shelled before it became too dangerous to come close to any of them.

In the villages the women take these Russians. I have heard of what they do to them, but have never seen it. Now, it is my chance, or so my friends tell me. When I ask why, they tell me to shut up and watch out when it begins.

We have taken one such pilot, a man in his early twenties, pale skinned and blue eyed, his physique ruined by poor diet and lack of exercise. He cannot walk because one of his legs is broken; we fashion a crutch out of a rifle abandoned by one of his dead colleagues and prod him on. He is exhausted and terrified, and protected only by a greatcoat – also acquired from one of his dead colleagues – he shivers so badly that I can hear his teeth chatter ten feet away.

We arrive in the dark, finding our way along the rocky paths with a torch. We are safe in the night; the Russians have no effective way of finding us in the dark. In the village, we wash and start on the meal prepared in our honour, thick naan and hot spicy mutton rich with fat. We sit around the fire and the women work on the captive with their knives.

This is no Islamic punishment, the slow incapacitation and then dismemberment that these women do to the Russians. I do not protest; I have seen what Russian helicopter pilots have done to the villages from the safety of their armour-plated craft, and I can understand the anger of the women.

November 2025

The train arrives at Chennai Central early in the morning, a few minutes ahead of schedule. I am tired, more from the illness than the stress of the long journey, and can't wait to get to Kabir's house, a flat in Nungambakkam. I usually avoid taking public transport here because I stand out – a tall fair-skinned man in a city full of short dark-skinned people – but this one time, I take the risk. A cab driven by a man who knows English takes me to Kabir's block of flats a little after seven, with the sun rising and warm despite a strong sea breeze.

I have never been here before. I got this address only a few months ago, after I met the doctor and thought of giving Kabir a surprise. I got it from someone who wouldn't tell Kabir he gave it to me. His apartment block is only five storeys, in a prosperous locality, far more so than I'd imagined. The people here are well dressed. Inside the gate are a couple of watchmen in smart uniforms. I'd never imagined Kabir lived thus. I'd have imagined he lived far more simply, sending his surplus money – if he had any – to his partners in the struggle.

At the entrance to the building, one of the watchman stops me, and I tell him I want to meet Kabir. I can manage enough Tamil to understand from the watchman's reply that Kabir is out. I tell him I'm Kabir's relative – he, too, is tall and fair-skinned – and the watchman smiles. From his gabbled reply, I understand that Kabir should be back in ten minutes, so I decide to wait at a café across the street. I have no idea how Kabir will react when he hears that a relative came visiting, so I tell the watchman not to tell him. He doesn't seem to understand at first, but when I tell him that it is a surprise, he seems to understand, and I leave it at that.

The café is full of the smells of frying south Indian food and asafoetida, which I don't like. But I've suffered worse smells without noticing them, so it's alright. I take a chair in a corner from where I can watch the gate to Kabir's building and settle down to wait. As I finish a cup of coffee, a taxi draws up at the gates of the building and drops Kabir on the pavement. I pay for the coffee and follow him in, waving to the watchman. In the lobby, I wait for the lift to disappear, and wait for it to return to the ground floor before moving on.

At his door I hesitate; I have never burst in on Kabir like this. We have always had to arrange our meetings discreetly so that our allies do not know. I ring the bell and Kabir opens the door. His eyes seem to cloud over when he sees me, but he doesn't say a word. He flings the door open, pulls me in, and shuts it behind me. 'Noordin!' he exclaims as we embrace. 'Noordin dear! How do you happen to be here without letting me know ahead?'

We speak in Kashmiri, his native tongue, my adopted one. 'It's a long story,' I tell him. 'I'm ill.'

'What do you mean you're ill?'

I explain to him what the doctor in Srinagar said and that I've come to live out the rest of my days here, with him. I tell him I think I've earned it.

'What about the job?' he asks instantly, by reflex.

'What job?' I ask. He's not supposed to know anything about this one.

He laughs. 'The current job, whatever it is. You're always up to something.'

Suddenly there is this gulf of suspicion between us. It's something new to me. Am I imagining things or is he hiding something? The way that question popped out of him makes me think he knows something about what I'm doing. He knows my sympathies, but no specifics.

I steel myself and smile back. 'Of course. I'm up to something that should be over in a month or so. After that I'm free. But before I go away, we have a few days alone, undisturbed. I thought I'd arrange it that way, just in case I don't come back... '

'Oh! Don't say that,' he says, distress clear in his voice. 'Don't even think it. You'll come back, and we'll go to the best doctor here, and you'll be well again.'

'Right,' I tell him. 'I'm a little tired now. I'll clean up and rest. We'll catch up after that, in a few hours.'

'Of course,' he replies. 'I have a few errands to run, so that's just perfect. What would you like for breakfast?'

Despite my objections, he has breakfast ready for me by the time I've finished having a shower. Toast and eggs and some beef, more than I can eat now. More for his sake than mine, I force myself to eat a little, and see him off on his errands before I lie down to rest.

In Kabir's bedroom, on his soft mattress, with the air conditioning keeping the temperature comfortable, I can't help dwelling on what he just said, about the job. For perhaps the first time in my life, I feel deep shame at my own weakness, my cowardice. I should have confronted him immediately, but I didn't.

I'm amazed that he lives in relative luxury. We, the brethren, spend when it's necessary to maintain a front. I used to, when I assumed the identity of Murad, but that was only from time to time, for a few days or a week at most. Kabir lives like this all the time.

Perhaps he moves constantly in circles where he has to maintain a standard of living, because I've lived with him in a hut in Kashmir and never heard him complain or shirk his part of the daily chores. Besides, he knows how to live simply. There's none of the hesitation you'd find in a city dweller used to electricity and running water. He knows where the water is, and the firewood, and he uses these with such economy, which you'd never find in a person used to running water and fire from a valve in a gas cooker.

My mood swings back and forth for what seems to be

minutes, but when I look at my watch, it's almost ten-thirty. He had promised to be back before eleven. It is time to make the most difficult decision of my life.

I have three days in which to find the truth about Kabir. If I cannot find out enough about him in this time, I will have to interrogate him, perhaps roughly, to get the truth out of him. Doubt is the greatest enemy, and I have to put it to rest at any cost.

There is a boulder in my chest that refuses to go away, but despite its weight, I drift off into sleep, and wake up only to the click of the front door being opened very carefully. I lie still with my eyes closed, breathing softly, pretending to sleep. He opens the door quietly, gently, and then, with a tenderness that breaks my heart, covers me properly with the sheet before padding out of the room.

This is not the way of the soldier. Dear God, forgive me my sins, my weaknesses.

∽

When I get out of bed half an hour later to wash up and join him in the dining room, he looks up at me with a smile that lights up his face. I have envied the clarity and sweetness of his smile, and though I smile back, I look at him with an inner confusion I have never felt before. Could someone with such a transparent smile be a traitor? Can anyone learn to act thus?

Chatting with him in that pleasant sunlit room, I have to be careful not to let my guard down. If at all anyone can be said to know me, it is this man. It is in him that I have confided matters that I have told no one else – matters about my childhood, about growing up in the cave, about my own fears and preoccupations. He has absorbed it all with patience and sympathy. I have felt from his eyes that everything that has pained me pains him when

I share it with him, that the few events that have brought me joy light him up as well.

How can I bring myself to set a trap for this man?

Three days is not enough for me to give him misleading information and wait for a reaction. Three days is not enough for any of the usual traps that intelligence men set. The only thing to do is to interrogate him. I'm only postponing the inevitable. I can't look to any of my brethren for help, or even advice. They will only tell me to deal with it on my own. I have only myself to blame for this, for I cut myself out of the circuit to spend time with him. I will, of course, search the house in his absence, but finding nothing won't confirm innocence… if I find something, it will only confirm his guilt.

Why am I postponing this?

Thus pass the most difficult days of my life. Every second, one voice in my mind – the one I usually listen to – says that I should take him now, immobilise him, and interrogate him. Another voice – the one I usually ignore – tells me to leave him alone. I tell myself I should be true, that I should take him, but I cannot bring myself to doing it.

We sleep together, but I tell him that my illness tires me out too much for passion, that my restlessness at night will only disturb him, so we sleep in the same large bed but not entwined as we used to. Perhaps he suspects something, but when a doctor confirms my illness on the first evening of my stay, he believes me.

I search the house. He has to go out for provisions in the evening, and I stay back. I wait until I see him on the road below, then look for hidden cameras and listening devices, and find none in the usual places. It's much more difficult these days to find really well-concealed devices, but I prefer to think like the other man and try to work out where he might have hidden them. I find none, and set about searching the flat, looking for markers that he might have left behind. I can't do a proper search – that would be destructive – but within the limits of my abilities and the time available, I find nothing. He has been careful, which is a part of his training, as it is a part of mine. I search carefully whenever he goes out, trying to put everything back in exactly the place in which it was when I started, but each time I find nothing.

On the morning of the third day, the last, I doze briefly after sunrise. I wake up to find him at my side. 'I've never seen you sleep this late,' he says. 'Is something wrong?'

His solicitude numbs me. I had planned to take him about this time – thus getting the entire day to work on him… but his concern deters me. I go to the bathroom to hide my confusion. I take my time over my ablutions, then settle down to pray, hoping for strength.

As I pray, my nerves steady. As I bow for the final time, I ask His forgiveness for sullying the prayer. This is a time of war, and a soldier needs some leeway. As I straighten up, I open my eyes, and twisting, lunge at Kabir, taking him completely by surprise.

His reactions give him away; he fights back whole-heartedly, clawing for my eyes. I have the advantage of surprise, however, and soon I have him out cold on the floor. When I rise, my chest heaving, and look down at him lying on the floor with his eyes closed as if in sleep, with a bruise just beginning to show where I hit him on the forehead, my resolve begins to weaken. I turn away and tear up a bed sheet into strips, with which I bind him tightly, at the ankles, the knees, and the wrists. I roll up a strip and stuff it into his mouth, then put a strip of gummy tape across it ensuring that he an't make a sound. For good measure, I blindfold him as well.

He is likely to be out for some time. These exertions have tired me, and I lie down for twenty minutes before returning to his prone form in the hall. Even though the last prayer was only half an hour ago, I go down on my knees and pray again, hoping for strength.

I do not get it, but I cannot postpone the action any longer. I drag him by the ankles to the bathroom, turn him over on his side, and tie his wrists to his ankles to restrict his movement further. I am not at my fittest best and have to make sure he can't get away. I dump him in the tub – such luxury – and turn on the tap. The thump on the tub bottom and the contact with the water wakes him up. He glares at me as the water rises up the walls of the tub, and struggles to get his head above it. He is awkwardly placed and has to struggle, but he does it, splashing water all over.

I put my hand on top of his head and push it downwards. He struggles some more, but his nostrils go under the water very soon. I keep him under for a while, then let him come up for one big breath before pushing him back under. I spend a few minutes doing this, then leave him alone – and helpless – to worry about what else I will do to him.

While interrogating someone under extreme conditions, it is always useful to hurt him.

It's always useful in interrogations to leave the prisoner thus for a while, especially when he has no way to track the passage of time. Isolation breaks his spirit faster than almost anything else. But silence is a double-edged weapon, and it works on me as well. What did I call Kabir? 'The love of my life.' Why am I doing this to him?

All kinds of questions race through my mind and all kinds of feelings rage in my heart as I lie on the same cool bed on which I rested after my journey. The strongest feeling is one of betrayal – how could he do this to me? I think it through some more and the feeling changes to one of contempt for myself –

how could I have let him dupe me so badly? Now there is only one thing to be done to contain the damage… I need to find out who he works for, what he knows, and what he has told others.

Regardless of what he knows, I must rearrange matters to cut down the chances of being caught. I will advance the date of both assaults by one day; that is likely to cause us some logistical troubles, but they will not be serious. I will call each of our men individually and make sure everyone knows. This is an option I haven't mentioned to anyone, so we might be able to evade patrols.

When I look at my watch after what seems to be an hour, I find it's been only half an hour since I left him alone. My sense of time is usually accurate to within a couple of minutes… but it's been an hour now, with Kabir in the bathroom… my sense of timing has gone awry.

As it did the very first time I used it.

January 2003

We are on our way across the AfPak border into Orakzai. In these mountainous parts, the border is but a line on a satellite picture. On the ground, during the harsh winter, it's notional. We are over a hundred strong.

Getting away from the Americans is simple once you get the knack. Unlike many others among the brethren, I have no contempt for them. They are in a strange land, among strange people with strange customs and a strange language. At home, their actions are being questioned openly by their own countrymen. They are hampered by their compulsion not to be caught breaking some of their own laws, about the killing or interrogation of non-combatants, and so on. Under such circumstances, they have done reasonably well.

Besides, it never makes sense to underestimate an opponent.

Overconfidence is the second biggest enemy after fear. We have been suffering from these for the past few days. Every now and then comes an air attack, too close to be by chance. We evade these attacks easily, traversing the tunnels, but even then, we need to emerge once in a while. When we do, we often find the Americans waiting.

Our group has been travelling independently, under my orders. I have been choosing our path carefully, giving orders every other day, breaking the group in four smaller parts and then meeting at appointed times at appointed places.

We have a traitor, and I have now figured out which group he is in. I think he's the leader. We are running too many risks, and I don't want to lose any more men. We have to stop the leak.

I have to stop the leak. There are no doors in the caves. When you want privacy, you ask for it, or you arrange it in other ways. I take the traitor into one of the chambers in the caves, and there I knock him out cold. I tie him up firmly, gag and blindfold him, and wait for him to come awake. After that, I spend several minutes beside him, in silence. When finally I ask him whom he works for, his mind is going. 'What do you mean?' he blusters when I remove his gag.

'Do you think I've missed the nature of the attacks on us?' I ask. Then I put the gag back on, and leave him alone, taking the lamp with me.

The dark helps to heighten his sense of isolation. My own reputation for ruthlessness – so far it's only been ruthlessness in action, not in interrogation – helps some more. None of these would be of any use without his fear. So you leave him alone with his deepest fears, with nothing to tell him whether or not they will come true.

The brethren have a terrible reputation for torture, gained mostly from accounts of how captured soldiers and helicopter pilots died in captivity. Well, we have no money for proper prisons, and we have to keep moving around to keep ourselves from being pounded to pieces. Are we supposed to take our prisoners along? We hardly have enough food and water for ourselves. How are we supposed to feed our prisoners?

Besides, we are angry people. We have been attacked for no reason, first by the Russians and now the Americans. We have no weapons with which to fight either of them, so we fight back with what we have.

The worst is reserved for the traitors amongst us. After letting him wait for what might be an hour, I go back to him. But I have timed my return poorly; in my impatience, he senses weakness. His resolve strengthens, and I have to use physical methods – messy and time-consuming under the circumstances – to get the truth.

When the work is done, I promise myself never to be in a position when I cannot tell the time. I have always kept a watch of some kind after that.

November 2025

When at last I go back to Kabir, the skin about his toes is wrinkled. I first remove his blindfold, ripping off the tape quickly, regardless of what skin or hair he loses in the process. I avoid looking him in the eye – his face is red and raw, and I can't help remembering his solicitude earlier, when he covered me up with the sheet. But then he has also betrayed me, and will perhaps cost me this operation, and thinking of that hardens my resolve.

When at last I look in his eyes I am surprised at the pleading in them. I rip the tape off his mouth and, keeping the muzzle of my pistol firmly between his teeth, remove the strip of bed sheet I'd stuffed into his mouth. 'Who do you work for?' I ask.

'Myself,' he replies.

'Who are you selling information to now?' I ask.

'To whoever pays for it.'

'Don't stretch this out,' I tell him. 'Don't make me lose patience.'

He smiles. 'Okay. For the past two years, I've been working for someone who seems to have an American background. I don't know his real name but he's old and behaves like a rich man. I think he works for their government.'

'What do you call him?'

'Rudra,' he replies. 'Just Rudra.'

For a moment, my control gives way. 'Why?' I ask. My voice is hoarse.

He looks away for a moment, then back at me. 'For us.'

'In what way?' I ask.

'We can go anywhere in the world. I have money in various banks, clear of taxes, with no trail, all over the world. I have identities. We can just leave all this alone and go live as we want… I've been meaning to tell you. That's why I was so shocked when you told me you were ill.'

'Suppose I don't want to go away? Suppose I believe in what I'm doing?'

'You're an intelligent man,' he replies. 'Just think, Noordin, just think. Who are you working for? For those crazy men in the mountains who can only think of fighting? For those fat cats in Pakistan who bray about Islam? For the Americans who love to see wars when they can sell weapons? For the Chinese who would love to see the Indians cut down to size?'

'I work for myself,' I reply. 'I do what I see fit.'

His voice turns bitter. 'You work for the good of the people? Don't you see, there'll always be a pecking order? There always has been. There always will be. You can't change it… no one can.'

He subsides, but only for a moment. 'Don't you know what you've done in Kashmir? Until you people started fighting for it, it was just another place. Then you went with the Pakistanis because you wanted the holy empire of Islam to spread. And what happened? Did it?

'Haven't you been there lately? The Indians might have done a poor job in Kashmir but the Kashmiris had a life; until 1989, when your people stepped in. Now what? The Taliban runs Kashmir. No women on the streets. Opium all over the place. Public whippings. Public hangings, like they used to have in Nazi-occupied territories in the early 1940s. And the Shariat, straight out of the seventh century. Were the Kashmiris better off with the Indians until 1989? Certainly. You destroyed Kashmir. So much for the people.

'Who do you think you are? Allah's custodian? If your belief were at all true you'd know that Allah doesn't need you to punish anyone. Allah created us all, and he can take care of the punishment. Don't you see that your faith is weak? If your faith had been strong, you would have let others make their own way.' He shakes his head and looks me in the eye. 'Tell me, Noordin, do you think you're working for Allah?'

When I cannot find an answer, he turns away. 'Don't you realise, Noordin, that I hate what you've done? Loving you is against everything I stand for. It's against my religion, and it's against my principles. I'm your prisoner in more ways than one.'

Again I cannot respond. The rock on which I thought I stood has turned out to be sand. I take my attention from him for a moment – I think I black out – and he seizes it. He goes beyond his pain, wrenches himself out of my grip, and, in a moment, has me down with the muzzle of my own pistol in my mouth.

He breathes noisily and heavily, for a moment. 'Noordin, you went a little too far with me just now for our relationship to be what it was before. I'm not going to kill you because of the good times we had, but I will disable you enough to get enough of a lead to get away. I don't think we'll meet again, Noordin, and I wish from the bottom of my heart that our last meeting were better than this, but this is what God's given us. At least I can be honest with you.' The pistol rises and falls, and everything goes black for a moment. I hear him scrambling away, but find myself unable to do anything about it.

ᔕ

After he leaves, I lie still, breathing deeply and trying to regain my strength. His questions and statements have stuck in my mind, not just because they seem to be genuine but also because I have thought about these matters for many years without arriving at any conclusions.

His conclusions disturb me. They speak of a weakness of the spirit that I find difficult to accept. Whose weakness? His or mine?

What disturbs me more is that he spared my life. He could have finished me off in that fraction of a second that I lost picking up my pistol. He knew it, and I know he knew it. I found him difficult to attack because of the depth of my love for him. Does he love me as much, to spare me thus?

What disturbs me most, however, is my own weakness, my lethargy in handling Kabir. By and by, I get up and search the flat thoroughly. I lock the door first – just in case there are unwelcome visitors while I ruin the flat – and look in just about every place where he might have hidden something. I break all the bottles in the kitchen and the fridge, tap the tiles looking for hollow spaces in the walls, rip open all the mattresses, destroy the wardrobes, and so on.

Of course there are things to be found. There is a stash of money in half-a-dozen currencies, and gold, all of which I will find useful. There is also a small bag containing four one-carat diamonds, and a bag of opium, which I destroy. There is plenty of liquor in the bar, and evidence that Kabir drinks, though I do not know for sure whether he drinks to keep up appearances or because he enjoys it.

And, in a small hidden cubby hole in the wardrobe, is a small handheld computer. Its battery is flat, but the charger lies next to it. I start it up, and it asks for a password. It's not much use to me because I know little of its technicalities, but I make one attempt to log in, using my own name as password. First I type it in the way I write it in English, with the first letter capitalised. Nothing. Then I try all lower case. Nothing again. Then I try upper case.

Ironically, it works. Kabir's password is my own name, in upper case. There is a lump in my throat when I discover this.

There's not enough time for more experimentation here. I must remove all traces of my presence here and leave before someone catches me. I'm sure they will in the next few hours, or days if I'm lucky. I put the computer in my bag, among my clothes, and move on.

The first thing to do is to find a hotel, to plan the next few steps. Meanwhile, I must also steal a cell phone to talk to my people. And I must find a computer with which to follow up.

I must also assume that Kabir will go to his paymasters, the Americans. They will probably come after me. If anyone from the Indian intelligence agencies intercepts him, they, too, will come after me. I must disappear by then. I have only hours, perhaps a day.

∽

It's the evening rush hour and the footpaths overflow. The light sea breeze reduces the discomfort very slightly.

I am tall and pale by Dravidian standards, but Chennai is cosmopolitan enough. There are plenty of tall pale youngsters on the streets, and I no longer stand out as I used to when I first visited the city in 2001. Plenty of youngsters carry backpacks not much smaller than mine, and I have no trouble merging into the crowd.

Chennai is full of little hotels where I can check in without any documentation. I find one such and pay for one night at the reception counter before a short dark man in shorts and a vest leads me up a dingy flight of stairs to a small room on the second floor. Inside is a bed covered with a sheet that hasn't been washed for weeks, covering a mattress I don't want to think about. I have to be anonymous for the next few days, and this is the best way to do it.

There are no bars on the windows. Around ten feet below is the roof of the porch at the hotel entrance, and the road is another ten feet below that. Getting away will not be difficult; I might stay here a few more days.

Kabir's words stick in my mind. What am I doing? What have I done to my adopted homeland?

I have considered this before. I have thought the Shariat was good, and because it is in place in most of Kashmir, I thought Kashmiris are better off than they were with the Indians, or by themselves. I thought that the lax form of Islam they followed was what weakened them.

March 2021

On this pleasant spring morning, I am in Srinagar to meet Anwar, a Kashmiri Talib, to arrange for the delivery of a consignment of RPG missiles for use at the border, against the Indian border guards. I arrived here in the morning, by road from Muzaffarabad, and have been with my hosts since dawn.

We finish our business, and towards mid-morning, walk in the sun by the Husseini Lake, formerly known as the Dal Lake.

It's the most beautiful time of the year in these parts, wildflowers everywhere. The city has begun to look very different now. The old ornamental gardens are gone, as are most of the houseboats and shikaras. Hardly any tourists come here; the only visitors are businessmen – traders come to buy rice and spices, and now opium that grow in these parts. There is more money in opium trade than there ever was in tourism, and now there are small factories all over where opium is turned into morphine and heroin for sale in cities in India and in Europe. A large part of it goes to Satan America, but the heroin sold there is of a higher grade than the heroin sold in India, and has to be processed in better labs, which are in India.

I am aware of the changes in Kashmir since the Indians left. When the Indians were around, spring brought colour, flowers, and clothes on the street. Now, spring is as dull as any other season. The city has taken on a uniform grey now, like most of Kabul, and many of the old chinar trees are gone. Gone, too, are the colourful clothes women used to wear. Now almost everyone wears dark, sober clothing. There are just a few women on the streets, and the ones we see are accompanied by men, as the Taliban have decreed.

Anwar is young and fierce, and leads a small group of youngsters, all Kashmiri, all proud of their status as young Taliban, itching to exercise their authority on the populace, which they are permitted to do despite the armed and khaki uniformed policemen. They operate much like the Saudi religious police, the Mutawa, except that they wear no uniforms, and need not report to any higher authority. They are free to hand out small punishments on the spot, much like Naeem Shaqeer's gang. Anwar, too, is waiting to exercise his authority.

It's just the same as it was in Jalalabad, where I first saw Shaqeer using his powers on the street. Kashmiris have been outside the Shariat all these years, and it takes a while for them to get used to it. They need time to change. They've had only a few years under the Shariat, and it's been followed rather loosely. I'd prefer to let people off with warnings a few times before punishing them.

As we reach the Hazratbal mosque, I see a teenage girl with an older man, possibly her father, hanging on to his arm and laughing, as I've seen daughters do elsewhere. Her veil rises for a few seconds, and her hair is exposed. Anwar leaps into action, but I grab his arm before he completes his first step towards the girl. He turns to me, anger in his eyes, but I keep my hold on him and he subsides. To anyone else, it would look as if I've put out a hand to guide him; only he and I know what has happened. He senses that, and when I tell him we will talk later, he nods angrily.

I explain to him later that being quick to punish minor offences, committed unintentionally, is unnecessary. He argues that larger offences come from small ones. I tell him that we want the people with us, not against us. He turns away, still angry, but I can see that he is thinking about it. I'm glad. This is a much better man than Shaqeer.

That night, as I prepare to retire, the image of the girl laughing up at her father looms up in my mind. It's as if a hand squeezes my heart; I wish I had a child to look up at me like that. I have refused to think of these matters until now. I understand that I stopped Anwar not because I wanted him to restrain himself but because I didn't want to spoil the moment for the old man and his daughter.

It doesn't have to be a daughter, I think. A son would also do. All the men I know say that they want sons to feed the jihad, but I know that most love their daughters too.

The image of the man by the lake comes up again. He seems to have brought her up with great love and care, perhaps even more care than he has exercised with his sons. What if she is raped? What if she can't find the necessary witnesses to testify for her? How will the father take it?

How can love be so warped?

November 2025

Now I am not so sure. Why now, I wonder, when I am in the middle of the biggest project I've ever been involved in. The answer comes on its own, emerging as if from hiding, from some unknown corner of my mind – this is the best time, because if you change your mind, you can still do something about it.

Think!

I can keep my thoughts at the back of my mind, but the project must continue. It's time now to contact some of the others, in the first group. Last-minute changes in the plan – I have kept the right to make them, on my own, and despite any leaks from Kabir, I can take the opposition off the guard. Surprise, at the very least, is my advantage.

Whom can I trust? After Kabir, I doubt everyone. Maybe Hameed? Abdul Hameed? Friend of my childhood. If he has turned, then the project is not worthwhile. Life itself cannot be trusted.

I must tell him in some way that only he and I can understand. I must tell him to meet me somewhere, sometime, that no one else will understand. For this, I must go back nearly forty years.

Autumn, 1988

We are lost, Abdul Hameed and I. We are not yet in our teens, and have already lived most of our lives in the caves in these mountains. Our point men, looking for water in the valley, have run into a Soviet patrol with armoured backup nearby. The backup, BMPs and some tanks, have arrived and begun to fire at the main body of our group, who number less than a hundred. We hide in a depression… we are trapped. Even as we watch, our numbers dwindle, from ninety odd to eighty, and, at the end of a twenty-round salvo, to just forty.

This battle is mostly long, quiet periods scattered with brief moments of noise, dust, confusion, and the smell of cordite, often followed by screams of pain and the smell of blood. Supplies are destroyed, people die, and the quiet after the noise of the shelling is harder than the shelling because that is when we take stock and each time we do that we discover the enormity of the damage done by their mortars.

But I find a quiet place inside me when the noise and dust and confusion begin. My mind flows with the tide of the battle, and I do things I cannot explain.

There is a crevice in a wall of rack at the south end of the clearing, not wide enough for a grown man to get through, but sufficient for a thin boy. At noon, Hameed and I make it through, and find a dead end just a few feet inside. I come back out, pick up two rifles and run back, noting the position of an anti-tank missile lying by a blanket. I leave the rifles with Hameed in the crevice, and return for the missile. I can't carry it, but by trying as hard as I can, I manage to drag it by one end back into the little cell. There, armed to the teeth, Hameed and I wait for the battle to run its course before we move.

We can watch the group from our hiding place. Our group members are overwhelmed, and the last fifteen-or-so survivors surrender when they run out of ammunition. Their food and water and supplies are gone, and not one has escaped injury. As we watch, the prisoners are led away, under guard, treated roughly, as was expected. But our leader, Shoaib, is badly injured.

He has to be taken back to base for treatment, for the Soviets want to interrogate him.

Minutes after the surrender, only seven men remain in the little clearing – Shoaib and six Soviet soldiers, including one junior officer, waiting for the helicopter to take them to their base camp. The Soviets, in these fading years of their version of communism, have few helicopters, and they send an Mi-24 gunship to collect their men and their prisoner.

The helicopter takes its time arriving. We wait for more than half an hour before we hear the throb of its engine. We see it settle, like some large clumsy insect. Hameed and I have a name for these craft – eagles. Like eagles, they fly high up, looking for prey, and when they spot something, swoop down for a kill.

The helicopter is loaded in less than two minutes; the Soviets do not want to hang around. From our hiding place, we see the doors snapping shut, and the helicopter, now heavy, rising slowly. I have the anti-tank missile ready, and braced against a rock wall. I have read the manual and know how to aim and fire it, though I have never done it before.

When the helicopter is thirty feet up, less than a hundred yards away, I get it in the cross hairs of the sight, and let it fly, as I have seen my elders do. The missile, a heat seeker, locks in on the helicopter's exhaust; and less than a second after I fire it, the helicopter is in flames. It falls in slow motion, reluctantly, bursting into flame as it does, with secondary explosions from the ammunition stored in it.

It crashes and burns. Two men emerge, their jackets on fire, limping.

They are the enemy, wounded or not, and they have killed my elders. I take aim and finish them off.

Night is upon us when we leave our hide. There is water in the valley, and we drink. We go to sleep hungry. At first light, we leave, following the stream, hoping to find a village by the water. We leave our weapons behind; if a Soviet sees us, we are boys who got lost.

We find no Soviets, but in the heat of the afternoon, we find a shepherd, who takes us to his village. There, we find friends of friends of friends, food and shelter, and some rest. Two days later, we are back in the caves, and I lead a small group of men to where I brought down a helicopter gunship. I show them the hiding place, and the launcher still there. I tell them what I did with Hamid's help, and how.

The evidence is in front of them. They hear me out in silence. Later, I discover that it is awed silence. From then on, grown men listen to me. They will not forget the day I brought down a helicopter.

Neither will I. It is a Saturday, the day after jumma, the day I brought down an eagle.

Hameed will remember it.

November 2025

I formulate the message in my mind. I will meet him at the day and time I brought down the eagle, outside Chennai Central Railway Station. He arranged a meeting for me outside Lahore Central back in 2015; no one who knows of that meeting is alive now. He should remember that. The time and day I brought down the eagle, the place at which he arranged the meet for me in 2015, but in Chennai instead of Lahore.

It takes me nearly half an hour to find a public telephone – they're increasingly difficult to find these days – and make the call to a relay who will then pass the message on to a series of other relays before it reaches Shahpur. It's going to be a day or two until Hameed gets it. Today is a Friday, so he has a week to make it. It's not much, but he will make it.

When he comes, I will speak to him without reservation. He will know what is best. He considers me inferior – weaker physically and mentally and less gifted with a firearm – but he is more honest with me than anyone else can even dare to be.

Seventeen

Ganesh

Getting into the DGCA will mean using up some of the leverage I've accumulated so far. But there's more.

Sridhar, the insomniac alcoholic physicist, told me quite definitely that if anyone's got any chance of getting into a nuclear power station and overriding safety mechanisms to let radioactive material loose, he's got to have someone inside – someone with training. Our nuclear power stations are all run by the government. Somewhere in the government is a database of all employees of these stations. I need to get into that.

Security at power stations is handled by the CISF, the Central Industrial Security Force. Senior officers in this are typically IPS officers sent to the CISF by rotation or by choice. Tenures in the CISF can be long – an IPS officer could choose to spend his entire professional life in it, but that's rare, because promotions only take you so far. Most officers spend less than ten years in it. I know only a dozen-or-so IPS men with 'weaknesses', and as far as I know, none is in the CISF.

I'm sure Anil will know someone in the CISF with enough pull to get me access to that data. There must be hundreds of

PhD-type scientists involved in the country's nuclear energy programme. I call him at seven in the morning, from a public telephone near my house. 'What do you want from me at this time of the day?' he asks, irritable because I woke him up.

'It's urgent,' I tell him. 'You know me well enough to know that I wouldn't disturb you without sufficient reason.'

'Alright,' he says. 'What?'

'We need to meet.'

'I won't ask why. Where? When?'

'As soon as possible. Wherever you like.'

'An hour from now. The hotel where we first met. The coffee shop on the ground floor.'

'Right,' I tell him, 'I'll be there.'

I arrive early, as usual, as does Anil. Even at this time of the day, he's got his dark glasses on. I wonder if he sleeps in them. His manner is pleasant though. 'What?' he asks, sitting down and ordering scrambled eggs.

'I need access to personnel files in our nuclear power stations.'

He smiles. 'What's in it for me?'

'Protection,' I tell him. I've got a disc in my laptop. I turn on the movie player, then turn the machine around so he can see it.

He watches himself in silence, and in a moment his shoulders sag. 'Where did you get this?' he asks. 'It's fabricated.'

'I got it off a SafeWrite I've stashed away somewhere. It's not fabricated. Do what I tell you and this stays with me. Otherwise I'll put it on the Internet, and someone will come calling for you soon.'

He takes off his dark glasses, and for the first time I see his eyes. They're red, and his rage shows. 'You don't want to make an enemy of me,' he says, his voice low but powerful. 'You have no idea what I can do to you.'

'Don't be a fool,' I tell him. 'Get me the information, and go back to whatever it is that you do. It ends there. By the way, I've got more surprises for you. I've got your daughter on another SafeWrite. More recent.' He purples now. I can almost feel his blood pressure rising. I pile it on with a tinge of glee. 'The press will have a field day. Paedophile father, porn star daughter. I've got myself covered. If anything untoward happens to me, like an unnatural death or an accident that leaves me paralysed, all this goes public. So get yourself together now. Get me what I want, and you'll be safe.'

'How do I know?'

'You know how old this video is. I had it made, so I've known about you for all these years, and you never heard a peep out of me. Did you?' He shakes his head, not speaking for fear of losing control. 'Well, I wouldn't have troubled you if it weren't serious,' I continue.

'Do you know what you're doing?' he asks.

'Yes,' I tell him. 'Your job.'

'What do you mean?'

'If you bastards had been doing your job properly, I wouldn't have had to do this. More than this you don't need to know. You need to give me access, safe access. If anyone gets to know I've access to that database and comes after me, this video goes on the Internet.'

'I'll get you one of these days, you know.' His voice is conversational again. He's recovered his cool.

I grin at him. 'Do. Anytime after the year-end. Just hold off until then.'

His brow wrinkles. 'I don't understand.'

'One more thing.'

'What?'

'I need information on helicopters. Private helicopters within the country, and any plans to acquire more. Not Air Force, not government. Private helicopters, parked in private residences or relatively low-security compounds. All over the country.'

'I can't help you with that right away,' he says. 'I don't have access, but I can get it in a few days.'

'That'll be too late,' I tell him.

I can see now that he's getting interested. He's intelligent and has experience. He's figuring it out. 'What do you know that I don't?' he asks. 'And how did you come by it?'

'None of your business,' I tell him, rising.

His eyes are hooded again. 'I will get you, you know. One way or another.'

'You repeat yourself,' I tell him, turning to leave. 'But if you come after me this year, I'll hand the SafeWrites to the noisiest TV channels we have, and put them on the Internet as well.'

'Wait,' he says. 'The best thing for me is that I don't have to do anything but breathe a word about your boast to Gowda. He has resources you can't even imagine.'

I turn. 'Like I said, do what you like. But if you do it this year, God help you.'

∽

Anil arranges access for me on the Internet. All I need to do is get into a website, log on with an ID and a password he gives me, and I'm into the personnel records of all nuclear power stations. I find I can access them by any characteristic – name, age, date of birth, broad qualification, caste, present posting, rank, length of service, marital status, and so on. So if I were a matchmaker looking for unmarried men over the age of thirty-five, I'd be able to find the right matches in a few seconds. There are brief histories, too, records of parents and schooling and so on – entire life stories, in fact, depending on how deeply I want to dig.

I've taken a room in a hotel using a false ID, using a computer

I bought a year ago using a false ID with a non-existent address, just in case someone digs out an IP address on the machine. I've been doing that regularly since I started working with Mahipal, to use the Internet with an untraceable computer.

The current roster holds several hundred nuclear physicists, all PhDs, learning and doing research on topics I don't understand. A few of them have police records, all prior to their joining the National Nuclear Power Corporation, all but two for traffic offences, mostly for parking in no parking zones. The two others are for possession of small quantities of hashish. A physicist taking an occasional sniff of hash doesn't strike me as unusual.

Among the data not available are political tendencies. There are hints, but none sufficient for me to decide whether following up on someone is worthwhile or not. When you don't really know what you're looking for, you need to look at the data again and again to see a pattern, and then a break in it. It can be a mind-numbing exercise, but it has to be done, and I do it with these records, starting by ridding my mind of any preconceived notions that might get in the way.

An hour and a half later, there's nothing to show. Then, more or less as a last resort, I look for Muslims among them, and the numbers drop sharply, to a couple of dozen. Most, I see, are from relatively privileged families. Five are not. Three of the five, I notice, two in Koodankulam, are from very poor families, all in Gujarat. The third is in Kalpakkam, also in Tamil Nadu. All three have had their studies paid for by an NGO, Jeevan Prakash Education Trust, based in Gandhinagar. They haven't stayed together after the trust found them; they went to different schools, lived with different foster-parents, but, after going to some very well-known schools, ended up at the same university, and lived in the same hostels, studied at the same college, and completed their doctorates within a year of one another.

Strange, how close their lives have been after the trust got to them.

I look up the trust on a search engine, and discover that it no longer exists. It went defunct soon after the three finished their master's degrees. The last managing trustee was a minor politician, brother of a major Delhi politician. He stole almost all the money coming in for a couple of years, got caught cooking the books, and, with his brother's help, fled the country to avoid going to prison. Someone caught up with him in Dubai and shot him dead. I can't make out whether or not there's a connection between his misdeeds here and his murder in Dubai. All this was more than eight years ago, and news archives carry conflicting reports.

His predecessor was a TV actress who, when she couldn't resurrect a failed career, tried to switch to doing good, but didn't do too well at that either. It was during her stint that these three young men were picked up. She, too, died early, in a car crash.

There are rumours that the money for the trust came from a London-based charity that also supported some questionable Muslim causes. From one of those increasingly common charities that devote eighty percent of their money to legitimate causes and the remaining to causes only they think legitimate.

The plot, such as it is, thickens.

The trust wound up a couple of years after the boys finished their master's degrees; two of the boys were bright enough to earn government scholarships for their doctoral work; and the third good enough to go to MIT. The trust's paperwork must be destroyed by now. There's nothing to be found about the trust's part in their lives.

Karim, Rustom, Adnan – they weren't even in their teens then, bright young lads from poor families, with little hope of doing better than their parents or their siblings. Someone opened a door for them all those years ago, which means all this came up all those years ago. Back before the second partition, probably when India and America signed their deal for nuclear cooperation. Somebody had it figured out then. Points to an agency with a long-term scheme, something more than the world domination thing that some Taliban talk about. Someone with intelligence, and money, and the will to find this NGO and take it over.

It seems beyond Pakistani intelligence. They don't have people with the kind of long-term planning ability that this requires. To find children, bring them up, indoctrinate them, and bring them to learn physics… it requires decades to bring something like this to fruition, and the backing of a very senior man. People in most intelligence services don't look beyond the end of their careers.

That's also why it's not been caught. They've insinuated themselves into the framework of the country so smoothly that no one's noticed them.

The simple thing would be to sequester these three physicists. Two of them are at Koodamkulam, which is probably where they'll attack. Koodankulam is right at the southern tip of the country, the power station less than twenty miles from the Vivekananda Rock Memorial at Kanyakumari. A few towns nearby, notably Tirunelveli and Nagercoil, have people wealthy enough to afford a helicopter.

They'll take a helicopter from somewhere near one of these towns, fly in under the radar, directly into the grounds. The physicists might even smuggle a couple of men into the compound, it depends on how lax their security is.

There is a last resort – I can take the physicists out. I would do that if I were sure they are the ones and that they're the only ones, but I'm not sure of that either. I have reservations mostly because I found these guys so easily; they might be a decoy, with the real insiders concealing their tracks some other way. There has to be a way to get more on the plan.

I need a policeman, someone senior and honest, with some resources at his command. That eliminates all my contacts – not one of them is honest. I give up on that lead for the time being and move homewards.

Sushil's taught me one thing – if you don't mind a bit of heat and dust and wind, a bike is the quickest way of travel in this city, with its wretched public transport, which is designed for the traffic load of ten years ago. Today, with no formal meetings coming up and no objection to heat and dust, I've been using a bike – a 10,000-km old green 450cc Kawasaki Ninja – to go to the hotel. It saves fifteen to twenty percent of my travel time and a whole lot of petrol, though I sweat a bit. I use a jacket and gloves and a full-face helmet with a dark visor to stay anonymous. I'm not particularly tall or fat or thin, just average, and in my very averageness lies the advantage of invisibility.

As I ride slowly out of the parking lot under the hotel – no one has parking on the ground level these days – I'm preoccupied with the thought of finding an honest policeman, but some old habits assert themselves. One thing I learnt from Granddad, and later from my sniper training is to spot patterns. There are patterns everywhere, and, when you get used to them, a break becomes very visible. In my rear-view mirror, I spot a small Fiat following carefully, staying within sight but a few cars away.

This bike sticks out in this sea of cars, making it easy to follow. As I watch the Fiat, another bike comes into view, a black Honda, its rider in a jacket and gloves and a full-face helmet, just like me. It doesn't make him completely anonymous because of his size and his paunch. The Fiat eases off after the Honda joins the stream of traffic. When I wriggle through gaps and leave a few cars behind, the Honda does the same. He's closer now and

I see he has a passenger, equally anonymous in a jacket and helmet, but with no gloves. His hands are tucked into his jacket.

They've been watching me. Anil's probably spoken to Gowda, and these are his men. I wheel into a mall with a large parking lot for bikes, and wait a minute or so for the Honda to show up. It doesn't. There are plenty of people around, so the bikers won't try anything here. I take the elevator to a food court on the third floor, duck into a service door, and wait ten minutes before emerging into the concourse. No trace of the jokers on the Honda. I go back down, decide to dump the bike, and take a cab home.

At home, which is a flat in a block with security that I've arranged to my satisfaction, I call Anil. 'Call off your dogs,' I tell him. 'Otherwise someone's getting hurt. And I've put the SafeWrites in a bank with instructions on what to do if something untoward happens to me. So just pray nothing happens, otherwise you and your daughter are going to be porn stars.'

He gobbles a little, and I imagine his face going red. 'They must be Gowda's men,' he manages a few words, finally.

'Then tell Gowda I have a SafeWrite on him, too.'

'Do you?'

'Yes.' I don't, but a man in Anil's position is easy to fool, and he can persuade Gowda better than I can.

A pause. 'But what if you have a real accident?' he manages another few words.

'That's what I told you earlier. Pray it doesn't happen. Tell Gowda to pray, too.' I hang up.

Eighteen

Thomas

December 2025

I spend an hour preparing the paperwork for a trip to Bengaluru, to visit my colleague Anil Krishnan and the colonel. I line up a couple of meetings with senior policemen in Bengaluru, speed the paperwork through, and take the night flight; one of the advantages of the position is that the state-owned airline will always make room for you, even if the others won't. I send word ahead of my arrival, and tell them that I need to be picked up at the airport.

I have bought a few cell phone sim cards under false names – names of people who have died or moved out of the country. The politicians have never been serious about a UID system under which every citizen has something like a social security number, so the system, while it exists, is far from comprehensive or watertight.

I call Anil Krishnan, on the cell phone number I got from the office. He picks up at the first ring, and I introduce myself. 'Can we meet?' I ask.

'Of course,' he says. I am, after all, senior to him in the service, and he has the toady's warmth. 'When and where?'

'Now, if it's not too late?' I ask. 'Anywhere at your convenience?'

He replies after a moment's silence. 'It's not too late. Would you mind coming over to a hotel?'

We decide to meet in half an hour at the bar in an upscale hotel in the heart of the town. I get a car, and, in the light traffic, get there a minute or so early. I know Krishnan's face from his photographs, but see no one like that in the dimly lit barroom. As I look around, a man approaches me, and when he gets within range, I see it's Krishnan. In his shirt pocket, he carries a pair of what seem to be aviator glasses; I wonder why.

We find a quiet table – it's crowded – and I order. The waiter seems to know what Krishnan wants – he must be a regular here. After the preliminaries, I come to the point. 'Do you know a retired Army type called Cariappa? Ganesh Cariappa?'

Krishnan nods, but I can sense he is tightening up. 'He came to me a couple of times after he retired.'

'Would you mind telling me why?'

Krishnan smiles and waves expansively. 'Of course not. He had quit the Army and was setting up his own business, a security concern. My cousin, who used to serve with him, sent him to me for leads.'

'And did you give him any?'

'One does what one can,' he replies. 'For goodwill.'

And a percentage, besides post-retirement options. 'So you've been in touch with him for some time?'

'Yes.' He shrugs. 'It's a sad story. He lost his wife and parents in the bombing of the Pegasus Mall. His daughter came away unhurt. But she died in a road traffic accident a few years later. Cariappa's alone now.' He pauses again. 'Why the interest?'

'Do you think he might be involved with any of these Hindu extremist outfits? The wild-eyed saffron types?'

He smiles. 'No. I don't think so. The man's too rational to get into any fundamentalist movement, and too good a businessman. I helped him out in the beginning, but now he's got a good name for himself and his company.'

'I've heard of them. They're supposed to be good. What about the death of the owner of the bus?'

Krishnan smiles again. 'A car crash, that's all. They went off the road at a hairpin. There didn't seem any doubt about it. And the man had plenty of enemies, not just Cariappa.'

'He never threatened you, did he, over that investigation into the bombing?'

He laughs now, softly, but the amusement seems forced. 'I was too valuable to him. He's a good businessman, like I said. Besides, I warned him off.' He takes a long sip from his glass. 'Did you come all the way here to check him out?'

'No, I have a few meetings lined up. But I'm curious about this man. There's something that doesn't quite fit.'

'I have a cousin who served with him in the Army. He was Cariappa's batchmate at the Police Academy and has served with him for six years. They're still close. My cousin's stationed here, with the MEG, a full colonel now. Would you like to meet him?'

'No. Your input is sufficient. I don't think I'll waste any more time on the fellow.'

'Good,' he replies, picking up his glass. 'All the best with that.'

Krishnan himself is well connected and intelligent. He must have some inkling of what Cariappa is up to, but isn't letting it out. I suppose I'd better speak to Cariappa.

After a farewell drink, I leave Krishnan at the hotel. All the waiters seem to know him – no honest officer with a wife and children, and no independent income can afford to frequent a hotel as expensive as this. He has made money, no doubt, but who am I to judge him on that?

I'm wondering whether to chase Cariappa tonight, at this awkward hour. I check my mail in the car, and find one important new message, from the field office in Chennai. It seems that one Ahmed Kabir, under surveillance for the last few weeks for associating with people who might be aiding terrorists, has been involved in a traffic accident – he was hit by a car as he ran across a street. The driver of the car, a lady, was busy talking on her phone and didn't see Kabir step out on to the street.

Kabir had $20,000 in cash in his backpack, and an automatic pistol from which the serial number had been removed. He was not coherent long enough to account for it. He is now unconscious, has gone into surgery, and will not be available for questioning for another twenty-four hours. There are so many different organisations trying to do damage here that it's very unlikely that Kabir has tied up with whatever Asif was up to, especially since they're in different cities, so I send back a message saying that I will be there the day after next to question the man, and that I am to be sent transcripts of any interrogations before I get there. Whether he is connected to Asif or not, I will be able to deal with him better after I speak to the colonel.

I find myself thinking about the man with some respect. If indeed he's been behind the removal of Asif's body from the morgue, it's likely that he sent the boy in there undercover. He is well off; he can certainly afford to send in another man or two undercover, so is this Asif the only one? If he did send Asif undercover, he's done better than the police have in all these years. He's found a weakness and has capitalised on it.

I tell the driver to stop, get out, go to a shop, and, offering a hundred-rupee note, ask if I may use the phone. The owner pushes his set across, and I dial Cariappa's cell phone number.

His voice is completely neutral. 'Hello?' he says. The unfamiliar number on his caller ID display has probably got him thinking.

'Colonel Cariappa?' I ask. 'Good evening.'

'Good evening,' he says. 'May I know who this is?'

'My name is Thomas,' I tell him, 'and I'm with the National Intelligence Agency. I'm in Bengaluru for some meetings which will keep me tied up all of tomorrow, so I was wondering if you could find time for me now.'

'Now?' A pause while I suppose he looks at his watch. 'It's well past ten at night.'

'Now would be perfect,' I tell him. 'I can drop in at your place, and we can chat. Of course, I could also invite you to our field office here, where we can have our chat, but perhaps the environment wouldn't suit you so well.' In my voice is a hint of thumbscrews – pure fiction, of course – but the threat seems to work.

'All right,' he says. 'Come now. Bring some ID.'

Twenty minutes later, I'm at the door of his flat, having passed through a metal detector in the lobby, after having Cariappa view me and my identity card through a video camera. A peephole opens first, then the door. Cariappa stands in the doorway, holding out his hand for my ID again. I give it to him, and he inspects and returns it before leading me into his austere home.

There's little furniture, but whatever there is looks very comfortable. I sink into a large armchair without waiting for his invitation, and he settles down facing me across a coffee table. 'What brings you here at this time of the night?' he asks.

'Curiosity,' I tell him, 'and a missing body.'

His eyebrows rise. 'What body? And what might I have to do with it?' he asks.

'Let me tell you a few things,' I tell him. 'Then I'll ask you a few questions. If we get through all that without trouble, I'll go away and never bother you again.'

'Alright,' he says. 'Let's get it over with.' I notice he's very still, and when he does move, he moves like a cat.

'To start with,' I tell him, 'I know that you got the fake Asif's body out of the morgue in Hyderabad. I've done some follow-up, and I know that you had Asif cremated here two days later, in the presence of his sister, who came in from England for that. I also know that you killed the owner of the bus that knocked down your daughter, and rigged it up to look like an accident. Right?'

'Let's say for the time being that you're right,' he says. 'You have no evidence, do you?'

'No,' I reply. 'Only gaps and coincidences. I'm sure I could get some circumstantial evidence at least, from interviews with the real Asif's people and the fake Asif's colleagues, but the forensics must be more or less destroyed by now. In any case, I haven't come here to take you to task for all that.'

'What have you come for, then?'

'You and I know that something ghastly is going to happen,' I tell him. 'What, when, where, and how can we stop it?'

'What makes you think I know anything of the kind?'

'You put Asif in there undercover. He must have found something, otherwise they wouldn't have killed him. Did he tell you anything?'

'Why should I trust you?' he asks. 'If you're like any of the police officers I know, I'd rather jump out of that window there than cooperate. I'm not going to talk to you. Do what you like. Call up your men. Arrest me. Whatever. But I won't come easily.' He sits back.

'I'm not here in any official capacity. I arranged a few meetings for tomorrow, but I've come all the way from Delhi to see you. None of this is official. I know what you're doing; I've come to help you. I've been sitting in Delhi putting two and two together, and the four tells me something is due, and it's slipped past all our barriers. You and I together, we have a better chance than you alone, and possibly better than the establishment, with all its creaky systems and leaky people. That's all.' I, too, sit back.

'Why?'

'I feel I must, that's all. I owe it to what's behind whoever's paid my salary these last few decades.'

'Would you like some coffee?' he asks, loosening up just a little.

'Yes, please.'

'Run-of-the-mill good coffee or something really special? The special has bite.'

'Run-of-the-mill, then. Thanks.'

A few minutes later, he hands me a fragrant cup. 'From your own plantation?' I ask.

'Yes... You did not tell me what put you on to me.'

I sip. It's good. 'A series of coincidences, your history, your present occupation. Patterns.'

'You must have found characteristics of the killings, and dug up my background. I've been waiting for a visit from the police for some time now. As for catching me, it helps to have access to some databases...'

'More or less. And a bit of luck. The man who did the autopsy on Asif is an old friend of mine, a professor of forensic pathology.'

He nods. 'What if we do this? Let's say we get through this bloody business that you say lies ahead. Then what? Do you haul me in for questioning about that series of coincidences?'

'No. God knows my own past isn't blameless. We'll let it lie. Besides, I really don't want you after me.'

'Okay. So let me tell you what I have. It's very little information, and a hunch.' He tells me of what Asif has given him so far, and his other informant – no personal details of this other man emerge in the conversation – and at the end of it, I can see that it's very thin, but it does make a kind of sense. Especially the bit about the physicists. 'What do you have?' he asks.

'Nothing yet,' I tell him. 'Any idea when this is going to happen?'

'If it's going to be in the near future, it'll be the Christmas-New Year week or Republic Day. From what I know, it could be either or something completely different.'

'Any ideas on who's behind it?'

'I know who's leading the attack – a guy called Noordin. An Afghan, a mujahid from Soviet days. They think he's some kind of superman.'

'Who's planned it out, figured out the money, the channels for paying for the physicists, all that long-term stuff?' he shakes his head. 'Could be some guy sitting in some town in Pakistan, maybe Islamabad. Someone in their military, because no one else has the kind of long-term vision that this requires. Possibly an ISI guy, serving or retired. Must be pretty high up to plan something as big as this, probably a general or at least a brigadier. Could be a chief or former chief of their operations directorate. That's a brigadier. Get lists of their officers out of our intel files, and we'll see if there's someone we can pin down. It has to go pretty far back. The time line should eliminate all but a handful. But I'd say these guys didn't start it all. That would have come from outside. I don't think anyone in their set-up looks twenty years ahead.

'If we get through this, then I'm going after whoever is behind this.'

'I've got some access to RAW files. Let me see if I can help.'

He comes back to the present. 'That might be useful. About the helicopter, get a list of all civilian helicopters around Koodankulam. Might be a magnate or two who has one, or maybe a politician. These days it's a status symbol.'

'That I can do.'

'My guess is that they'll have three groups. One, physicists inside the reactor complex, people who know what to do with the nuclear cores. Two, people they infiltrate from the helicopter, who will enter the compound and disable security systems at some entry point. Three, a larger group who will enter, get through the security apparatus, and take control.

'It's complicated, but there's no simple way to get into a nuclear power station anywhere.'

'How do we stop it?'

'Just us? No other help?'

'I don't know. Unless we have more information, no more.'

'The simplest thing would be to block off the infiltrators. Shoot the damn helicopter down.'

'That'll likely kill everyone on board. What if they take hostages?'

'Take them on the ground. Before they take off. More complicated, riskier, but we can try to minimise civilian casualties.'

I can't help smiling at that. 'Obviously you don't think of yourself as a civilian.'

He looks strangely at me. 'No. No, I don't. I can take care of myself, after a fashion. I'm familiar with cleaning up after violence.'

'Miss the Army?'

'Sometimes. Less now than before. They have systems to help you deal with loss.'

'I can see that.'

'What chance do we have?'

'A good chance of stopping it. It's the getting away afterwards that's going to be tricky.'

'What about weapons and so on?'

'I have some, and can get some more. Enough, I think. Look, these little helicopters won't carry more than four or five people. If we take them by surprise, we can throw their timing. Enough to get the security on the ground going.'

'Just the two of us?'

'One more possible. A youngster. The one who got me some of the information. But we assume it's just the two of us.'

'Can't we just tell the local police to watch out?'

'Based on what? Our conjectures? Besides, I wouldn't be surprised if there's a leak in our intelligence services. You tell a colleague some of these things and it could all just get back to the invaders, and then where would we be?'

'Local police, I said. Not the higher-ups. An anonymous call.'

'That'll get some constable driving by. One more casualty, that's all. I don't think they'll have the systems to deal with an attack like this. Not, say, a hundred kilometres from the power station.' He smiles. 'But we need to know when they plan to hit the place. Without that, all our planning is just pie in the sky.'

'Right. I'll get you the DGCA lists, in any case. Anything else?'

'What if there are two – or more – private helicopters in the area? Of the same type we're looking at?'

'I don't know... We'll have to see who's more vulnerable, who's more likely to lend his helicopter to someone for a bundle of cash, and so on. The first thing we do is compare security arrangements. The timing will certainly matter. When do you think they'll hit?'

'We have to find out. I guess it'll be around Christmas. During the week after, when everything is closed down, and people by and large are off the guard.'

'Yes. I'll see what I can do.'

'If we can find out about the helicopter, we're fine. The worst case is that I get someone to camp near the gate every night until the attack happens.'

'We'll see.'

∽

Back in my room, I can't sleep. Cariappa has been a surprise, but not quite. He is competent, apparently casual and light hearted, but very thorough and very committed. He seems to take my presence at his side for granted. I haven't a hundredth of his experience with violence, or its aftermath.

I last held a firearm outside the firing range many years ago, in 2004, when I led a team that raided a house where a Lashkar man was hiding out.

November 2004

November can be one of the most pleasant months in Delhi, not too cold and not too warm. At this time of the year, the action shifts out of Kashmir – which is too cold – to northern bits of India, and, despite the pleasant weather, we are on high alert. I am in a tedious meeting when the emergency call comes – there is information that an injured Lashkar operative is holed up with a sympathiser somewhere in South Delhi.

The informant is a middle-aged surgeon, one Dr Khatri. He claims to have been waylaid on his way home from work, at about midnight. He was blindfolded at gunpoint, and then taken to a location he can't identify, a private home, where he operated upon a bearded young man, no name offered, with a bullet lodged in his hip. In a half-an-hour procedure conducted on a dining table in a most unsterile atmosphere and with only the relatively crude anaesthesia that he himself could administer, the surgeon removed the bullet and dressed the wound. He was then told that his daughter would be killed if he didn't keep his mouth shut, knocked out cold by a blow on the head, and then dropped off near a bus stop in Najafgarh, some twenty-five kilometres away from his hospital.

He woke with a headache, in a strange place, just before dawn, but managed to find a taxi. The driver hesitated to take him in, but changed his mind when the doctor showed his identity proof.

At the sympathiser's home, Khatri had displayed some initiative. His kidnappers, not used to kidnapping, had only taken his phone, and not his wallet, which held a small pencil. Khatri used the pencil to write a note on a sheet of toilet paper. He transferred the cards and ID in the wallet to his pocket, wrapped the wallet – with some cash still in it – in the toilet paper note, and managed to toss it out of the barred toilet window with his fingers. The note simply said, 'Keep the wallet and the money, but call 9101010011 and tell whoever picks up the phone the place where you found this. Please help!' The number in the note was his wife's cell phone number.

A sharp-eyed ten-year-old boy found the wallet next morning and followed instructions, calling from home when his parents were out. He didn't want his father grabbing the money. Dr Khatri, who had been in touch with his friend in the IB, swallowed some aspirin and discreetly led his friend to the sympathiser's home.

The man in the IB put the data together and concluded that the injured man was Abdul Wahid, a member of the Lashkar, shot in an attempt to murder a politician in Bihar. Since the people who had waylaid the doctor seemed to know his route and his rough schedule, besides knowing how to change dressings, the IB man decided that the sympathiser was likely to be a hospital employee. Sure enough, the address was that of a male nurse at the hospital.

Since the case involved a possible terrorist who had fled from another state, the CBI – I, in effect – was called in. There are occasions when the bureaucracy works fast, and this was one, because everyone involved left the paperwork for later and used the telephone instead. Just seven hours after the little boy called Dr Khatri's wife, I am in an anonymous white SUV parked three houses away from the sympathiser's, self-consciously holding a firearm, wearing a flak jacket, and trying to work out the best way to burst into the house.

Sadasivan, too, is there, similarly armed and attired. 'Not sure what to do?' he asks.

'Yes,' I say.

'Leave it to the inspector,' he tells me. 'Believe me, he knows how to deal with this better than us. He's done it before. You and I should watch and help when we can.'

Fifteen minutes later, Abdul Wahid, in great pain from his opened wound, is carried away on a stretcher. The only shots fired have come from the police team – warning shots that have hit no one and done little damage.

December 2025

It's a long time since I've done any criminal work or serious detective work on my own. I've got used to having an organisation, labs and technicians, and officials who file reports working for me. I've become a bureaucrat like almost anyone else in the government – reading files, absorbing data, trying to figure out what will help me and what won't, rather than what's happening. I suppose all senior policemen get to be like that, with a few special skills.

But now, without that organisation backing me up, I am at a loss. At point nonplussed.

Just then, it hits me. I know the man I need to talk to – Sadasivan. I'll call him as soon as I talk to the man in Chennai. And finding him is easy enough, as I'm discovering, thanks to my friend Ajmal, who opened up the various databases for me.

Nineteen

Noordin

December 2025

Abdul Hameed meets me at the right time. We embrace outside the bookshop. For this meeting so far from home, we are both clean shaven and dressed conventionally, so as not to attract any attention, in jeans and T-shirts, and we speak English. Two lean, graying, fiftyish men dressed thus and speaking English hardly stick out even in Chennai, even if they are fair-skinned.

We go to my hotel – I've shifted hotels again since I sent him the message – and find a quiet corner in the restaurant below. Hameed's eyes are dull, not entirely from fatigue. I ask him why. 'They took away Abida, you know,' he replies.

Abida is the woman who looks after his granddaughter, a widow. 'Who took her away?'

'Fareed and his lot.' The enforcers, who come down once in a while from Srinagar to collect money or produce, and to enforce the law. Fareed has enough armed supporters to have his womanising ignored by the elders, and Hameed knows that Abida has turned down Fareed's advances more than once.

'Why would they do that?'

'Blasphemy.'

'But that's ridiculous!' I say. 'Abida's a good, hard-working woman.'

'I know she is. That's why I trust her with Fatima. I've known her since she was a baby. I knew her parents, her husband Hussain, everyone. And it's not just me: the whole village knows what she is.'

'This is strange. How did it come to this?'

'Fareed raped her one night while I was away. He forced his way into her house, stuffed a gag in her mouth, and raped her. Then he went away. She went to the council when she could, and they, seeing that Fareed was the accused, raped her in a different way.'

'What do you mean?'

'They told her to produce four male witnesses to the rape. She said, 'How can I? The man forced his way into my house at night while I was alone and raped me, so where do I get four witnesses from?"'

'And?'

'They said, well, the Book says you have to have four witnesses, otherwise you're lying, and the penalty for lying like this is death. It's like blasphemy.'

'What could she do?'

'Nothing. They gave her four days, and of course she couldn't produce witnesses. So now she's on trial for defaming Fareed. Knowing that bunch of old men, they'll finish her off just to please Fareed.'

'I'll try to get this sorted out when I get back there.'

'She won't live that long.' Hameed looks dispirited. 'No, Noordin, no. All I want you to do is promise that you'll look after Fatima. No matter what happens to me, you look after her.'

I'm tempted to tell him I myself haven't very long but seeing the frozen look in his eyes I have to agree. 'I promise,' I tell him.

'Alright. I have more things to tell you.'

'What?'

'Noordin, Abida was like my daughter. They took her away. They'll kill her. I know one of them… she'll die quickly. What did she do to earn death, Noordin?'

'Nothing.'

'There you have it, Noordin. Fareed isn't the only one doing this. The council is a curse. They make us grow the poppy or whatever fetches them money in the market, and they give us a fraction of what they get. They keep the rest, live like kings, and claim to be defenders of the faith. They do what they like, listen to men like Fareed, and enforce the Shariat on people like Abida who can't fight back. Or Karim, who got flogged for talking back to Fareed.

'They make their living out of the poppy. Do you think that's right according to the Book? I don't.'

'I will go back and talk to them. I'll make them listen.'

'If there's anyone in this world who can make them listen, it's you. But I think it's gone beyond all that now. I don't know what to do.'

'Whatever we do, we do together. Okay?'

'Okay.' For a moment, I see in him the little boy who kept me company in the caves, and I am lost in a wave of tenderness for him. I see the damage that his body has taken for the cause, and I am appalled at the treatment his people have gotten. I am appalled that a bully like Fareed can get away with such ungodly behaviour. But not everyone on the council is like that, a voice tells me. We have to build the empire of God, and though a few will take the wrong route, we will make it, by and by.

I don't know what to say to Hameed. I do now know what

will console him… I hope that the promise about Fatima would have done a little. I stay silent, and prepare to listen, and to think, for if at all I have shared my life with anyone, it is with this man. If there is someone I want near me at the end of my life, it is this man.

Twenty

Ganesh

December 2025

Despite knowing that Thomas of the NIA is after me, his visit takes me by surprise. What he says during his visit surprises me even more. I can't help wondering why he is working unofficially on this one. He seems to be a man with a conscience, and strikes me as sincere, certainly more so than Anil or others of the police service.

His support makes all the difference. We will find that helicopter base, and we will stop the attack right there, before it gets to the power station. I'm not telling him everything though, as he might get tempted to use his official position, and there's no telling about leaks in his office. I'll arrange for some backup in a day or two; on principle, it's better to keep the arrangements as late as possible.

All through the next day, I reschedule meetings and finish off paperwork to be free for a couple of days after that. I sit late, briefing Ashok on matters that might need my attention or his when I'm away, and get home only about nine in the evening. Skipping dinner, I find that Thomas has mailed me a transcript of his meeting with one Rahul Sadasivan, one of Thomas's mentors, who retired from the police service as the deputy chief of the IB. Sadasivan is well-known for turning down post-retirement quangos, living in anonymous retirement near his hometown, but his help is of dubious quality – if he has to tell serving policemen about what he's looking for, then all this work is going down the tubes.

Next morning, despite being short of sleep, I'm up at the usual hour of five, before the first light. I get to the office earlier than usual, finish off some paperwork, and wait for Jai, who arrives at half past eight. I tell her that I'll be out all day, and that I should be disturbed only in an emergency.

For a moment, I lose myself in the faint brotherhood of my partners. They all have some inkling of what I'm up to, especially Ashok, but they haven't said a word. I won't involve them in these troubles, but if necessary, I will take money from them, money I think they'll be glad to give up for the purpose. I'm especially grateful for Ashok's presence, for he's freed up half my time.

I message Sushil, telling him to make himself free and pick a place to meet at noon. He picks a trucker's stop where he knows we can speak without disturbance or fear of being overheard. It's two hours away, but the security makes the distance worthwhile. Twenty minutes later, I'm on the highway going towards Salem. We're meeting a few kilometres past the border with Tamil Nadu; we pick a place like this because it's easy to spot and lose pursuers at the checkpoint.

Again I spot a tail. This time, too, it's a bike, another Honda, a CBR 600 from its appearance, yellow in colour. Two anonymous men on it, the pillion rider is also wearing gloves, but plain leather ones and not riding ones with reinforcements at vulnerable spots. They can go much faster than I can, and the men are fit, unlike the couple of fatsoes they used last time.

I've got a weapon, too, a pistol that I've filed the foresight down so it won't snag on clothing when I draw it. It's a Glock, expensive, smuggled, and, I hope, untraceable. It's got a 15-round magazine, and I've a spare in a holder down my back. I don't like automatics because I don't need to spray and pray.

Do they know where I'm going or are they just following?

If they have lethal designs, I know just the spot they'll try something. Just this side of the border with Tamil Nadu is a lay-by where they park trucks and wait for papers to be cleared before they cross over. There's a football-ground-sized apron, which has anything up to a few hundred trucks parked on it anytime, with no fencing and no guards. Since trucks are usually crewed by two men – sometimes more – there's no real need for guards because one of the crew is by the truck all the time. Traffic past the checkpoint is usually thinner, and since private vehicles aren't stopped at all, the pair on the Honda – it's probably got fake number plates – can get away easily into Tamil Nadu, and return at their leisure in another vehicle.

An option is to get them off on to a poor road where their bike, with its low ground clearance and hard suspension will no longer have the edge of speed, especially with a passenger moving around on the hard little pillion seat. I don't know of any such road this side of the border, so I need to be comfortably ahead at the lay-by, just before Hosur.

I cross the lay-by with the CBR twenty metres behind me and gaining speed, but on the open stretch past the border, I keep myself within a knot of cars so he can't get up to anything funny. We grind up the hill to the Ashok-Leyland factory, the flyover past the exit to the town, and on to the six-lane road to Krishnagiri.

Eight kilometres out of Hosur, when the factories and the

little residential areas end, I drive off the highway on to a side road that cuts through fields and a banana plantation beyond it. It seems we've suddenly gone back two decades because the pace of life here has slowed down, with next to no traffic and the sharp smells of fertiliser borne on the wind from the east.

I have to brake down to forty to keep the bumps bearable, and to keep my centre stand from scraping the ground. The pair on the CBR behind slows down even more, and I see them receding in my monitor. Three kilometres off the highway, we're running along a five-foot hedge around a coconut plantation with pepper vines climbing up the palms. At the end of the plantation is a narrow path to the left, a blind curve. I take it, drop the bike off the path, run back to the corner, and duck behind an old acacia.

I don't want to use the pistol now for the fear of attracting attention. The protective gear they wear will absorb much of the impact of a blow or even a knife thrust, so I have to get them off balance if I want to take them without pulling the pistol.

They come by seconds later, slowing to less than twenty kilometres an hour to handle the bumps, and I step out from behind the tree and hop on to the passenger's back. That unsettles both of them, and they fall, the engine first roaring as the rider turns the throttle, but I'm intent on the passenger, who I know is armed. As he falls, I roll off him and stamp on his right hand in its plain leather glove, then kick him in the groin. The rider is now off his bike and I kick him too, in the groin. By the time he straightens up, I have the Glock out and ready. I bend down and find the pistol in the passenger's belt, a Hi-Standard .22 with a silencer.

'Take off your gloves, helmets, and jackets,' I command.

The rider's gloves come off first, then his helmet, and then, with his assistance, the passenger's, with the jackets coming off last. I don't recognise the men – they're medium-grade toughs, perhaps with some martial-arts training and some discipline. I walk over to the CBR and shoot out the tyres. I take their cell phones and shoot through them, too, with their pistol. I unscrew the silencer and toss it into the field, with the pistol following. I take their wallets, with their driving licences, credit cards, and cash, and stuff them into my own jacket. I make them take off the rest of their clothes and crawl naked under the fence and lie on their faces before I get on to my own bike and start for the highway after tossing their clothes into a small pond.

Back on the highway, I stop to call Anil. 'A couple of goons followed me today,' I tell him. 'I got rid of them. Now take your pick. Who's going to be the famous porn star? You or your daughter?'

'Wait!' he says. 'I told Gowda to back off, and he assured me he would!'

'Who sent these guys then?' I ask.

'Which guys?'

'Get a piece of paper and a pencil.' I give him the names on the ID in their wallets, and the CBR's registration number.

'It's going to take me a few hours to find out,' he says, pleading. 'Just hold on until I get back to you. This evening, at the latest.'

'Okay,' I tell him, and hang up.

I'm twenty minutes late for the meeting with Sushil. He's waiting at a table at the back when I ride in. 'This is the first time you are late,' he says as I sit down across him.

'The unexpected happened. I saw two guys on a bike chasing me. Took a detour and chased them down instead.'

'Where are they now?'

'They must have retrieved their clothes from the pond and walked up to the highway,' I tell him. They must be looking for a public phone now.

He laughs. 'What's to stop them from sending more guys?'

'Nothing,' I tell him. 'I'll be careful, and I'll have someone follow me so if anyone suspicious gets after me, he can let me know with a call on a dedicated mobile line.'

'Sure,' he says. He's matured since we started working together. He's much more relaxed and confident. Overly so? I don't know.

'I'm not sure I should be asking you to do this,' I begin.

'Would you do it in my place?' he asks.

'Yes.'

'Well, then I will.'

'You know most of it. Helicopters. Suits. Radiation. The whole lot. A policeman got in touch, one Thomas from the NIA. He followed up with Mahipal's body. I've been expecting him, but he surprised me anyway. Said he knew some of the things I've been up to, but didn't want to make trouble about that. Said he wanted to help.

'So I told him what I knew. He's promised to get me info about the helicopters and so on. That shouldn't be a problem. The only thing we don't know is when will they hit the helicopter base. That's also not a big problem. We can just watch the place.

'The thing is, we've got no one. There's Thomas, and I don't know how good he is at this kind of thing, and there's me, up against an unknown group of men. Not many – certainly not more than five, that's the number of people that can go on the chopper. But it's still dicey.

'Would you like to come in? You're underprepared, I know, but if you keep your cool, you will be able to help.'

'I'm in,' he says. 'Tell me what I must learn. We have a couple of days, right?'

'Right. So you're in. You're young, you're fit, and you don't lose your head easily, so we're already more than halfway there. If there's a firefight, it'll last only seconds; anything more will attract attention, and we will ultimately lose the game to them.

Everything's in our favour… it's just that I'm not sure whether we can get out in one piece.

'I want you for backup. Thomas doesn't know about you. If he's turned, or leaked, you're still the ace up my sleeve. Okay?'

'Of course. Just tell me what to do. You don't have to go on and on about how bad it can get. I have some idea.'

'Fine. So you're going to practice with different types of weapons for three hours a day from now on. I'll pay for it. Okay?'

My cell phone rings – it's Anil. 'That bike's number plate is fake,' he tells me. 'The number belongs to an ambulance. The license numbers that you gave me are real, but the addresses don't exist.'

'Anyone can fix a fake number plate. Gowda can fix the papers.'

'He does it through me, and I assure you I haven't fixed these.'

'He could have got them done elsewhere. Don't like to think of that, eh?'

He's pleading now. 'I checked. These guys got their licenses outside Bengaluru, and I haven't done any papers outside for a long time. And I checked with Gowda. He tells me they weren't his men. He's pulled them off. He doesn't know what you have about him on your SafeWrite.'

'I'll think about it,' I say, and hang up. Let him stew awhile.

I, too, am stewing. If it's not Gowda's men, who could it be? I have enemies, but why should they surface now? I turn back to Sushil. 'So you go to Virajpet now, where I'll leave instructions that you should be shown around and permitted to use the facilities. One of the guys there, the estate manager, is a former para NCO from our side. He'll show you what you need to do. Okay? And I'm borrowing your bike for a day or two.'

∽

Back at home, I'm beginning to think I haven't thought this thing through, so it's back to basics. There's a complex system of work that the Pakistanis have created here. They did it in Kashmir, and now they're doing it here. They're learning all the time. They learnt methods of protest from the Palestinians in Gaza. They learnt evasive tactics from the Afghan mujahideen. They learnt to run a clandestine nuclear arms trade from the likes of Adnan Khashoggi. They learnt drug smuggling from the Afghans again. They've learnt from the Bangla HuJI, the Indonesian Jemayat, from everyone. They learnt to separate their channels – arms one way, communication equipment another way, men a third way, all with backups, all meeting at a staging point – from armies all over.

That's when I begin to think beyond the immediate operation. These are just the heads that we're looking at. The monster is behind – learning, growing new heads when necessary.

Twenty-one

Thomas

December 2025

I am in Chennai, preparing to interrogate the man they've caught with weapons in his car. He's sustained some injuries in the crash that first got the police interested in him, but he's recovering well from those. I will talk to him in the government hospital where ailing prisoners are kept, in a separate ward under guard.

There is much background work to be done before interrogating a suspect. I like to know the suspect as thoroughly as possible. Information about family helps confirm identities. With present-day computer systems, there's often no need to track down people physically. With the UID system, we can look at bank records, hospital records, deaths, and so on without moving out of our chairs. People have protested that the system gives the government a lot of power without responsibility, and they have a point – people in the government have been known to sell information from the UID database.

There's much that they didn't tell me. Besides the weapon

and the cash, he's got four sets of identities. One is Kabir Ahmed, the name he gave the doctors at the hospital, which checks out completely. Two others are obviously quick fixes – the fingerprints and other biometric details don't match. The last one, under the name Rajesh Shivpuri, is another complete match, biometrics and all. Different hometown, of course, and parentage and everything else. It's a complete set, with a passport and a driving licence and even a bank statement with a photograph.

The Shivpuri passport hasn't been used ever, the Ahmed one has been. Since there's a little more data on that identity, I assume, for purposes of reference, that it's his real one. By that, he's in his late forties, Kashmiri by birth, businessman by profession, and doing quite well trading in commodities. He's travelled abroad several times, mostly to Europe and the Middle East, all but thrice on business. But even a wealthy commodities broker shouldn't be wandering the streets with $20,000 in his backpack.

He has some police record of sorts. He was taken in for questioning once, many years ago, on the possible charge of having helped in financing the explosives purchases by a Chennai-based Muslim fundamentalist group. There are notes on where he was held, and of each session of interrogation, but the content of the interrogations is missing – the voluminous transcripts have not been kept because the man wasn't even charged, far less convicted. But I can see that he was picked up for questioning some fifteen times.

The police have to do that sometimes, to put pressure on a suspect – especially when they can't use third degree – and I've found it worthwhile in my entire career to avoid anything even approaching coercion in interrogations. Repeated polite and persistent questioning often achieves results bluster doesn't, especially when combined with sufficient research to give the suspect that impression that the interrogator can read his mind.

So I look for whatever background I can get of the man.

The picture that emerges from the police files is bare and one-sided – because there are no personal pointers by interrogators – and I have to be satisfied with that. I complete my reference work at the field office before moving on to the hospital to talk to the man. Interrogating a man in a hospital isn't all that different from interrogating him in a prison or a police station. The room they've made available to me for the purpose is just as unprepossessing as interrogation rooms in prisons or police offices are, but it doesn't have the purpose-built furniture. Since Kabir has just had some surgery done on him, and seems to be in pain, I don't think he'll escape; the pair of armed constables at the door should be able to handle any escape attempts, and there's a husky sub-inspector – also armed and ready – beside me to foil any attempts at violence or hostage taking.

He's reclining, arms limp at his sides – two attendants wheeled him in on a gurney, and dumped him on a bed, raised the back to a semi-upright position, and fled – when I finally get to him. The sub-inspector has already checked under the sheet for concealed weapons and takes his place on a chair inside the door after I sit by the bed.

I have never interrogated a suspect like this one. He is sunk in depression, uncaring. His life seems to have lost meaning and when I ask him questions he answers like an automaton. When I ask him his real name, he replies, 'Kabir Ahmed.'

'This is not a third-degree interrogation,' I tell him. 'I am looking for information to prevent a major crime. If you help me, we will see how we can help you. But even if you don't, there will be no compulsion. You can stop talking when you wish, and if you want a break or a glass of water, you only have to tell me. Is that clear?'

He nods listlessly, and I ask him, 'You had four sets of identities on you when we got you. How did you get the false papers?'

'The regular way. You apply for the papers. You pay money as you go along, and you get the papers.'

'What was the purpose of getting all these false identities?'

'Why are you asking me all this? I already told the other policemen whatever I know.'

'You are now in the custody of the police because you have been found with an unlicensed firearm and a large amount of foreign currency in cash. Just that much is enough for us to arrest you on a non-bailable warrant and keep you in custody for two weeks, with extensions up to three months. Believe me, I can outwait you. But if something terrible does happen while we wait, you will be in real trouble. So don't ask me any more questions about why and so on. Just tell me what you can. Clear?'

He nods, and I continue, 'So what was the purpose of those false identities?'

'I usually don't carry all those papers, I just carry enough to get me through.'

'Why were you carrying all of them, then?'

'I was running away. I had to take everything important, so I took all the cash I had and those papers.'

'What were you running from?'

He is silent and I can see the ache in him. 'I can come back later, if you like,' I tell him.

Sympathy seems to work where threats don't. He shakes his head. 'That won't make a difference. It won't bring back what's gone.'

'What has gone?' I ask.

He looks up. 'Okay. I've thought about it. I'll tell you the whole thing. Just give me some water and a few minutes alone.'

'I can certainly give you water and leave the room, but I can't leave you alone.'

'You don't have to leave me alone. Just hold your questions for a while.'

He sips his water slowly, and, when he's done, puts the glass carefully on the floor. 'I'm ready now.' I turn on the recorder and my cell phone as well, so I have a personal copy of what he's said.

What follows over the next few hours is a complex tale, a lot of information that will take a team of investigators months to backup. Kabir really is a commodities trader who had made his pile by the time he was forty in perfectly legitimate activity, for which he has a knack. He told me that by the time he was thirty-five, he was earning more in a month that his father earned in a lifetime of hard labour.

The twisted bits began some fifteen years ago. In 2010 in Dubai, a friend – more of an acquaintance, really – came to him with a sob story. A relative of this friend, one Rahim Khan from Chennai, was seriously ill, and needed money immediately. The money was available, but it was here. Could Kabir carry the money to Chennai and hand it over to the ailing Rahim's parents? He did, handing the packet over to a young man who claimed to be Rahim's younger brother. A week later, his friend in Dubai e-mailed him, thanking him, telling him that Rahim and his family were grateful.

Two months later, the police turned up at his doorstep. They took him in for questioning, not to a police station but to the police headquarters in Chennai. There they told him that they had evidence that he had helped a Chennai-based Muslim fundamentalist group in purchasing explosives. He understood that he had been let down by his 'friend', and that there was no ailing Rahim Khan. Thinking that the simplest way out of his troubles was to stick to the truth, he cooperated with his questioners. He told them about his friend, gave them the address at which 'Rahim Khan' lived, descriptions of the young man claiming to be Rahim's brother, and so on. He told them how to trace his 'friend' in Dubai, and everything else they asked him.

He was let off soon, but the case didn't end there. For the next couple of years, every now and again, without warning, he would be carted off to a police station or to the headquarters, where he would undergo more rounds of questioning. There was no physical discomfort; nothing but the disgrace of being taken away by the police from time to time, the fear that he was in trouble without really knowing it and the possibility that the police might involve his family in the case. He kept cooperating for almost two years, until he found his friends shunning him, his neighbours whispering behind his back, and his business failing.

He began to think that they were picking on him because he was a Muslim. He had never been a devout man, but these troubles turned him devout, and, on visits to a local mosque, he began to meet others who had suffered as he had. The talk of the imams got him to think that he was being targeted because of his religion. He did not, in any case, understand that the real culprit, the 'friend' who sold him down the river, had gotten away easily and would probably repeat his skulduggery with others.

On a business trip to Dubai, where he still had some contacts, he met people who proposed that he uses his business to launder their money. He looked at their proposals in detail, and figured that the risk to him was minimal. He accepted, and soon his bank balance revived, and although his commodities business flagged, his money-laundering operation kept him going. Soon his income was far more than it had ever been.

But now he was hooked – he was a white-collar criminal and his partners abroad made it clear to him that he couldn't walk out on them. In any case, he didn't want to. They 'suggested' he broaden his activities, and he did, and soon he was helping develop a pipeline to deliver illegal weapons into the country… in small quantities, mostly to be stockpiled.

He didn't care about what he was doing. His parents were

dead, his siblings had severed ties with him when he was being harassed by the police, and he wasn't married because he was a raging homosexual. He was still in the closet, and showed no external signs of being gay. However, the talk of the imams, all of whom condemned homosexuality as unnatural and ungodly, made him question the basics of his religion. There he found much doubt.

And then he met Noordin. He had no idea who Noordin was, except that he was a legend among the mujahideen who had freed Afghanistan, and, later, Kashmir. There was a spark between them, and within hours of their first meeting, they were in a relationship of a kind neither had ever known before. They met when they could, savouring their days together, understanding that these days had to be few and far between.

A snake had crept into this Eden in the form of a gentle blackmailer who wanted information. Anonymous, completely forgettable, and extremely professional, the man – he called himself Rudra, as convenient a name as any other – mined Kabir for all the information he could get on arms shipments and possible 'projects', in return for which Kabir got a promise that Rudra wouldn't tell the police about his other activities.

Kabir has been speaking for nearly three hours, and asks for a break. I, too, take a break, in which I ask for a secure room and use my laptop to get on to the database to try to double-check Kabir's story, which sounds genuine. The case is too old though, and I cannot find transcripts of interrogations, which are not retained more than ten years unless the accused is prosecuted.

But he has given me names and descriptions. I will take my laptop with me to the interrogation room and show him photographs of people who could be the ones he's named. It's highly irregular, of course, and there will be a witness – the sub-inspector assigned to take care of my personal safety – but I am past caring about all that.

As I start for the interrogation room, the SI salutes me. 'Do you speak Tamil?' he asks in Tamil.

'Yes,' I reply in the same language.

'Your interrogation is very good,' he says. 'You have seen that man's mind. We are never taught these things. We learn to use other methods. But your method is best.'

'Thanks,' I tell him, obscurely pleased by praise from a junior. 'Learn what you can from observation.'

Back in the interrogation room, Kabir is still sunk in misery as he resumes his tale.

Three months ago, he had heard from his friends that Noordin was up to something dangerous, involved in his biggest 'project' so far. He had no idea what the project is – all he knew was that it was big, in the south, complicated, and would be decisive.

I have two leads to follow up. First, the snake in Eden, the gentle blackmailer; and second, this Noordin. I try Noordin first, asking for more details. Noordin is fiftyish, tall, lean… much leaner now, and weaker than before, probably ill. 'How do you know?' I ask.

'Who do you think I'm running from?' he asks in return. 'Noordin sensed something in my behaviour… I don't know what. He stayed in my flat, and on the third day, he attacked me. I was able to get away, as you can see. If he had been as he usually is, I would not have got away. Besides, he told me that he's dying. He's got a cancer that's beyond treatment.

'Do you know why I'm telling you all this? He's gone, and so am I. Really. I have nothing to lose.'

'Did you have anything in your flat that might tell Noordin more? About the blackmailer?'

'Not directly, no. But I left a computer. He might pick up

hints about Rudra. Rudra is South Indian, and could be any age between an elderly forty-five and a vigorous sixty-five.'

I take Kabir through the photos I have, but nothing clicks. Half an hour into the session, he picks out Noordin, who is on record as an Afghan national settled in the new Kashmir, a hero of the Afghan war against the Soviets, a ranking Talib who has been only occasionally active for the past fifteen-or-so years, but is still one of the most capable and effective men we know. Also one of the most feared.

He doesn't recognise Rudra, the gentle snake, from the photos, but insists that he has seen photographs of the man somewhere, he doesn't know where. That nags at me.

By four in the afternoon, Kabir is drooping with exhaustion, pain, and depression. I give up, and send him back to his fate. He has to be in custody for another couple of weeks, which the magistrate will most likely extend by another couple of weeks, by which time this whole thing should have blown over.

I mail my notes to Ganesh first, leaving out some of the details of Noordin's illness. But it's Rudra who worries me most. Who is he working for? Certainly not Indian intelligence. Certainly not Pakistani intelligence either, because they have direct access to the project Kabir might know about. But then, intelligence has become such a complex game, with freelancers and double- and triple-agents and spies who've turned…

Time to move on. I call Sadasivan.

∽

Sadasivan is as simple and unruffled as ever when I visit him at his home in a gated township some thirty-five kilometres out of Chennai, near Sriperumbudur. When I tell him I'd like to visit him, he says I'm welcome, takes my car's registration number, and says he'll tell the watchmen at the gate to let me in without fuss.

He's been told that I've entered, for I find him by the door of his compact villa, dressed as usual in a bush shirt and comfortable slacks. He leads me into his simple drawing room and offers me a drink, which I turn down and ask for a cup of coffee instead. It's not as good as Cariappa's home-grown, but then it's not meant to be. I sip it slowly while it cools, and, when the temperature is right, gulp it down. He watches. Then, in his quiet way, he asks me what he can do for me.

'I came for some advice,' I tell him.

'I'm a dinosaur,' he tells me, smiling. 'I've no idea what you people have done with technology since I retired, or with forensics, or even with law. I've been out of touch, you see. Vegetating. I have learnt quite a lot about lawns though.'

'It's nothing to do with technology,' I tell him. 'More about looking at matters with a clear mind, which I don't have.'

'What matters are we talking about?'

The secrets I've carried all these years suddenly weigh a tonne. 'It's a long story,' I tell him.

His grin still carries mischief and makes him look ten years younger. 'I have nothing but time now, Thomas. Go slowly. Have a drink. Get your breath back, and your perspective. Then we'll see.'

I take his unhurried advice, sit back, take a deep breath, and tell him everything – starting with Nancy, then Mridula, without naming her, the diversion of money, and Tony McAuliffe. Finally, I tell him about Cariappa and what he's found, about Asif, and the helicopter-borne assault team that he plans to intercept at the staging point.

'I don't really know what to tell you,' he says when I'm done. 'I never did anything as big or as important as this. I can't even begin to think of intervening without official backing. Do you think they might have suborned the owner of the helicopter? If they've done that, they can hide out at the hangar and be fresh when they arrive at the power station. One less obstacle. And one more for you if you happen to hit the helicopter base.'

'We did think of that. Cariappa thinks he can handle it regardless.'

'What do you think of the man?'

'Oh, he's dangerous, resourceful, and committed. You see, he has nothing to lose. No family. He's handicapped because he's alone in this. His business seems to be a separate part of his life and he won't use his resources there for this. I suspect he doesn't mind dying for something like this – he just doesn't care.

'He thinks there's someone behind the Pakistanis, and he's going to follow up on that. I think whatever he is going to find out will be interesting.'

Sadasivan's phone rings, and while he's busy answering it, I happen to look at my watch. I'm surprised to see that I've been here for more than an hour. I feel lighter after telling him all that I have, and find a sense of perspective returning. When he returns, I thank him for hearing me out. 'Don't go yet,' he tells me. 'I might be able to help.'

'I have other work, and, in any case, we can be in touch on the phone.'

'Of course,' he says. 'Go ahead. From what you say, I gather that two pieces of information are crucial to your plans – where the helicopter base is, and when they'll take it. The rest your man Cariappa should be able to handle.'

'Exactly.'

'I should be able to help you zero in on those two.'

'How?'

'The present DGP of the state is an old student of mine. I can ask him to look for unusual activity in some of these places where there might be a chopper. He won't ask me too many questions, so he needn't ever know about the plans to attack the nuclear power station. He might come up with something. He does have an intelligence network, you know. I also know the man who runs the IB field office, another student. That's all I can think of for now.'

'That's quite a bit,' I tell him. 'I, too, would have helped you, if I were in their position. Thanks a lot.'

He seems lonely, and urges me once again to stay for a meal, but I have other things to do now. He accepts that. 'I'll call you the moment I have something,' he tells me at the gate.

As I near the police headquarters in Chennai, I develop a headache, but I choose to ignore it and continue working. Cariappa must have my notes on Kabir as soon as possible, as well as what I got from Sadasivan. I manage to send him a transcript of my chat with Sadasivan, and then call Mridula for some relief from these pressures. The headache grows. When I get to the guest house, I swallow some aspirin and fall into a deep sleep.

When I wake up, it is dawn. The headache is gone but there is a foul taste in my mouth. I clean up and prepare for the journey back to Delhi, to Nancy. And, thankfully, to Mridula.

Twenty-Two

Noordin

20-26 December 2025

We are in place before the first attack, in Goa; travel afterwards will be difficult because the security men will be on full alert. These last few days before the raid, there is little to do but prepare. Eighteen members of the team, about half the total, have all assembled some thirty kilometres north of the southern town of Kanyakumari – travelling as tourists, arriving in three groups, by bus or by cab, each group led by one who speaks Tamil. We live in a large, isolated farmhouse in the windy, hilly country of the Kanyakumari district, found for us by a sympathiser from the adjoining state of Kerala. We have rented the farmhouse for two months from an absentee landlord. To one side of us, along the valleys, are rows of disused wind turbines, remnants of an experiment that the Indian government has given up.

The rest are in a similar house some forty-kilometres away. We will all assemble in the grounds here on the night of the operation, an hour or so after dark, which is at quarter past six in December in these parts.

Hameed is in a hotel nearby. He speaks English well enough to escape suspicion. Immediately after I reach the farmhouse, before anyone else arrives, I visit him. I tell him about the plan, about how there will be a massacre of sorts in Goa followed by this takeover of the power plant and the threat of letting loose a cloud of radiation over the peninsula.

Hameed hears me out, asking no questions. At the end of the recital, he asks, 'Why are you telling me all this?'

'I am not sure how much longer I will live. I want someone I know to share the burden of this knowledge. I have only you, so I told you.'

'You know that knowledge is like toothpaste? Once you take it out of the tube you can't put it back in?'

I grin. Hameed has a strange sense of humour. He grins back, and I tell him, 'Do what you will. I can trust you to do the right thing.' I leave it at that and return to the farmhouse.

I have a room to myself; the rest share the three other bedrooms or sleep in the hall, which is large and airy. My room overlooks the back garden – an extensive young coconut plantation, too young to be harvested. The weapons have already arrived, brought in by a different group, and cached in a shed at the back of the house. There is enough space to practice with silenced weapons without raising suspicion in the neighbourhood. We increase the volume of the television in the room nearest to the road so that any sounds from the back will be further disguised.

The owner of the helicopter has arranged for a van to transport eleven of us to the main gate of the Koodankulam nuclear power plant, and a car to take the other four to the staging point. He will report both vehicles stolen the day before we use them, and leave the town for Chennai immediately after that. Two armed men guard the hangar, and another two the only gate to the compound. They have been told to expect us, and not to resist; we have arranged for one of them to be injured to add verisimilitude to their story.

The regular pilot of the helicopter will not be available to fly us into the compound. Hamdan, one of our groups, will fly the helicopter there. His flying skills are not reliable enough for him to guarantee to get us there in darkness, flying on instruments, but we are willing to risk it; he thinks he has had sufficient instruction to get us there, even if he can't guarantee a take-off after his landing.

In the hall downstairs, Hamdan has set up a plywood model of the nuclear facility. He brought it along in two boxes, in pieces, and took over three hours to set it up. It is detailed, and from the time we reach the farmhouse, we go over it again and again, until we are familiar with the layout, and the points of entry. The helicopter will land on a lawn just inside the gate that leads to the reactor towers, which are a distance away from the administrative buildings, with another ring of security in between.

The helicopter, with the proper ID, will come in on a Mayday call. Men from the helicopter will use an anti-tank missile to get rid of the security office inside the gates, which should draw the attention of the platoon at the main gate. The thirty men outside will blow their way in after this; we expect the security men at the gate to focus on the mayhem at the blockhouse on the inner ring. They will enter in their vehicles – normal thin-skinned civilian ones, taking the guard by surprise, aided by RPGs or small one-man missiles. We expect the men at the guardhouse to have radio communication with a nearby base, but expect that support from there, by road, will take at least thirty minutes to get to the site.

We should be inside the plant in much less time than that – we are simply capitalising on the Indians' tendency to have highly visible security, which makes them concentrate on the perimeter.

Security inside the perimeter is electronic, which Rustom and Adnan will take care of.

We expect there will be at least a company of paramilitary guards – over a hundred men – on site with another two companies available in half an hour. Of the hundred odd men on duty at the site, one ten-man section will be in the administrative block, another ten-man section at the main gate, and a third at the blockhouse. The rest are typically distributed over the facility, in teams of two or four, with no man alone.

We have chosen to hit reactor number 1, the oldest. From what I gather, it is middle-aged – it was completed fifteen years ago, and commissioned soon after. Tower 2 is a couple of years newer, towers 3 and 4 are under five years old, while 5 and 6 are still being tested. The boys have detailed plans of the tower complex, with its water pumps and steam turbines and the reactor itself. They have also been briefed on the safety mechanisms, which come into effect automatically. The most technical part of the operation is the plan to override the safety measures, and that is for the two physicists.

They will not be able to do it on their own, for there are security cameras all over the control room and the critical areas of the complex. There are also people in the control room who might override what Adnan and Rustom do – we have to take them out. Over the last few months, the two have smuggled in tiny detonators, over ten kilos of plastic explosive, and various other things they will need to improvise small bombs. However, if the CCTV monitors catch them, as they almost inevitably do, they will be under attack from about half the security men on site – about fifty or even more. That is where we play our role; we have to hold off the security men long enough to enable the physicists to disable the safety mechanisms and set up a remote-controlled bomb that will release nuclear material into the atmosphere. Once the bomb is set up and the safety systems are overridden, I will negotiate with the government.

Ten of the men are familiar with the workings of pressurised water reactors. Every power station has its own instrumentation and routines, but we have enough material on this one to familiarise our men with what they need to do. There are the two bright boys inside to tell them exactly what.

The signal to the men outside will be the first missile hit on the guardhouse, but we will back it up with a prearranged radio signal. The men will come through the gates and make straight for the entry to tower number 1.

I have set up routines with Hameed, who will be behind us at the helicopter staging point. I send him messages at random times of the day, coded innocuously as always. He replies in similar fashion. I will meet him once to brief him before we actually hit the helicopter base. I want him in, on this operation.

We go out in small numbers, always with one of the three who speak Tamil. We pretend to be tourists visiting the Cape from which you can see the sun rising from the sea in the morning and setting into it in the evening. It's the first time I've seen such a thing; and once again, I find myself amazed at the wonders that God has created.

We meet Adnan on the 21st, the last Sunday before Christmas. He has settled down remarkably well. He knows his way around, and explains to us how to get about, how to get to the staging point, and the security protocols around the helicopter, which belongs to a rich local businessman who also happens to be a member of the state's legislative assembly. It is worth a mention that he is the most successful drug dealer in the state. It is through his channels that the weapons have arrived; he is part of the network and cannot expose us without exposing himself and his two sons to long prison sentences.

We should be secure, but some events disturb me. On the 24th, we have a surprise. My illness keeps me awake, and I slip out of my room to the unkempt garden in front at about four in the morning. I doze off sitting on the cool grass, and wake up to the opening of the gate for a visitor. I can hear voices – it's Raza, talking to Aslam and Hamdan, who are on guard. Aslam stays outside, while Raza and Hamdan go in. I see lights come on, and then more talk. I wait for some time before returning to my room through a window at the back that I have left open to avoid disturbing my colleagues.

When I come down for breakfast in the morning, Raza is at the table, as cool and collected as he is in Islamabad. 'I dropped in for a last-minute check,' he tells me, 'and to give you some disturbing news.' I wait in silence, and he continues. 'Our Goa operation might be blown.'

'Why do you say that?' I ask.

'Yesterday,' he replies, 'a group of men in plain clothes came sniffing around the place where we were supposed to cache the arms. They said they were looking for drugs. When they look for drugs in Goa, they always have people from the local narcotics units, but these were all outsiders.'

'We have a leak somewhere?'

'Either on the weapons pipeline or at the centre...'

Thinking back, I don't understand how Raza got news of Goa being blown ahead of me. He didn't even know about the Goa operation until I told him. Did Ghani Khan tell him or is there someone else I don't know about? It is time to change the topic, to not let him know that I have these suspicious thoughts. 'How did you get here so fast?' I ask.

'I was in Delhi anyway. Scouting. Collecting fake identities. I took a detour, and thought I'd let you know. I got tickets for the last flight to Kochi and then drove down here. Got here early in the morning.'

Hamdan hadn't seemed surprised to see Raza. In this world of shadows, there is no such thing as trust. What is Raza doing here, and why – and how – did he tell Hamdan that he was coming? I smile. Raza is no different from me... I have Hameed looking after my back, don't I? In any case, the important question is, who sent Raza?

I spend the rest of the morning briefing Raza, who seems distracted. It is perhaps the danger; his father once told me that he is not an operations man. But I think it is something deeper. My feeling that this cannot be a Pakistani idea grows. Someone planted the idea in the brigadier's head.

I had thought that the execution of the plan lay in my hands, and mine alone, as the brigadier had said. Now it is clear that there are other hands involved, and I do not know what they are doing.

Again and again, I ask, who gains? A few threads don't fit the pattern of operations that I've seen launched from Pakistan – Sohail's death, for instance. This operation has been planned from outside. The brigadier was only the front end. Who was behind him? The only answer I can think of does not seem possible. I must spend more time on it.

When I am with the others, the adrenaline runs high, but when I retire to my room, the weakness takes over. Now, with all this manoeuvring going on, it is even more important that no one else knows that I am unwell. I am glad I've managed to keep it to myself all this while.

By late evening, I am worn out and go to bed, and, surprisingly enough, go off to sleep. I wake up in the middle of the night, slightly refreshed, mind active, and wonder what it is about Raza and the plan that disturbs me.

January 2011

I am in Muzaffarnagar, preparing to shift my permanent base to a small village in Indian Kashmir. I no longer participate regularly in the Taliban fund-raising activities, which, being based on drug sales, is increasingly repugnant. However, there are other means available now, one being the destruction of NATO convoys.

NATO supply convoys are soft targets. The trucks and tankers are run by local contractors, with hardly any provision for security – a convoy might have one or two rifle-bearing guards, if at all. The border crossing between Afghanistan and Pakistan at Torkham is mostly open to pedestrians, if you like, which most Afghans and North Pakistanis do, you can just walk past the checkpoint without being challenged. Having a laden mule or donkey makes a check even more unlikely. The policemen simply don't have the time to check the IDs of all the passersby, and there are plenty of people higher up who have simply not got identity papers, so the bureaucracy doesn't operate well here.

Getting a team together to hit a convoy is no problem. People used to do it and sneak past the border after caching their weapons. These days, they don't even bother with crossing over because there's no serious investigation except by the Pakistani Army, who are our friends, or ISI, who are often our sponsors.

The great joy in hitting a NATO convoy is having the local population join in when the first truck goes up. But the greater joy is in the money. We can often persuade drivers to lighten their loads – we remove fuel and oil and whatever halal food there is – before destroying the convoys. NATO officials, in the absence of NATO troops to guard convoys in Pakistan, hire men from local contractors to provide security. These are often our men, so we get paid for offering them. They are armed at NATO expense, and they let us through to the convoys, because once a truck is destroyed there's no easy way of telling whether it was emptied first or whether the locals stole the supplies. So we get money and supplies from NATO, and use the money to create more alliances.

I participate in a raid, just to see what it is like. It's far less risky than anything we did in Afghanistan, and I see that the youngsters tend to lax. I am only an observer and happen to mention this to one of the elders, Rehmatullah, who laughs. 'It doesn't matter,' he tells me. 'They'll harden up with time.'

Later, we run into another group in the mountains, among whom are three white men. They all claim to be Muslims, and true mujahideen, but I notice that their enthusiasm for prayer decreases as we march on. They are clearly unused to hardship. Later, I ask Rehmatullah about what they're doing here. 'Volunteers,' he tells me. 'They came in from Germany. They've brought in money, and some medicines. They're weaklings, and when they find the going too difficult, we send them back, but we keep what they've brought. The ones that stay, well, they can continue with us.'

Bombing a NATO supply caravan doesn't bother me... this does. Our leaders are going down the same route as the enemy... doing anything for money. The more I see of it, the less I like it. The more I see of it, the more I wonder how the money for my long-term operation will come through. I know little of finance. I have always depended upon others for it, but now I am beginning to see that too much dependence on finance leads, eventually, to greed. And if we become greedy, how are we different from the enemy?

The enemy is within us.

24-26 December 2025

I know what to do. In the quiet of the night, I stumble upon the right question – who gained the most from everything I've been involved in all these years?

Early next morning, I corner Raza and take him out into the garden where we can talk undisturbed. 'Who sent you?' I ask. 'Who's behind this operation?'

'You know,' he replies. 'My father.'

'This is too big for your father,' I tell him. 'I've worked with Pakistanis for decades. There's no way this would have stayed under wraps for so long. He might have started it but now it's been taken over by someone else.'

'Don't be silly, Noordin,' Raza says.

I cut him off. 'There is no one left of the original group. Sultan was never in it, and, in any case, he is dead. Sohail is dead. Masood is dead. And where did all the money come from, Raza? We used to be short of money for food and medicine, but Adnan, Rustom, and Karim went to college. There's been equipment for me whenever I like. There's been money to train these thirty people, arrange transport, weapons, paperwork, everything. Money to get these farmhouses and to get the team all the way here without being spotted. Money for the Goa operation, for six people to live it up in a big hotel for a week! I don't believe any Pakistani intelligence operation could last so long without being spotted… unless it was run from the outside from the very beginning.

'You and I, we're the only ones left of the original group. I don't know who's running this operation. I'm not. You can't, though you might pull strings at the back. So who is it?

'I'm curious. I want to know who I work for, and what he stands for. I want to see how strongly he's committed to this. So I want him here before we leave. I'm going to put a bomb on you that won't be able to get off, and if he doesn't turn up, you're gone. One of my men will be watching you all the time. Put a foot wrong and you're dead.'

Twenty-Three

Ganesh

15-26 December 2025

My plans grow more detailed every day. The first steps are obvious. We have to stop the helicopter. We have to keep those men on the ground. We have to alert the security at the perimeter of the power plant about the presence of the attackers hunkered down somewhere near the main gate. If I'm not mistaken, they'll have the men ride in open trucks in dirty clothes, pretending to be a gang of construction workers – or even farm workers – in their way to a new project. They'll wander about a little, and perhaps coordinate with the helicopter by coded messages on an open radio frequency. The helicopter will probably send a Mayday signal before touching down in the power plant lawns, with insufficient warning to get more than the company on duty into play, which means that if the pilot brings the helicopter down within a hundred-metres-or-so of the gate, a man-portable missile should be able to take out the gatehouse entirely in a few seconds. That'll also be the signal for the men in the truck to come in.

The obvious thing is to take the helicopter out at the hangar, before it gets anywhere near the power plant. Without the helicopter-borne team, there's little the men on the ground can do.

I'd have preferred something like an RPG to do the job but the helicopter, being a civilian craft, will be relatively easy to bring down – tracer bullets in the fuel tank should do it. Anyone with a little practice and a steady hand can put a bunch of tracer bullets in the right place. This is a civilian helicopter, with no armour and the usual Perspex windscreen and windows, so we should be able to knock out a few of the occupants as well. I have a sniper rifle and a submachine gun and Sushil and Thomas for backup and one of us should be able to get the job done. Thomas's police training certainly involves exposure to small arms, and I've made sure Sushil knows how not to shoot himself in the foot – the day we spent in Virajpet, he seemed to be talented with firearms, with steady hands, a good eye, and a steady heartbeat. He has made himself comfortable even with the big .50 calibre rifle.

Ideally we should get there late in the evening. These guys probably plan to attack the power plant at three in the morning, when the biological rhythms of the men on guard are approaching their lowest ebb. They'll take off in the helicopter maybe an hour before that, though it's only a fifteen-minute flight to Koodankulam.

Sushil, the amateur, is probably the weak point. He's never been in a firefight before, and doesn't know how much of a mess it can be, and how quickly it can all be over. I don't expect it to last more than about ten seconds, if that much. He doesn't know that battles involve mind-numbing preparation, long spells of even more mind-numbing waiting, the short, sharp, noisy confusion of battle, and then the consequences – the ones that are sometimes more hurtful than battle itself.

But he has nerve, I know, he doesn't buckle under pressure, and is fit for his age. He thinks out of the box and isn't afraid of anyone or anything. Just the right kind of combination to come out well. I take him off to Coorg where he can learn to shoot better, and, over the next few days, try to toughen him up as much as possible.

Thomas calls. His contact at the DGCA has got him a list of the two private helicopters in two adjoining districts, Tirunelveli and Kanyakumari, from where the attack might be staged. One is eliminated straight away because it's a Eurocopter, completely different from the JetRanger, on which the attackers trained. This one sits in Kanyakumari, some eighteen kilometres from the atomic power station – just ten minutes for a helicopter flying at well over a hundred kilometres per hour.

The owner is a businessman-turned-politician from Kanyakumari, and has been representing his constituency in the state assembly for the past eleven years. As a businessman, he made large amounts of money, and has been making it hand-over-fist after getting into the assembly. He and his twenty-year-old son have been named – but never convicted – in cases of murder, kidnapping, rape, smuggling, and extortion. Over his years in politics, he has spruced up his ancestral home, set in the midst of some thirty acres of coconut and other plantations, and bought a helicopter on a whim. He's also bought some luxury cars, including a Rolls and a top-end Mercedes.

The helicopter, being noisy, sits in a compound of its own, some 200 metres away from the house, and adjacent to the coconut plantation. From a SafeWrite 'friend' at the National Remote Sensing Agency, I get recent satellite pictures of the house and the hangar.

The hangar is a large shed with forty-foot wide, twenty-foot high collapsible doors that open silently, which is operated by a remote control device, and is powered by a 3,000-watt motor. Directly in front of the hangar door is a square, thrice the size of a basketball ground. From ground surveillance – courtesy Sushil – we've discovered that the hangar compound is surrounded by a nine-foot wall surmounted with broken glass – a primitive system that I would have replaced with a set of small hidden cameras. The owner, sensibly enough, doesn't consider modernisation necessary. Only a few people would know what to do with a helicopter even if they got into the compound.

Since at least four men will enter the compound, they're likely to do it through the main gate – the side gate is from the house – rather than over the walls, because lugging weaponry over the walls is a tricky business and the guards have been suborned anyway. The simplest thing would be for me, alone, to sneak into position after dark, armed with something like an RPG, and blast the attackers as they enter, but we don't have an RPG or anything like it. I think I'd be able to stop the chopper with a rifle, but can't be too sure of being able to handle four or more heavily armed Lashkar-trained men, even with the advantage of surprise. And this place is too far away from Koodamkulam for an incident here to set off alarm bells at the power plant.

So we have to go in. The wall is definitely an advantage. I can go in the back way, lay a strip of tarpaulin across the broken glass, and get Thomas and Sushil in with me. That changes the odds considerably in our favour. The thing is, they'll have something like an RPG, and we have to disable them before they can bring it into play. The best I have is a regular anti-materiel rifle that will deal with the helicopter. It's heavy and unwieldy, with its built-in bipod and clunky ammunition belt, but nonetheless, it is worthwhile. Disabling a helicopter with one shot from a regular rifle is a chancy business… you have to get a vulnerable spot. The .50 calibre, with its vastly more powerful round, offers a much wider range for targets. The best bit is that Sushil knows how to use it, just in case I can't.

I plan to get in early on the morning of the 26th, rather than in the evening, and stay hidden for something like eighteen hours. I've done it before, and can do it again. From the satellite pictures, I can see that there are plenty of trees in the compound, and a shed, perhaps a tool shed, besides the hangar. It is big enough for me to stay under cover. Except for the guards, no one will be around during the vacation, not even the regular gardeners, and the risk of being caught is negligible.

On the 24th, Sushil and I leave – separately though, he on his bike and I by train and taxi – for Kanyakumari. We will stay in different hotels in the town and communicate on untraceable cell phones. I have shown him models of the hangar, told him how to equip himself, and described how we will make contact outside. There is no need for anything else unless something goes wrong, in which case I will send him a prearranged message on the neutral phone.

Twenty-Four

Thomas

20-26 December 2025

It has been extremely difficult to maintain anything like a normal demeanour at work since I got back from meeting Sadasivan, Cariappa, and, of course, Kabir. I spend a few hours with Mridula when I can.

The Goa police get news, through an informer, of a cache of arms hidden by the coast, in a house near Mobor Beach, near Margao, and the report arrives at my desk – on my computer terminal – on the 22nd. It needs immediate follow-up, with Christmas a few days away, and I have no time to deal with it directly. I pass word on to my colleague in charge of operations, and to the Mumbai field office, who jump at the opportunity to do something big. Between them, the operations chief and the officer-in-charge of the field office will take the credit for it. The ops chief even agrees to keep me in the loop as long as I don't interfere. 'Sure,' I promise, and, mystified, he takes my word for it.

They find a cache of small arms, ammunition, and different

kinds of grenades, fragmentation, flash-bang, incendiary, and tear gas. In a separate cache is a quantity of American C4 explosive, with timed detonators and fuses. The small arms, unusually are German and Belgian – because they tend to be more expensive than the East-European or the Russian-makes – and the grenades from all over the world, including South Africa. The people at the cache have no idea what they're going to be used for, but they're to be picked up by a group of guests at a nearby hotel, the luxurious Leela.

I mail Cariappa, using code, as always.

On the morning of the 24th, the operations men from the Mumbai field office zero in on the guests, a group that has just flown in from Kuala Lumpur. Their passports seem valid, but their accents don't match their purported backgrounds, and, despite their claims of innocence and evidence that they have been guests at the hotel before, they are taken into custody. There are six of them, three men and three women – couples.

Soon the plan emerges. They are supposed to open fire at the expensive Christmas dinner at the hotel, where their fellow guests will include many of Page-3 kinds. They are supposed to use the grenades and improvised bombs to keep rescuers at bay, take hostages, and do the best they can to bring the administration to its knees. Needless to say, all are willing to die in the attempt.

Now that we have prevented the attack, my mind moves on to other questions. Where did the information come from? When I ask the Goa police for the informer's identity – on the grounds that he might come up with more information that affects an investigation I have on hand – they refuse, quite politely. I ask them if the informer has helped them earlier and meet a stone wall again. I have no intention of being high handed, of using my position with a central agency to press the police of a small state, but they leave me with no choice. I ask the DG – now happy with me because the Goa op has made him look good, and I haven't got in the way after handing over the information – to check with the National Security Adviser to get the information.

He makes a few calls, and tells me that the informer was a regular, on the payroll of the Goa police. He in turn got the tip from someone who told him the exact spot where the weapons were cached, in a garden. He followed up, found that the place had been dug up, saw men he knew were involved in smuggling weapons, and passed on the information for money.

'What have they said about whoever informed the informer?' I ask.

'Nothing yet, except that the man is credible, and probably an insider.'

'Well, why haven't they followed up on the insider then?' I ask.

There is no reply. He postpones, saying that he'll deal with my questions after the Christmas-New Year week. For the rest of the year, we must concentrate on what we've got on our plate, which is more than enough, thank you.

I tell him I've asked for leave now, and he tells me that I can go ahead, but must get back by the 29th. I don't expect this Koodamkulam operation to go beyond that, so I agree, and take the evening flight to Thiruvananthapuram, and a cab thence to Tirunelveli, where Cariappa is waiting for me.

In the cab, lying quietly on a comfortable rear seat, I snooze briefly, and wake up to find matters becoming clearer. The two outrages, the one in Goa and the one at the power plant, must be connected. The first is a petty act of war, a slap in the face, especially after what the Pakistanis did in Mumbai all those years ago. The second, with its threat of a nuclear disaster, makes war impossible. The Pakistanis can't have done all this on their own. They might think this up but they can't plan that far ahead because whoever is in power has a limited horizon. So someone's been holding their hand, telling them what to do... someone with a bigger budget than the ISI.

Who?

If they're connected, why did they tell us about the Goa plan? If they told us about the Goa plan, will they also tell us about the other one? Why?

The only reasons I can think of are commerce and credibility.

My mind wanders. Even in these mild latitudes, December sunsets come early. The road winds through the hilly country, and the effect is hypnotic. Now we're back to the old question that Sadasivan used to keep harping on. Who gains? Cui bono? There are, unfortunately, too many answers. The Chinese, for instance, or the Bangladeshis, the Nepalis, the Sri Lankans... we've made enemies of all our neighbours, and I wonder how. Our own foreign policy is appallingly incompetent, and opaque, so no one with a good idea can get anywhere near the ministry.

My mind is foggy, and again I sleep, and wake up only at the hotel in Tirunelveli town, a small one near the bus-stand used mostly by commercial travellers, where Cariappa has arranged for me to stay. He will stay in another hotel nearby, and we will meet for a meal at yet another hotel. He is buying us some time, just in case someone comes after us.

I check in and proceed to my room. With a cell phone that Cariappa has given me, I call and tell him I'm at my girlfriend's house – the prearranged code phrase – and he replies that he will probably be there by ten in the morning.

We are to meet for a late supper at another unremarkable restaurant which is a five-minute walk from the hotel. Away from work and family, living anonymously in a small hotel, I feel strangely free on the road, still crowded with people heading purposefully towards the stand or going wearily away from it.

The restaurants are still nearly full, and noisy with conversation. I realise I haven't been in such a place for decades.

November 2020

An interrogation takes me to Lucknow. The suspect in the case is the private secretary of a sitting member of the legislature and former minister. The MLA has been charged with providing refuge to a terrorist, and his defence is that he meets dozens of people every day and cannot be expected to know the antecedents of each of them. He claims that his secretary arranges all the meetings, and that the video footage – not on SafeWrites, unfortunately – that shows him partying with the alleged terrorist has been fabricated.

The MLA, one Shambhu Nath, has a point. Busy people depend on their staff to vet visitors. Anyone who gets through the cordon of private secretaries and assistants is assumed to be safe. There are no inconsistencies between the secretary's story and the MLA's. However, the instinct of the officer who has conducted the interrogation so far is that the MLA and the secretary have been coached by someone, most likely a defence lawyer; their accounts are a little too perfect. My instinct says much the same. I have to pick a hole there somewhere.

This is not just another case. If we find enough evidence to prove Nath guilty, then we have to find a way to prevent this from recurring. It's important that I look at other means of finding an inconsistency.

I do, eventually. I pull up the background on the secretary, one L.V. Prasad. An inspector accompanying me finds that Prasad, who is married with two children, has a mistress, who in turn happens to be married to an influential building contractor known for his short fuse. Accompanied by a lady inspector, I pay her a visit and pick her up for questioning. No paperwork is necessary at this stage. I take her to a safe house – in this case, a government guest house an hour away from her house on the outskirts of the city – and, for a couple of hours, question her in some detail about her meetings with Prasad. I let her know that if she answers my simple questions, we will not inform her husband that she has been seeing another man. She asks about having to testify. I assure her that if she gives me leads to other witnesses, she would not even figure in the case.

From her we discover that Prasad was with her on the afternoon on which he claims to have taken his terrorist friend to Shambhu Nath's office. We also discover that videos exist of Shambhu Nath with the gentleman in question at a wedding that took place three weeks before he claims he first met the man. Access to the guest list at the wedding is no problem, and since the legislator is a VIP, plenty of people remember him.

Confronted with the new evidence, Prasad breaks down. He had no idea the man was involved in anything more than a little 'harmless' drug peddling, he says. I tend to believe the man, and leave the rest of the investigation to the field office.

The local police wouldn't have dared question the wife of the contractor, or taken the line I did. The people involved are all far too influential. As it was, I got several calls from politicians in Delhi telling me to be careful.

The evening before I return to Delhi, I stay at the guest house where I took the secretary's mistress, and take a walk in the grounds carpeted by falling leaves. As dusk comes, my depression deepens. All through the case, I have been weighed down by a sense of futility and my own inability to take a stand on the investigation. I have no idea what will come of the case against Shambhu Nath, or whether what I've done – threatening a defenceless woman – is justified. What overwhelms me is the intricacy of the web of deceit in which we operate, in which I, too, am trapped. From a professional standpoint, I can define the boundaries of cases and declare them closed, but no case stands in isolation. We cope as best as we think we can, that's all.

24-26 December 2025

That same sense of futility weighs me down as I walk towards the restaurant. As I enter it, someone waves at me from a dimly lit table at the back. It's Cariappa, sitting in the back, from where he can look out without being seen easily. I join him with relief. I have few doubts now. From any official point of view, what I am doing is completely wrong, but there is a growing certainty that I can do nothing else, even if it's all futile.

Our voices are drowned out in loud chatter from surrounding tables. This is, after all, a tourist town, with many temples besides the memorial out in the sea, and it's the time of the year when people come visiting. We sit side-by-side, not face-to-face, because speaking across the breadth of the table would mean talking loudly, which we do not want to do.

He tells me what I need to do. I have kept myself fairly fit, and carry no excess weight. I can find my way around an infantry obstacle course if need be, though I will probably be too slow by a matter of seconds. Doing what Cariappa expects of me should be no problem. I have never fired a weapon except on the police ranges, and there my performance has always been just sufficient to pass, no more.

'I believe the objective of good policing is to minimise the need for weapons,' I tell Cariappa.

'Exactly,' he agrees. 'Just like the idea of having an effective army is to prevent war. But then wars happen. So does violence. When it becomes inevitable, do the best you can.'

'I couldn't get six years' worth of your service records,' I tell him.

'I was doing the best I could,' he says. He smiles. 'It's not heroic, or glam, what I did in those years. Most of the time, I was waiting; and the rest of the time, I was afraid. Leave it.'

He deflects praise and sympathy, I notice, and concentrates on the matter at hand. At the end of half an hour, with the crowd ebbing away, we are done. He settles the bill, and we leave, walking slowly along the emptying streets. On impulse, I tell him, 'If I don't survive this, you must do something for me.'

'A message for someone?'

'Not a message. Just visit someone.'

'Sure,' he replies.

I give him the details. 'Shouldn't I ask if there's something you want done in case you don't make it, and I do?'

He looks me in the eye, suddenly sombre. 'Nothing,' he says. 'Nothing. I've got no one.'

'I thought as much.'

Suddenly he smiles. 'Makes it easier, you see. Nothing to lose. So I can just go for it, no matter what... good night.' He turns, and, in moments, to my surprise, has disappeared into the shadows.

Twenty-Five

Noordin

There is a small change of plan. Raza, obviously terrified, has been speaking to someone on his cell phone. I have left all his electronics untouched – it's too late for him to do anything but call off this project. He tells me that his handler won't be able to make it to the farmhouse because there's not enough time, but can be at the helicopter hangar by the time we leave, and will have a group of his own men with him.

I tell him that I don't mind, and that I, too, will have backup. I want Hameed in the meeting in the hangar; he can leave afterwards, if he wishes, or could carry on from there.

In the last few hours, I rest as much as I can, eat lightly, and listen carefully. We leave the farmhouse at sunset in a small van, cramped because each of us is carrying plenty – a pistol and a submachine gun per man, ammunition for the lot, a man-portable RPG with a dozen shells, grenades, shaped charges to blow doors, plastic explosive and detonators and fuses of different kinds, a relatively light anti-materiel rifle for locks and lightly armoured doors and such, communicators, and medical packs with pressure bandages and painkillers.

Over the years, the men have developed a buddy system – they're paired off, and each man checks his partner's weapons and kit. No one usually checks mine, though. I have not allowed it since a careless check of my Remington some decades ago knocked its sight out of alignment, and I missed two crucial shots. But now, I ask Hameed, much to his surprise, to check my pack. He does it quietly and efficiently, without asking questions, and then shows me his own pack for me to check.

Some of the younger men find the waiting difficult and keep fidgeting with their kit; the older hands are used to it. At dusk, it is time to move on. Even though the guards have been bought, something might go wrong. Someone might stop by the gate to chat with one of the guards at just the wrong moment; we could have passersby noting awkward details; or a hundred other things going wrong. The action begins at the hangar, and the tension starts these last few minutes before it.

It also keeps fatigue away. I have been dosing myself carefully, not quite following the doctor's instructions, which are aimed at long-term palliation. I am not particularly concerned about what happens after the next few days, a week at most, so I double the prescription without hesitation.

We will hit the power plant at three in the morning, and the helicopter needs ten to fifteen minutes to cover the distance. We will fly it as fast as it can go – terrain permitting. The area is under radar and satellite surveillance, but the terrain is hilly and the radar is unlikely to amount to much. The flying time is too short for satellite surveillance to catch us and call up air or land support, so we should be safe.

We need to be at the hangar at least forty-five minutes before take-off, so that Hamdan can make sure everything is as it should be. We need only about twenty minutes to get to the hangar at that time of the day, so we need to leave only after half past one in the morning.

The van is ready, as arranged. We have changed the number plate so a passing policeman who knows that the van has been 'stolen' won't stop us to ask for papers. The equipment fits in the back, under the cover, but it's heavy, and the van is awkward to drive. We all pile in – Hamdan at the driver's seat, I on the front passenger seat, and Raza somewhere in the middle of the rear seat – and we leave at twenty minutes to two.

The sentries at the gate are prepared. We tie them up, and Irfan knocks them out, none too gently, for their injuries must be real. We shut the gate, leave the four men to a side, and, as the van enters the compound, we are surprised – a row of floodlights comes on, illuminating the front of the hangar and the landing area.

Raza straightens up. 'Noordin, take it easy. Your man is here.' The hangar door opens a foot, and a dark-skinned man steps out. He has an AK-47 in his hands, but it points upwards, and he waves us on. 'Keep going. It's all under control.'

The man keeps watching quietly, his weapon neutral, as we drive up. As we exit, he lowers the weapon one-handed, relaxing when he sees Raza. We enter the hangar, which is brightly lit, and see the helicopter, painted blue and white, in the centre, with a small glass-walled office in a corner, and supplies and spares stacked along one wall.

Most importantly, there are other men standing by all over the hangar, all armed, all weapons pointed downwards. Two men – one Caucasian, the other Indian – sit in chairs by the small office. As I look around, the Caucasian stands, extending his hand to greet. 'Well done, Noordin. You figured it out. I thought you would.' He is middle-aged and trim, and speaks with a pronounced American accent.

'Who are you?' I ask.

'My name doesn't matter,' he replies. 'Call me Charlie. Or something else, if you prefer. I've been looking after everything you needed.'

'Old Ghani Khan didn't say anything about anyone like you.'

'Old Ghani Khan was out of his depth. He underestimated the amount of money you needed, and we made it up for him after he died.' He smiles. 'There were others in the ISI who wanted to take it over, but we kept them off.'

'What about the Goa operation?'

'What about it? We lost it. There must have been a leak somewhere. We don't have the time to go into all that now. Look ahead.'

There is only one leak that I can think of, but this is not the time to mention it. 'I am looking ahead,' I tell him. 'I just wanted to make sure it's going to proceed as we had planned.'

'Oh, it will, don't worry,' he says.

'I want to make sure.'

His tone hardens slightly. 'Let's not take that attitude with each other. You took out Mike, which is enough to get any American agency mad at you. You had a special friend, Kabir... that's enough to get all your own people mad at you. Start with this – I haven't said anything about Mike to my people, and I haven't said anything about Kabir to yours.

'I want the same things you do. So let's just do it, okay?'

Gunfire erupts briefly from somewhere in the compound. The weapons might have sound suppressors, but they still make a lot of noise. My own weapon comes up but Charlie waves a casual hand. 'I have more men out there. They've found something interesting.'

'What?'

'My friend here,' he waves at his dark-skinned companion,

who is still seated, 'tells me that a couple of men might try to intercept you. We're waiting for them, but I sent my men out to look for intruders anyway. Sounds like they've found someone. We'd have come earlier, and found them before you got here, but I took time getting the team together.'

'What intruders?'

'A policeman and an old soldier. We intend to finish them off and leave them behind for the police to find. That'll lead them far away from where they should be looking. I'm here with my friend to make sure the details are fine.'

Moments later, the door opens again, and some of Charlie's men drag in two prisoners. They're both on their feet, not tied down, and apparently in good shape. 'Here are the intruders,' Charlie tells me.

One of the prisoners looks at Charlie and his companion in shock. 'What are you…?' He regains his poise, and turns to his companion. 'Meet James Carver of the US Department of State's Consular Operations. Also Rahul Sadasivan, formerly Deputy Director General of the IB.'

Charlie smiles at me. 'Mr P. Thomas, Chief of Investigations, NIA, and Ganesh Cariappa, ex-Army man.' He turns to Thomas. 'Sadasivan started "The Fund", you know. That man you met in Mumbai, well, he's just a gangster who used to have a uniform. Meanwhile, meet Noordin. One of the most painful thorns in your flesh when he's in action.' He smiles, as if he can't help crowing a little, and adds, 'He's been one of our most productive assets in the region these past few decades.'

I know of Thomas, of course; he is known to be intelligent, and as far as I know, honest. Ganesh, too, I know. He has fought us in Kashmir, and he was behind Asif, the mole in Hyderabad. I am confused for a moment. Then I remember Shahryar, and ask myself, 'who gains', and suddenly a lot of history becomes clear. Involuntarily I turn to look at Hameed, standing three feet away, armed, like myself, with a submachine gun. I could never understand what Charlie or the Americans have against the Indians, but now I do. I also know what to do.

'I'm glad you turned up,' Charlie continues talking to Thomas. 'They'll find your bodies here, assume all the wrong things, and go haring off in all sorts of wrong directions. I told my men to be gentle with you – despite your known tendency for violence in these situations, Colonel, because I want to decide exactly how you'll go.'

From outside, less than fifty yards away, comes the thunder of a big rifle, a .50 calibre firing powerful armour-piercing rounds. The door, which has been left unfastened, swings open with the first shot, and, as we watch, the helicopter's engine disintegrates and the rotors tilt to a side.

In less than two seconds, someone with a big rifle has finished off the work of a decade and a half, and I do not regret it. In any case, we're all busy looking after ourselves, going down for cover. Out of a corner of my eye, I see Ganesh swinging away to club one of Charlie's men and take his weapon; and Thomas, the policeman, taking a shot in the leg. Then I get busy firing at Charlie's people. 'Take the white man's men!' I shout to my own men, and they, following my lead and Abdul Hameed's, do just that.

I leave Charlie for the last, for he is unarmed, and can do little damage by himself. His men, expecting attack from outside the hangar and support from us, are taken completely by surprise in the first few seconds after that first shot that blew the door open, but they recover quickly. There is sporadic gunfire from all directions, and Hameed goes down beside me with a chest wound.

Ganesh, still uninjured, helps Thomas away, keeping low, maintaining fire single-handedly, and finds cover behind a large, heavy crate of helicopter spares. Fifteen seconds have passed since that first shot… and now comes a silence.

Everything has changed. My aims now – first, finish Charlie and his accomplice, then get away. Hameed is down, as are the rest of my comrades. Outnumbered and outgunned, they have acquitted themselves very well. I would gladly have given my life in place of one of them, but the Almighty decrees otherwise.

Meanwhile, for the time being, Ganesh, my old enemy, is an ally.

Twenty-Six

Ganesh

25-27 December 2025

I scale the wall in the wee hours of the 26th. The getaway car, a Ford hired earlier under a false ID, is parked half-a-kilometre down the road, and a spare key is already with Sushil. I'll have to stay in the compound for close to twenty-four hours, but it's worth the wait. I've prepared for this carefully, eating carefully the day before, and drinking plenty of water. Besides the weaponry and the medic pack, I have a water bottle and sugar pills – low blood sugar makes me trigger-happy. I cache weapons for Thomas and Sushil in the compound, digging shallow pits with a spade I've brought along.

Security is lax, as I had expected. The family is away for Christmas, and the servants are taking it easy. It's easy to cross over from the farm to the helicopter compound and back, and I find a secure corner in which to sleep in the afternoon. I'm not even particularly cramped; I can get up and walk around without being seen, because the servants start getting drunk early in the evening.

Meanwhile, I hear activity in the hangar. Two men in overalls enter the hangar, leaving the huge doors open – to air out the place, I assume – and I get a good look at the machine. The men are mechanics, who are inspecting the helicopter. They walk around it, looking at the rotor assembly and the engine underneath it, then climb in and spend a few minutes laughing and doing god knows what, and then they put on earmuffs. The engine comes on with a rattle that turns into a roar. They run it for a few minutes before turning it off, and leave after closing the door behind them and locking it with a huge padlock.

But now I know where exactly the helicopter is. I wait for dark, and find a spot for the .50 calibre, some thirty feet from the nearest gatepost, by a mango tree, from where a direct hit on the helicopter is easy. If it comes to that, Sushil will do it. With a belt full of armour-piercing rounds, even the closed door won't make a difference. For a moment, I consider disabling the helicopter now and walking away, but give up the thought almost immediately – I want to see Noordin.

Sushil comes first, at nine. We speak softly on short-range radio communicators. I throw a rope across the wall, and he climbs over, using a sheet of Kevlar from a bulletproof vest to handle the broken glass on the wall. I take him on a quick, silent tour of the compound and show him the .50 calibre. 'They'll take time to load up and get going,' I tell him softly, 'and all the while the doors will be open. You'll see the chopper clearly. Aim at the centre of the rotor blades, and at the engine, which is just below it. You have an area of nearly a square metre at a distance of under fifty metres, so it shouldn't be a problem. Do it before the thing starts moving; it'll be very difficult after that.'

'Got it, Chief. Centre of rotors and just below. Shoot before they move. And what will you be doing?'

'If you have to shoot this thing, I'll either be gone or be in their hands. Once the chopper is out of action, you get out of here. Don't think of anything but your own skin after that.'

'Sure, Chief.'

'If people come looking for you, climb this tree.' I point at the mango. 'Watch out for the ants. If Thomas and I get caught, you finish the job and then run for the car.'

'I'll be okay, Chief. Don't worry about me. Find someone else to hassle about.'

I'm not sure how well he'll follow the instructions, for he has a mind of his own. At this moment I'm glad that he, like me, has no one to mourn him. 'This is it,' I tell him. 'Good luck.'

Thomas comes at ten, clambering across, breathing hard, lands heavily, and twists his ankle badly. He is fit for his age, but no longer nimble, and his eyesight, especially his night vision, is fading. He gets to his feet on his own, but is in trouble. I tell him to stick by my side until I go down; we can't have him bumbling off into the dark on his own. There is little else I can tell him; he knows enough about these operations – theoretically, at least – for me not to have to instruct him. From what I know of him, he will keep a cool head and do his best.

At one, the activity begins. A van-load of men arrives – a dozen of them. The gates swing open, the van enters the compound, and the gates close behind it. The hangar doors open, the lights go on, and a dozen men, most of them armed, go in, while the van is driven off, to be parked to a side of the hangar. Nothing else is unloaded; the men have nothing bigger than an assault rifle.

I have no idea what's going on, but these aren't the men going to Koodankulam. Even if they are, there are more vehicles coming with equipment. There are too many of them for me to take, and if we go in now, the odds are heavily against us. I elect to wait until more happens.

Ten minutes later, six of the men, all armed, emerge in pairs.

I notice they've got flak jackets on, bigger and better than ours, and helmets. One man in each pair has strap-on night vision goggles and the other a communicator on his belt. They fan out in the compound; they're looking for something. I boost Thomas up into the lower branches of a tree beside me, and follow him up, but his foot gives way and he slides heavily down.

The searchers have heard the sound. I hear the soft muttering as they speak on their radios, and then silence. They don't use flashlights because they don't want to be seen, and the night-vision goggles give them a huge advantage. We pad silently away from the tree. They've anticipated that. They don't know of Thomas's injury, and probably expect us to get further away than we do.

Some twenty minutes after the first, a second, smaller van drives up. The van is let in through the gate and is parked by the doors, in a brightly lit area. Five men emerge, all in black uniform, all armed. They carry more arms out of the back of the van. I see what seem to be an anti-tank missile launcher, an RPG, a big rifle, and some boxes. They've also got supplies of food and water.

These are the men going to Koodankulam. I don't want to play hide-and-seek in this compound. I can take down some of the men, certainly, but that'll endanger Sushil and the backup plan.

We move away from the tree as softly as possible, looking for cover, but it's not much of a contest. I can't help feeling that we've been given away somehow; there can't be any other reason for them to come looking for us. Only Sushil and I know of his role here; they won't know about him. If they find us, they'll stop searching for more, and that'll leave Sushil a clear field of fire when the doors do open.

When they do find us, it's an anticlimax. Very soon after the second van arrives, a flashlight comes on, pointed in our faces, blinding us. One of the searchers fires a brief burst of his weapon, aimed a foot to my left. I feel the bullets kicking up earth as they hit the ground near my hip. 'Drop your weapons,' a voice says softly. 'Stand up, hands on your heads, and come forward slowly. Three paces forward, no more. Then stand still.'

We follow instructions, Thomas rather slowly, limping on his twisted ankle. Someone steps up behind me and I feel my flak jacket being unfastened. I shrug myself out of it; and a moment later, I'm on the ground, breathless and unable to speak due to a massive kick in the kidneys. I curl into a ball before the next kick arrives, and take it on the shoulder. Thomas, beside me, gets much the same treatment, except that he gets the second blow too, in full measure.

They have no handcuffs. Instead, they take us as policemen take prisoners, with a man at each side, grasping each of my hands, with a pistol in his free hand. They judge they've done enough damage to keep us quiet, and I go along, pretending to be a little more badly damaged than I am.

They lead us to the doors and inwards, into the glare of the lights inside, and we see before us about a dozen men in two separate groups – the men who have just arrived are clearly separate. I hear a sudden faint intake of breath from Thomas, and then he says, 'What are you…' His voice trails off, and he turns to me. 'Meet James Carver of the US Department of State's Consular Operations,' he says, his voice level. 'Also Rahul Sadasivan, formerly Deputy Director General of the IB.'

Carver looks at the leader of the second group. 'Mr P. Thomas, Chief of Investigations, NIA, and Ganesh Cariappa, formerly of the Indian Army.' He turns to Thomas. 'Sadasivan started "The Fund", you know. That man you met in Mumbai, well, he's just a gangster who used to have a uniform. Meanwhile, meet Noordin, one of the most painful thorns in your flesh when he's in action.' He pauses, gloating a bit. Then he continues, 'He's been one of our most productive assets in the region these past few decades.' Another pause. 'I'm glad you turned up. They'll find your bodies here, assume all the wrong things, and go haring off in all sorts of wrong directions. I told my men to be gentle with you – despite your known tendency for violence in these situations, Colonel, because I want to decide exactly how you'll go.'

There's little time to react to Noordin's presence. I pray for Sushil to keep calm. There's nothing else on my mind at the moment when, just seconds after Carver finishes speaking, the .50 calibre goes off, the bullet swinging the door open. I feel one of the hands holding me relax, and I get myself free. I slam into the man on the other side, clawing for his eyes with one hand, going for his weapon with the other. Rifles have already begun to fire, and I have a weapon and am rolling free when Thomas goes down from a hit below the chest.

Then, to my surprise, Noordin, who's dived to the ground, shouts something and opens up with short, aimed bursts – no spray and pray for this man. His companions also turn on Carver's men, and out of the corner of my eye, I see both Carver and Sadasivan go down. Ten feet away is a large crate of spares. Thomas is still, his face a mask of agony. I think he's been hit in the spleen. I drag him away, get him behind the box, and hunker down behind it. Only then do I see that the helicopter is disabled, its rotor axle shot away, the blades drooping irregularly.

No one's flying out of here tonight.

The priority now is to get out of the hangar. Sushil will have taken the car, but there are two vans outside. I must get Thomas to one of them. Fourteen men in the hangar besides Thomas and myself. When I take a look around, I see ten bodies. No Noordin. He's made it to cover.

I wonder why he turned at this moment. Then I see movement behind another box in a corner as Noordin lobs a grenade at the helicopter, and in the bang and the fires that follow. I grab Thomas in a fireman's lift and head for the door. Noordin and I have spotted each other, and neither of us has made an offensive ove. My move is followed by a burst from his rifle… he's covering me. I have barely covered a few steps beyond the door when I hear two more rifles opening up. Thomas is hit again and then something hits me, an almighty whack on the side of the chest… I stumble. My arms are turning to jelly and I let my grip on Thomas loosen, knowing somehow from his limpness that he's dead.

Another bullet hits me in the thigh and the pain lightens up as I fall. Then the blackness comes up and the last thing I remember feeling is relief that I won't have the job of telling Thomas's mistress that he's gone.

31 December 2025 – 25 January 2026

My three weeks in the hospital passed uneventfully. The fourth day after surgery, I was permitted visitors, a newspaper, and an hour of TV that I let pass because of an unrelenting headache.

Several pompous senior policemen camped in my room the whole day, debriefing me in a hostile atmosphere. The knives were out, and all had the same name – National Security. The debriefing was followed by instructions not to talk out of turn. Perhaps because of my worsening headache, I told them that I had ten copies of a file in a foreign bank with instructions to let the noisiest newspapers and TV channels have a copy apiece if anything untoward happened to me. A burst of good sense followed, however, and I told them I'd keep shut if they made sure Thomas was treated honourably. They hemmed and hawed and left without committing themselves, hanging on to their pomp with their fingertips.

One of them, perhaps a little less unsympathetic than the

rest, stayed back to fill me in. The mystery of the dead American, he told me, remains partly a mystery. His fingers and eyes were destroyed, but DNA samples identified him as one Anthony McAuliffe, a businessman with interests in mining and contacts with some extremely unsavoury members of the Chennai underworld. He was killed, most unfortunately, in the events at his host's house. A 'facilitator', a retired senior policeman, one Rahul Sadasivan, apparently a business associate of McAuliffe's, was killed with McAuliffe.

While officialdom said nothing, there was some speculation that they were kidnapped and killed in a botched rescue attempt. In the absence of threats or traces of ransom demands, nothing could be confirmed. The US government didn't comment at all.

Then came Sushil and filled in some of the gaps. He hid behind a tree while the men were searching for us. He came back down when Carver's men dragged Thomas and me into the hangar. He couldn't see much after that, but the door was open a few inches and he saw activity. He had some trouble getting the rifle set up in the dark. It wasn't lined up with the opening and the helicopter rotors, so he took a few steps right, saw the chopper, got back to the rifle, lined it up with where he thought the rotor would be, and let fly. The first shot banged the door open and he saw the helicopter. After that, he just fed the whole belt into the gun.

There were several bursts of firing inside the hangar after that, but he did nothing because he didn't want to risk shooting Thomas or me, so he just kept still. Then he saw me getting out with Thomas, and joined us just before I got hit the second time. He saw Noordin emerge and bring down the man who'd shot us.

Noordin saw me going down, stopped, put a pressure bandage on my abdomen and a tourniquet on my leg, and lugged me into the van in which he and his men had come. Sushil and Noordin got me to the car, and thence to a hospital, in time. Sushil stayed with me long enough to ensure that the police follow-up didn't threaten my life any more. The doctor reported my wounds to the police – doctors are required by law to report gunshot wounds – but the follow-up didn't touch me because I was in intensive care, and the doctor, who went by the book in reporting the wounds, was equally uncompromising in keeping the police out of my hair. Noordin didn't wait for Sushil's thanks; he disappeared as I was being loaded on to a gurney at the hospital. But he did leave behind a small hand-held computer, which Sushil handed over to Ashok. I told Ashok to get it cracked – there is software to unlock encrypted computer files, and we have all the time in the world.

A few days later, the Home minister at the Centre visited me in the hospital, preceded by the usual hordes of hard-eyed, gun-toting men in black looking for intruders. They found none, and the minister, all smiles, presented me a shawl. Mixing his metaphors, he told me that rocking the boat is bad for the state of the nation, and spoke vaguely of handing out consulting contracts to the appropriate people. I heard him out, smiled back, and wished silently that he would take his execrable presence away, which he did, after ten minutes of non-stop natter.

Ashok came a bit after he left, with no smiles but active concern instead. 'Everything is under control,' he said, and I was to concentrate on getting well before returning to work. Sushil came again, casual as ever, offering anything. I told him to be patient, and to look for a regular job. His eyebrows rose. 'Make me an offer,' he said. I did, and he promised to consider it.

Anil dropped in to bury his hatchet, and to sniff for more SafeWrite threats. He lightened up when he discovered there were none. He had heard rumours of all kinds, and wanted to know if there was any truth in them, and, more importantly, anything in it for him. He learnt quickly enough that there wasn't, and left – eyes neutral behind dark glasses – after telling me that Gowda intended to hold his peace. The SafeWrites keep both at bay.

Meanwhile, the cracked computer, which turned out to belong to Kabir, Noordin's friend, displayed evidence of more bent policemen and officials, and turned up another arms smuggling pipeline. It turned up a photograph of Sadasivan, who must have been Rudra, who haunted poor Kabir. It also turned up dozens of photographs of Noordin, in many different poses, in many different guises, most of them showing him happy and relaxed. I thought hard before deciding not to hand the computer over to the police. I hoped Noordin had found his way to days as happy as the ones he seemed to have enjoyed in the photographs.

There was no scandal because of a few deaths in a dusty little town by the tip of the peninsula. Gang-war, said the government, reaches everywhere. Quietly, the cover-up consumed a few victims. A dozen junior officials lost their jobs, and a few senior men retired early from the police services and the bureaucracy, mostly on grounds of poor health. Thomas was reported to have died in an accident while on a fact-finding tour in Kanyakumari. Since he died on duty while in harness, he would be given an official funeral, and his widow a full pension. A parliamentary committee was pressed into service to review security procedures. The committee's title is long and impressive, and it has a year in which to report. Meanwhile, it's been business as usual.

It's been business as usual for me, except for a little break. A few days after leaving the hospital, with the bandages and aches and pains mostly gone, and only a limp and a walking stick to remind me of the damage, I set out to do something I hope I never have to do again. I take a flight one night to Delhi and check into a hotel near the airport. Next morning, towards eleven, I take a cab to an upper-middle-class locality in Gurgaon, and by noon, in the warm winter sunshine, find my way to a quiet block of flats. I offer my ID to the security man in the lobby, knowing that he is a colleague. He recognises my name, snaps an enthusiastic but sloppy salute that would have gotten him a reprimand in the Army, and calls the person I've come to visit.

She lives anonymously on the fourth floor. Greying and dignified, a little gaunt about the cheekbones, she invites me into her modest flat and I offer condolences. She accepts with grace. It's been almost a month now since Thomas died, and she seems to have got used to the hole in her life. All around the room are photographs of the two children growing up. Her own photographs, some obviously recent ones, show her with fuller cheeks and black hair. In all the lot, there isn't a single one of Thomas. She busies herself with tea, and, when she serves it, senses what's on my mind. 'I couldn't acknowledge him because of the children. He knew and accepted it.'

'I thought as much. It doesn't matter.'

She sips. 'He spoke of you the last time we met. Then I heard that you'd been in a hospital for some weeks; they said you'd been shot. I was wondering whether you'd come by, actually.'

'I had to,' I reply. 'I was with him through that night. His last thoughts were of you. He was a good man, and a courageous one. You already know that, but I still have an obligation to tell you… in the end, he was one of the best.'

She squeezes a handkerchief and begins a smile that twists in fresh, tearing pain. 'You wouldn't be here if he weren't…' After a brief silence, she asks hoarsely, 'Did he suffer much?'

'No,' I lie unhesitatingly, remembering the utter helpless agony of his last few minutes. 'He just bled out. I don't think he felt any pain at all.'

She sits bowed, plying the handkerchief, sniffing. Slowly her composure returns. 'He was concerned about you. He told me that if he didn't come back, I'd still have the children. And you?'

'Good question,' I say.

'You're young yet. Get someone.'

'I'll try,' I promise, and leave her to her memories and her children.

Epilogue

Ganesh

February 2026

Sunday morning drags, the seconds plodding by with agonising slowness. I wish, as I do every empty holiday, that Noordin had just gone away that night instead of lugging me out to the van – then guilt twinges. He took a huge risk doing what he did. How can I be so contemptuous of what he's done for me?

My life has changed since that night. Mahipal's death remains unavenged and will remain so. Revenge, I've discovered, is a dish best left untouched. It gives sleepless nights and grief. I've given up what I used to do in my spare time, and now those hours hang heavy on my hands. Time has turned leaden.

At ten, the intercom buzzes. It's the watchman, from the lobby, saying I have a visitor. A face floats on to the video screen – it's the man himself, Noordin. 'Send him up,' I tell the watchman, leaving the front door ajar.

Two minutes later, he's in the doorway. He's down to skin and bone, his clean-shaven face chalky pale except for dark circles under the eyes, his clothes hanging loose as if he's lost a lot of weight recently. 'Noordin,' I say. We stand for a moment, measuring each other, and then I take a step forward, holding out my hand. 'Welcome.'

He takes a tentative step inside, shakes my hand, and looks at the sparse furnishings for a moment. 'I was not sure you would let me in,' he says. His speech is stilted and formal, like his manner.

I smile. 'Why not? Last time we met, you saved my life.' I look him up and down. 'You're very thin. Have you been well?'

He nods, waves a hand around the flat. 'If I had a place of my own, it would be like this,' he says, finally. 'We might be more similar than you think.'

I can't help smiling at that. 'I have a few questions about that night.'

'I thought so. Some I can anticipate. Abdul Hameed tipped off your police about Goa. Also about our operation, but only about the power station. By the time we met, I was already thinking of doing what I did. What the American said only made me sure I was doing the right thing.'

'Why did you change your mind?'

'I became a Kashmiri. I got to like the place, and love its people. It's a gentle, rich version of my homeland, Afghanistan. Then I saw what we did to Kashmir, just to enrich a few Americans. Abdul Hameed made sure I did. That was enough.'

'Thomas told me a lot about you; about Kabir.'

He waves a hand. 'None of that matters any longer.' Momentarily, his control deserts him. 'I have come to ask a favour,' he blurts.

Admitting any kind of weakness is difficult for him, and asking a favour next to impossible. 'I'll do what I can,' I tell him.

'It is important and very big.'

'I'll do what I can,' I repeat. 'I really will.'

'I have no children, but Abdul Hameed has a granddaughter.

He is gone now, but he was more a brother than a friend. She is a year-and-a-half old. She is in my care.' I nod, and he takes a deep breath before he continues. 'I would like you to look after her.'

'It's time you retired,' I say. 'Why don't you do it yourself?'

He hesitates. 'Only the professionals know of this yet, the doctors.' He forces himself to go on. 'I do not know how much time I have left. Months, perhaps a year at best. I cannot go back to my people after what happened when we last met, you know that. I cannot think of going to your government, or to the Pakistanis. I could think of no one but you.'

Thomas's notes mentioned this illness of his. 'I'd heard you weren't well. What is it? Is there anything I can get done for you? I know some of the best specialists in the country.'

He shakes his head. 'There's nothing to be done. It is a cancer that has spread, from my liver to my stomach and now to my lungs.'

'Have you done what you can about it?'

'It is too late.'

Conflicting thoughts chase each other around my mind. A little girl, especially one from a different culture, a different place, will be extremely difficult. Doesn't matter, a voice shouts in my head, no more empty Sundays. All of a sudden there's a lump in my throat. 'I don't know how she'll turn out,' I manage. My voice is a croak.

'She is with a widow in Delhi, who keeps her because she does not object to making a profit out of a small child. Her papers are all ready. You will have no trouble with all that.'

'Another of your bright children, like the boys in the power station?' I ask.

'No! Her grandfather died at the hangar that night. He was by me. Remember?'

'Yes.'

'She has no one else. I promised him I'd take care of her... I told you, he was my closest friend, my brother.'

'You know I'm alone.'

'So was my father! And you had a daughter. Does it matter?'

'Not at all... I'll do it.' The words emerge before I know I've said them.

Six weeks later, Fatima comes home – small, pale, silent and a little hostile in the manner of small children with strangers they don't quite trust. From silence, she progresses to wails and tantrums, refusing to eat or sleep. The thought of all those empty Sundays keeps me patient, and slowly she unbends, to me and to Usha, the woman who used to look after Gayatri. I've brought her back from Virajpet, to take care of Fatima during my hours of work. Over the weeks, she begins to eat well, to sleep through most nights, and, early one morning, smiling, steals my heart. Time begins to race past, and a child's laughter once again brightens my house.

Noordin is in a private nursing home. When I visit him first, I know, as he has known for some time that he won't leave it alive. He is fed through tubes because his gullet is blocked, and he is drowsy from painkilling drugs. In his hospital bed, tethered to all those bottles, he is helpless. I wish I had known him better.

Fatima and I visit him every morning, until, one day, he seems to be improving. He recognises me, holds her hand, and with an effort, makes small talk. We linger, until he goes to sleep. That night, we get the news – he never woke up from that sleep. In the morning, we follow his cortege to the cemetery – the only mourners. Fatima doesn't understand, but senses the solemnity of the moment, and my own sadness. At the graveside, she begins to sob, and, for the second time, I dry a little girl's tears at a funeral.

It's been a long, tiring morning. On the way back home, in the car, stuck in traffic, she eases up into my lap, and thumb in mouth, goes to sleep. With Noordin's death, she has found her new home in every sense. He would have been pleased.

∽

Acknowledgments

Thanks to Dad, who retired from the Army in 1971, and my cousin Biju, a serving soldier, who helped with all kinds of information. Also to Altaf and Mohammed, who accompanied me around Kashmir some years ago, sometimes into places none of us should have been in.

Thanks to Prita, for support, as always.

Thanks also to a couple of old doctor friends in my hometown, Drs K.P. Shantakumar and P.M. Madhavan, for unstinting moral and spiritual (and occasionally spirituous) support.

Thanks to Jay, for friendship and for running around.

Thanks to Rashmi, for the editing and so on.